Essence

THE EVE SERIES
BOOK 1

A. L. WADDINGTON

3rd Edition

Cover Design by Greg Simanson

This is a work of fiction. Names, characters, places, brands, media, and incidents are either the product of the author's imagination or are used fictitiously. Any resemblance to similarly named places or to persons living or deceased is unintentional.

PRINT ISBN 978-1-948143-00-4

EPUB ISBN 978-1-948143-04-2

Library of Congress Control Number: 2014900487

Acknowledgments

A very special thank you to Beth Neil-Beliveau for your compassion, for keeping me grounded, and for listening to countless hours of my rambling. You have been a great friend and mentor over the years. And to Cindy Williams for all your help in the historic elements of this story; you are truly a kind person who always has a smile for everyone! Also, to Kevin Rand for his proofreading skills and objective eye; you are an amazing professor! A huge thanks to Pat Clark for your patience and tact during a crisis, for being my lifeboat, and for drilling me endlessly on the suspension of disbelief. "Essence" would not have been the same without your input and feedback, and I love you for it! A giant thanks to Larry Cooper and Tony Gude for your unbelievable patience, skills, and talent in photography and design. You put so much passion and care into your work and did an amazing job. A big thank you to Max Engling for being the role model and inspiration of the type of man I inspired to create in Jackson. You are a true gentleman! Also, a huge thank you to my fabulous editor, Melinda Reuter for her patience, comic relief, and putting a shine on my words.

CHAPTER 1

Saturday, October 10, 2015

I SLAMMED MY HAND across the top of my alarm clock as it started blaring at me, waking me at seven. I kicked off my covers with a groan and headed to the bathroom. After pulling my long, reddish-brown hair up in a ponytail and throwing on an old pair of gym shorts and a T-shirt, I headed for the kitchen to scrounge up some breakfast, still half asleep.

My father, Shane, greeted me from behind his morning paper and coffee. "Good morning, sleepyhead."

"What are you doing up so early?" I asked while I got out a bowl, filling it to the top with cereal before drowning it in milk.

"Your mother wants me to clean out the garage today. It's going to be an all-day job," he grumbled.

"Good luck with that!" I sat down across the breakfast nook.

"Did you sleep at all last night? You look really tired." He looked at me for the first time.

"Yeah. Just slept hard, I guess," I answered before taking a bite.

"You should go to bed early tonight. Get some rest."

"Okay, Doc." I smiled at him.

"I'm telling you as your *father*." He smirked back at me.

My dad worked at the hospital but strictly handled the business end of it. He had his doctorate, not his medical degree, unlike my mother, Amy, who was a pediatrician. He was some kind of vice president of compliance. I honestly had no clue to what he really did. Nor did I really care.

"Well, I've got to get going. Can't be late. Coach Smith is on a rampage because of Thursday's meet."

I sighed heavily and put my bowl in the sink. "I don't know why she's making us practice on a Saturday. It's ridiculous!" My dad laughed from behind his paper. "Just because Jessica screwed up, we all have to pay the price."

Jessica, whose mother worked in the school office, was only on the volleyball team because of her mother's association with the school; she had no coordination whatsoever and had nearly blown the meet for us, almost ruining our perfect season.

"It's part of being a team." My dad glanced over the top of his paper with a slight smile. "You driving Jenna?"

"I think so." I fumbled around, looking for my car keys.

He put his paper aside and followed me out to the garage. My best friend, Jenna Burk, was already waiting in the driveway for me; she only had to walk over from next door.

The chilly October morning was crisp with the ground completely covered with morning dew. The sky was a pale gray with a hint of rain hanging in the air. The leaves were starting to turn a brilliant array of gold, yellow, red, and auburn. The plush green grass was littered with scattered leaves drifting away with the summer sun. I pulled my jacket closer around me, thinking of the Indian summer that had ended two days earlier. Fall had now settled in for the duration. Days of cute tank tops and shorts were over until next May. Despite my love of fall with all its brilliant colors, I loathed winter with a vengeance.

We climbed into my maroon, 2004 Grand Prix that I'd gotten for my seventeenth birthday.

"Good morning, chica," Jenna greeted me happily as she climbed into the passenger seat.

How anyone could be so happy so early was beyond my comprehension.

I grunted and half grinned in response, pulling my sunglasses out of my purse even though there really wasn't much sunshine. I pulled out of the driveway and drove the short two miles to our high school.

We joined the rest of our sleepy teammates in the locker room. The stale air stank of sweat socks and grim that clung to the dingy gray walls. I was sitting down on the bench, putting on my knee pads, when Jenna sat down beside me, grinning from ear to ear.

"Did you notice the *sold* sign on the Davison estate? Can you believe it finally sold?" She raised an inquisitive eyebrow at me.

"Huh?" I looked over at her, confused. My brain hadn't begun processing anything yet.

"The Davison estate across the street finally sold." She beamed.

"Oh."

The Davison family had moved out midsummer, leaving the beautiful, old mansion empty after the discovery of a racy scandal between the married Mr. Davison, a high-profile business attorney, and an up-and-coming assistant district attorney who was at least twenty years his junior.

"I wonder who bought it," she said, more to herself than me.

"Don't know," I muttered and shrugged.

Three and a half hours later we dragged our exhausted sweaty selves back to the locker room. My legs felt like rubber as I wiped the sweat off my forehead with the back of my hand. It had been a long day already and it wasn't even noon yet. Everyone was anxious to leave and get on with their Saturday.

"Any plans for the rest of the day?" Jenna asked.

"Caitlyn and I are heading over to Cody's around two. He and Zak were talking about maybe going to a movie or something later." Hilary Wade kicked off her shoes.

Hilary's boyfriend, Cody Porter, was our football team's star wide receiver. Caitlyn Buchanan's boyfriend, Zak Engling, was the starting varsity quarterback and team captain.

"So, are you and Zak back together?" I inquired.

"*Again.*" Hilary laughed aloud, causing Caitlyn to glare back at her.

Caitlyn was head over heels for Zak, and we all knew it. However, his standing on the football team had inflated his ego to the point that it was causing problems in their relationship. He would do or say something stupid, and Caitlyn would break up with him. But in the end, she always took him back.

"Yeah. He's trying to behave," Caitlyn muttered under her breath. Eager to change the subject, she turned her focus in my direction. "So, when are you going to start dating, Jocelyn?"

I was placing my knee pads and shoes in my battered blue locker when her words caught me completely off guard. "Haven't found anyone I'm interested in," I casually responded, shrugging my shoulders. "Besides, I really don't have the time."

I knew they didn't buy my excuse. In all fairness, there wasn't anyone at our school I was interested in. I had been asked out by several guys in the last couple years, but I'd always found a reason to turn them down. I was tired of all the immature high school crap, and the way couples only lasted briefly. The couples who did stay together always seemed to fill their relationships full of petty drama, and I didn't want to waste my time.

"You're just being too picky, Jocelyn." Jenna teased, putting her things in the locker next to mine. "There are some really cute guys here, and you could have any one of them."

I glanced over at Hilary, rolling my eyes and making her giggle.

"I saw that," Jenna scolded.

"You want to walk home?" I teasingly asked Jenna, who playfully shoved me in return.

"Sure." She stuck her tongue out at me over her shoulder in a purely childish gesture before walking over to the mirror to check her reflection and adjust her long, brown hair, which was pulled up in a ponytail that hung several inches past her shoulders.

Caitlyn joined her briefly to make sure her own blonde locks were in check. Caitlyn really should have been a cheerleader. Her tall, thin stature made us all envious. She probably would have been if it weren't for the fact that Taylor Perry was the captain of the squad. If there was anyone who truly believed she was queen of our school, it was Taylor; and her little crony, Dakota Anderson, was certainly the princess.

Hilary popped in between the two of them, making a face at the reflection that stared back at her before she quickly turned away. Hilary, who was shorter than the rest of us, hated her shoulder-length, unruly, curly, red hair. She would have killed to have Caitlyn's gorgeous hair more so than the rest of us.

Once back in my car, I was eager to get home and jump into the shower. I felt so gross covered in sweat. The sun had partly come out flirting with the clouds as they danced across the sky. I pulled out my shades and started up the car. Jenna flipped through the radio stations absentmindedly.

"Are you spending the day with Kyle?" I asked, pulling out of the school parking lot.

"Probably," she shrugged.

Jenna and Kyle had been dating since the beginning of our freshman year, and she was crazy about him. He was only a couple inches taller than her five-foot-seven-inch frame with dirty-blonde hair that had the longer, messy look to it; and his light-brown eyes were almost golden. Despite having the build, Kyle didn't play football. His sport of choice was tennis, but he would occasionally play basketball with Jenna and me in my driveway.

Kyle and his family had moved in next door on the other side of me when we were all in the second grade. After growing up with him always around, I looked at him as more of a brother than anything else and was shocked when the two of them had started dating.

The hot water from the shower soothed my aching muscles as I absorbed the heat. I remained there until all of it was gone. I climbed out of the tub very aware of the fact that my legs felt like rubber and were in constant pain. My arms felt sore and stiff.

I tossed the wet towel across my desk chair and scrounged though my bottom drawer for my old cut-off sweat shorts. I climbed into them and grabbed an old T-shirt out of my closet. I sat down at my vanity and ran the brush roughly through my wet hair. My stomach grumbled, and I realized I hadn't eaten anything since breakfast. I sighed heavily and set the brush down making a face at my reflection in the mirror.

I stood up and realized how strangely quiet the house was for a change and smiled. I rarely got the house to myself. I stepped into my booty slippers and went downstairs to search for some lunch.

I settled on the couch in the sunroom with a smoked ham and provolone cheese Panini, carrot sticks with ranch dressing, and a cold glass of peach tea. I flipped on the television and surfed through the channels and found *The Breakfast Club* just starting. It was one of my favorite movies.

Once I finished my lunch, I placed the plate on the coffee table and rolled over to get even more comfortable. The silent house was incredibly peaceful, and the warm, afternoon sun was glowing through the windows. It wasn't long before I drifted off into a sound sleep.

A short time later, Jenna abruptly awakened me. She jumped on my stomach, scaring me half to death.

"Ah! Get your fat butt off me!" I smacked her across her back.

"Are you going to sleep all day?"

"What do you care?" I glared up at her before rolling over with my back to her. She knew how much I hated being woken up.

But Jenna was dancing with excitement, barely able to contain herself. "I care because there's something I want to show you."

I didn't bother to roll back over. "Nothing is that important."

"Ah. Come on. The new neighbors are here."

"Who?"

"Across the street." Jenna bounced.

I was too tired and worn out from practice to care about who was moving into the old Davison mansion.

"The moving truck arrived, and they started unloading it around noon today. I've been watching them from my house, but I can't see anything." Jenna's voice picked up an octave. "Come on," she begged. "I can't even tell who's moving in."

I tried to rub the sleep out of my eyes. "What time is it?"

"Three-thirty."

I reluctantly rolled back over to face her. "Explain why I should care."

"Because I do." Jenna danced out of the room to the front room.

I reluctantly followed only to find her perched over the back of the couch, peeking through the drapes.

"Are you sure you don't want to sit out on the front porch or perhaps the lawn?"

"I would if it wouldn't look too obvious." She glanced over her shoulder with a wink.

"If my mother catches you in here, you're going to wish you had chosen the porch or lawn," I stated sternly.

Our front living room, or the parlor as my mother liked to call it, was her favorite room in the house. We rarely used it except for special occasions.

Our house was built shortly before the Civil War. It was huge, old, and drafty. It was whitewashed with black shutters and a grand porch that was wrapped around the front and sides of the home. My parents bought it when my mother was pregnant with me. It was a great place to grow up, especially to play hide-and-seek in. There were three floors plus a full basement.

Outside stood a detached, three-car garage that was apparently servants' quarters at one time. It had been converted into a garage long before we ever bought the house. There had been an old stable barn in the opposite corner of the backyard where the yard supplies, carriages, and horses were housed but it had burned down sometime in the 1930s, or so I was told.

The main floor of the home was open and airy. It was the kind of house with an old-style charm. I loved it. My mother's room was professionally decorated with timepiece antiques from when the house was built.

The outside wall was home to a large fireplace that still had its original mantel. It was the one-piece mother would not budge on remodeling. It was nicked, had dated initials carved into it from the original owners, and nails to hang up stockings at Christmas. Somehow, it made the room feel like home. Mother's grand piano in the front corner sat unused since her failed attempt to talk me into taking lessons when I was a child.

I was staring at the piano when Jenna turned back to the window to peek out the drapes. "Your mom went shopping about an hour ago."

I walked over and sat down beside her, pulling back the curtain a little to have a look. I couldn't see anything, but the moving truck parked in the driveway and men unloading it.

Jenna let go of the drapes. "I still haven't seen the new people."

"What does it matter? Why are you so curious?" I leaned back against the cushions and sighed heavily.

"Because nothing ever happens around here. This is exciting." She cooed.

"You realize that it's probably some couple with a bunch of little kids who will be running around screaming and riding their bikes in the street, so we'll have to watch out for them. Yes, it'll be so exciting."

"Agh. You're probably right." She snorted. "It's just so boring around here."

"How can anything be boring with you around, waking people up?" I playfully smacked her again on the arm.

Just then, Kyle walked through the front door. He never knocked. Neither did Jenna. Of course, I didn't knock at their houses either.

"What's going on? Already spying on the new neighbors, I see." Kyle chuckled at us perched behind the drapery.

"Trying to, but I can't see because the front yards are too big and there's too many trees." Jenna glared.

Kyle and I laughed at her.

"I'm sure we'll find out soon enough who they are. Something like this is not going to stay quiet too long in this neighborhood." He came over and sat down in the armchair. "I already heard my mom tell dad this morning that the realtor who's a friend of hers said the husband is a lawyer and the wife is a novelist. They have three kids. Two are grown and still back east. The other is in our grade." He sat back with a satisfied smirk.

"Really? I wonder." Jenna looked lost in thought.

"What?" It was unsettling to imagine what could possibly be going on in that head of hers. Nothing good usually came out of her meddling.

"I was just thinking…" She pondered.

That could be dangerous.

Kyle stood back up. "Tell ya what. Why don't we shoot some hoops?"

"Sounds good." I stood up and pulled Jenna's arm.

The three of us went out to the driveway and started shooting around. Kyle, despite being athletically built, was not a basketball player and fumbled the ball several times. Jenna and I had no problem stealing it from him or blocking his shots.

We were enjoying ourselves and acting stupid when a voice spoke up behind us.

"Excuse me. Mind if I join?"

I took an unintentionally deep breath when I caught sight of where the voice came from.

He was over six feet with broad shoulders and muscular stature. His dark, wavy brown hair was glistening in the afternoon sun, giving it almost copper-colored highlights; but the most striking feature was his piercing, emerald eyes. I don't believe I'd ever seen eyes so bright and dark at the same time.

The mysterious person stood near the birch tree on the edge of the flower garden, looking somewhat uncomfortable; yet there was an air of confidence about him. Kyle walked over to him and extended his hand.

"Sure. Glad to even the odds." Kyle smiled, breathing heavily. "They're killing me. Kyle Clausen." Kyle shook hands with the gorgeous stranger.

"Jackson Chandler. My parents just bought the house across the street." He slowly walked onto the asphalt driveway as Kyle tossed him the basketball.

"This is my girlfriend, Jenna Burk. She lives next door." Kyle pointed to Jenna's house. "And this is Jocelyn Timmons. This is her place. I live over there." Kyle nodded in the direction of his home.

"Nice to meet you both." Jackson smiled at Jenna and me.

"You too." Jenna walked over and shook his hand while I remained rooted where I stood.

His presence bothered me a great deal. I couldn't explain it, but I could feel it, like I'd seen him before even though I was positive I hadn't. I felt like I knew him.

Jackson smiled in my direction and suddenly a wave passed over me, making me very lightheaded and dizzy. I took a step back. Feeling nauseated, I leaned against the basketball goal post. My breathing quickened. I could hear the three of them speaking, but the sounds were muffled like there was cotton in my ears.

I slowly slid down the post and sat on the grass, wrapping my arms around my knees, and closed my eyes, resting my head down upon them, trying to block out the world around me. My breathing slowed, but the nausea and lightheadedness continued.

"Are you alright?" It was Jenna's voice.

I nodded as best I could.

"Are you going to get sick?"

I shook my head and looked at her kneeling beside me.

"Guess I'm tired from practice this morning." My voice sounded foreign in my ears.

Her face was full of concern. "Are you sure? Do you want me to get you anything? Some water?"

"Yeah. Some water would be great. I can get it. Just give me a hand."

I held out my hand and she helped me to my feet. As I regained my balance, I noticed that Kyle and Jackson were hovering right behind Jenna.

"Are you okay?" Kyle asked.

I nodded at him, purposely avoiding looking at Jackson.

I headed into the house. "I'm fine. Just need some water."

Jenna followed, and the boys began shooting hoops again.

"What's wrong?" Jenna asked once inside the kitchen.

"Nothing. I just got lightheaded for a second. I'm probably just worn out." I got some water from the fridge door and had a long drink.

"Are you sure?" Jenna eyed me suspiciously with her head cocked to the side.

"Yeah. I'm fine. Really." I nodded again.

"So, what do you want to do tonight?" She perched herself up on a bar stool.

"I don't care. I don't have any plans. Aren't you and Kyle doing something?"

"Nothing concrete. Why don't we call Hill, Cody, Zak, and Caitlyn and see if they want to watch a movie or something?" Jenna shrugged. "Just hang out. Nothing special."

I leaned my head against the cool side of the fridge and started to feel a little better. "All right." I continued sipping on my water. The lightheadedness was almost completely gone.

"You go lie down for a while. I'll make some phone calls."

I nodded as Jenna bounced back out the back door while I stayed in the kitchen long enough to pour a third glass of water. I sat down at the breakfast bar, wondering what had come over me so quickly. I had never experienced anything like that in my life. There was a thin layer of sweat across my brow that I wasn't sure was from the episode or basketball. I wiped my forehead with the back of my sleeve and rested my head on the counter.

The nausea began to subside a little, and the cool counter felt welcoming on my face. I just wanted to lie there and not move. Maybe I was getting the flu or something.

A few minutes later, my father arrived in the kitchen to scrounge for a snack. He was sweaty and dusty from cleaning out the garage most of the day.

"Hey," he patted me on the shoulder. "You okay?"

I looked up at his face and gave him the best smile I could muster.

"Yeah. Just tired from practice," I replied, sliding off the stool.

He stood there with a box of Wheat Thins in one hand and a Diet Coke in the other and nodded as he munched on some crackers.

"Hey, Dad? Do you care if I have some friends over tonight just to hang out and watch movies in the basement?"

Our basement had become a popular hangout in the last several years. My parents had remodeled it years ago, turning it into a recreation room with a large television, oversized sofas, a pool table, and a bar in the corner.

It seemed everyone enjoyed loitering around our place mainly because my parents weren't typically as bad as others in letting us just hang out and be stupid. They checked on us, but not that often and don't come unglued about couples snuggling during a movie, although they do the occasional *'hand check'*, which had become a running joke now within our group.

"Whatever," he muttered and waved, leaving me alone for half a second.

"Cool. Who's coming over?" Ethan, my younger brother, entered the kitchen from the other entrance. His dark, blonde hair was a mess and in dire need of a trim.

Ethan was only a year behind me in school. A fact I truly hated sometimes. He was also on the football team and constantly wanted to hang out with my friends and me.

"Just the usual." I turned toward him. "What are *your* plans?"

"Not much. Movies maybe. Mariah and I were talking about doing something with Haley and Corbin. Who knows?" He shrugged and reached into the fridge. "Did you meet the new guy across the street? Seems like a nice enough guy. He's out in the driveway with Kyle, shootin' hoops."

"Yeah. I was out there a little while ago. I really didn't get the chance to talk to him."

"I guess they're from Boston."

"Boston?"

"That's what he told me just a minute ago. He also asked me about the team. Guess he played wide receiver at his old school. That should make Cody happy." Ethan smirked and pulled out of the fridge with a Coke in one hand and a chicken leg in the other. He took a big bite of the chicken and grinned at me.

"You're disgusting," I slapped him on the shoulder. "Get a plate, you pig."

Ethan held the chicken in his teeth and grabbed the half gallon of cookie dough ice cream out of the freezer, placing it on the breakfast bar. I rolled my eyes at him and left the kitchen. He always ate like a pig, but it got a lot worse during football season when he was training hard. His metabolism raced, and he ate nonstop.

I retreated to my room to change and fix my hair before my friends arrived. The episode in the driveway was now becoming a faded memory. I felt embarrassed about the whole thing.

What an impression I must have made on the new guy. It was probably just caused by all the long hours of practice and the late nights I'd been up studying.

Jenna arrived shortly before Caitlyn, Cody, Zak, and Hilary; and the six of us headed downstairs, where my mother had left out chips and pizza rolls and stocked the bar fridge with sodas. We all got comfortable lounging on the oversized sofas, chatting about school, when Mariah, Haley, Corbin, and Ethan came down the stairs.

I looked up, giving Ethan a dirty look; but the four of them made themselves comfortable and joined in on the conversation. None of my friends really minded my brother; and our friendships did overlap, but it made boundaries blurred, secrets and privacy a joke. The guys decided that we were going to watch *Ironman*, which none of us girls minded because we all loved Robert Downey Jr.

About an hour into the movie, I heard footsteps on the stairs. I was curled up in the corner of the sofa with my arms wrapped around a pillow and covered by a throw blanket. I was enjoying the movie when Jenna, who was sitting next to me, smiled as Kyle came into view.

Turning, I realized that Jackson was with him and immediately, the same nausea and lightheadedness I had experienced earlier swept over me. I closed my eyes, regretting the pizza rolls I had just eaten. Then Kyle and Jackson, much to my horror, squeezed in between Jenna and me on the couch.

Kyle made brief introductions to everyone while my eyes remained closed. I tried hard to give the impression that I had fallen asleep. I didn't want to move. I tried to convince myself that if I remained still with my eyes closed, I would not vomit all over Jackson.

I just had to pretend that this beautiful creature was not only inches from me, so close I could barely move my hand and be touching him. I struggled to breathe.

"When did Jocelyn fall asleep?" I heard Caitlyn ask after some time had lapsed.

"She wasn't feeling well earlier. I think she's just worn out," Jenna replied.

"I hope that someday I might actually get to meet her," Jackson said.

"She's really nice. Honestly." Hilary spoke up. "She's just a little shy sometimes."

"Shy?" Ethan challenged. "My sister? Hardly. She's never shy when she's yelling at me!"

"That's only because you're a constant pain in her ass," Jenna piped back.

I knew she was giving him her smart-ass grin and I had to fight not to smile myself.

Finally, I heard everyone say their good nights and climb back up the stairs. I had no idea what time it was. I had kept up my sleeping impression for the rest of evening since the nausea and dizziness would not subside.

When I was sure that the basement had emptied, I was glad to finally be alone. I slowly opened my eyes and stretched out my cramped legs. The lights had all been turned off except for the small light over the bar. I decided I would be much more comfortable in my own bed and climbed up the stairs.

But as I opened the basement door, standing there in my kitchen was Jenna, Kyle, Ethan, and Jackson. I froze and tried to act casual.

"Hey sleepyhead. Did you realize we left you?" Ethan smiled over at me.

"Yeah," I covered my mouth, pretending to give a big yawn. "I think I'm going to head to bed. See you all tomorrow."

I moved a little faster than I intended, but the uneasy sick feeling had returned full force. Strangely though, by the time I reached the second floor the feeling had completely subsided.

I crawled under my covers and buried my face in my pillows, feeling dumbstruck by what had occurred.

Am I coming down with something? Or is it just pure exhaustion?

I had never experienced something so powerful in my life. How something could sweep over me so quickly but then leave just as fast left me with the oddest feeling.

My mind continued whirling with various possible explanations and scenarios until I finally drifted into a deep, dreamless sleep.

CHAPTER 2

Sunday, October 13, 1878

I FELT A SUNBEAM flowing through the lace curtain on my windows and breaking through the veil of my sheer canopy to warm my face. I smiled to myself and stretched, thinking about Jackson. The light felt refreshing on my skin and filled me with the last heat of the summer before autumn took its full hold.

Mimi was beside me as soon as I opened my eyes, smiling down at me. "Gud mornin,' Miss Jocelyn. Did ya sleep well?"

I nodded and pulled myself up on my pillows. My down, ivory, lace quilt stretched out around me, lying gracefully upon my bed.

"Morning, Mimi. Is everyone up?" I watched her for a moment while she laid out my things for the day.

"Yes, ma'am." Mimi nodded. "Dr. an' Mrs. Timmons ar alreada eaten n' da' dinin' rum, an' Mr. William wus headin' tha' way win Ah's com up."

I climbed out of bed and walked over to the water basin to wash my face and brush my teeth. The fresh water was chilly and instantly brought me back to life after my deep slumber. Mimi helped me into my corset, and I held my breath as she tied me up. I truly hated this torture device. At least that's what it felt like to me.

I climbed into my dark, cornflower blue gown with the ivory lace around the cuffs and neckline. The weight of it covered me like a thick blanket as it billowed out around me. I spun around before the full-length mirror, smoothing out the front of my heavy gown. The corset was so tight it made it a little difficult to breathe deeply, but it made the dress so flattering.

Once at the vanity, Mimi began brushing out my long, thick, wavy reddish-brown hair. Sunlight filled my room, making my hair look almost red. It always looked red in the sun.

It was my pride and joy, and Mimi always took such loving care of it. She was very graceful despite her years.

Mimi had been with my family for as long as I could remember. She told me once that she had taken care of my mother's family before she married my father and then came to live with them after their wedding. She was likely the oldest of all our servants except for perhaps her husband, Eddie. He and the others answered to her and Mother. But Mimi was clearly the favorite and most loved by me and all four of my older brothers. She loved us all; but my being the only female child in the house, she was always the one who dressed me and fixed my hair.

However, now that I am turning eighteen in less than two weeks and finishing my studies at school, she was more of a confidant than anything else.

"How are you feeling today, Mimi?" I noticed her rubbing her lower back as her wearied face winced. She was probably somewhere in her late sixties or mid-seventies; but since there were no records of her birth, no one was sure.

"Jus' m' bac gettin' wurs." She continued rubbing the small of her back.

"I'm sorry you are not feeling well." My eyes met hers in the mirror. Lately, I was beginning to really worry about her. She seemed to be tired all the time.

"Jus' gettin' ol'." She gave me a half smile and continued twisting my hair into curls.

"Not you, Mimi. You are not allowed to do that." I smiled lovingly at her reflection.

I watched silently as her skilled fingers twisted my hair up in curls and ringlets that clearly flattered my face.

Finally satisfied, she smiled back at me. "Dere. How's tha'?"

"Beautiful." I beamed. She was so warm and loving. "As always."

"Now, ya'd betta scoot fo ya breakfas'. Sara's bin cookin' all mornin'."

I joined my brother William at the dining room table. His tall, stocky frame was buried behind a newspaper. My parents had already finished and left the dining room. His dark, blonde hair was neatly combed, and he was already dressed in his Sunday attire. I could see his crystal-blue eyes absorbing every word across the page, and I wondered what held his attention so fully.

"Good morning, William." I tried to interrupt him.

"Morning, Jocelyn," he muttered, not bothering to look up from the paper.

"Anything interesting in the paper?" I inquired.

"Not really. Just much of the same." He remained behind his paper.

William was my favorite brother and the closest to my age. We had always been close growing up, but now he was gone throughout the week at Northwestern University, studying to become a lawyer. I was so envious of him and my other brothers for being allowed to continue their education that I practically pounced on them when they came home for any information, they would give me about all the things they were learning.

"Tell me about it anyway," I half-pleaded with curiosity.

William placed the paper down on the table beside him. "Later, Jocelyn." He laughed and rolled his eyes at me. "Give me a moment to wake up and enjoy my coffee, please."

William ran his fingers through his hair, and for the first time I really noticed the dark circled beneath his eyes. They looked tired and worried. His studies must be taking a lot out of him with midterms right around the corner.

"Fine," I playfully pouted to lighten his mood. He knew I'd continue pestering him until he talked. It was a constant game between us.

"You should hurry up and eat. Jackson will be here soon to pick you up."

I took a bite of my eggs and watched William help himself to another cup of coffee and spoon in one too many teaspoons of sugar before taking a sip.

"What time?"

"I am not sure, but soon I would imagine. It is almost eight already." He picked at his food but didn't take a bite of it.

I continued watching him, feeling that something was off with his behavior. Typically, William was the free-spirited one of all my brothers. It was almost impossible to catch him without a mischievous grin across his sculpted face. Something was bothering him, but I couldn't figure out what it was.

I played with my food for a few more minutes and finished my coffee while William disappeared once more behind the morning paper. I wasn't hungry, just anxious to see Jackson. He too was gone all week at the university with William, so I treasured my time with him on the weekends. We were to be married this Christmas, only ten weeks away. Shortly before then, he would be finished with his studies and become an attorney and take his position at his father's firm.

Finally, I gave up on having a conversation with William and went back upstairs to retrieve my capelet and bonnet before Jackson arrived.

I sat down in my window seat that faced our front yard with a book in my lap. I looked over toward the Chandler estate across the way.

The large, red-bricked, mansion appeared silent in the midmorning light. I wondered if Jackson was even up yet. Perhaps he was just as tired as William from his studies. Yet, he was much further along than my brother. William had only started his studies this fall, and the two young men shared a room at the university and were close friends. However, William had said that the workload was much more challenging than anything he had ever encountered before.

I spent the next half hour trying to read, but it was impossible. Every two sentences, I glanced over at the house across the way.

Finally, I saw Jackson emerge and make his way toward our home. As excited as I was, I did not want to appear overly anxious. So, I hid behind the drapes and waited for him to reach our door before I got up.

Eddie approached the door to welcome Jackson in but before he could reach it, William pushed past him and flung the door open.

"Good morning, Mr. Chandler." William was smiling at his own humor and mockingly bowed to Jackson. "Please come in."

I watched the scene from the top of the stairs with curiosity as William's mood completely shifted.

His playful antics always irritated Eddie, which only fueled William's behavior. Eddie did not believe it was proper for a housemaster, even a young one, to open his own front door. He flashed William a stern look as he held out his hand to receive Jackson's hat.

"Thank you, Mr. Timmons." Jackson laughed at William. He enjoyed William's playful nature; and in truth, Jackson behaved like him when scorning, older eyes were not upon him. Jackson gave Eddie a nod as he crossed the threshold, pausing in the foyer.

William gestured in a playful proper form to his right with a wide grin. "Will you not join me in the parlor while you wait for Miss. Jocelyn?"

"Certainly," Jackson replied, leading the way with William in tow.

I paused on the staircase, observing their charade with Mimi. I smiled at their playfulness while she shook her head with disapproval.

As I reached the first floor, Missy, one of our downstairs housekeepers, was already carrying a tray of coffee into the parlor for our guest. I entered the room, and both young men stood. Jackson crossed the room, taking my hand, and kissing it lightly.

"You look lovely this morning, my dear."

His piercing, emerald eyes gently held mine. My heart skipped a beat at the touch of his lips on my skin.

I curtsied slightly to him, returning his smile. "Good morning, Mr. Chandler." I continued their mocking charade.

Jackson's dark, gray suit looked stunning on his muscular frame. His dark, wavy, brown hair was slightly tousled, giving him an almost-boyish appearance. I loved the way it glistened in the sun, giving it copper-colored highlights.

"Won't you please join us?" Jackson gestured to the lounge.

"Thank you."

I crossed the room and gracefully sat on the edge of the lounge, careful not to wrinkle my gown. The full skirt ballooned out around me, draping almost the entire area of the lounge. Jackson sat down next to me a couple of feet away, taking care not to touch my skirt but still close to me. William took a seat in a chair across from us while Missy served us all coffee.

My parents arrived within moments, informing us it was time to leave. Jackson and I rode together in his carriage behind the one carrying my father, Patrick, and my mother, Annabelle, and William driven by Eddie.

I sat on the hardwood oak bench next to Jackson, listening to Reverend Jacobs preach about Cain and Able. It was a story I have heard a thousand times before, making it impossible to hold my attention. My focus instead was on Jackson and the gentle way his hands were holding mine. My eyes could not escape his face this morning as the sunlight brilliantly danced off the colors of the stained-glass windows across his cheeks, making it difficult for me to look elsewhere.

Jackson glanced over at me with the corners of his lips curled up ever so slightly. He refocused his attention forward, although I couldn't command myself to do so. William, on my other side, elbowed me in the ribs. I flashed him an annoyed look as he grinned.

Jackson and I rode together with our neighbor and my closest lifelong confidant, Olivia Adams, and William back to our home for Sunday dinner after services finally concluded. I was surprised when William asked Olivia to join us and eyed him suspiciously, but William paid me no attention.

He had never shown much interest in Olivia before except for pulling her braids when we were much younger. I was intrigued as to whether I was missing something between them. Certainly, Olivia would have told me. After all, she and I spent our weekdays together at school.

Olivia believed school to be a waste of time and did not enjoy our studies nearly as much as I did. She was a good student but felt that it was trivial for women to receive an education beyond a certain point.

It was one topic she and I did not agree upon. I adored learning and dearly wished I could continue my education. I had never voiced that opinion to anyone except Jackson and William since it was unheard of in our home.

My father was a firm believer that a woman's proper place was in the home, attending to the needs of her husband and children, coupled with hosting tea parties and cotillions. Women simply did not read newspapers or discuss politics or anything beyond the occasional appropriate novel. He had commented before that I was too curious for my own good when I had remarked on something about a new industrial machine.

He sternly informed me that such subjects were too complicated for me to understand and for me not to worry about anything beyond the scope of my course studies.

However, I knew that recently a few women were now attending the same university as my brothers and Jackson and even graduating. Yet, as far as my father was concerned, it was not even a consideration for me. It truly depressed me the way he wanted to limit my education simply because I was female.

My four brothers were either attending or had attended and graduated from college. It simply was not fair. Although I believed his point of view to be so old-fashioned, he knew there was no way I would defy his wishes.

The autumn sun was warm and peeking out from the puffy white clouds that drifted across the clear blue sky. The breeze added a chill to the air, kicking up the fragrance of ripe apples and hay. The leaves were beginning to fall and cover the pathways just enough to remind me that the long summer days were now only a fading memory.

Jackson placed a hand over mine while his other guided the reigns. I pulled my capelet closer around my shoulders to block out the cold. From the front of the carriage, I could hear Olivia and William speaking softly to each other; but I could not make out the words being spoken. Instead, I turned my attention back to Jackson.

I was immensely curious by this change of events. "Did you ask my brother to invite Olivia for dinner?"

"No. He asked me last evening if I would mind if they joined us, and I did not believe you would disapprove." The expression on Jackson's face told me he knew more than he was saying.

"No. Of course I do not mind. I was just unaware that William had any intentions toward her." I did my best to keep my eyes forward and not turn around to question the two passengers behind us.

"I know that they have been exchanging letters frequently since classes resumed this fall." He continued to look straight ahead, but I saw him raise his eyebrows a little.

"Really? I was unaware." I muttered softly so our passengers couldn't overhear. I couldn't believe it. "Neither of them has spoken of word of it to me. If Olivia was interested in my brother, why would she not have spoken to me about it, and why hasn't William mentioned it either?"

"I believe they both were concerned that you would be unhappy about their relationship. They did not want to upset you."

Jackson patted my hand in a reassuring way that made me even more upset. I felt like I had been deceived by all of them. I gently removed my hand from his, pretending to readjust my capelet again.

"Why would I be unhappy about a relationship between them?" I inquired, attempting to keep my voice smooth.

"I am not sure. I spoke with William about it. I informed him that he was truly being foolish for hiding his relationship with Miss Olivia from you. But he assured me yesterday that they had decided to tell everyone that they intend to be married."

Jackson's voice was cool and calm, but I was suddenly frozen to my seat, immersed in shock and anger.

"Married?"

"I know they are intending to speak with us about it, although I promise you, I am unaware as to why."

I sat in silence, fuming beside him.

Sometimes I truly despised the role I was born into. Men could openly express their displeasure in any situation, and no one ever thought differently of them. But being a lady, it was improper to do so without the world's judgment falling upon me.

I remained silent and fumed only to myself.

Our dining room overflowed with friends and family as we all gathered around the table. My mother was bursting with happiness, as I expected. She loved entertaining and felt completely satisfied when the house was filled with family and friends.

The men were discussing federal and state politics, the growing industry of the railroads, and the problems with some outlaw down in the New Mexico Territory. I sat and listened to them as they talked about this William H. Bonney person and his Regulators and what President Hayes intended to do about them. But I was not allowed to join in the conversation.

By early evening, Olivia, William, Jackson, and I settled on our front porch to escape the others. William had invited us with Olivia and him to discuss what Jackson had informed me of earlier. I sat next to Jackson and waited anxiously for what was coming next.

"As you probably have already guessed, Jocelyn, Olivia and I have become very fond of each other." My brother began nervously.

"I feel terrible that I did not share this with you sooner, Jocelyn." Olivia looked down at her hands. "It was only that I was unsure as to whether or not you would feel comfortable with my involvement with your brother."

"Why would I mind? It does not concern me. Obviously, no one thought so, or I would have been informed long before now." I could no longer hide my displeasure.

William interjected, "Now, Jocelyn, it was not like that at all." He placed his hand over Olivia's.

"Really now? Did it ever occur to either of you that I would be happy about your relationship? Apparently not, because both of you, and shall I say all of you," I looked directly at Jackson, "found it necessary to deceive me for the last several months." I fired back angrily and stormed into the house. I ran directly up the stairs to my room, slamming the door behind me.

I paced around my room with my thoughts racing. I hated being upset with Jackson. But I hated even more the feeling that he had betrayed my confidence by keeping a secret from me. I could not believe my best friend had been sneaking around with my brother behind my back for months and lying to my face the whole time. I realized that I was truly the last to know. I felt as if I was being laughed at for being the only one kept in the dark.

They all betrayed me.

In my pure disgust with all of them, I picked up my hairbrush off the vanity and threw it against the wall. The loud noise that followed enabled me to release the tears I had been fighting back. They poured down my face, as I threw myself atop my bed. The light outside my windows began to grow darker as the shortened day ended.

A few minutes later, I heard a knock at my door. "Jocelyn?" rang Olivia's voice. I remained silent. "Jocelyn, please," she called again.

I said nothing. A few moments later, I heard her footsteps retreat down the hall.

Shortly thereafter, heavy footsteps raced up to my door, followed by William slamming my door open.

I jumped off my bed and screamed at him, "How dare you barge into my room without knocking!"

He stood just inside my doorway, red-faced with his hand on his hips, glaring at me.

"How dare I? You, ridiculous child! Olivia is downstairs in tears because of you and your selfish behavior. You should be ashamed of yourself!" William pointed his finger at me.

I glared back at him. "Do not raise your voice at me, William. I am not the one who deceived you! I was not sneaking around with your best friend behind your back for the last several months, making a fool out of you!" I had never been so angry with him before.

"You had best come downstairs now and apologize this minute," he stated through gritted teeth.

"Me? Me apologize? Certainly, you cannot be serious!" My jaw dropped at his audacity.

"I most certainly am! Olivia tried to apologize, but you would not open your door and give her the chance to explain. Instead, you decided to behave like a child."

His words stung, and he knew it. He constantly teased me about being a child simply because I was the youngest.

"Get out of my room, William, or I shall tell Father that you barged in here without knocking. He will skin you alive for it," I taunted because he knew it was true.

None of my brothers were ever allowed to enter my or our mother's bed chambers without knocking and being verbally told they could enter. It was a rule that was strictly enforced and respected in our home.

William's eyes narrowed as he looked at me with disgust before he stormed out of my room, slamming the door behind him. I whirled around and threw myself back across my bed as the tears returned full force.

I lay there, sobbing, for what felt like an eternity when a soft knock on my door brought me back to reality and out of my selfish tears.

"Jocelyn?" My mother's soft voice called through the door.

"Yes, Mother?" I sat up, wiping the tears from my eyes.

She slowly opened my door and, with all her grace and beauty, entered my room. My mother was slightly taller than me with long, golden, blonde hair with crystal-blue eyes and was blessed with fair, porcelain skin. Even for a woman of her stature, she had a petite and delicate grace about her that made every woman in her presence take note. Her quiet demeanor and gentle smile yet firm hand commanded respect from everyone who came across her.

"William explained to me what happened." She sat down on the corner of my bed, placing her hands over mine. "I believe William and Olivia were only concerned about hurting your feelings." Her soft, blue eyes were filled with sincerity.

"Perhaps." I sobbed as she handed me her handkerchief. "But what bothers me the most is that they all deceived me. They made a fool of me."

My mother wrapped her arms around me and let me cry on her shoulder. "I do not honestly believe that was anyone's intention. And no one believes you to be a fool."

"But Jackson did not tell me. And for William and Miss Olivia to…" I sobbed. "Jackson, he's supposed to be in love with me, tell me everything. There are not supposed to be any secrets between us. I would never do this to him; betray his trust like this."

She finally released me and wiped the tears off my cheeks. She smiled lovingly cradling my face in her hands. "Jocelyn, you are a smart, beautiful, young lady, and I understand why you feel hurt and betrayed. You honestly have every right to, but downstairs there are three people who are hurting because they hurt you." She sighed.

I could only hope that someday I would have her grace, patience, and objectivity.

"I believe now is the time for forgiveness, to remember how much each of them means to you and how much you mean to them."

I nodded my head, understanding exactly what she wanted me to do.

"Now, let's clean up your face. Everyone is wondering where you are. Of course, I told them that you were tired and decided to lie down for a while." Mother's eyes gleamed gently. Her comforting smile gave me the strength to stand.

I returned to the porch to find the three of them still there. Olivia was sitting on the swing next to William, who had his arm around her.

William and Jackson rose as I approached, while Olivia still cried into her handkerchief. Jackson slowly approached me with a distressed look on his face.

He led me over to the double lounge rocker by the porch swing. Olivia looked over at me as I sat down.

"Jocelyn," she began, "please try to understand."

But I wouldn't allow it.

"Olivia, please."

I held up my hand to stop her from continuing. "I can handle tears from anyone, but you. You have nothing to be upset about. I behaved badly, and for that I apologize. I understand why you all had your concerns." Although I honestly didn't. "But I am truly happy for you both." I did my best to smile and put the circumstances of the evening, along with their deception, out of my mind and attempted to focus on the joy of the situation.

"Jocelyn," William began, still holding Olivia in his arms.

"William, seriously, it is all right." I had had more than enough for the evening. Thankfully, Jackson leaned over and asked me if I wanted to take a walk alone with him.

The full moon glowed off the cobblestone walkway, illuminating the path before us. The air was crisp and clean, and the smell of autumn was thick. I linked my arm through his as we walked slowly, enjoying the peaceful time we shared alone together.

"Jocelyn, will you please allow me to explain my actions?"

I opened my mouth to stop him, but he paused and placed his finger to my lips. I smiled and kissed his finger before he lowered it again.

"As I mentioned earlier, your brother and Olivia have been writing to each other since the fall term resumed. William apparently began courting her shortly before the end of summer, and they are happy. I believe it is wonderful after all that she has been through since losing Sean."

Olivia had been in love with Sean Donavon for three years before last spring when he passed away from pneumonia. They had gotten engaged the summer before, and she was devastated when she lost him. She had stayed in bed for months, and only toward the middle of the summer did she begin to rejoin social gatherings.

Jackson sighed deeply before continuing.

"William makes her very happy, and they seem very much in love with each other. I know they were concerned that with you and William being so close and her being your dearest friend their union might upset you. Neither of them intended to hurt you."

That sounded a tad bit flimsy, and I didn't buy it. There had to be something else, but I held my tongue. Instead, I wrapped my arms around Jackson's neck and kissed him on the cheek.

"Thank you for being honest with me."

I stepped back, looking at his beautiful smile. His dimples deepened as his smile reached his eyes.

The wind gently blew through his hair, lifting it slightly. It added emphasis to the slight curls in his hair. His hat shifted a touch, causing him to readjust it. I laughed at him as he cocked it to the side and gave me a jaunty grin.

"I love you, my darling," he declared in the moonlight.

"I love you too," I whispered back, completely in awe of him.

"Do you realize that in just over two months we will be husband and wife?"

"I cannot wait."

Jackson held both my hands in his as we stood facing each other. He finally turned, and we slowly resumed our walk.

"You realize that it is going to be an enormous affair." He glanced over at me, and I could feel he was heading somewhere with this. I nodded to gently urge him to continue. "Well," he stammered, and I knew this could not be good. "How would you feel about us having a double wedding?" He spoke very quietly.

I unsuccessfully attempted to conceal my shock with my sharp intake of breath.

"Seriously?"

He nodded with a weak smile.

I stopped cold in my tracks and stared at him. He did not seem to grasp the seriousness of what he was asking of me. For as long as I could remember, I had been dreaming of my wedding day. Now that it was so close and already painfully planned out with almost every little detail attended to, he wanted to alter everything.

"Are you asking me if I mind if William and Olivia have a double ceremony with us?" I could not believe my ears.

Please let him be kidding.

"Yes, I am. Your brother asked me several weeks ago when he proposed."

"William has already spoken with her father?" This was also news to me. Jackson barely nodded.

"When?"

"Almost a month ago, I think. He spoke with Mr. Adams and proposed to her one weekend when we came home from school." Jackson looked at the stones, refusing to meet my eye.

"So, then everyone knows about this?"

Jackson nodded slightly without looking up at me. I truly was the last one to know. The full degree of their deception grew a hundredfold. Suddenly, I was angry and hurt all over again.

"Yes," Jackson replied in a weak tone, "and now William has asked me, well, us, if there is any possibility that we could have a double wedding."

I started to speak but again, he placed his finger up to my lips.

"Now before you get upset, think about how much you love them," he pleaded. "I understand that our wedding is the most important day of our lives for us, but I was thinking that it would be even more special if we shared it with the two of them." He looked deep into my eyes, begging me for compliance before he finally kissed the top of my head.

I felt trapped in an impossible situation with no way out. I was so hurt and angry that I could not find the right words to say. So, I smiled and nodded.

What else could I do?

We wandered back up the cobblestone pathway toward my home. I did my best not to focus on the entirety of the situation. It felt like a nightmare I could not awaken from. I could not believe they would even consider intruding on our special day. Doing something like that to someone else was inconceivable to me.

How could they both be so thoughtless and inconsiderate? Especially Olivia. Certainly, she of all people understands what my wedding day meant to me.

Upon our return to the house, I played my part by smiling and being gracious and polite. I hugged William and Olivia and expressed my delight in their nuptials. I also informed them that I would be thrilled to share my wedding with them. Before retiring for the evening, I smiled accordingly when my father formally toasted the announcement of our double wedding. I did not want to feel this selfish, but I simply could not fathom why they were in such a rush to be married and could not wait and plan their own ceremony at some other time. I hated being manipulated into sharing my wedding.

CHAPTER 3

Sunday, October 11, 2015

I WOKE EARLY TO THE SOUND of the basketball bouncing off the asphalt driveway and laughter outside my window. I crawled out of bed and over to my bay window seat to peek through the blinds. Kyle, his younger brother, Brandon, Ethan, and Jackson were shootin' hoops. I considered opening the window and shouting at them for being so loud this early in the morning, but instead I sat there, watching them for several minutes before making my way to the bathroom.

After breakfast, I decided to go outside and practice hoops with everyone. Much to my pleasant surprise, Jenna also appeared. It shocked me, considering she never rose before noon on a Sunday. The incredible noise the guys were making must have awakened her also.

I crossed the porch to the driveway, and I could already hear their juvenile antics. Jenna saw me coming and threw the ball at me. I caught it and expertly hit an easy three-point shot. The boys laughed, and Jenna gave me a smirk.

"Show off!"

I glared over at my brother. "What's with all the noise so early in the morning?"

"Just havin' fun." He gave me a brotherly shove.

Jackson approached me with an amazing smile on his beautiful face and his hand extended. "Sorry. I haven't gotten the chance to properly introduce myself. I am Jackson Chandler."

His hand barely brushed my fingers in his attempt to shake mine when complete darkness overwhelmed me. Suddenly, my head hit the asphalt with a loud thump.

I woke up on the sun porch lounge with everyone standing over me like I was some specimen to be studied. As I slowly opened my eyes, the nausea took a strong hold of me and everything I had eaten for breakfast instantly came back up and landed on the rug. The cold sweats and uneasiness were holding a firm grip over my entire body. My mom touched my forehead with a cool washcloth.

"It's okay, sweetie. Don't worry about that. I'll clean it up."

"I'm sorry," I barely muttered as she hurried away to retrieve the cleaning supplies and bucket under the sink.

Jenna came over and sat down beside me. "Are you okay?" Her face was full of concern.

I nodded.

"Is it the same as before?"

Again, I nodded.

"I think you have the flu." She speculated.

"Probably."

"Well, at least this will get you out of school tomorrow." Jenna laughed. "And nice bump." She touched the side of my face, which hadn't hurt at all until her fingers brushed it.

I winced in pain. "Ouch."

"That's gonna leave a mark. Just in time too for the homecoming dance. But I'm sure we can cover it with some makeup."

My mom returned and cleaned up the mess I'd made, bringing with her a smaller, plastic wastebasket to sit beside me.

Jenna and the guys lingered about the sun porch, discussing the upcoming game on Friday and Jackson's first day of school tomorrow. Jackson sat directly across from me on a wicker chair with floral cushions, looking completely comfortable and at ease with my friends and family. It seemed rather odd to me that he just melted into our group the way he did, like it was the most natural thing in the world.

By noon, my mom insisted that I retreat to my room for the remainder of the day. The boys returned outside to shoot hoops, but at least Jenna came with me to keep me company.

I hated being isolated in my room during the day. My attempts to reassure my mom that I was now feeling better were completely fruitless. Jenna had let it slip that this wasn't the first incident, making my mom even more concerned.

"If it happens one more time, I'm taking you to the office for an examination."

There was nothing worse than that. So, I remained banished to my room on probably the last beautiful Sunday of the year, and I was not happy about it. I flopped down across my bed in frustration and flipped on the television, but as usual, there was nothing good. So, Jenna put in a movie.

I picked up one of my pillows and threw it at Jenna. "This sucks! I feel fine now. Why did you tell her about yesterday?" I knew Jenna had the best intentions, but it still made me upset that her little comment put me in my room for the rest of the day and probably tomorrow as well.

"I'm sorry. I just wanted her to know that this happened before."

"I know."

She folded her legs up under her, sitting on the side of my bed. "So, what do you think of Jackson?"

"I don't know," I shrugged. "I haven't even talked to him yet."

"He's really nice. And, man, is he gorgeous!" Jenna eyes widened with excitement.

"Jenna!"

"Oh, stop it. Like you didn't notice. I might have a boyfriend, but I'm not blind." She laughed. "He's asked me all kinds of questions about you." An evil grin spread across her face.

"Really?" She nodded. "Like what?"

"Oh, just the usual ones like, 'Do you have a boyfriend? What do you like? Do you play sports?' All that kind of stuff." She bounced around on the corner of my bed.

"What did you tell him?" I hated to admit I was curious.

"I told him you're great, that you play softball, basketball, volleyball," she paused, laughing, "and that you are very available."

"You didn't! How could you do that to me?" I could already feel the blood rushing to my face.

"I didn't say anything that wasn't true," she defended. "Besides, he's gorgeous and new in town, which makes him even more mysterious. He's from Boston, so he has that sexy accent. He's tall and built. What else do you want, Jocelyn?" Jenna could be so impossible sometimes.

"Are you kidding? I don't even know him. I've never even spoken to him." It was just like her to do something like this, always messing with things that weren't her business.

"But that will soon change. Besides, did you notice last night that he sat beside you on the couch?"

The coy look on her face was starting to make me nauseous again, but not in the same way.

"That doesn't count. I was asleep," I lied.

"He was also one of the last to leave last night. He was here first thing in the morning to get Ethan and Kyle to play ball. Plus, he was the one who carried you inside after you passed out." That I didn't know.

"Yeah. Well, he also saw me throw up. Very romantic." I covered my face with one of my throw pillows.

She shrugged her shoulders casually. "True. And believe me, it's unfortunate, but at least he didn't leave. That's a good sign."

She tried to reassure me, but I wasn't quite convinced. Something like that was truly tragic in front of someone you're trying to impress, not that I was trying to impress him. Well, not really.

"Yeah. A great sign," I grumbled at Jenna, who, in return, tossed a pillow at me. I fell backward against the bed when it hit me.

"You know, it's not so bad having a boyfriend living so close by." She walked over to the bay window and sat down to watch them for a few minutes. "It's comforting to know he's so close."

"Jenna, I'm not," I paused. "I'm not looking for a new boyfriend. I just want to finish high school and go off to college. I don't have time for all the drama of a boyfriend."

"Jocelyn, you haven't had a boyfriend since our freshman year." She came back over to the bed and sat down beside me. "I know how hard it was when Danny moved, but that was a couple years ago."

"You know he still emails." I had never shared that information with her before. I knew she'd be too judgmental and thought I was holding on to him and the past.

"You're kidding."

I shrugged casually. "Every once in a while, but not very often anymore." Which was true. Danny moved on with his life. He'd posted a junior prom picture of him and his new girlfriend on Instagram. It ripped my heart out to see him with her, but he did look happy. We had been together for three years when his dad was transferred to California.

Jenna broke my train of thought. "I'm sorry. Why didn't you tell me?"

"'Cause, I knew you'd think it was a bad idea."

"I do.

Judgmental.

"Well, don't worry 'cause, he's moved on and has a new girlfriend. I'm over him. My goodness. We were kids, Jenna. And, seriously, my not wanting a boyfriend has nothing to do with Danny."

However, she and I both knew that wasn't entirely true.

Jenna and I spent the remainder of the day watching movies and talking. We were both so bored, and I truly appreciated that she spent her day keeping me company rather than enjoying her Sunday with everyone else.

For the next several hours, we could hear the boys outside, but as the sun began to set on the long day, the hollowness of the house disappeared and became alive with laughter and conversation from the rooms below.

After six, Jenna left me to join the others before she headed home. I spent the next hour negotiating with my parents until I managed to convince them that I felt fine, and it was just a twenty-four-hour bug.

I desperately wanted to go to school tomorrow after spending the day confined to my room. I was restless and going stir crazy, so much so that I was even happy when Ethan came to see me before he went to bed.

His hair was wet, and he smelled like soap from the shower as he sat down at the foot of my bed.

"Feelin' better?" I nodded. "Mom says you want to go to school tomorrow. Sure, that's a good idea? You've been sick all weekend."

"I feel fine, E. They're being overcautious. I'm so sick of being in this room I could scream."

He gave me a sympathetic look. "You really didn't miss anything today anyway."

I'm not sure what bugged me more, his sympathy or his attempt to be casual.

"Jackson seems to like you," he added, ignoring my pouting.

"Why do people keep saying that? He doesn't even know me!"

Ethan rolled his eyes but smiled. "He asked me about you."

What is it with this guy and his determination to get to know me?

"Does it really matter? I'm not interested. Besides, I'm sure after tomorrow he will have his choice of any girl in school." The truth of that statement bothered me more than I cared to admit.

"Yeah. I can see that. But he really seems interested in you."

"I wouldn't know." I shrugged helplessly. "I keep passing out every time he's around."

A fact I had not completely realized before it hit me right in the pit of my stomach. It was true. The only time I felt lightheaded, or nauseous or got cold sweats was when Jackson was near me, and the only time I had fainted was when he touched me.

That little piece of information had completely escaped my consciousness before but was alarmingly true.

Ethan reached over and touched my shoulder, which was rare for him. "Hey. Are you okay? You're really pale. Should I call Mom?"

"No. Don't. I'm fine," I lied. "I think I need to get some sleep." I leaned back against my pillows. "I'll see you in the morning, E."

"Holler if you need anything," he offered with a sincere grin.

"I will. Good night."

"Night." He flipped off my light as he closed my door.

I tossed and turned for the next several hours, unable to find a comfortable position. My mind raced beyond my control.

How can this be possible? Is it Jackson who is making me sick?

The mere thought of it sounded ridiculous even to me. One person simply being near another could not make them physically ill in that way. And of course, no one else had any reaction to his presence. It was clearly a coincidence, nothing more.

Still, my mind wouldn't calm itself. There was something missing. And even though I couldn't explain it just yet, I was determined to figure it out.

CHAPTER 4

Tuesday, October 15, 1878

CLASSES WERE, FOR ONCE, UNINTERESTING. I struggled to grasp the world slipping away around me. Concentrating on anything my teachers were saying was impossible.

Olivia was sitting two seats down from me and instead of looking happy about the upcoming double nuptials, her face looked pale and depressed. We had not spoken much all morning because I could not think of anything to say to her. I knew she had to be aware of my displeasure with the change in plans. She had been beside me since early May when Mother, Jackson's mother, Emily, and I had begun making all the wedding arrangements. It had taken months for me to have my dress made and take care of all the details. Olivia was supposed to be my maid of honor and William was to be Jackson's best man.

How was this going to work now?

As we began our walk home after classes, the wind picked up considerably. Dark clouds hovered over us looking angry and overburdened. They fit my mood perfectly. My step quickened as I wanted to reach home before the sky opened and poured down upon us. I walked quickly beside Olivia, whose step was rapidly increasing the closer we got to home.

"Olivia." I struggled to keep up her pace as my gown brushed heavily against my legs. "Will you please slow down?"

"It looks like it might rain any moment," she hastily answered without bothering to look at me.

"I know, but could you please slow down? I cannot talk to you at this pace." I finally stopped, making her pause beside me.

"Jocelyn, I do not want to get wet." She flashed me a hostile expression, catching me off guard.

"Neither do I," I retorted, "but you have been avoiding me all day. What is wrong?" I was torn between anger and concern. Something was obviously bothering her a great deal.

"Nothing," she fired back and started walking again.

I picked up my pace to match hers. "I am not an idiot, Olivia. I can tell when something is upsetting you."

"You could not possibly understand, Jocelyn. So please do not ask me questions that I cannot answer." She looked like she might burst into tears at any second.

"There is nothing you cannot discuss with me. I promise to be understanding," I assured her.

She stopped and turned, giving me an angry look. "I am sure you will. Just like you were so understanding about my involvement with your brother and how you have given me fake smiles since Jackson talked you into the double wedding. Do you really think I do not know how upset you truly are about sharing your wedding day with me? I can see it in your eyes every time I look at you. You hate the thought of sharing your wedding day, and you have every right to be upset. I, of all people, know how long you have been waiting for this and here I am, ruining it for you."

"All right. Yes, I am upset with you, but you would feel the same if our roles were reversed."

"Our roles would never be reversed," she fired back.

I felt the tears stinging up in my eyes from both anger and confusion. "Olivia, I am trying. Truly, I am. I want to be happy for you and William. Honestly, I do. I only feel like everyone has had time to adjust to all of this, and I just found out. I need a little time. Please try to understand how I feel."

Olivia stared down at the walkway. "I do understand, Jocelyn. Better than you realize." Her voice was dry and hollow.

"Then why are you angry with me?" I did not understand. I was the one who should be angry, not her.

"I am not angry with you. I am angry with myself for doing this to you."

"I do not understand what you mean."

"It makes no difference. Let's get moving now before we get rained on." Olivia started walking again.

She remained silent the rest of the way. She waved a quick good-bye without a word and headed up the pathway toward her house.

I was surprised to find Jackson waiting for me in the kitchen, talking with Sarah and Mimi.

"Hello, my love." He walked over, taking my hand, and kissing it softly. "You look lovely today."

"Thank you. What are you doing home this evening?"

"I was just telling Sarah that I could smell her good cooking all the way at my dorm and had to come." He smiled over at Sarah, and she laughed, tossing a dishtowel at him.

"Ya git outta of ma kitchen', Mr. Chandler. Ah'll fin ya win suppa's dun."

He placed the rag down on the table, laughing at her. The two of them constantly tormented each other in good spirits.

"You had better." Jackson took my hand. "Would you like to have a seat by the fire?"

"Of course."

Jackson rarely came home through the week. Something else was amidst, but I had no inkling what was behind all the deceptions and secrets. For once, I just wanted someone to be honest with me for a change.

We walked over to the front room and sat down next to the roaring fire in the hearth. It felt wonderful to feel the heat on my face after shivering all the way home. Jackson walked over and turned on the phonograph; beautiful, soft music flooded the room. He came over and sat down beside me.

I curled up in his arms. "I am surprised you came home this evening. I thought you were studying for your midterms."

"I am, but William wanted to come home to speak with Miss Olivia. She is really upset, and he wanted to check on her." Jackson stared over at the fire as if lost in his own thoughts.

"Well, I wish him luck with that. I tried to speak with her on the way home, and she would hardly talk with me. I have no idea what is wrong with her." I wanted to put her and William out of my head.

"She will be fine," Jackson assured me.

"What is going on?" Curiosity was getting the best of me.

"That is between the two of them. I am sure everything is all right."

I sighed heavily and shook my head slightly. "Why can you not be honest with me for a change? I know something is going on that no one will discuss," I grunted, "with me anyway." I paused for a moment waiting for Jackson to respond, but he didn't. "Olivia said she was angry with herself, not me, and that our roles could never be reversed. Whatever is that supposed to mean?" I had absolutely no clue what was going on with Olivia. Nothing about her behavior made any sense to me anymore.

"That is a strange thing to say," Jackson continued, staring at the fire.

"She is not acting like herself," I commented, watching his face intently.

"Perhaps she is a nervous bride. After all, you have had some time to digest the concept of it all. Miss Olivia really has not. This is all very fast for her," he speculated.

"I remember being terrified last spring at the thought of being a wife and running my own household. But now I cannot imagine anything I want more." I placed my hand over his. I smiled up into his eyes, recalling how apprehensive I was last spring.

"I am happy to hear that. You sure you are still not scared?" He narrowed his eyes at me with a mischievous grin.

"Looking forward to it," I assured him. "I wish the wedding were tomorrow."

"I do too. It will be wonderful to come home every evening to your beautiful face and to someday have a family of our own." He gave me a gentle squeeze.

Jackson placed his arm around my shoulder, and I leaned my head against his chest. I could hear his heart beating through his shirt and vest, steady and strong. The smell of his skin was intoxicating. I closed my eyes, imagining how wonderful it was going to be to get to share every evening with him for the rest of my life.

The music drifted me off to another place where my worries were gone and there was nothing but our perfect wedding day, our anticipated wedding night, and a lifetime of happiness ahead. It all felt so close. I could almost reach out and touch it.

We heard the front door open and shut loudly, bringing heavy footsteps into the foyer outside the room. Jackson and I both turned toward the noise to discover William standing in the doorway.

"Sorry." He looked embarrassed. "I did not mean to interrupt."

"Please, come in," Jackson offered.

William and I hadn't spoken since his departure Sunday evening, and I could feel the tension between us rising as he took a seat across from us by the hearth. He truly looked tired and worn out, more so than I had ever seen in my entire life. My love for my favorite brother overcame my anger, and I felt myself softening toward him.

"Is everything all right, William? You look tired."

"Just classes. Midterms," he muttered back, leaning forward, and resting his head on his hands with his elbows on his knees.

"You look like you need to sleep." He had prominent, dark circles under his eyes.

"I do. However, I cannot seem to shut my mind down long enough for a good night's rest." He shook his head wearily. "Please, excuse me. I need to go cleanup for supper." William got up and hurried out of the room as quickly as he had entered. He and Olivia were behaving so strangely.

Supper was delicious and full of chatter. Jackson's parents, Robert, and Emily had joined us at Mother's request, so that wedding arrangements could be settled. As our mothers began discussing a new formation, it seemed strangely both sad and odd, especially since I felt that Olivia and her mother, Harriet, should be present for this conversation. However, neither Mother nor Emily ever acted as though it mattered that they were not present.

My heart and mind were, for once, not on my wedding. Instead, I was intently watching William's behavior. He would occasionally comment on the conversation among the men over politics and President Hayes, but it was obvious that he was not really paying much attention. I could not help but wonder what was going on in his mind.

The gentlemen were having a heated discussion over the immigrant problem developing in the inner city of Chicago. Apparently, the current housing structures were not suitable for so many individuals and the mix of poverty and poor relationships between the various cultures were causing problems for a great many people. I found their conversation intense and more intriguing than Mother and Emily's. I had almost overnight lost interest in my wedding details simply because I truly believed my opinion no longer mattered on the subject.

Everyone retired around the hearth after dinner to have coffee. I excused myself for some fresh air, picked up my shawl in the foyer, and stepped out onto the front porch. The rain had finally started and was dancing softly off the shingles. The evening air was cold, giving the wind a solemn feel.

I leaned against the railing, watching the raindrops splash upon the cobblestones, when a voice came up behind me, startling me out of my solace.

"Mind if I join you?" Emily Chandler came up beside me.

"No, not at all. Please do."

"Are you getting excited about the wedding yet?" I nodded silently. "I am sorry so many things have to be switched around, but I am sure your mother and I can get things settled to your satisfaction." She gave me a warm, motherly smile.

"Honestly, it does not matter so much anymore." I hated that I sounded so shallow about it, but it was truly how I felt now. I looked down at my hands, trying to hide my true disappointment.

"Why is that? You have been so excited about this since your engagement was announced."

"I feel as if now it cannot possibly be the wedding that I have always dreamed of; therefore, the details do not matter so much anymore." I did not want to come across ungrateful, and I knew Emily would understand my disappointment.

"Jocelyn, your wedding will be beautiful and everything you have always wanted, I promise." I wanted so badly to believe her, yet I knew that it simply was not a possibility.

"But how? My maid of honor is now also a bride in the ceremony." I took a deep breath and exhaled slowly. "Honestly, I am trying not to be selfish. I dearly love Olivia and my brother, but I do not understand why they find it necessary to intrude on my wedding. Especially when both know how much Jackson and I have been waiting for this day."

"Perhaps they love you both so much that they feel that combining the ceremonies will make the day more special for the four of you."

"I know, I sound terrible." I looked down at my hands resting on the porch rail, feeling ashamed and wishing I had not been so honest.

"Not at all. You have every right to be selfish about your wedding. I know you have been anticipating it for a long time."

"Yes, I have." *Too long.*

"I also know that in the end it will not matter what kind of ceremony you and Jackson have. You two have a very special kind of bond, a love so deep that nothing could possibly taint it." She reached over and gently touched my arm.

"Thank you, Mrs. Chandler. I appreciate that."

CHAPTER 5

Tuesday, October 13, 2015

JACKSON WAS AN INSTANT SUCCESS at school. The girls stared at him as he walked down the halls with Kyle or Ethan and his friendly personality drew everyone to him, especially Taylor, which truly burned me although it had no reason too. Jackson was free to date anyone he wanted. I certainly had no say in the matter. But there was something about him that made me feel like he'd been a part of my life from the beginning.

I couldn't explain it. But I knew I had to stay away from him. He was like a poison to me and would surely cause me nothing but heartache and trouble. I had an important volleyball match on Thursday, and I couldn't afford to miss it. I was positive that if I fainted one more time there was no possible way my mother would allow me to participate.

Jenna waltzed giddily up to my locker right before lunch, more excited than I had seen her in a long time. "Guess what Kyle just told me."

"I can't imagine." I truly was not in the best of moods since it seemed in the last two days Jackson had quickly become friends with everyone in my world, making it near impossible for me to go anywhere without him being there already. Since I was purposely avoiding him, it was rapidly making me an outsider.

"Jackson told him this morning that he is going to ask you to the homecoming dance this Friday." She bounced up and down as I rolled my eyes, looking inside my locker to avoid her excitement. "Isn't that great?"

"Yeah. Wonderful," I muttered under my breath.

Why can't he focus on someone else and realize that I don't want anything to do with him? Is he that blind or just that stupid?

"So now we can all go together."

I slammed my locker closed and confronted her.

"Look, Jenna. I'm not going to the dance with Jackson or anyone else. I don't want to go to some silly dance. Seriously, let it go." She looked shocked and annoyed at my lack of enthusiasm.

"Jocelyn, you really need to lighten up. You're quickly becoming an old shrew!" Her forehead wrinkled, give me a stern look of disapproval.

"Thanks. I appreciate that." I walked away, leaving her standing by my locker, looking completely flustered.

"Are you coming to lunch?" she hollered after me down the hall.

"Can't. Studying." I didn't turn around to look at her but raised my calculus book back over my shoulder as I headed off toward the gym.

I took a seat about halfway up the bleachers in the empty gymnasium. I knew students weren't supposed to be in here during the lunch period, but I couldn't stand to be around anyone. I opened my calculus book and laid it out on the bench below me.

I situated my notebook and started working on the assignment given to me earlier, so I wouldn't have to take it home. I rested my head in my hand and slightly brushed the fading bruise and knot on the side of my face. It was still tender from the fall, and I looked like someone had punched me in the face.

I had gotten numerous inquisitive looks in the last couple days, but no one had directly approached me about it. I winced in pain and readjusted myself. The last several days hadn't exactly been the best.

I took a deep breath and tried to focus on my calculus but couldn't concentrate to save my life. It seemed I was rapidly approaching complete frustration with almost every aspect of my life. I knew Jenna was upset with me and utterly confused by my behavior, and I didn't know how to explain any of it to her.

I willed myself to focus on calculus and got my homework done in record time. Whether it was correct or not was another story. I was good at calculus, but today I just wanted it done.

I spent the rest of the day avoiding my friends or looking at Jackson, who was not only in my morning AP biology class but also turned up in my AP psychology class at the end of the day.

Great. Now I have two classes with him. Just what I wanted.

Since we didn't have assigned seats, I managed to stay across the room from him by the windows and did my best not to look in his direction.

Our psychology teacher, Mr. Rand, was finishing his lecture on personality disorders while I stared out the window at the football field, only half-listening. I glanced at my watch every five minutes, anxious to get out there and away from Jackson. I wanted to hurry to get to practice so that I could run out my anxiety and clear my head. What I wasn't looking forward to during practice was being confronted by my friends and having to explain my behavior for the last two days.

I changed my clothes as fast as I could in hopes of getting out onto the court before the three of them arrived in the locker room. However, as I sat down to tie my shoes, the three of them surrounded me, cutting off my escape.

"Jocelyn, what's going on with you?" Caitlyn was the first to start the inquiry.

"Nothing." I wanted to act as casual as possible.

"Why did you skip lunch today? And yesterday you left five minutes into lunch?" Jenna was clearly annoyed.

"I went to the gym to get my calculus done so I wouldn't have so much homework. I have two big tests next week, and I'm trying to be prepared." That much was true and the fact that they all knew I was a closet bookworm helped cover my actions.

"But you've never done that before." Caitlyn narrowed her eyes at me suspiciously.

"Seriously. Nothing's going on. Why all the questions?" I wanted to sound as innocent as possible.

"I'm not buying it." Hilary rolled her eyes at me while changing her clothes for practice. "Something's not right here."

"Maybe she's sick. She did pass out a couple of times this weekend, and she slept through Saturday night."

Jenna spoke to the other two like I wasn't even standing there, which really annoyed me more than it should have.

"Stop it! I'm fine. Let it go!" I pushed my way around Jenna and stormed out of the locker room.

I avoided any type of questioning throughout practice, which wasn't too difficult since Coach never gave us a break long enough to chat. For once, I was extremely thankful.

By the time we ended at five, I was completely drained both emotionally and physically. I knew I was supposed to be riding home with Jenna, but I really didn't want to get in the car with any of them.

I followed the three of them out the school doors and paused, making them turn to look at what I was doing.

"I left something in my locker I need, so go on. I'll see you all later." I turned to walk back into the building. Although I hadn't left anything, I didn't want to get into it. I'd rather walk home than be in the car with them.

"S'okay. We'll wait." Jenna shifted from one foot to the other.

"Nah. Don't be silly. Head on home."

I started to walk back into the building, but Caitlyn caught my arm. "How you gonna get home?" Caitlyn inquired, raising her eyebrows at me.

"I'll walk." I pulled my arm back gently.

"Don't be silly. It's too far. We'll wait," Hilary stated.

"No. Really. It's fine. I want to walk."

I gave them the best smile I could muster as they all stood there, staring at me with puzzled looks on their faces.

"Fine." Jenna was the first to turn and walk away. "Come on!" She hollered to Hilary and Caitlyn over her shoulder when they hesitated. "If she wants to be alone, let her."

I could hear the anger in Jenna's voice, but I didn't care. She couldn't possibly understand what I was going through, even if I attempted to explain it to her.

I waited inside the school and watched the three of them drive away before I set out. It was a cool, cloudy evening, the perfect setting for my mood. The air held tight to a blue-gray tinge masking the brilliant colors that were long lost with the summer sun.

I turned down the corner of our street, and I could already hear the basketball bouncing off the asphalt.

Great, he's back again.

Coach Shelburne certainly isn't giving the boys hard enough football practice if they still have the energy to shoot hoops afterwards.

As I got closer to my house, I could see Ethan, Jackson, Brandon, Kyle, and Jenna goofing around and laughing. The scene in front of me literally made me sick to my stomach. Last week it was me instead of Jackson out there doing the exact same thing. I couldn't even explain why Jackson's presence in my life upset me so much. Something deep inside me screamed for me to stay clear of him, but another part was so drawn to his presence.

I walked slowly up the walkway and the bouncing immediately stopped. Everyone turned in my direction and stared.

"Hey, Jocelyn. Join us so our teams will be even." Ethan smiled and so did everyone else, except Jenna.

I only shook my head and walked to the front door as fast as I possibly could. Jenna rolled her eyes and followed me into the house.

"Hey!" She reached out, grabbing my arm, spinning me around. "What the hell is your problem? You've been acting like a bitch for the last several days."

"I'm just not in the mood to shoot hoops. What's wrong with that?"

Jenna let out a deep breath, letting go of my arm. "Jocelyn, what's wrong?"

"I'm just confused about something. Seriously, it's no big deal."

I stumbled upstairs to my room with Jenna in tow.

I threw my things in the corner and flopped down on my bed. She lingered in the doorway, staring at me like she'd never seen me before and at this moment, I wasn't sure I disagreed.

"Jocelyn?" Jenna approached me with caution. "I don't understand what is going on with you lately."

"That makes two of us," I buried my face in my pillow, unsure if I was going to scream or cry.

"I'm serious." She sat down on the edge of my bed, and I sat up to look directly at her.

"I am too. I can't explain any of this either. Something's changed, and I don't know what it is."

"Why have you been avoiding us for the last two days?"

"I haven't."

"Oh, come on. You have so. You went to the gym for lunch, and don't give me this crap about studying." Her eyes narrowed. "I know you study more than the rest of us, but you have never gone down to the gym to study during lunch."

"I know." I looked away from her. She was right.

"So, what's eating you?"

"Honestly?"

"Yes."

"Why is it that every time I turn around, Jackson's there? I'm sick of the way he's always hanging around." I got up and peered out the window. Down below, I could see him out in the driveway with the rest of them. "I mean, it just seems like the last several days he's been glued to us. I'm tired of it." My tone got harsher.

"Really, Jocelyn? How petty can you be? The guy just moved here. He doesn't know anyone, and he lives across the street. Of course, he's going to befriend Kyle. They're the same age and have several classes together. And Ethan is only a year behind. Jackson's only trying to make friends in a new place. That can't be easy."

"I know," I agreed with harshness still in my voice.

"I could understand it more if it was a girl trying to move in on your life, but why do you care so much if he hangs out with Ethan and Kyle?" Jenna cocked her head to the side and studied me closely.

"I don't know. There's just something about him, and I can't explain it. I'm not sure what, but I get this weird feeling about him. He's different from us." I couldn't come up with the right words to tell her exactly what I was feeling.

"Yeah. He's from Boston. He's sexy, gorgeous. Not at all like the normal jerks that we have around here." Jenna joined me at the window and watched the guys for a moment. "Honestly, Jocelyn. He's really nice. The only strange thing that I've noticed about him is that he actually has manners, and his grammar is flawless." She smiled at the image below us. "I mean, have you heard him speak? Seriously, it's like some Jane Austen novel. Well, if that's what you call weird, then yeah; I supposed he is. But we're all weird in our own way, right?" Her logic made me smile.

"True." I let out a weak laugh, hoping she was right.

"Are you okay?" She turned and faced me. All her anger had turned to concern.

"Much better. Thanks." Jenna placed her arm around me and gave me a gentle squeeze.

"Come on. Let's join the guys and show them how it's really done."

We headed back downstairs, but.as we reached the edge of the driveway, the heavy, dark clouds finally broke loose and dumped their showers, ending any prospects of a three-on-three match.

"Let's get in the house!" I shouted at Jenna.

We broke into a sprint, reaching the sun porch already soaked to the skin.

Jenna shook her hair and shivered from the cold. "Well, I think I'm gonna head on home. Are you gonna ride with me in the morning?"

"Of course." I nodded. "Hey, sorry for being such a bitch lately, and please let's keep everything I said between us, okay?"

"Always." Jenna smiled before she retreated outside, making a mad dash between the yards toward her own back door.

I stood out there for a minute longer, realizing I was immensely curious about the boy across the street.

Gathered in the living room with our TV trays, Ethan gave our parents an earful of his day. I only half paid attention, listening to him ramble on endlessly about football practice as our dad added in his two bits between sentences. It wasn't until Ethan started discussing his afternoon with the guys and Jackson's name was mentioned that my ears perked up.

"I swear Jackson is such a character." He snorted between mouthfuls. "After it started raining, we headed over to Kyle's to play some *Halo*, and Jackson accidentally knocked over a Coke on their living room carpet. Kyle's mom comes running in with paper towels, and Jackson said, 'I am so sorry, ma'am. I honestly did not mean to soil your carpet. I will clean that up for you'." Ethan did a poor imitation of Jackson's Boston accent. "And he takes the paper towels from her and cleans up the mess. I swear Kyle's mom was so stunned she just stared at Jackson, but no words came out of her mouth. It was hilarious. I don't believe I've ever seen her speechless before."

He and my parents laughed, considering Kyle's mom was notorious for her big mouth.

My parents started discussing their days and my mind immediately tuned them out, wandering back to what Jenna had said earlier about Jackson's proper grammar and manners. It made me smile to think of how different he was indeed from the other guys we knew. He was special. That was for sure. Perhaps I was wrong to judge him so harshly.

Ethan came into my room right after I had climbed under the covers. I snuggled down with my well-worn copy of Anne Rice's *Interview with a Vampire* when he appeared, taking a seat at the foot of my bed.

"You were quiet at dinner tonight. Are you sure you're feeling all right?" I could tell he was fishing, only now I wasn't sure for who.

"I'm fine."

"Why didn't you and Jenna come back out and shoot hoops with us?"

"We did, but it started raining and we saw you guys run over to Kyle's."

"You know, Jackson was asking if you had a date for the homecoming dance."

"What did you tell him?"

"That you didn't."

Great.

"You couldn't have lied or something?" I didn't want to come across to available.

"Why would I lie? He's a nice guy?"

"I'm tired." I placed my book back on my nightstand and slid farther under the covers. "Can you turn the lights out on your way out?"

"Sure." Ethan stood up and walked over to the door. "Hey, can I ask you something?"

"What now?"

"Why don't you like Jackson? I mean, even as a friend?" He scrunched his eyebrows.

"I don't know Jackson. Why does everyone assume I don't like the guy?" This sentiment was getting old fast. "It's not true and turn off the lights." I smiled at my little brother.

"Sweet dreams."

"You too."

I laid there, wide-awake, watching the shadows dance across my walls, letting my mind wander endlessly until I finally drifted off into a dreamless sleep.

Chapter 6

Thursday, October 17, 1878

OLIVIA IGNORED ME ALL MORNING through the duration of our classes. Even during lunch, she sat quietly while I spoke with our friends — Elizabeth, Laurie, Christina, and Maryanne. They were so excited about the Autumn Festival coming up on Halloween weekend. In their eyes, it was terribly romantic and spooky. The perfect night to have a man by your side to dance with at the evening party and enjoy all the games and spooky activities.

There was always a hayride, bobbing for apples, a pie eating contest, dancing, bonfires, and a haunted maze where people dressed up in costumes and tried to scare the life out of you as you tried to find your way out. The annual event had become a favorite tradition for everyone in town.

I did my best to share in their enthusiasm while I continually glanced over at Olivia. I was quickly growing more concerned about her. Once again, she looked pale and fragile sitting there across from us, refusing to speak or make eye contact with anyone. Although I was still upset with her odd behavior and deception, I was trying my best to be polite; except she was making it difficult by her continued silence.

After lunch, we made our way to our next class when Olivia quietly announced that she was not feeling well and had decided to walk home. Without as much as a goodbye to any of us, she simply turned and walked away. The other girls and I stood there, looking after her, completely stunned.

"Olivia, wait." I called.

She did not bother to slow her pace or acknowledge my voice.

"Olivia, please." I slowed down beside her as we passed through the school doors. "What is wrong? Are you ill?"

"I need to lie down, Jocelyn. Go to class." She still refused to meet my eye.

"No. I want to walk you home. If you are not well, I want to make sure you get home." Her coolness toward me was making me more upset by the minute, and I struggled to remain polite if only for William's sake.

"Please, Jocelyn. I want to be alone." She picked up her pace.

"Olivia, this behavior of yours is ridiculous and frankly, I am getting tired of it." I could feel the anger boiling to a head inside me and the struggle to be polite was almost impossible.

"Then go to class and leave me be!" She practically screamed in my face.

"I do not know who you think you are talking to, but I am done with your childish antics. You are so selfish, and the last thing I want to do is share my wedding day with you!" I shouted at her, making her stop in her steps.

She turned and glared at me coldly. "That is fine with me. I do not care, nor do I want to be a part of your wedding in any fashion either as your maid of honor or another bride!" she shouted back. "Now leave me alone!"

"I cannot believe the sheer amount of audacity you have! You spend several months sneaking around behind my back, seeing my brother, writing him letters, and now you are the one intruding on my wedding and you are mad at me! How rich!"

"You have no clue what you are talking about. I do not want to share my wedding day with you any more than you want to share it with me!" Her harsh tone raised yet another octave.

"Wonderful. It is settled then, and you can tell my precious brother your spin on it, making it look like my fault, as always!" I could not imagine the wrath my brother was going to bestow upon me for this.

"Do you honestly believe he cares? He does not want our wedding with yours any more than I do."

Now I was stunned.

What in the world is going on that I do not know about?

"Then why are you doing this to me? I do not understand you at all."

"And you never will." Hatred blazed from her eyes.

"What is that supposed to mean?" I shot back, glaring at her. I was so sick of her games and wanted some real answers.

"Jocelyn, you live in your perfect little paradise with your perfect little romance and perfectly planned wedding, and you have no clue whatsoever what life is really about!"

"What is wrong with you? How dare you talk to me like that!"

"You have spent your life in your properly sheltered bubble without any idea of what a relationship truly entails!"

Tears rolled silently down my cheeks as I stared at the face of someone who had once been my dearest friend and now, somehow, turned into someone I did not recognize at all. Thankfully, there was no one around to hear her nasty words since our afternoon classes had already resumed.

"Your life has been just as sheltered as mine," I mumbled.

"You know nothing," she spat back.

"What did I ever do to you, Olivia?" My voice was now weak. All the anger had disappeared, and all I could feel was pain.

"Nothing, Jocelyn! Nothing! You are perfect! Always!"

The hatred remained in her eyes, and it made no sense at all.

"I am not perfect, Olivia. You of all people know it," I said softly.

"Oh, yes you are, and I am so tired of living in your shadow!" she shouted back.

Her words totally surprised me. I never had any idea she felt that way. "When have you ever lived in my shadow?"

"Ever since we were little kids. Now, when someone close to you wants to be with me, you cannot stand it!" I could see her hands trembling as if she wanted nothing more than to reach out and strike me.

"What are you talking about?"

"William!"

"William has nothing to do with this. I could care less that you are marrying my brother. I was upset because I had no clue what a backstabbing sneak you are! If you were going to be with my brother, you could have at least told me instead of hitting me with it out of the blue."

"Oh, and you would have given us your blessing, right?" Tears started rolling down her cheeks despite her anger.

"I would have if it made you both happy, but now I could care less if either of you are happy. Actually, I hope you make each other miserable!" I shouted my anger at her before leaving her standing alone on the walkway.

I hastily walked back into the building, knowing too well that I was very late for my next class. I considered going home myself, but I was determined not to let Olivia ruin my entire day.

Elizabeth and Maryanne, both gave me inquisitive looks as I joined our history class that was already in progress. Mr. Grahame glared his disapproval at my tardiness while I quickly took my seat in the second row.

"Nice of you to join us this afternoon, Miss Timmons." He tapped his fingers on his desk as he always did when he was annoyed.

"I apologize, Mr. Grahame. I wanted to make sure Miss Olivia made it home safely, sir. She is not feeling well." I tried to make my voice as calm as I could, and it was extremely difficult.

"Fine. Now may I return to the Continental Congress?"

"Again, I apologize, sir." Mr. Grahame glared at me a moment longer before he cleared his throat and continued with his lecture on John Adams's contributions to the Continental Congress.

I stared at the clock on the wall, convinced that it was not working properly. Frustration continued to build from deep within me. My argument with Olivia was harsh in the way that only a close friend can truly hurt. I did my best to pay attention to the words spoken by Mr. Grahame, but it was pointless.

Maryanne cornered me after the final bell. She and Elizabeth had witnessed the beginning of my argument with Olivia, but had left to get to class on time, therefore missing the entirety of the disagreement.

"Are you alright?" Maryanne rushed to my side for all the juicy details, as I had expected. Her brown eyes were full of anticipation as she flipped her dark curls over her shoulder.

"I am fine. Miss Olivia and I just had a disagreement on a personal matter." I wanted to sound as casual as possible.

"We heard." Maryanne paused outside the front door. "Is it true that you are having a double wedding now?"

I nodded, looking down because I did not trust myself not to cry if I looked in her face.

"I cannot believe she would do that to you." Elizabeth, who always desperately wanted to believe in the good in all people, looked baffled. "Is she really marrying William?"

Again, I only nodded.

"I was unaware he was even courting her."

"Me too, before last weekend. Apparently, it has been going on for a while now, at least since last summer," I stated in a flat tone.

"Really?" Maryanne was utterly stunned.

"How could she do that to you? You two have always been so close." Olivia's act of betrayal clearly upset Elizabeth.

"I know, and I am afraid it came as quite a shock." I let out a small, hollow laugh that sounded more like a cough. "Not one that I reacted to very well either."

"Well, I would be livid if I were you, Jocelyn. I mean, not only does she sneak around behind your back with your own brother, but now, to top it off, after months and months of painstaking planning and details, she wants you to compromise and share the most important day of your life." Maryanne was getting redder in the face with each passing moment.

I thought at least for Olivia's sake it was a good thing she had gone after my brother and not Maryanne's. I believe Maryanne would have physically hurt her for it.

"Well, I must be getting home. I need to get my hair washed this evening before Jackson comes home tomorrow." I descended the front steps.

It was a small lie but a good excuse to get me away from Maryanne before she could inquire as to whether Jackson knew what was going on between Olivia and William. I knew she was aware that the two were roommates at school, and I did not want to admit that Jackson had kept this a secret from me. Maryanne would have surely gone into the entire trust issue and the depth of Jackson's role in this deception. It was a subject I could not stand to touch on with her.

Elizabeth followed me down the stairs since she lived only a few houses from me and was going in the same direction.

"I am so sorry, Jocelyn." Elizabeth and I slowed down our pace as we hit the cobblestone pathway.

"I am doing my best to work through it, but to be honest I am really upset about the whole situation." The entirety of the day's events finally hit me, and I felt overwhelmed with sadness. I no longer had the energy to be angry. It was all simply too much.

"That is understandable. You feel betrayed and hurt by people you love and trusted." Elizabeth reached over and put her arm around me, squeezing my shoulder as we walked.

"I am glad at least one person understands." The tears started, and I quickly whipped them away. "I truly am trying, Elizabeth. I am. But I am so hurt and angry that it has clouded everything else. I am so tired of hearing my mother and Jackson talk down to me like I was a child and tell me that they kept this from me because they did not want to hurt me. That is such a lie." The sobs started coming out from all the frustration and anger I had experienced over the last several days. "Why would I be unhappy about Olivia and my brother? I would have given my blessing. Honest I would have."

"I know. I wish I had some words that would comfort you, but I cannot think of any. I do not understand why they did not confide in you right from the beginning." Elizabeth's delicate frame shivered in the cold breeze. Her light-brown hair was covered by her maroon bonnet that perfectly matched the beautiful gown she was wearing. She was such a quiet girl and so awkwardly shy that it usually caused her gracefulness and beauty to go unnoticed.

However, I knew at one point in time a few years back, William had noticed her and really wanted to court her. Unfortunately, she was much too shy for his rambunctious personality. I wished now that he had pursued Elizabeth instead of Olivia.

"That makes two of us." I tried to smile but did not quite pull it off.

"Perhaps there is another reason for all this secrecy."

"Maybe." I shrugged. "Who knows anything anymore? Apparently, my opinion and feelings do not count for much these days." I looked over at her elegant face. "Do you believe I am being selfish about the wedding?"

"No. I would be hurt and very upset if I was in your situation and it was my wedding," she stated softly.

"You upset? I cannot imagine." This time, I truly did laugh. The idea of Elizabeth being angry over anything was amusing.

"I would." She smiled widely. "I would be very angry, actually." Her face then filled with a full blush from the confession.

"That I would like to see." I laughed wholeheartedly for the first time in what seemed like forever, and it felt wonderful.

"Jocelyn, I was raised that a lady never gets angry," she explained in her soft voice. "My mother always said it was very bad manners. But in this situation, I do believe it would be warranted. I know how much you have been looking forward to your wedding, and to have someone intrude upon it in such a forceful manner is unthinkable. I cannot believe your mother can be all too happy about it."

"I think both my parents feel torn between me and William and what we both want."

"Yes. I would imagine so," Elizabeth said thoughtfully.

"However, as far as my father is concerned, I do not believe that he understands my feelings on the situation. I do not believe men fully grasp the importance of a wedding day and what it means for a lady." I turned toward Elizabeth as we walked. "I have thought about this day for as long as I can remember. I grew up having a crush on Jackson. I always believed he thought I was too young for him and when he finally noticed me, I mean really noticed me, I had this perfect idea wedding encased within me. And now, when it is so close, poof! It is gone!" The tears returned, and all the anger I felt for Olivia and William returned.

"It will all work itself out. I promise."

"I hope so, although I do not see how at this point."

"It will. You must have faith. I know it looks bleak but look at what you will be getting when all is said and done — a wonderful husband. Jackson is a truly an exceptional man, and he dearly loves you." Her words comforted me a great deal.

"I know. You are right. And I truly love him. I cannot wait to his wife."

Elizabeth and I stopped in front of my house. I could not help but glance over at Olivia's, not sure exactly what I was expecting to see there. But the house was silent and dark.

"Are you going to be all right this evening?" Elizabeth asked.

"Yes. I will be fine. I am sure my mother and Mrs. Chandler have already worked out all the final details with Olivia and her mother. I will remain silent and go along with whatever they decide." I took a deep breath and exhaled slowly, looking back up at Olivia's house again. "What other choice do I have?"

"I will be home if you need me. Come down after supper if you would like to," she offered and hugged me tightly.

"Thank you. Perhaps I will." I was thrilled to know I still at least had one person whom I could really count on to be honest with me.

Elizabeth continued down the pathway, while I walked up to the porch. I was half expecting William to come running out of the house to read me the riot act for my confrontation with Olivia earlier, but I knew he would not be home until tomorrow, for which I was truly glad. I did not want to deal with him today also.

CHAPTER 7

Thursday, October 15, 2015

I CAUGHT MYSELF STUDYING JACKSON carefully throughout our morning biology class. I was sitting two rows back across the room from him, studying the way he sat in his chair; straight with perfect posture, not slumped over the way most of the class did. He held his head up with pride without appearing arrogant. The line along his chin was smooth, soft. He also had the sexiest little dimple in the cleft of his chin like John Travolta. I loved watching the way the light from the windows played with his hair, making copper highlights appear in his black waves.

I barely heard Mrs. Neal-Beliveau's lecture on cell biology. Luckily, I was doing well in the class, but I realized that somewhere between the Golgi apparatus and mitochondria, I was going to have to do some extra reading to compensate for my lack of attention this hour.

During lunch, I sat several seats over and across the table from Jackson. I was watching him laugh and carry on a conversation with Cody and Zak, and although I couldn't make out exactly what they were discussing, I knew it had something to do with football. However, as soon as I took my seat, I began feeling sick to my stomach and very warm. The lunch on my tray looked more unappealing than usual and I felt a strong urge to move, to lie down on a cold surface. I looked over at Jenna with pleading eyes.

"I have to go to the restroom."

Her eyes flashed concerned when she saw the look on my face. All the color had completely drained, and I sat there as pale as a ghost.

"I'll come with you," she said and helped me out of my chair. She held on to me as we walked between the tables out into the hallway. Caitlyn and Hilary followed right behind us.

Once we left the cafeteria, the cool air flooded over me, and the color slowly returned to my face. I leaned up against the wall to steady myself but instead slid down the wall, resting my head on my knees and wrapping my arms around my legs.

"Maybe we should try to get you to the nurse's office." Jenna's voice was low with concern.

"No. I'm fine. I just need to rest for a moment. It will pass."

"One of us should go get the nurse." Hilary looked frightened.

"No. Seriously. I'm fine." I tried to reassure her. "Just give me a minute."

The three of them sat down on the floor next to me and began to chat about the dance the next evening. They were overly excited about their new dresses and numerous accessories purchased for the event.

"Has Jackson asked you yet?" Caitlyn inquired a few minutes later.

I looked up at her with my chin still rested on my knees. "No. Why?"

"He told Zak he was going to," she replied.

"Yeah. Cody told me the same thing," Hilary added.

"Kyle too," Jenna chimed in. "You know you're the only one who hasn't gotten a dress for tomorrow night. We'll all have to go shopping before the match this evening and find something."

"No. Seriously, Jackson hasn't asked me and even if he did, I'm really not up for it," I concluded. I wasn't ready to admit I was attracted to him. I knew they'd blow it out of proportion.

"Are you sure?" Caitlyn asked, placing her hand on my shoulder carefully.

"Why would you turn down a chance to date Jackson?" Hilary looked confused. "I mean, I know I'm with Cody and I do love him, but man, I'd have a difficult time saying no if he asked me. Actually, I'd have a difficult time remembering Cody's name if Jackson asked me out." She laughed, and we all joined her. It was true. He was hard to resist.

"I know, but I haven't been feeling like myself and I really don't want to go with Jackson or anyone else."

Three sets of eyes stared at me, secretly judging.

Thankfully the bell rang, and Jenna cautiously held my arm, making sure I wouldn't fall as I tried to get back up on my feet.

"Thanks. I'll see you later." I waved to the three of them and mixed in with the crowd coming out of the cafeteria on my way to my locker.

Mr. Rand was in full swing today as he started his psychology lecture. Although I was feeling better, I still didn't trust myself to be close to Jackson. It seemed my theory was becoming more of a reality, and it terrified me. But it also made me extremely curious. I wondered what would happen if I walked over to him and placed my hand on him.

Our match that evening was a particularly difficult one. Despite coming out victorious, it was too close to bring any comfort to the team. I could see my family and Jackson sitting up in the bleachers throughout our game and the junior varsity's match.

They even came out victorious with a much greater defeat than our own. We should have been elated, but the shadow that had fallen over my existence was somehow affecting the spirit of the entire team. Their laughs sounded hollow in my ears and their voices muffled as we made our way back to the bus for the short ride back to school.

Chapter 8

Friday, October 18, 1878

THE DAMPNESS OF AUTUMN had settled in overnight, and the rain off the great lake had picked up vigorously. A gray haze settled over Chicago, reflecting my emotional state of mind. William and Jackson were due to be home that evening and for the first time in a very long time I wasn't terribly excited about their homecoming. Instead, I just wanted to be alone.

I decided after my final class of the day that I had caught a cold and would retire early without visitors. I knew I was not in the right frame of mind to be around anyone involved in this mess. I decided to wait until the morning when clearer heads would hopefully prevail.

I made my excuses to Mimi as soon as I arrived home and hid in my room for the duration of the day.

I sat in my bay window, looking out at the graying sky that threatened downpour at any moment. Jackson's home across the street was peaceful and inviting. I noticed several oil lamps lit throughout the downstairs, illuminating a soft glow through the curtain-drawn windows. I saw shadowed movements stirring about, and I wondered if something was amiss or if it was just the normal activity of the household.

I watched Jackson cross over the lawns shortly after supper to see me. I listened to his knock on the front door and heard distant voices from downstairs as he spoke with William. I could even hear from a distance the anger in William's voice. Clearly, he had already had a conversation with Olivia, and she had given him her side of our argument. I was half-tempted to confront him and inform him of my version, but I also knew in my heart that it was pointless, so I remained where I was.

I suppose that the two men had gone somewhere else in the house since I could no longer hear them, and it was hours later before Jackson finally left. As he walked down the walkway in front of our house, he paused for a moment and glanced up toward my bedroom window. I knew he could see my figure behind the lace curtains, but I did not bother to pull them back.

I was afraid that if I made eye contact with him, I would rush to him. After a few minutes of waiting to see what I would do and receiving no response, he turned and walked away, looking disappointed.

CHAPTER 9

Friday, October 16, 2015

MR. RAND ANNOUNCED at the start of class that we were going to begin our discussion on schizophrenia and the current research involving twins and genetic components.

"Yeah rah," I muttered to myself and turned toward the window.

Doesn't he realize that no one in our class is paying any attention to him?

It seemed the whole school was buzzing about the homecoming game that evening and the dance following. Nothing else seemed to matter to the entire school, yet neither of them held any appeal to me.

I had avoided Jackson all week. I was set on not giving him the opportunity to ask me to be his date for the dance, and it made me more determined to avoid being anywhere near him. He had tried to approach me on several occasions, but I continued to give him some excuse or another and always from a distance before quickly disappearing. With his absence, the symptoms had also disappeared.

I rushed home after the last bell with Jenna and Kyle to get ready for the game. Coach Smith had thankfully canceled practice because of homecoming and after a week of grueling practices, she was behaving more humane.

The football players all stayed at school as they normally did on a game day, and it was a nice retreat not having Ethan give me the third degree about why I was being so rude to Jackson. Especially now, since Jackson was part of the team and the two seemed to have become fast friends. According to Ethan, Jackson was even better than Cody. He had replaced Trey as the other starting wide receiver on the varsity team.

As I had accurately predicted, Jackson had become extremely popular with the girls at school. Since his first day, he had every head turning between classes and received constant stares during. Of course, Taylor was by far his biggest fan. She was constantly making a complete spectacle of herself when he was anywhere near, especially in the cafeteria. It was almost comical watching her and him seemingly to not even notice. Jackson's obvious lack of interest was killing her. Instead, it seemed he was always watching my every move.

Kyle, Jenna, and I joined Hilary and Caitlyn in the stands right before kickoff. It was freezing out, and the wind cut right through our clothes. Luckily, the rain held off and for that I was grateful. Despite the weather, it seemed that most of the school had turned out. The excitement was contagious as the game finally got underway.

By the end of the first quarter, I had to admit Ethan was right; Jackson and Zak were a perfect match. The other team didn't seem to have a prayer of stopping the two as they stomped them into nothingness. The excitement consumed the crowd as everyone rose to their feet and remained there throughout the entire second half.

Caitlyn was beside herself screaming for Zak while Hilary, though excited, was getting aggravated by the end of the third quarter because Zak had not thrown Cody the ball once during the game. She had decided to vent her frustrations to everyone present in the car on our short ride home.

"I don't care who Jackson thinks he is or where he's from. Cody was here long before him, and they have been playing together since grade school." She pouted from the backseat with Kyle and Jenna.

Caitlyn, who was riding shotgun, rolled her eyes at me. "Don't worry about it. We won. That's what matters," Caitlyn hissed.

"I know that, but Jackson had no right bumping Trey out of his position and then hogging the ball the whole game."

"Cody just couldn't get open. The other team had him covered all night. I'm sure that's why Zak didn't pass to him." I tried to reassure her and put an end to this.

Thankfully, she let it drop, and we rode the rest of the way in silence. When I pulled into my driveway, I was glad to see we'd beat my parents back to the house, so I could have dibs on being the first to take advantage of a hot shower.

Everyone piled out of my car still chilled to the bone from the game. Both Hilary and Caitlyn were headed over to get ready for the dance at Jenna's and for a moment, I almost reconsidered joining them. Then I remembered all the reasons I couldn't and felt almost sad.

Why does the one guy that I want to be with have this kind of effect on me? It doesn't seem fair.

"Are you sure you won't go?" Caitlyn paused in the driveway.

"Yeah." I shook my head. "I'm really not up for it tonight." I mustered my best smile for her.

"You really should come. It's going to be great," Hilary joined in.

"Thanks, but I don't think so."

I waved them off and retreated into the house to avoid any more questions.

I soaked in a steamy, hot bubble bath for a good thirty minutes. Ethan took a quick shower in my parents' bathroom, since I was in ours, before getting ready for the dance himself. It felt so childish hiding from him, so he wouldn't have the chance to give me the third degree before he left. I knew I was being a coward, but I just didn't want to hear the same crap from him as I had from my friends. It was too pathetic, and I was already consumed with self-pity.

I waited until I was sure he was gone before I ventured downstairs. My parents were busy watching television in the family room, so I fixed myself some microwave popcorn, grabbed a Coke, and headed down to the basement.

I put in one of my old favorite DVDs, *St. Elmo's Fire*, and settled back on the couch to enjoy making a pig out of myself and some peace and quiet.

Shortly thereafter, the basement door opened, and I heard someone walking down the stairs. I didn't bother turning around since my parents were the only one's home, so it took me by surprise when an unexpected voice rang out in the room, making me almost choke on a mouthful of popcorn.

"Hello." Jackson's voice filled the empty space. "I hope you do not mind. Your parents let me in," he remarked when he saw the look on my face.

"What are you doing here? Why aren't you at the dance?" I questioned, feeling sicker with every step he took toward me.

I leaned my head against the back of the couch, waiting for the feeling to pass. I tried my best to fight off the lightheadedness and nausea. I couldn't do anything about the cold sweats. I felt miserable.

He cautiously took a seat in the recliner across from me, looking a bit apprehensive. "I wanted to ask you to go with me to the dance, but I haven't been able to speak to you all week."

"How come you didn't take Taylor? She seems crazy about you." A small laugh escaped from me before I could stop it, but he only smiled.

"Taylor is not my type."

His words sounded muffled in my ears as he sat there with almost-perfect posture, looking irresistible. I had to consciously divert my eyes, so I wouldn't stare at him.

"Oh." I still wasn't feeling well and was hoping I had it under control. "You did great tonight. Impressive." I babbled like an idiot.

"Thank you." He flashed his irresistible green eyes at me with a brilliant smile, making me feel even weaker than I had a moment ago.

Several minutes of silence passed with neither of us knowing what to say. We both turned our attention to the movie to ease the awkwardness.

"I like this movie." Jackson broke the silence.

I could only nod in agreement since I didn't trust myself to speak. I felt sick to my stomach and deeply regretted gorging myself on popcorn.

I sat there, feeling like a complete moron, and believing he was thinking the same thing. I knew I had to at least muster up the strength to make small talk or he was never going to speak to me again.

"So how do you like it here?"

"Everyone seems nice. I am still getting used to it." He kept his eyes on me, making me incredibly self-conscious.

"It'll take a while," I tried to say but my voice cracked. This was turning into a nightmare.

"Have you always lived here?" he asked, although I was pretty sure he already knew the answer.

"Yeah. Same house, same people, everything."

"And you like that?" His head cocked slightly to the side as if he was interested in my response.

"I guess. Never really given it much thought."

"Where do you plan to go to college?"

"I've applied to several different schools this fall. It depends." I shrugged. "You?"

"Same. I am hoping to go to Boston U like my brother and sister." He paused a second and then got up and walked over to the couch I was sitting on.

Instantly, my head began to spin like I was intoxicated, and all sound became distant and faded.

Jackson sat down on the other end of the couch, leaving only a three-foot gap between us. I felt like I was going to vomit and swallowed back the vile bitter taste in my mouth.

"Can I ask you something? Why do you not like me?" His voice sounded like he was speaking through a tunnel. Then he inched a little closer and placed his hand on my shoulder.

"Hey. Are you alright? You're really pale?"

His voice faded out, and the room turned black.

I felt the coolness of a damp cloth on my forehead as my head started to become clear again, I didn't want to open my eyes. I knew if I saw him, it would begin again.

"Do you want me to get your mother?"

I shook my head. She was the last thing I needed.

"No thank you. I'm fine." I tried to sit up, but as soon as I opened my eyes, my head started swimming again.

"Not so fast."

I could hear the smile in his muffled voice, and I rested back about the cushions.

"This is why," I stumbled.

"Why what?"

"Why I can't be near you," I muttered, feeling foolish even with my eyes still closed.

"You are kidding? I thought you just did not like me." His hand reached toward me, but he pulled it back when I cringed.

"Go sit across the room. Now! Please!" I begged, raising my voice at him. I instantly felt bad about doing so.

Jackson hesitated then finally moved back across the room. The cloud began to lift, and the fog cleared, but only a little. I slowly pulled myself into a seated position, feeling extremely embarrassed and nauseous.

"I'm sorry. I didn't mean to offend you," I apologized.

"I am not offended. I am just happy to know you do not hate me." His green eyes held mine with sincerity, making me even more nervous.

"I don't hate you. I don't even know you," I stated flatly on purpose.

"So, do you do this around all guys, get nauseous and pass out?"

"No. This has never happened to me before." I wanted to sink into the floor and disappear.

"Maybe it means you really like me." His smile widened.

"Or that I'm allergic to you." I gave him a coy smirk.

"Ouch!" He laughed.

"Well, what do you want me to say?" My body felt completely drained.

"Nothing, but it would be nice to be around you without making you physically ill."

"True. That would be a change." I couldn't help but laugh.

Jackson stayed across the room from me for the rest of the evening, and we managed to pull off a conversation so long as he kept his distance. He thoroughly enjoyed the fact that his presence had such an effect on me, although I didn't find much humor in it.

I found out that he had an older brother, Alex, and a sister, Phoebe, who had both remained in Boston. Phoebe had graduated recently from law school, and Alex a couple of years before her. When his father, Robert, had accepted the position at the law firm in Chicago, neither of his siblings wanted to uproot their lives and move to the Midwest. I couldn't blame them. I wouldn't have wanted too either. He told me his dad, Robert, was an attorney and his mother, Emily, worked from home, which I already knew from Jenna but didn't tell him that.

Jackson was, in fact, very sweet and even somewhat funny. I really enjoyed spending time with him, although it was weird having to keep such a distance between us just to have a conversation.

He went home a little before eleven. I waited downstairs until he was gone before slipping upstairs. I wanted to hide before Ethan came home to give me a full report. I changed quickly and hid under my covers with the lights out, knowing he wouldn't bother me if he believed I was asleep.

My unexpected evening turned into a grossly conducted experiment that unfortunately confirmed my initial theory as to Jackson's effect on my physical being. This newly confirmed knowledge left me feeling restless and even more baffled than before.

How can a guy I don't know cause me to experience such symptoms? Why do I feel like there is something missing?

Although I still couldn't explain what was going on, I had a strong suspicion that Jackson knew more than he was telling me and that left me feeling even more uneasy than nausea.

CHAPTER 10

Saturday, October 19, 1878

I AWOKE FEELING REFRESHED and in much better spirits than the day before. I decided to have breakfast in the dining room. I hoped to find William, so I could discuss with him what truly happened between Olivia and me on Thursday before the tension between us grew worse.

My parents were already out on their morning walk, enjoying the last remnants of the morning sunshine. William was sitting at the table, buried behind the newspaper and I was glad that I had the opportunity to speak with him alone. However, William could be very challenging to talk to about certain subjects and relationships were one of them.

I sat down in the chair across from him and smiled politely. He seemed engrossed in the morning paper and ignored my presence.

"Good morning, William. How was school?" I was hoping to ease my way into a conversation, but he was not going to let me off so easily.

"What do you want, Jocelyn?" he asked without looking up.

"William, please. I would really like to talk with you. Can you please put the paper aside for a moment?"

William's eyes were blazing as he hastily put the paper on the table. "What?"

"I wanted to apologize for my behavior. I admit I was very surprised by your news and did not handle it well."

"That is an understatement," he huffed.

"I realize that, and I am sorry."

"Plus, you go and start an argument with Olivia," he accused.

"I did not start that argument, William. I tried to make sure she was all right, and she only wanted to insult me." I attempted to defend myself, but the excuse did not even sound plausible to my own ears.

"Really?"

"Yes." I started feeling betrayed by him again. "William, you could at least listen to my side of the story."

"After all you have done lately, why should I bother?"

I quickly got up from the table and rushed out the front door. I practically collided with my parents on the steps, only pausing long enough to escape around them. They gave me a puzzled look but said nothing as I ran down the walkway and out the front gate.

I ran along the cobblestone to the little, white gazebo in the park where Jackson had proposed last spring. The air had a chill that blew through my gown, and I had left the house without a shawl or capelet. The sun was flirting with the clouds, providing only momentary glimpses of light and warmth.

The flowers around the gazebo had long since died away with the summer heat. Now nothing was left but the decaying remembrance of happier times. I sat down on the little bench that surrounded the inner-lying perimeter of the gazebo and dropped my head against the railing. I let the tears roll freely down my cheeks feeling completely defeated and spent.

"Are you going to hide here all day?"

The sound of his voice startled me. I looked up to see Jackson as he approached the steps of the gazebo.

"I am considering it," I answered through my sobs.

Jackson sat down next to me and handed me his handkerchief. "Dry your eyes, my love. I hate to see you crying."

He slipped off his overcoat and wrapped it lovingly around my shoulders. His fragrance lingered heavily on the fabric, along with the heat from his body instantly filling me with warmth.

"How did you know I was here?" I asked as I wiped away my tears.

"William came over right after you ran out of the house. He told me what happened at breakfast, and I knew you would be here. This is our favorite place, after all." Jackson leaned over and kissed me on the cheek. "I believe you caught him off guard this morning. He and Olivia are dealing with a lot, and I know that they both want to talk with you."

"What about now?" I could only imagine another harsh exchange.

"Jocelyn, your brother, and I are roommates. During the week we spend a lot of evening breaks between studying and discussing different things. And trust me, I have asked him not to confide in me things that he is not ready to tell you about, but sometimes he does not listen so well," Jackson began.

"Exactly what are you not telling me about now?"

"I need you to remember how much I love you," he began after sighing audibly.

The fact that he started out with this statement only reminded me again of his role in their deception. I immediately stood and started to walk away. There was no way this was going to end well. Jackson reached out and grabbed my hand to stop me. I gently tugged it away and descended the gazebo steps.

He followed.

"Where are you going?" he inquired with haste.

"I believe I have heard enough. I am sorry, but this is more than I can deal with." The tears started coming even harder and were beyond my control. I took off his jacket and tossed it back at him.

"Jocelyn, you don't even know what I am talking about."

But I kept going.

"Will you please stop?" Jackson stopped along the path to make me pause also.

He slowly approached me and gently wrapped me in his arms, kissing the top of my head. I wanted to push him away but could not bring myself to do it.

"There is so much more to this than you realize. If you will please just calm down for a moment, I would like to share with you the entire story."

I nodded my head stupidly as I drowned in his bright emerald eyes.

"I should not be the one to share this with you. It should be your brother and Olivia." He took a deep breath.

"Please, just tell me the truth." I sighed heavily. "It would be nice if someone was honest with me for a change."

"Two Thursdays ago, after we had dinner at your house and William and I returned to our dorm room, your brother said he needed to speak with me. I knew they had been seeing each other and writing letters for the last several months and I knew it was getting serious between them. But I had not realized exactly how serious they were. William was very upset and had been for a while and he had disappeared a couple days earlier in the week."

"Monday and Tuesday, right?" I interrupted him. Strangely, Olivia had also missed the same days.

"Yes. Olivia too?" I nodded. "William and Olivia had apparently taken a trip to South Bend."

"Why?"

"To go somewhere where no one knew them to see a doctor there."

"Doctor? But my father has always taken care of them. Did he send them to a specialist or something? Which of them is sick?" The words were all rushing out of my mouth without pausing to give him a chance to answer. My mind was whirling with every possible horrible illness, but reality and the simplest explanation never even registered.

"Here, let us sit down." Jackson led me back over to the gazebo steps and sat down beside me wrapping his jacket back around my shoulders. "Olivia is pregnant, Jocelyn." His voice was low and calm.

"What?" I shouted. Now it all made sense. The quick engagement, the sneaking around, the invasion of my wedding.

"I guess it happened over Labor Day weekend. Obviously, it was unplanned and now they need to get married quickly," he explained.

"Olivia is pregnant," I muttered. It would not sink in. This sort of thing did not happen to properly raised young ladies. Her parents must be furious. I could not believe she had not been disowned. "Who knows?" I looked back up at Jackson.

"Only the four of us. For obvious reasons, they would appreciate your silence in this matter. Neither of them is dealing well with it. William is terrified since he still has several years of college left and is in no position to support a wife and baby. He has no idea what he is going to do."

"I cannot believe this." I shook my head numbly. I could not comprehend the fact that Olivia had sex with my brother. I had barely kissed the man I had known my entire life, dated for more than four years, and had been engaged to for the last six months.

I sat there in Jackson's arms as the world that I had always known and trusted disappeared around me.

"Everything is going to be all right, sweetheart." Jackson gave me a gentle squeeze and kissed my forehead.

"How can you say that? Everything has changed." I looked at him, stunned with disbelief.

"They are still the same people, even if they did not wait. It happened, and we cannot shame them for that."

"You know I feel so foolish. I had confided in her all my fears about our wedding night the weekend after Labor Day, and here she had already..."

"Fears?"

I suddenly felt my face burning with embarrassment. "Nothing. Forget I said anything."

"What fears could you possibly have about our wedding night?"

"Please, Jackson. It is nothing." I felt so stupid.

"My darling, you are going to be my wife and we should be sharing everything with each other. No secrets." I unintentionally scoffed. "Now I realize that as of recently, you have every reason to be upset with me regarding that, but I promise you from this day forward I shall never keep anything from you ever again. I hope that you can understand the reasons I had to keep all of this from you until now."

I nodded in understanding, although I truly did not.

"Please, explain to me what fears you are having."

"Jackson, I am sorry, but I simply cannot." My face burned.

"There is nothing you can say that will upset me."

"It is silly. Honest." I looked at him with pleading eyes, begging him to let it go, but his interest was not going to wane until I confided in him.

"If it concerns you, then it cannot be silly." I took a deep breath, wishing I had kept my mouth shut.

"You are going to laugh at me. And trust me, this is not something that is proper for me to discuss with you."

"I will be your husband in a few short weeks."

"Eight weeks," I corrected him.

"Alright. Eight weeks. Still, it is almost here. Proper or not to what society believes does not apply to us. We can discuss anything and everything. I promise you all that we discuss will stay between us and no one else." Jackson squeezed me tightly.

"I am afraid I am going to disappoint you on our wedding night. There. I said it." I covered my face with my hands from sheer embarrassment.

"Why in the world would I be disappointed?" He gently removed my hands and turned my face to look at him. His voice was soft.

"Because...you know." I could not bring myself to say it.

Jackson placed his hand under my chin, gently forcing me to look him in the eye. "You are referring to us being together as man and wife for the first time."

My face was scarlet, and I wanted to crawl under the gazebo and disappear from humiliation.

"Why in the world would you ever disappoint me?" Then he let a small chuckle escape his perfect, soft lips. "If we are being honest, I am actually afraid *I* am going to disappoint *you*."

Now he was the one with the red face, which made me instantly smile.

"Well, at least it should be an interesting night with us both sharing the same fear." Secretly I was thrilled that he was as nervous as me.

"It is silly that we both have been raised not to discuss such important aspects of our lives. But you know, this relationship is solely between us and what we discuss is just between us. No one else needs to know. So, if we have fears about sex, then let us discuss them instead of hiding from them. It is the only way either of us is going to feel better." His words were so comforting and sincere. I instantly felt so much better.

Jackson kissed me gently on the lips, sending a fire of passion through me like no other. I reached up, caressing the back of his head, pressing him to me. The intensity grew stronger as his arms pulled me closer to him. I could feel the warmth of his body against mine. The chilly air disappeared as the heat from his body flowed through mine. Our breathing grew heavier and more intense, and I could feel his heart beating rapidly through his dark blue vest. I too felt as if my heart was going to leap out of my chest. I reluctantly tore myself away from his clutches.

"We cannot do this." My breathing was intensely labored.

"I know. I am sorry." His face was as flushed as I was sure mine was.

"My love, I am sorry also."

"Well, I do believe that chemistry will not be a problem on our wedding night." Jackson gave me the cocky smile that I loved so much, showing off his dimples. "Waiting, on the other hand, that could be a bigger problem."

"Waiting will certainly not be a problem; need I remind you of whom we are having a double wedding with?" He laughed and playfully scooted away from me on the step.

"No. I do not have a problem with waiting." He squeezed my hand. "I guess we had better head back to the house. We have been gone long enough, and I am sure your family is probably starting to worry about you."

William stayed over at Olivia's house for the remainder of the day and even through dinner. I was glad since it allowed me the time to fully process everything Jackson and I had discussed. The day had been truly overwhelming. The knowledge that I had gained scared me, because I knew in my heart it could have just as easily had been me instead of her.

I understood that fire, that passion, that overwhelming lust and the difficulty of stopping. It was impossible for me to feel superior to her in any way. The only difference between us was truly my fears, and even those had been lessened immensely today with the knowledge Jackson shared with me.

William and Olivia made their appearance shortly before seven. Jackson and I were sitting in front of the hearth in the parlor, listening to him read *Walt Whitman* aloud. He stopped, causing me to look up when the two of them entered the room. Jackson stood and gave a short bow as William bowed and Olivia curtsied.

"Please, come and join us. We are enjoying the works of *Whitman* and the fire. Has it turned colder outside?" Jackson was always the perfect gentleman.

"Thank you." Olivia took a seat on the lounge across the room from us, but still did not make eye contact with me.

"Yes. It seems the temperature is dropping quickly, and winter is well on its way. Hopefully not early, though. I am not ready for the snow." William took a seat beside Olivia and took her hand in his.

The two of them did look sweet and appeared to be in love. I looked at the two of them sitting across from me and could see the terror in both their eyes — terror of the present circumstances they were now facing and of the future, which was still unknown to them. I knew they were both worried about the assumptions and accusations people were going to make when the baby arrived early. I knew the concerns they both had about the shame that this was going to cause both of their families and my heart went out to them.

"Did you both have a nice day?" I didn't know what to say to either of them. They nodded but remained silent.

After a few minutes of deafening silence, Jackson began to read aloud again. By nine, it was time to draw the evening to a close. The four of us had avoided any new type of conversation that would have helped ease the tension that hung over the room.

It was an awkward good-bye as William set out to walk Olivia home and I escorted Jackson to our front door. He had promised me that he would be by early in the morning to pick me up for church services. We kissed and hugged briefly. All romance felt earlier in the day had somehow disappeared with the sunshine and with the reality that William and Olivia were now confronted with.

Mimi helped me undress and climb into my nightgown. She looked as tired as I felt and was moving about slowly and uneasily.

"Are you feeling all right, Mimi?"

"Jus' hurtin' a lil ta-nit. Bin a long daz," she replied as she draped my dress over the vanity chair.

"Amen to that. I did not believe this day was ever going to end." I slumped down on my bed and threw myself back against the mountain of pillows.

"Wha's got ya so upset, Miss Jocelyn?" She turned and offered me one of her motherly smiles.

"There are some things I honestly wish I did not know about. I believe sometimes ignorance is bliss."

"Ya wanna talk 'bout it?"

"I really wish I could, but I promised not to say anything." She sat down on the corner of my bed and patted my hand.

"Evera-dang's gonna be fine," she assured.

"I certainly hope you are right, because if you are not then things could get very ugly very quickly." I threw my hands up over my eyes.

"Are ya sur huney da' ya don' wanna talk 'bout it?"

"Yes. Of course, I want to talk about it, but I cannot. I promised."

"Well, Ah believe da' promises onlee 'plies ta dos who'd poss'bly tell some'um els, an' da's not may. Now ya kno' Ah's neva says a wor' ta no'um 'bout dangs ya've tol' ma."

And that was true. She was the one person in the world I could completely confide in my deepest and darkest secrets in without fear of being judged or betrayed.

"I know, Mimi." I paused and settled down under the covers. "I am sure that you have heard about William's proposal to Olivia and that we are now having a double wedding?"

"O' course." She nodded.

"Do you know why they want to intrude upon my wedding day?" Tears spilled over the brim of my eyes, and there was nothing I could do to stop them.

"Miss Livia's wif chil'." I looked up at Mimi completely stunned, and she laughed. "Ah, honey. Do ya believe da' dis a sakret? Evera'um no's but is bein' too kine ta say nothin' 'bout it."

"But why? If everyone knows, then why do they feel like they have to hide it?"

"Cuz yun ladies don't git 'n a family wa befo' tay weddin'. It jus' ain't proper, so evera'um's pretendin'." She smiled and kissed me on the forehead.

"I understand that it is not proper, but what is done is done. They are going to be married shortly anyway. Surely, she won't be showing by then?"

"Probably, but only a lil. She shud ve able ta pull it off. Ah's hope so anyhows." She smiled.

"Me too, Mimi. Me too."

"Now, darlin', dis time fo ya ta git sum sleep."

We hugged each other tightly. I loved her so much. She had always been here for me through all the trials of my life. It was difficult for me to imagine going off and starting a new life without seeing her every day.

"Thank you, Mimi. I love you."

"Ah's luv ya too, Miss Jocelyn." She blew out the oil lamps and closed my door on her way out.

I lay there in the dark, watching the shadows dance across my walls. The big tree in the front yard outside my window was blowing in the breeze, making bizarre shapes by the light of the moon dance across my walls. With Halloween such a short time away and the Autumn Festival around the corner, the weather was perfect in every fashion; dark, cold, and dreary with the smell of frost that had not yet decided to settle in for the winter stay.

My bed was warm and comforting, but I still could not find any solace beneath the troubles that weighed so heavily on my heart. I could not imagine what must be going on in Olivia's mind as she lay next door in her bed, waiting for sleep to take away her pain.

My heart went out for her in her confusion between the joy of her upcoming nuptials along with the arrival of her baby and the certain shame and fear she must be living with every minute that our families and the world would discover her secret. I wondered if she loved William the way I loved Jackson. I truly hoped she did.

I wanted so badly to speak with her, to offer her comfort and understanding. I also wanted to understand how she could have been so foolish.

When sleep finally found me, my heart was still heavy with grief and my head still whirling with thoughts I could not escape.

CHAPTER 11

Saturday, October 17, 2015

UPON RETURNING TO MY ROOM after breakfast, my cell phone was buzzing on my nightstand. Thinking that it had to be Jenna anxious to give me a full report of the dance, I flopped across my bed and reached for my phone.

"Hello," I answered, expecting to hear her launch into all the latest updates.

"Good morning. Are you feeling better today?" It was Jackson.

"How did you get this number?"

"Your brother. Is that all right?"

How could it not be? God, I love his accent.

"Sure," I muttered like an idiot.

"Are you feeling any better?"

"I feel great. How are you doing?"

"I am wonderful," he teased. "I am not the one passing out all the time."

"Very funny."

"What are your plans for today?"

"Studying. We have a psychology test on Monday. I was thinking about getting a head start on it." I wanted to come across as nonchalant as possible, afraid that he could see straight through me.

"That is right," he paused. "We do have an exam on Monday. I had forgotten."

"Pathetic. Mr. Rand reminded us yesterday before the bell, remember?" My attempt to tease him did not come off as well as I had hoped.

"Do you want to study for it together? I could really use your help. I am a little behind since I was not here for the first part of the semester and some of that material will be on the exam."

"I'm not sure if that's a good idea." I took a deep breath. I honestly did want to see him again, but I didn't do so well with him around. I was sure I wouldn't be able to concentrate with him making my head swim. "I don't think I'd be able to focus clearly." I tried to choose my words carefully.

"Jocelyn, I enjoy your company and I would like to get to know you better. Plus, if I am going to have any chance of passing this exam, I am going to need your help."

Why does his voice have to be so irresistible?

"All right. We'll try it."

"Thank you. What time do you want to get started?"

"Noon-ish?" I had a horrible feeling in the pit of my stomach that this was a really bad idea.

"Great. I will see you then."

I hung up and scurried over to my closet. I wanted something casual but amazing. I wanted to look like I wasn't trying to impress him, although I really wanted to. I tossed jeans, skirts, and an array of shirts and sweaters all over my bed but couldn't decide on anything.

I grabbed my cell and called Jenna. She finally answered after the third ring.

"Yeah?" She sounded groggy.

"Get over here." I was starting to panic. "I need your help. Jackson is going to be here around noon, and I can't find anything to wear. I need to look spectacular without looking like I'm trying to. You know what I mean? Help!"

"Calm down." She sighed. "I'll be there in ten."

Jenna strolled into my room with her hair pulled back in a ponytail and sporting an old pair of sweats. She must have had a good time last night. She burst out laughing when she saw the mess I'd made with my clothes.

"Care to tell me again how you're not interested in this guy?"

"Oh, shut up." I smirked as she started sorting through the pile. "I don't know what I'm doing."

"Beginning to live again." Her coy smile told me how happy she was to see me in such a state.

"Don't start that. I shouldn't even have agreed to help him study."

"Study? Is that what this is about?" She held up a sweater for a second before putting it back in the pile.

"We have a psychology test on Monday. Since he missed the first few chapters that will be covered on the test, he asked me to help him." I shrugged casually and held up a shirt in front of me, but Jenna shook her head.

"You know he didn't even show up at the dance last night." Her eyes gleamed.

"I know." I sat down on the corner of my bed.

She narrowed her eyes and studied me for a moment. "How'd *you* know? Ethan tell you?"

"No. Jackson was here, watching a movie with me."

Jenna's eyes got wider, matching her grin. I shrugged like it was no big deal. She didn't buy it.

"Really?"

"It wasn't like that. I didn't even invite him. He just showed up and my parents let him in, not me."

"So, anything interesting happen?" She was grinning from ear to ear.

"No."

"Nothing?"

I shook my head again.

"How disappointing," she replied, sitting down on the bed. "So, you need something that looks great without looking like you're trying to look great, right?"

"Exactly." She shuffled through the pile of clothes again.

"I'd go with this." She held up a pair of jeans with a hole in one knee, a teal sweatshirt that zipped up the front, and a dark blue tank top that matched the lettering in the sweatshirt.

"You sure?" Jenna knew style better than anyone I knew except for my sister, Sidney, but it looked overly casual.

"Of course. The jeans fit perfectly, tight but not too tight. Zip the jacket about halfway up and push the sleeves up. Trust me." She tossed them at me.

"Okay." I slipped into the clothes.

"You want to look casual and comfortable. After all, you're just studying, not going on a date."

I spun around in front of my full-length mirror before turning to her. "How do I look?

"Fabulous. But you might want to work on your hair and makeup." She laughed.

I hadn't as much as run a brush through my hair and had only washed my face and brushed my teeth.

"Just a little." I couldn't help but laugh at my reflection. "Hey, thanks."

"No problem. What are you doing tonight?" Jenna fell back on the pile of pillows on my bed. She looked as if she could have fallen asleep at any second.

"Who knows?" I sat down at the vanity and started brushing my hair.

"Want to have everyone over?"

"Seriously? I hate always hanging out here."

"It'll be fun. Besides, Cody's parents are back in town for the next couple of weeks, so his place is out." She tossed one of my pillows at me and laughed when it hit me from behind while I was fussing with my hair.

"All right." I threw it back, but she ducked out of the way.

Jenna climbed off my bed and stood beside me in the mirror. "Well, I've got to go. I'm going shopping with Kyle for your birthday."

"Ah, Jenna! Don't!"

"Too bad." She laughed as she waltzed out of my room.

My eighteenth birthday was coming up on Wednesday and Jenna always made a big production out of birthdays, as did my family. Every year, she did something to horribly embarrass me.

When Jackson rang the bell shortly before noon, I had already placed all my notes and study materials on the dining room table. My parents were out playing golf, so the house was empty except for Ethan. When the bell rang, he beat me to the door.

I snuck back into the dining room, so I didn't appear overly eager to see him. I heard the two of them chatting in the kitchen while I pretended to be reading about psychological disorders and their classification in the DSM. I could hear them discussing the upcoming game on Friday. I was doing my best to block them out and concentrate on my textbook when Jackson finally entered the room.

He placed his study materials down on the table, taking a seat in a chair at the other end. As usual, all the symptoms flooded over me as soon as he entered the room. I rested my head on top of my book, waiting for the feeling to pass. Jackson remained silent but looked at me rather curiously.

Slowly, he got up and walked very slowly to my end. As he approached me, I could feel darkness coming closer and felt his hand touch my shoulder. Then, as if in a distant fog, I swear I could hear myself laughing; only it couldn't have been me. But it was, and I was in this house, running toward someone — a boy who was a little older than me and very strangely dressed in old Victorian-style clothes. I followed him out onto the front porch.

"William, wait up. I want to go too!" I cried after him. The boy slowed down for a moment. "Jocelyn, go back and play with your dolls. Girls do not fish." I felt myself start crying from his rejection. "William, please," I begged him, but he only smiled sweetly at me. "Why don't you go ask Olivia if she wants to play?"

His sandy blonde hair was a mess, and he had a little bit of dirt smeared across his cheek. He shifted his fishing pole to his other shoulder and gently put his hand on my arm. "We will be back soon and bring lots of fish for Sarah to cook for dinner." And with a gentle squeeze of my arm, he grinned and took off running to catch up with the other boys down the pathway. I was left standing there, crying on the porch of the house, this house, my house!

Slowly, I opened my eyes and lifted my head off the table. I was confused, terrified, extremely nauseous, and very sweaty; and my head was suddenly killing me. Jackson's hand was inches from my shoulder, and he was looking down at me with a puzzled expression on his face.

I slid out of the chair and backed away from him.

What in the hell just happened?

My mind was racing. Nothing made sense.

How can I see a memory of a past that doesn't belong to me?

I heard my own voice as a child speaking to someone, I could feel was important to me, but whom I was positive I didn't know. I stared at Jackson as I backed myself against the dining room wall.

"Jocelyn, are you alright? You look as if you have seen a ghost."

I held my hand out to keep him from approaching me. "I'm fine. Just keep away from me." I couldn't shake the feeling of loss left by the memory.

"Are you going to pass out again?"

I shook my head slightly.

"Please sit down. You do not look well." He politely pulled the chair out in offering.

"No, I, I need some water."

I covered my mouth with my hand and fought the urge to vomit. I stammered and stumbled over my own feet through the doorframe and fell into the kitchen.

I quickly got myself a glass of water from the fridge door, knowing Jackson would soon join me in the kitchen. I needed a moment alone to collect my thoughts and clear my head.

None of this made any sense at all.

Jackson walked into the kitchen, pausing in the doorway. His bright, green eyes were filled with concern.

"Jocelyn, are you sure you are all right?"

"I'm fine. Really." I took a deep breath and refilled my glass. "We should get to work." I smiled at him, desperately trying to convince myself that everything I had just witnessed had to be a product of my overactive imagination and nothing more.

"All right, but only on one condition — you join my parent's and me for dinner this evening. They have heard me speak of you and would like to meet you." He smiled brightly.

"Dinner with your parents? Are you serious?" I looked at him as if he'd lost his mind. "You want me to have dinner at your house with you and your parents?" There was no way I was eating dinner with his parents.

"Why not? You are going to meet them eventually anyway. They do live across the street, you know." He flashed his irresistible cocky lopsided smile.

"I know, but why now?" I wondered if they would affect me the same way as their son.

"Now is as good a time as any." He shrugged his broad muscular shoulders a bit.

I could think of several reasons but was too afraid to voice them. I was already terrified that he thought I was crazy. "For the obvious reason."

Like the fact that I don't want to black out and then vomit all over your parents' dinner table.

"Nonsense. Trust me. You will love them. They are great people."

That's a change. I don't believe I've ever heard any of my friends refer to their parents as great. Even if they personally thought it, they would never voice it to their peers.

"Okay," I relented setting my glass down on the island. "Now let's get some studying done." I did my best to put my apprehensions behind me.

We returned to our respective places at the table and opened our textbooks.

"So, you missed chapters four, five and most of six, right?" I confirmed.

"Yes," Jackson flipped his book open to chapter four.

"Have you read them?"

"I have read four and five, but I have not started on six."

We studied for the rest of the afternoon. I'm not sure how much he benefited from it, but I felt much better about the exam than I had previously. I had never studied for an exam using these types of techniques, but I had to admit it was quite effective.

Before I realized it, the time had quickly come when we had to leave for dinner at Jackson's. Strangely my parents hadn't returned from their day on the golf course; so, I left word with Ethan to tell them where I was.

As uncomfortable as I now felt with him, I wanted him to walk a short distance from me just to be sure the symptoms did not become worse again. I seemed to be all right if he was at least an arm's length from me, which was progress. There was simply no explanation for it.

We crossed the street into his front lawn. The house looked strange after spending months in darkness. There were curtains hanging once again in the windows, chairs on the porch, and wind chimes singing from the flowerbeds. The house was alive once again.

Jackson's house was a large, two-story mansion covered in faded, red brick with a blanket of greenery climbing up part of the front porch and covering the east side. The shutters were a forest green, and the brick archway leading to the front door now held a welcome sign on a post. Two ancient looking lanterns stood on either side, lighting our way.

The inside of his home was gorgeous. It was decorated in earth tones and brick reds and held an old-fashioned feel to it. His mother, I assumed, collected antiques and oil paintings. There were flowers everywhere in colorful vases and jars.

It instantly gave me a feeling of warmth and comfort. It was impossible to tell that they had lived here barely more than a week. There were no scattered empty boxes or stacks of things lying about. Instead, the home was neatly organized and beautifully decorated.

We walked into the kitchen unnoticed, finding his mother standing at the counter range, stirring a sizzling skillet while his father was chopping an onion on a chopping block beside her. The aroma flowing from the steamy pots was enticing.

Their kitchen was beyond anything I had ever imagined. I only hoped my mother would not see it; I knew if she did, we'd be redecorating immediately. The cabinets were a dark cherry with a glass front that would never have worked at our home. We were much too messy and unorganized. Their counters were dark green marble, and all the appliances were stainless steel. Even the floor was slate, old, colonial style, which added just the right character to the room.

His mother realized we were standing there when his father playfully kissed her on the cheek.

"Oh. Excuse me." She walked forward with her hand stretched toward mine. "I am sorry. We forget sometimes that we are not alone." She had a very warm, motherly smile. I liked her immediately. "I am Emily, and this is my husband, Robert. Welcome to our home."

She was about my height and very beautiful with dark brown eyes that were soft and warm. Her brown hair hung loosely over her shoulders and a little way down her back. I couldn't believe how youthful she looked for someone who had three grown children.

"Thank you." I shook her delicate hand.

"It is nice to meet you finally, Jocelyn." Robert smiled and approached us to shake my hand before placing his arm back around his wife. Jackson was obviously an exact copy of his father, with the same black hair and sparkling, green eyes. Although he got the waves in his hair from Emily, his stature was all Robert.

It was wonderful to see two parents who seemed happy together. My parents hardly ever showed affection in front of us children.

"You too." I couldn't stop grinning.

"We have heard so much about you and your family. I must apologize, but we have been so busy trying to get the house in order that we have not had the time to come over and introduce ourselves to your parents," Robert explained.

"That's okay. They understand."

I wasn't sure why they would even do that. No one who moved in ever did. People in our neighborhood usually met when they bumped into each other outside or one of the guys needed to borrow a tool or something. The welcome wagon was a thing of the past.

"Please, make yourself at home. Would you like some apple cider? I just picked some up this morning at this little farmer's market outside of town. It is fresh and very delicious," Emily offered.

"Wonderful. Thank you." I followed them into the heart of the kitchen. "It smells amazing in here. Is there anything I can do to help?"

"Just have a seat and relax."

Robert poured Jackson and me a glass of apple cider as we sat down across from them at the bar side of the island. His parents resumed cooking dinner, asking me all kinds of questions about the neighborhood and school.

The food was outstanding. I couldn't get over how well it tasted. My own mother was a horrible cook. Nothing she had ever created came close to this. Emily even topped off the meal with an apple pie that she'd made totally from scratch that afternoon while we were studying.

I had to admit it. Jackson was right. His parents were fabulous – not at all like my other friends' parents, who were nosey and always trying to act like they were still cool or something.

By eight o'clock, Jackson suggested that we all go over to my place, so we could introduce my parents to his and I suddenly remembered that Jenna was going to have our friends over. I hadn't talked to her since before noon. Normally, she would have called sometime throughout the day to confirm plans. Since I hadn't heard anything from her, I assumed her plans had changed.

However, when the four of us walked outside, there was a line of cars parked up and down our street, and my driveway was completely full. I was trying to recall if my parents had mentioned having company over for a dinner party or something, but I was drawing a blank.

We entered the house, and it was unusually silent. We found my mother in the kitchen, making popcorn, and looking annoyed.

"Jocelyn Alyssa, where have you been? Do you think that it's all right for you to invite your friends over for the evening and then leave? Your brother has been downstairs, entertaining your friends for you instead of going on his date with Mariah!"

"I'm sorry. I lost track of time and Jenna didn't confirm anything, so I wasn't sure if anyone was coming over." I felt baffled.

Why is she angry? Surely Ethan doesn't really care. He is always hanging around my friends.

She dumped another bag of microwave popcorn into the large bowl. "Well, you'd better get downstairs and apologize to your friends, not me."

"But, Mom, I wanted to introduce you to Jackson's parents, our new neighbors across the street. This is Robert and Emily Chandler."

They exchanged hellos and shook hands.

I excused myself to retreat to the basement and beg forgiveness, but the four of them followed me.

When I reached the bottom of the stairs, the basement that had appeared empty seconds before sprang to life in an instant.

"Happy birthday!"

I turned to the four guilty people standing behind me, before scanning the room for the other guilty culprits: my dad, Jenna, Ethan, and probably Kyle. This was so typical of them.

"You planned this all along, didn't you?" I eyed my mother.

"I had some help." She looked at the three standing beside her. "And Jenna, Ethan, and Kyle were in on it also."

Everyone was all smiles and excited. Even my older sister, Sidney, had returned from Northwestern. She and my father were hiding amongst the crowd in the basement. The basement was filled with balloons, streamers, and there was a table in the corner covered with cake, food, beverages, and dozens of gifts. It was a ridiculous scene, and I happily drifted off into the crowd to mingle amongst the guests. The music was blaring, making it difficult for anyone to carry on a conversation in a normal tone.

Pretty soon, people began moving the furniture against the walls and started dancing. With so many people, no one was really coupled off, making it possible for everyone to have a great time without leaving anyone on the sidelines.

I finally made my way over to the guilty culprits in this little scheme, giving each of them a playful tongue lashing for their troubles.

The party continued right up until curfew for most of my friends. However, I was surprised when people began leaving that Hilary, Caitlyn, and Jenna stayed behind. Apparently, they had stashed their overnight bags in my room while I was gone, having planned a genuine grade-school slumber party.

We all pitched in and helped my parents clean up the mess before we retreated upstairs to my room for the remainder of the evening.

Jenna flopped down across my bed while Hilary immediately started rummaging through my wardrobe and Caitlyn began riffling around in my accessories. I flipped on some music before taking a seat in my desk chair. "You guys are the best! Thanks so much for the party."

Caitlyn spun around, sporting a black fedora and hot pink scarf. "You're welcome. Now I want to hear what's going on between you and Jackson."

"What? It's nothing. We're just friends." I tried to sound convincing.

"Yeah right. I saw how he was looking at you tonight, and that's not how you look at a friend." Hilary held up one of my outfits in front of her in front of my full-length mirror with a wide grin across her face.

"I noticed that too," Jenna joined in. "He's very interested in being more than just your friend."

"His folks are great. And their house is simply gorgeous." I paused, looking directly at Jenna. "Hey, how were they in on the party?"

"Oh, that. Apparently, they came over and met both our parents while we were at volleyball practice. The guys didn't even know about it until tonight." Jenna smirked, completely proud of her deception.

"Oh, come on. You are not going to sit there and act like you're not interested in Jackson. I have known you since kindergarten, Jocelyn Timmons, and you are not that good of an actress. I saw the way you were looking at him tonight *and* the fact that you were purposely avoiding him all evening!" Caitlyn pointed her finger at me, now modeling my old lace gloves that I'd worn for Halloween a couple years back along with an old pair of purple sunglasses.

"What? I'm not saying he's not good looking. I mean, how can I? That much is obvious. But I told you all before I'm not looking for a boyfriend." I flopped down across my bed.

"Yeah yeah. We all know you're concentrating on school and sports, blah, blah, blah." Hilary mocked from my closet floor, sorting my shoes, and trying them on. "Oh. I love these. Can I borrow them this week? They would go great with the outfit I just bought."

"Sure. Now will you get out of my closet?" She was always borrowing our things.

"Fine." Hilary pouted but put the shoes in her bag.

"He's really nice," Jenna stated. "You can't tell me that you're not the tiniest bit interested."

"I'm not." I got up and walked over to my DVD case. "Anyone want to watch a movie?"

"Stop trying to change the subject, Jocelyn," Caitlyn interjected.

"Fine then. I'm putting in *Sixteen Candles*." It was the perfect slumber party movie. I switched off the stereo and started the movie. "Come on, guys. Let it go, please."

"Not until you admit that he's the perfect guy for you. I mean, really, it's our senior year. It's time to have a little fun, enjoy life. Besides, it would be nice if we could all couple together." Hilary sat down on the bed beside Jenna after changing into her sweats.

The rest of us followed her example and put on more comfortable nightclothes and got ourselves cleaned up for bed. I was hoping they would let the subject drop, but no such luck. They continued to badger me up until the moment we fell asleep.

CHAPTER 12

Sunday, October 20, 1878

SUNDAY SERVICES WERE LONG and eventless. I watched Olivia and William out of the corner of my eye. They both were looking tired and apprehensive. I couldn't help but wonder what was going through their minds. Even Olivia's parents looked particularly upset this morning, and I wondered if they knew. From the expressions on their faces, I imagined they did. Even my parents seemed a little more fidgety than normal throughout the sermon.

After services concluded, my mother approached Jackson and me as were exiting the church. "Excuse me, Jocelyn, Jackson, could you two please return to the house and inform Sarah that supper needs to be postponed about an hour, maybe two?"

Jackson nodded, but I wanted more information. "What is going on, Mother?"

"We are staying after to speak with Reverend Jacobs. William and Miss Olivia and her parents will remain behind as well."

I nodded knowingly. Mother turned and rejoined my father, who looked agitated.

Jackson helped me climb into his carriage and promptly joined me. He draped a blanket across my legs to shield me from the bitter wind that had sprung up last night,

"I am glad I am not in there for that conversation." Jackson looked at me with wide eyes.

"For once, so am I."

"I guess their secret is out."

"Mimi told me last night she knew," I confirmed.

"Really? I guess everyone knows but is being too polite to say anything to either of them." Jackson held the reins steady as the horse began to trot.

"My father looked really upset." My father was normally such a calm and reasonable man that I worried when he got upset.

"He is. You missed a huge argument last night."

"Really? I did not hear anything."

How did he know about an argument in my house when I did not?

"That's because it was behind closed doors in your father's study, on the other end of the house. But I guarantee anyone in the near proximity heard plenty." He grimaced.

"Were you in there?"

"Yes. William, both your parents, and me and it did not go well. Your mother cried a lot and even slapped William across the face when he told them." I unintentionally giggled and Jackson gave me a look of disapproval, which I ignored. "Your father shouted at him about honor, duty, responsibilities, and restraint. I have never seen your parents so upset. It was ten times worse than when the whole studying law thing broke."

We arrived at the house and left the carriage out front. Both of us were unsure what to do until the others arrived. We spent the next two hours pacing around the family room. Jackson would occasionally stoke the fire just for something to do with his hands. I watched his movements carefully, wondering what it would be like to be with him finally. I quickly dismissed the thoughts from my mind and focused back on the situation at hand. Clearly, those types of thoughts were what caused this situation in the first place.

I walked over to the piano and sat down. I fumbled a few times before I could get my fingers to play a solid melody that made any sense. Jackson continued to pace the room while I attempted to play. Both of us remained silent. I had no idea of the amount of humiliation my parents must be experiencing at this moment, nor could I imagine the state they were going to be in once they returned home.

I could hear whispers from the staff in the kitchen. Each of them clearly had overheard the argument last night. There were many speculations flying about. Sarah came in occasionally to see if we needed anything or to refresh our tea, but neither of us were hungry. Time crawled by as we both stared at the clock on the mantle.

Three hours. Nothing.

Eventually, I gave up on trying to play anything that resembled a song. I got up and paced the room restlessly with Jackson.

Finally, at about five o'clock, everyone arrived home. The tension rolled in along with the group, and there was an awkward silence that filled the room. Father immediately walked over to the bar and poured himself a scotch and one for Olivia's father, Benjamin. They both gulped it down. My mother did not bother to remove her shawl or bonnet before she stalked off into the kitchen to check on supper. Her face looked tired and drained. Jackson and I stood in the middle of the six individuals, feeling completely out of place.

"Is anyone hungry?" Olivia's mother, Harriet, asked, removing her shawl. She was attempting to be polite, but I could tell her actions were forced.

"No thank you," my father answered. "I have lost my appetite." He glared at William, who was staring at the floor, looking utterly ashamed.

Olivia did not look any better than William. She still had tear streaks on her face, and her eyes were red and swollen from crying.

Mother reentered the room, finally removing her shawl and bonnet and handing them to Eddie. "Now let us not make this any worse, Patrick. Everything has been said and done. This is the time for us to calm down. We have another wedding to plan and not much time to do it in."

My father let out a grunt of disapproval but followed her into the dining room with Olivia's parents.

Jackson, Olivia, William, and I stayed behind, not sure whether to follow or not.

"Well, you got your wish, little sister. Your wedding will be a solo event and as perfect as you planned."

William was the first to break the silence between us. His expression toward me was one of pure hatred.

"What happened?" I whispered more to Jackson than to Olivia or William.

"We cannot get married in the church or by a minister. We have disgraced our families and shamed ourselves, but your day will be perfect. Happy now?" William stormed out of the room and left the house, slamming the front door behind him. Jackson reached over and squeezed my hand and took off after my brother, leaving me alone with Olivia.

"I am so sorry, Olivia." It was the truth.

"Please, do not apologize. You did nothing wrong. I am the one who is sorry for my behavior."

I reached over and wrapped my arms around her, hugging her tightly. Her tears fell upon my shoulder as she sobbed in my arms.

"I cannot believe this is happening to me. How could I have gotten myself in this situation?"

"It is all right. Everything is going to be all right." I tried to comfort her.

"How can you say that? Everyone is going to know now. Reverend Jacobs yelled at us, saying that we had disgraced God and our families by our lustful actions, and it was a sin against God!" Her crying was uncontrollable. "Everyone is going to judge me." She sobbed. I wanted to reassure her, but I knew she was right.

"No one is judging you on anything." I knew as I said the words that it was a lie.

"Yes, they are, and they will. Everyone will, and you know it."

I tried to remain clear-headed and calm her down. I walked her over to the lounge and made her sit down beside me.

"Olivia, you have to relax." She slowly nodded her head. "Tell me what happened."

"I can't. I don't even know myself." She blew her nose with her handkerchief. "It was Labor Day weekend and we had just left the picnic with everyone, remember?" I nodded. "We walked down by the lake and sat out under the stars, and things just got out of hand." She cried harder again. "I am so sorry. I know I should have stopped him, but I have been so lonely since I lost Sean, and I was sure that I was never going to love anyone again."

"I understand, Olivia. I honestly do."

I sat there in silence with her for some time, holding her while she cried. Everything now made perfect sense to me. I could no longer be upset with her or William.

Jackson and William returned shortly after dark. I got up and let William take my place holding Olivia, who was still crying. I took Jackson's hand, and we walked over to the foyer and sat down on the bottom of the stairs.

"Is William all right?"

"No," he whispered.

"What did he say?"

"Just a lot of rambling. He is really beating himself up over this." Jackson put his arm around me, and I leaned against him.

"So is Olivia."

"Did she finally talk to you?" He kissed my forehead lightly.

"Yes, a little." I looked up into his beautiful, emerald eyes and saw how tired they looked. This entire situation was taking its toll on all of us.

"You both okay now?" He kept his voice low.

"Much better." I mustered a smile for him.

"I am glad to hear that. She needs you right now. She feels as if everyone is judging her."

"I know, and the sad thing is, she's right. Everyone is going to be talking."

We both knew it was true. Everyone loves a juicy story, and this had all the right ingredients.

"Yes, but we can at least do our best to be supportive of them. You really need to try to patch things up with William also."

"I will, but he is more difficult than Olivia. I know that I should not, but a small part of me is still blaming him for this. I am so disappointed in him for doing this to her."

"It takes two, Jocelyn. She is as responsible for this situation as he is."

"I know, but he had to realize that she was still struggling with everything since losing Sean and was feeling all alone. I cannot help it. A part of me feels like he took advantage of that."

He gave me a coy smile that said something I did not quite understand. "I see why you might think that, but he truly did not."

"She told me how she was feeling that night by the lake."

"He told me also that they had discussed Sean, but they also were falling in love with each other for some time before that evening, and William did not force himself on her. Your brother is not like that. You know that, Jocelyn."

Truly I could not imagine my hyper yet gentle and loving brother forcing himself on anyone. "I know."

"The best thing we can do now is to simply let them both know that we are here for them without judgment." I nodded, resting my head against his shoulder.

We sat there for a while, during which both sets of parents stayed in the dining room. At one point, my father passed by us and went out the front door without a word and returned several minutes later with both of Jackson's parents. They proceeded to follow my father into the dining room without as much as a hello to either of us.

A half hour later, Emily motioned for all of us to join them in the dining room. Everyone was seated around the table, and the four of us reluctantly joined them. Our parents all held the same sullen expressions.

"As you all might have guessed, we have been trying to find a solution that is most suitable for everyone in this situation. Some difficult decisions have been made." Benjamin started off the conversation.

He and my father sat opposite each other at the end of the table. Both men looked terribly upset and as if they were struggling to control their anger. William and Olivia both stared at the table, waiting for their fate to be decided for them. My heart went out to each of them.

"Since it is now impossible for you two to marry in a church or by a Reverend, Mr. Chandler has graciously agreed to reside over a small ceremony that will take place on November second at our home. It will be a quiet affair with only immediate family, no friends. An announcement will be released after Thanksgiving, not before."

"There will also be no mention of this wedding before it takes place to anyone outside the immediate family." My father joined in, looking particularly annoyed. "William will remain in school and finish his degree. Olivia, you will not return to school after the wedding. You both will reside within this household since it will be easier to conceal the pregnancy for as long as possible so that dates can be rearranged without much notice. Your siblings will remain in the dark for the sake of their innocence."

"Once William finishes school, he will take a position at Mr. Chandler's law firm and work alongside him and Jackson. At that point in time, you will proceed to purchase a home for you and your family." Benjamin glared so hard at my brother I swore it bore a hole straight through him.

William only nodded and remained silent, looking at the table.

Jackson and I sat quietly, absorbing our surroundings with despair. I held his hand under the table and gently squeezed it from time to time as the fathers' tones became harsher and harsher.

Olivia and William were seated across from us. Olivia had silent tears rolling down her face. I noticed my bother reach over and place his hand over hers and squeezed it gently to comfort her. They both looked so young, not even close to adults at all and certainly not ready for the life that was now being carefully planned out and laid down before them.

"Any questions?"

But both remained silent and only shook their heads.

"Fine. You kids can leave now."

I looked over at Jackson, who hesitated a moment before rising himself. I could tell the insult my father just stated upset him, but I guess he figured now was not the time to say anything.

The four of us exited the dining room and wandered into the kitchen. It had finally occurred to me that I had not eaten since breakfast. Sarah quickly assembled a makeshift dinner out of leftovers for the four of us. Jackson and I both ate everything, but William and Olivia barely touched their plates.

"Are you feeling all right?" I looked over at Olivia.

"I will be fine. I just need time to adjust to all the changes." She gave me a weak smile.

"It will take some time." Jackson tried to soothe her.

"I guess. I suppose you are thrilled with this turn of events, Jocelyn?" William glared over at me.

His comment took me by surprise.

"Now you get to have your perfect solo wedding just the way you always wanted it." He threw down the dinner roll he was playing with and suddenly Jackson's face turned scarlet with anger.

"That was uncalled for, William. Apologize now!" Jackson raised his voice through gritted teeth.

I had never really heard Jackson speak in such a tone before, and I could tell he was struggling to control his temper. I had been arguing with my brother for as long as I could remember, so his comment had not bothered me much. It was typical of William to project his anger when he could not confront the real source of it.

I placed my hand on Jackson's arm, trying to calm him down. "Jackson, please. Let it go," I whispered.

"Me? What about your little princess? Her behavior has been unforgivable for over a week, but she gets her way in the end, as always!" William shouted at Jackson.

"Sir, you apologize now or step outside!" Jackson's voice reached a new level.

"No stop it, boys. Ya'll is not chil'en anymo," Sarah scolded in a firm voice, stepping in between the two in an attempt to save her kitchen.

Olivia and I could only stare. I had never seen them argue, let alone get into a physical altercation.

"Outside," William growled with his nostrils flaring.

Jackson immediately threw off his suit jacket, turned, and stormed out the back door with William right on his heels.

The two stood under the cover of darkness in the middle of a light rain. Jackson barely had time to turn around to confront William before William swung a cheap punch in Jackson's face, catching him off guard. Jackson returned with a quick jab to William's jaw. William tagged him in response and the two men fell to the ground, screaming horrible insults at each other while the punches flew.

Olivia, Sarah, and I stood on the back patio, too stunned to say anything. I had witnessed many fights over the years between my brothers, but none had ever escalated to this level before. I had no idea what to do to stop them. I was afraid to get in the middle for fear that they would accidentally take a swing at me also.

Soon, our parents surrounded Olivia and me, along with Eddie and Mimi. Benjamin took a couple of steps toward William and Jackson, but Robert grabbed his arm.

"Let them fight it out. William needs this."

"You cannot be serious?" Benjamin looked livid.

"Yes. Very much so." Robert held firm to Benjamin's arm.

"Benjamin, I agree. William needs to work his anger out, and Jackson is letting him." My father stood on the other side of Benjamin, making sure he did not interrupt the fight.

I stared at our fathers in disbelief. Perhaps William needed to work out some anger, but why did he have to use Jackson as a punching bag? I did not want William to hurt him, nor did I want to see my brother hurt. I could certainly understand why he was so angry. The entire course of his life had been dramatically altered, and he was helpless to fix it.

"Father, please do something! Stop this!" I approached my father and demanded.

"Jocelyn, they are fine. Trust me," he responded softly.

I stood there, helpless, watching William and Jackson rolling around, soaked to the bone with blood and mud smeared across their faces and clothes.

I could hear Olivia's sobs behind me and our mothers' small noises whenever another punch was thrown by one of the boys.

All of us were getting drenched as the rain picked up its momentum. The intensity of the screams from both Jackson and William began to slow, along with their movements. Jackson had worn William out to the point that William laid on his back in the yard and gave way to a burst of hysterical tears and sobs. Jackson rested beside him in the rain, purely exhausted.

Robert gently guided Benjamin's arm and then my father's. "Let us leave them alone. It is over. They need some privacy."

Olivia and her parents bid us all good night and went home. I knew Olivia had wanted to speak with William about everything that had been decided for them, but she would have to wait a little longer.

William and Jackson should have left for school hours ago, but the events of the day had prevented their departure. I was not even sure if they would be returning tomorrow morning or what their plans were. I wanted to wait for them to come inside, but my mother sent me upstairs to bed.

I soaked in a hot bubble bath for a while, trying to warm myself back up from the freezing chill and wetness outside. I hated myself for being so thankful that I was not Olivia and facing what lay ahead of her and William. But I also felt guilty because I knew in my heart it could have been just as easily Jackson and me instead.

Mimi came in and brushed out my hair as I sat on the corner of my bed. I could no longer hear any voices from downstairs, and I wondered if Jackson and his parents had gone home as well.

"Long dae," Mimi stated rather than asked.

"Yes. I suppose you heard everything." I laughed. I knew she had. She always did.

"Yes'm."

"What do you think about all this?" Her opinion truly mattered to me. She was a very wise woman who had seen so much in her years.

"No m' place ta say." Mimi sat down beside me and lovingly took my hands in hers.

"I am asking."

"Ah's think tha' Miss Olivia is n' fo' a vera long pregnancy, but it'll elp a grate deal havin' ya ere wif er."

"I am not so sure. She is not exactly happy with me these days."

"She jus' needs sum time ta ajus." Mimi patted my hands assuredly.

"I know. We spoke a little today, and that helped, but I know she cannot be thrilled at the prospect of living here as opposed to her own house."

"Er fatha will not allow er ta live at home. So's yar ma offered er ta live ere. Mr. Adams is a grate mo' upset dan he's lettin' on, n' Mrs. Adams is a mighty cold woman n' mys opinion." She looked deeply disturbed.

"This is such a mess. Have you seen William and Jackson since they came in? Are they alright?" I asked softly.

"Fine. Fine. Jus' sum bruises n' scratches. Nothin' bad." She laughed. "Boys'll be boys."

"I suppose." I sighed.

I still wanted to see Jackson to make sure he was fine. I was not even sure when I would get to see him again.

I snuggled down into bed while Eddie came in and stoked the fire to break the chill out of the night air. Within minutes, Mimi turned out the oil lamps and closed my door. I strained my ears to see if I could hear anything from my parents.

I was positive that they were still awake but probably had retreated into Father's study. The entire house was silent except for the scuffing movements of our servants. At moments like these, I hated having such a large home. It made it impossible to hear what was going on.

CHAPTER 13

Sunday, October 18, 2015

JACKSON CALLED MY CELL AT ONE, waking the four of us. I hadn't realized how late it had been when we finally drifted off and couldn't believe we'd all slept in so late.

"Did I wake you?" he asked when I answered. Clearly, he could tell.

"Yeah." I rubbed the sleep out of my eyes.

"Sorry. I figured you would be up by now."

"Normally I am, but Jenna, Hilary, and Caitlyn spent the night." I did my best to stifle back a yawn, but it escaped despite my best efforts.

"Not gossiping about boys now, were you?" he teased.

"Why would we waste our time?"

Two can play this game.

"I am hurt. I just thought that perhaps since you all had boyfriends it might be a topic of conversation." I could picture the smile on his lips, and it instantly brought one to mine.

"*They* have boyfriends."

"And you do not." He attempted to sound hurt. "Really?"

"Certainly not."

"Now I am hurt and offended." He laughed. "Then what am I?" I could tell he was enjoying himself.

"Just a friend who lives across the street." I teased, enjoying myself.

"A friend? Is that all? You really do know how to hurt a guy." He continued laughing. "So, you are not mad at me?" He inquired.

"No. Should I be?"

"No."

"Then why are you calling?" I teasingly demanded.

"Wow. Now look who is being rude." The giddiness in his voice returned.

"Sorry, but you are the one who just woke me up. Plus, you woke up my friends," I pointed out.

"I am sorry. I honestly did not mean to." He paused, and I rolled my eyes to the three sets that were on me. "But I was calling to see if you wanted to help me catch up on biology and review a little more for the psychology exam."

"Seriously? I haven't even showered yet, and you're already talking about studying?"

"Okay fine. You shower and throw on something comfortable, and I will fix you something to eat so you do not have to study on an empty stomach. How does that sound?"

I shifted the phone to my other hand, trying to turn away from the eavesdropping group beside me. "Are you serious? You want me to come over there and study and you're going to fix me some breakfast?" All the eyes upon me widened, as did their smiles. Immediately, their heads began shaking for me to say yes. "All right. Fine. Give me about an hour."

"Wonderful. I shall see you then." He hung up before I could say anything else.

I set the phone back on my nightstand and all three of my friends jumped up, fully awake and absolutely thrilled.

"Oh, my God!" Hilary started in. "This is great!" She jumped around the room and then headed for my closet. "We've got to find you the perfect outfit. Something he hasn't seen you in yet." I rolled my eyes behind her laughing at her enthusiasm.

"You want to tell me again how you're not interested in him?" Caitlyn smirked.

"Really," Jenna agreed.

"It's studying. That's all. Now I'm getting into the shower."

I left the three of them all giddy like junior high girls over a boy's phone call.

Jackson answered the front door wearing jeans and a cream-colored, long-sleeved, cotton shirt with three buttons at the top. Two were undone. The shirt really emphasized the muscular structure of his frame. His smile was warm and welcoming.

He stepped back and let me pass and of course, the now-familiar symptoms returned full force as I crossed over the threshold so close to him. I was suddenly extremely thankful that I had an empty stomach, but somehow, that did not stop the nausea. I became so lightheaded that I grabbed the doorknob to maintain my balance, accidentally brushing against him. The muffled fog completely engulfed me again as I hit the floor the voices and images returned.

"Mother, Olivia invited me over this afternoon. May I please go?" I heard myself saying.

A woman was standing next to the fireplace in what appeared to be my mother's living room, but it was different. I scanned the room, noticing all the variations. Then I really looked at who I had just addressed as Mother. She was not my mother, and her clothes were from the Victorian era. The woman wore a beautiful, blue, full-length skirt and a long-sleeved, white blouse. Her golden blonde hair was pulled up in a bun at the nap of her neck.

This was wrong — the room, the woman, all of it. The woman turned to me and smiled.

"Yes, Jocelyn. But please return before supper. You know your father will be upset if I have to send one of your brothers for you again." She cautioned.

Brothers? What? I only have one brother. What is going on?

"Jocelyn, are you alright?" I felt Emily dab my forehead with a cold washcloth. "Sweetheart, you fainted. Do you want me to call your mother?"

I slowly opened my eyes to find out only Emily kneeled beside me but Robert and Jackson also.

I was so embarrassed.

"No. I'm sorry. I'm okay. I must just need to eat something." I lied.

The last thing I wanted to do was put something in my queasy stomach. My head was still spinning, and everything sounded muffled in my ears.

I wish Jackson would back away from me.

I sat up slowly, feeling completely foolish.

"There is no need to apologize, Jocelyn." Robert held out his hand to help me up.

I was thankful it wasn't Jackson's, because I had a feeling that if I touched him, I would be right back flat on the floor again.

"Easy now." Robert's eyes were soft and caring, just like Jackson's.

"Thank you." I stood. "Really, I'm very sorry. I feel so foolish." I covered my face with my hands. I'm sure it looked as if I was trying to hide my embarrassment, but I was really trying to get my head to stop spinning.

Jackson picked up my scattered books and papers that had fallen across the foyer when I fell. "I will put these on the table for you."

He walked out of the room, leaving me alone with his parents. Strangely, I felt comfortable with them, even more so than I did with Jackson.

"It is all right, really. No need to feel foolish," Emily reassured me. "It happens. There is no reason to be embarrassed." She wrapped her arm around my shoulders and guided me into the kitchen.

I sat down at the breakfast bar, where Jackson or Emily or perhaps even Robert, I didn't know which, had made brunch. There was a plate with scrambled eggs, a slice of ham, sour bread toast, and a bowl of fresh fruit waiting for me.

It looked fabulous, but my stomach was still too uneasy, and I didn't trust it.

Emily and Robert hung around the kitchen with us, probably just to make sure I wasn't going to fall off the bar stool and crack my head open on the tile.

I picked at my food, eating only a little of the fruit and taking a couple bites of toast. The sight and smell of the eggs and ham were making my stomach sick. If I was home, I would have put them in the trash to get them away from me, but since I wasn't, I tried not to breathe through my nose so as not to be rude or insulting to my hosts.

"Is everything okay, Jocelyn?" Emily noticed I was only picking at my food.

Immediately, I sliced the ham and took a bite. "Yes. It's delicious. I love it." I lied, not wanting to hurt her feelings.

His parents hung around, making small talk until we finished eating.

Jackson finally announced we needed to start studying for our upcoming exams. His parents excused themselves to the family room while we disappeared into the dining room.

Sitting in seats opposite of each other made Jackson a constant distraction for me. Every time I looked up, I could see his gorgeous face looking back at me, making it impossible for me to concentrate.

"Did you hear that Cody is having a costume party at his place on Halloween?" Jackson asked, flipping pages without really looking at them.

I tried to act like I was reading in our textbook. "Hilary said something about it last week. Are you planning on going?"

"Only if you agree to be my date." His smile was irresistible.

"Your date? You're not going to make me dress up in some ridiculous costume, are you?" I smirked at him.

"Absolutely," he flashed his lop-sided grin that I loved.

I tapped my pen to act like I was bored with the idea. "What did you have in mind?"

"Actually, I was thinking of something classy rather than silly or scary."

"Like what?"

"Want to do an era piece?"

"Depends on the era. I am not putting on a toga or something equally ridiculous. And I'm not going to dress up as Pebbles to your Bam Bam either." I chuckled at the notion.

"Duly noted. I was thinking that we could dress up in something from the late 19th Century. What do you think?" He tilted his head to the side, his eyes glistening.

"Late nineteenth century?"

Not exactly what I had in mind.

"Mid to late," he shrugged. "Sure. Why not?"

"Isn't that like *Gone with the Wind,* classic Victorian style?" I was pretty sure but not positive. History wasn't exactly my favorite subject.

"Exactly," he beamed.

"I own absolutely nothing that would fit that kind of criteria." I shook my head. "Sorry, but we'll have to come up with something else."

"Please think about it. My mother loves to sew and be creative. She said she will handle everything. Trust me. You will not have to worry about anything." He bragged lovingly.

How can I say no to that smile?

"Okay, but are you sure she won't mind? I don't want to put her out. I mean, the party is only two weeks away. That's not a lot of time to create two costumes from scratch."

"Trust me. My mother truly enjoys these kinds of projects." Jackson winked across the table, and my heart melted.

"Fine, then. I'll go with you."

"As my date?"

"Yes, as your date." I smiled back.

"Thank you. Now if you will stop distracting me, I have an exam tomorrow to study for." He winked again with a smile, causing my face to instantly burn red.

"Oh. Sorry." I threw my pen across the table at him.

Emily announced that dinner was ready around five, forcing us to take a short break to eat. It felt so natural being here in this home with his family, almost like I'd been here numerous times before.

We studied both psychology and biology until almost seven in the evening. I don't think I'd ever had so much fun studying before, nor have I ever felt so prepared for exams. I was positive that at least in these two classes, if Jackson and I continued to study like this together, I was going to ace them.

The air was clear and crisp. The stars were shining brightly against the darkened sky as Jackson walked me home. I wanted so badly for him to put his arms around me and hold me close. I wanted to snuggle up in his arms, run my fingers through his dark hair, and feel his lips touch mine. But I knew it was impossible with these constant episodes every time he touched me.

We stood on the front porch of my house, neither of us knowing what to say. It should have been an awkward moment, but oddly, it wasn't. I fought against myself not to reach out and touch him, but there was no way I could risk fainting here.

To break the silence, I gestured toward the swing. "Do you want to sit down for a minute?"

"Sure."

Even though the swing boards were cold through our clothes, I didn't care, and Jackson didn't seem too either. I didn't want to leave him even though I was chilled to the bone.

"Thank you for helping me catch up this weekend. I appreciate it. I had a really great time getting to know you better."

I gazed over at him, feeling such a fire burning deep within me. It seemed so unfair that I had to have such negative side effects from him.

"You're welcome. I had a good time too. Besides, you were right. Your parents are the best. I really enjoyed getting to know them and spending time with you also."

"Do you feel ready for the exams?"

"Very." I nodded stupidly.

"Me too."

"We should do this before every exam."

"I agree."

We sat in silence, each on opposite ends of the swing. Jackson seemed nervous about getting too close to me. He smiled over at me, sliding his hand only inches from my hand that was rested on the seat. Reluctantly, he stopped with a disappointed look on his face.

"I am sorry, Jocelyn. I do not know what to say about these, um, episodes that you are experiencing whenever I am near you. Are you all right now?"

His face was full of concern, so I nodded with a smile. Oddly, I was getting accustomed to the constant nausea and slight dizziness I felt around him.

"Good. Just making sure." He smiled. "But I have to admit that it is very intriguing."

I certainly didn't think so. "And why is that?"

"I suppose every man enjoys a challenge." He grinned slightly.

"Is that what I am to you? A challenge?" I wasn't sure if I was insulted or flattered.

"I do not mean that in a bad way. What I mean to say is that I like you very much and these little episodes are quite inconvenient." He laughed but not really.

Jackson turned toward me, almost taking my hands in his, but, once again, he hesitated and placed them back in his lap. "Do you have any idea how much I want to hold you in my arms?"

I was speechless. I wanted him to sweep me up in his arms, but I was terrified as to what the effects would be.

"What do you think would happen if I did?"

"To be honest, I'm trying not to think of it." And that was the truth. If I gave it any more thought, I just might be tempted enough to try it and to hell with the consequences. At that moment, I wouldn't have cared if my mother dragged me kicking and screaming to the hospital if I had the chance to feel his arms around me just once.

Jackson's smile widened at my response, which made it even more difficult to hug my end of the swing. "And why is that?"

"I believe you already know."

"What, you are not attracted to me? Is that what you are saying, and you just want to let me down easy, right?" He pretended to be hurt.

"No." I shook my head, smiling. "Well, how could this work? Every time we get close, I feel nauseous, get cold chills, and feel lightheaded. When you barely touch me, I faint." My voice sounded whiney to my own ears.

"Jocelyn, every relationship has some obstacles." He tossed his hands in the air for emphasis.

"Couples don't usually throw up or black out when they're near each other."

"True. But I honestly believe we can push through this. It is just a matter of mind over obstacle. If we really like each other, and I truly believe we do, we must trust that we can get through this. We will take it slow and enjoy getting to know each other. What do you think?"

His words were more comforting than anything I had ever felt before.

Jackson stood up and faced me. "May I drive you to school in the morning?"

His offer touched me. He was willing to give this a go despite the obvious.

"Sure, but I have practice after school." I shook my head slightly at my own stupidity. "But then again, so do you."

"I shall see you in the morning, then. Good night." He paused for just a moment at the top of the steps. "And sweet dreams."

Jackson walked down the steps and across the yard. I watched him until he reached his front door. We waved once more to each other before disappearing into our homes for the evening.

CHAPTER 14

Wednesday, October 23, 1878

I LAY IN BED LISTENING to the patter of the raindrops falling on the roof and not wanting to get out of my warm bed. The soaking rain was so befitting after all that had happened in the last several days. Even though Olivia was supposed to remain in school until the wedding, she had not returned since she walked out last Thursday. I had not even spoken to her since Sunday. I had gone by her house the day before to drop off some schoolwork she'd missed, but her mother informed me that Olivia was not feeling well and was unable to receive guests.

I had also not spoken to Jackson since Sunday. He had not called, which was understandable since I knew he had examinations this week, but I honestly had hoped to hear something from him since we did not even get the chance to say goodbye. I wondered what was going on between him and William. I was curious if they'd made up yet or if things were still very tense between them. Although I had never seen their dorm room, because females are not allowed in the building, Jackson had told me it was very small. I hope they were at least getting along somewhat better.

I gathered with my friends on the steps for lunch, taking advantage of the respite from the rain. I only picked at my food. Everyone, except me, was in good spirits and excited over the upcoming festival despite the persistent showers.

"Have you seen Olivia lately?" Maryanne asked between bites of her sandwich.

"No. I went by her house yesterday and Mrs. Adams told me she was too ill to have guests. I left her homework material with her mother." I shrugged trying to act casual.

"I hope she is not too ill," Elizabeth stated in her soft voice. "Do you believe she will make it to your birthday party on Saturday?"

My goodness. I had completely forgotten that today was my birthday, and my family was hosting a party to celebrate it on Saturday. "I hope so."

"Do you have any idea what Jackson got you?" Christina inquired.

"No. He is being very secretive about it, and it is making me crazy." I let out a low chuckle of frustration.

"I do." Laurie smirked. Her father, Henry Cain, owned the local mercantile, and she almost always knew what went on in her father's store. "He ordered it a couple weeks ago and swore me to secrecy."

"I suppose I will find out soon enough." I tried not to give it any thought with everything else on my mind.

"Do you know who all is going to attend on Saturday?" Elizabeth piped in.

"Mother made up the guest list, so I would imagine it will be grander than necessary, knowing her." I tried to laugh and act like everything was normal.

I looked back down at my food and drifted away from the conversation. I listened to them speculate about the cake and decorations and discuss what they were going to wear. I wanted so badly to be as enthused about my party as they were, but my heart was not in it.

It was strange. A month ago, I was looking so forward to my eighteenth birthday. Now it seemed rather trivial. My family had not even acknowledged it this morning before I left for school. I wondered if they even remembered it. Funny enough, I had not.

I let myself become engulfed in my afternoon studies. It was a welcome reprieve from everything else that had been consuming my thoughts of late.

I found myself emerged in the accomplishments of Thomas Jefferson as I sat through my history class. Jefferson was truly an amazing individual; and I found it intriguing that both he and John Adams, who were lifelong friends and eventually enemies, had managed to revive their friendship during the last years of their lives by writing letters to each other.

It was curiously odd that the two famous men passed away on the same day only hours apart and odder still that the date happened to be the Fourth of July.

That short piece of history seemed to strangely give me some hope that there was a small chance that Olivia and I could mend the wounds between us and become close again, especially since in ten short days we would be considered sisters.

Eddie picked me up from school since the rain had returned and increased in intensity. Normally a very quiet man who rarely spoke, it surprised me when he wished me a happy birthday while opening the door for me. I smiled politely, nodding, and said, "Thank you" before taking my seat.

I wondered if I should attempt to visit Olivia again this afternoon. I had another packet of papers for her from school today. Then I reconsidered and thought that perhaps I should allow Eddie to drop them off for her. I figured if she wanted to speak with me, she certainly knew where to find me.

Upon our return home, I climbed out of the carriage and handed Eddie the packet and asked him to please drop it off over at the Adams estate for Olivia. He nodded quietly and escorted me inside my house.

Sitting on the bottom step of the stairs in the foyer, much to my surprise and delight, was Jackson. "Happy birthday, darling," he sang out and rose to greet me. He picked me up and wrapped his arms around me. I embraced him tightly, not wanting to let him go.

"You left without saying goodbye." I playfully complained, fighting back tears of joy and relief. My emotions were so all over the place I felt like I was living constantly on the verge of tears or hysterical laughter, and one word could send me swinging in either direction.

"I am so sorry about that, my love. I was a little preoccupied with William at the time." He laughed, setting me back on my feet.

We sat back down at the bottom of the steps, and Jackson kept his arm draped around me.

"How is he?" I was still somewhat upset with him for using Jackson as a punching bag.

"Better. He needed to rumble to rid himself of the anger. He is doing better now," Jackson said as if he were reading my thoughts. I guess he knew me too well.

"Good. And you?" I glanced over his face to see if there was any evidence left of Sunday evening. I saw only a light bruising on his left cheek and a scrape above his left eyebrow. *No worse for the wear, I suppose.*

"I am fine. William looks much worse than I do."

That made me laugh and feel better.

"Good. Serves him right." I tried not to show too much enthusiasm for my brother's injuries. "Is he home also?"

"No. He decided to stay on campus to study for midterms, but he does send his best wishes for your birthday. He also told me to tell you that he is sorry for the way he acted Sunday evening and that he promises he will be home for the party Saturday."

"Really? Is he planning on attending, or is he going into hiding with Olivia?" I could not mask the sarcasm in my voice.

"Is Olivia in hiding now?" Jackson raised his eyebrows.

"Apparently. She has missed classes all week and when I went over there yesterday to bring her the material she missed, Mrs. Adams said she was too ill for guests."

"That is strange. I thought she was going to attend until the wedding."

"So, did I. Has William spoken to her since Sunday?" All of this felt wrong to me and the more I thought about Mimi's words, the more it bothered me.

"No. She called twice, but he made me tell her he was at the library, studying."

"You lied to her for him?"

His embarrassment for his actions was more than obvious on his face. "I know I should not have, and I repeatedly asked him not to place me in the middle, but you know how your brother is."

"True, but you should have made him talk to her or at least tell her his own excuses. I am sure she is suffering too. She's reaching out to him for comfort and reassurance." William's childish behavior truly irritated me. "So, is my birthday the reason you came home?" I shifted the subject in desperate hopes of not ruining the evening with him.

"I also missed you and wanted you to know that I love you." He brought his lips to mine, and I could feel the desire starting to burn inside me.

"I love you, too. I am so happy you came home." The butterflies danced deep within me as I kissed him passionately.

"Now you need to put your books away for the evening, because I am taking my lady out for a special dinner in the city." Jackson raised his eyebrow in mysterious amusement.

"Are you serious? But it is dreadful out."

"I traveled all the way from school in this mess to take you into the city to one of the finest restaurants and you are going to complain about the weather? You should have been born in July if you wanted perfect birthday weather." He laughed and playfully pushed me away from him, making me giggle at his childishness.

My parents came in together, looking better and happier than I had seen in days. Mother walked over and embraced me warmly. "Happy birthday, darling. You look lovely today."

"Thank you, Mother. So, do you." I hugged her tightly.

"Are you two ready?" Father stepped forward and gave me a tight hug. "Happy birthday, darling. I cannot believe you are eighteen years old. It seems like only yesterday you were just a baby." He kissed my forehead, making me feel like a child again.

"I was not aware that you both were joining us. This is wonderful." I stepped back, looking at my parents. "Is anyone else joining us?" I asked, thinking of my brothers and their families.

"They will all be here Saturday for your party." Mother grinned and placed her arm through Father's as Eddie opened the front door. I smiled at Jackson, taking his arm.

The carriage ride lasted about half an hour. Mother and I sat silently while Jackson and my father discussed his studies and Jackson's preparation for his upcoming bar exam. The law courses he was taking honestly did not hold a lot of interest for me. I was more excited about science and biology. For the last six years or so, I would sneak around and read my father's books in his study when no one was around. I was thankful that Jackson loved these traits about me and encouraged my thirst for knowledge. I was looking forward to the time I would be able to sit in a rocking chair by my own hearth and read without fear of being discovered.

The restaurant was crowded with various businessmen and society elites. The place itself was elegant and beautifully decorated. Low-lit oil lamps hung along the walls and each table was draped with off-white, linen cloths where little candles burned brightly in the center. The silverware sparkled in the soft lighting. There were flowers everywhere and the strong aroma of various complementary spices hung in the air.

My father ordered for us all, along with a bottle of their best red wine. He poured each of us a glass and rose to his feet, raising his glass. He had a gleam in his eye that I had not seen in a while.

"Tonight, we celebrate one of the most joyous occasions in my life; the birth of my only daughter, Jocelyn Alyssa." He turned toward me, and I was surprised and deeply moved when I noticed his eyes tearing up. "May you have a long and happy life, my darling, and never know sorrow any one moment of it."

We all raised our glasses and had a drink.

"Thank you, Father." I choked back the tears welling up in my eyes.

He settled back into his chair. "Let me also say that I am very happy with your choice of a husband." He looked over at Jackson. "Jackson, you are a very fine young man and I know that I will sleep peacefully at night with the knowledge that you are taking care of my little girl." He gave Jackson a warm, fatherly smile.

"Thank you, sir. I truly appreciate that. I love Jocelyn very much. I promise to do everything I can to make her happy." Jackson placed his hand lovingly over mine.

"I know that son." My father raised his glass slightly toward Jackson and took another drink.

"And I know you two will have the most beautiful children." Mother beamed.

A gray façade clouded over my father's face. "Please only wait a while for that. I do not believe I can handle any more shocking news. Of course, it would be different with you two, at least being married first, but just the same."

Mother placed her hand over his. "Patrick love, not tonight. You promised."

"Yes, dear. I apologize. I am afraid I am having a difficult time understanding how this could have happened. I had always thought so highly of Olivia, but now," he stammered.

"Father, I understand. I am having the same difficulty myself. But people make mistakes, and we must be understanding, forgiving. All we can do now is make the best out of the current situation. Also, William is just as responsible for this as she is." I spoke gently and chose my words very carefully.

However, I knew as I said them that the same standard did not apply to men as they did to women. A double standard I hoped someday would change.

"Men are always going to be men, but I had thought we raised William better than that. I am quite disappointed in his behavior as well," he stated.

"Patrick, we did raise a good son." My mother's voice was barely a whisper.

"It shows."

In a quick turn of events, my glorious birthday dinner was now filled with uncomfortable tension.

"Let us not think about it this evening. We are here to celebrate after all." Jackson attempted to lighten the mood.

"How do you think your parents would have reacted if it were you and Jocelyn instead?" My father gave Jackson an inquisitive look.

"Honestly, sir, much the same as you have, I would imagine."

As the words came out of his mouth, I seriously doubted him. His parents were such compassionate and loving individuals that I could not ever believe either of them would behave in such a manner.

Father grunted in agreement and took another long drink of his wine, emptying his glass, and immediately helped himself to another. I looked over at my mother, who held an apologetic expression on her face.

"Proper young ladies do not engage in such activities until they are married. It was not as if they were even engaged when this occurred." Father took another drink of wine. "I am sorry, but it does call into question as whether she participated in such activities with Mr. Donavon or anyone else, for that matter."

It was then I realized we were all thinking the one thing that none of us were willing to state. I wanted to trust that my dearest friend would never be like that, yet now I honestly had to admit that even I was unsure.

"Are we even sure if this child is William's?" My father's words surprised me.

"Of course, it is, Patrick. I do not believe Olivia would be dishonest about something like that."

Yet it was Mother, not I, who spoke up to defend what was left of Olivia's honor.

"How can we be sure?" He looked truly disgusted.

"We have no other choice but to trust her. We cannot dishonor our family any more by not making William take responsibility for his actions," Mother gently explained in a soft voice.

I looked from my mother to my father, amazed that they were having this conversation in front of Jackson and me.

"I believe there is enough dishonor going around that no one is immune." My father gave me the oddest look.

"Did I do something wrong, Father?" I immediately became alarmed.

He shook his head at me, but his expression did not change. "Of course not, darling. I know that you were just as surprised by these events as the rest of us."

"Yes, I was," I replied.

"Do you know of her doing anything like this before?" My father inquired, looking at me intently.

"Not to my knowledge. I cannot believe this happened either. I admit that I was extremely upset when I found out." I let out a deep breath and looked down at the table, ashamed of my recent behavior toward the couple. "I am afraid I did not handle it gracefully."

Jackson and my mother both chuckled, which broke the tension, if only slightly. My confession was a slight understatement, and they both knew it.

"Well, I must say that I am happy there will be two weddings instead of one. I never did agree with that when William and Olivia suggested it." Mother smiled sweetly over at me.

"I agree."

"Me too," Jackson chimed in.

"Well, I can say that if Harriett pushed it any further, I was about to give her husband his half of the wedding bill. You are an expensive child, Miss Jocelyn." It was wonderful to hear my father tease me again. "Now I am truly glad that you are my only daughter. I would go broke if we would have had all girls." He placed his hand over my mother's.

"It is not fair of you to complain about the wedding expenses, Patrick. You told me to spare no expense to give our little girl whatever she wanted for her wedding." She gave him a coy smile.

"And you certainly did not." Father's smile broadened with love.

"Either way, I appreciate it. Our wedding is going to be exquisite." I looked around the table at the three most important people in the world to me.

"Speaking of exquisite," Jackson reached into this pocket and placed a little, dark-blue velvet box with a pale-blue ribbon in front of me.

I slowly cracked the small jewelry box to find a sterling silver ladies' pocket watch resting on the velvet. It was truly gorgeous. The numbers were inlaid on the cover in striking detail. I lifted it out of the box and examined it closely.

"It is engraved on the back," Jackson added brightly.

Turning it over, I saw *"Time will reveal my love"*.

"It is gorgeous. Thank you! I love it!" I could not imagine a more perfect gift; a beautiful token of his love that I could carry with me always.

I leaned over and kissed Jackson on the cheek. He and my parents looked most pleased with my reaction as I handed the watch over to my mother. She looked at it adoringly.

"It's lovely," she remarked handing it over to my father.

"Very nice," he concluded and handed it back to me.

"My father had one made for my mother before they were married, as did Alexander for his wife. It has become a tradition in our home, and I wanted to share it with my beautiful future wife." Jackson explained.

"What a beautiful tradition," Mother beamed.

"If we are giving out gifts," Father placed a small, black jewelry box next to my plate. "This is from your mother and me."

I opened the box slowly, unsure what to expect. My parents had never given me jewelry before. My breath caught in my chest.

"Oh, my goodness." There on the soft, green, velvet lay my grandmother's broach. I had seen my mother wear it on very special occasions, and I loved it dearly. I had asked her numerous times to wear it, but she would always politely explain that it was expensive and rare and held a great sentimental value that could never be replaced. She had promised me that someday it would be mine, but I had never expected it to be so soon. "Are you sure, Mother?"

"Yes. I believe you will treasure it as much as I have," she answered sweetly.

I looked adoringly over at Jackson and explained, "It was my grandmother's. I remember her wearing it when I was a small child. She gave it to my mother before she passed away. I have always loved it so."

I ran my fingers over the delicate, white gold and inlaid emeralds and diamonds. The craftsmanship was amazing. I knew that it was passed down through the women of our family and my grandmother had gotten it from her grandmother. As old as it was, there was still a rich shine about it. Obviously, it had been handled with loving care throughout the years. It was a true treasure.

"Thank you both so much." Tears filled my eyes. "I promise I will take care of it and someday pass it on to our daughter as well."

The ride home was incredibly cold. The night air had taken on a frosty element that chilled me down to my bones. I huddled close to Jackson, wrapped in a blanket, trying to stay warm and keep my teeth from chattering.

Chapter 15

Wednesday, October 21, 2015

I HIT THE SNOOZE BUTTON on my alarm and snuggled back under the covers. Today was my eighteenth birthday. I couldn't believe it. I was now legally an adult. But today I still had to go to high school and take an AP biology, and I still had a volleyball match tonight.

So much for welcome to the adult world.

It took me longer to get ready because I had to French braid my hair with a blue ribbon intertwined for our meet tonight and wear our goofy-looking team sweatshirts. I applied my makeup carefully. I wanted to make sure I looked my best, not because of school, but for Jackson.

He had been driving me to school all week, and of course, my friends had noticed and were giving me a hard time with it. At first, they were giving me grief about no longer participating in our carpool and recently shifted to teasing me about my apparent 180° turn about wanting a boyfriend. All three of them were almost as giddy as I was about my crush.

Jackson was already downstairs, sitting at the island with Ethan, who was hitching a ride to school with us. Very romantic. I could have killed him for it. The two of them were laughing about something that had occurred at football practice the day before and stuffing bagels in their face. I quietly slipped in and filled my travel mug with coffee and an abundant amount of sugar and cream.

"Good morning, doll." Jackson was all smiles.

Morning people truly baffle me.

"Good morning." I smiled back as I reached for a bagel.

"Did you sleep well?" He inquired as my brother rolled his eyes.

"Okay. I'm out." Ethan grabbed another bagel and headed out the front door. "I'll be in the car."

This had quickly become our routine. I loved it because I got to sit next to Jackson both on the way to school and home and in two of my classes, plus lunch. Also, I hated it because despite how close we had gotten, we remained literally worlds apart.

Jackson's effects on my physical being hadn't lightened up in the slightest and even though I was rapidly becoming accustomed to the onset of symptoms, they quickly worsened if we pushed the envelope ever so slightly.

The distance between us at times was perhaps maybe a foot, but it felt more like a mile. I loathed the fact that we still hadn't kissed or even hugged. It was true that we were narrowing the gap, but only by a few inches. Whenever we got closer than the typical personal space, my symptoms overwhelmed me.

Thanks to Jackson, Mrs. Neal-Beliveau's biology exam was incredibly simple, and I breezed through it during our second-period class. Jackson smiled over at me on his way back to his seat after turning in his exam. We studied together on Monday and Tuesday evening in the same fashion that we had over the weekend. He gave me a soft wink, making it difficult for me to keep a straight face while the rest of the class finished their exams.

Our group gathered at our usual table during lunch. I was glad now how my friends had quickly integrated Jackson in such a short amount of time. The only damper was the constant barrage of dirty looks I was receiving throughout the lunch hour from Taylor and Dakota. Caitlyn, in true form, did offer to slap the look off their faces, which was extremely tempting. However, since we had a big match that evening against our county rivals, Coach Smith would have killed Caitlyn for missing the game over something so immature. So, I told her to hold off, for now.

Mr. Rand passed back our psych exams during last period. As confident as I had felt previously about the results, I had butterflies in my stomach as he started passing them back. Jackson got his first and turned his exam toward me with an extremely proud smirk.

Jackson had gotten ninety-eight percent. I grinned back at him, but now the pressure was on.

I held my breath as Mr. Rand came back around the room, crossing through the aisle in my direction. He handed me my exam face down, which was never a good sign. I slowly turned it over while Mr. Rand hovered.

"Nice work, Jocelyn. Only perfect score." He grinned and walked away.

"Show-off." Jackson chuckled.

"I couldn't have done it without you."

When the final bell rang, I was so thrilled with my exam score I wanted to throw my arms around Jackson's neck and celebrate. But of course, I couldn't.

Jenna, Hilary, Caitlyn, and I went out to Subway before the game. We had a short break before we had to return to school for the home meet.

"So, you have to tell us. How good of a kisser is he?" Caitlyn started in as we squeezed into one of the tiny booths. "He's got the most luscious lips." She glanced to see my reaction. "I'm sorry, but it's true." She shrugged without apology.

"A lady doesn't kiss and tell." It was all I could come up with before quickly taking a bite. I was not about to admit that we had only touched by accident, and when we did, I had visions and heard voices.

Yeah. That would go over well.

"Then spill the beans, honey, because there are no ladies here," Hilary said.

"Wow! I resent that!" I acted offended.

"Well, I can say that my love life has died down since Cody's parents are back in town. I can't wait until they leave. I'm tired of making out in his car." Hilary pouted.

We all stared at her with disbelief.

"TMI, Hill." Caitlyn rolled her eyes, poking Hilary in the ribs.

"Oh, like that ever stopped you from giving me the gritty details about you and Zak." Hilary narrowed her eyes.

"Okay, okay." I waved my hands in the air over the table. "Before a cat fight breaks out, let's change the subject. Now, what is everyone dressing up as for Cody's Halloween party?"

"Aladdin and Princess Jasmine." Caitlyn shrugged. "Zak picked them out." Caitlyn looked thoroughly disappointed as she sulked in her drink.

"We haven't even started looking yet," Hilary explained. "Every time I suggest something, Cody rolls his eyes at me. We'll probably end up not coordinating our costumes at all since we can't agree on anything. He makes me want to strangle him most of the time." She playfully acted out her definition of strangulation, making us all laugh.

"I'm not telling anyone what we're going to be," Jenna taunted. "I want it to be a surprise."

I glanced down at my watch. It was already four-thirty. "And as stimulating as this conversation is, we'd better get back because I'm really not in the mood to get yelled at."

The locker room was consumed with its usual hot and musty air accompanied with that stale, funky smell when we arrived for the game, yet tonight, something felt different. As I passed the first couple rows of lockers, I noticed there were brightly colored balloons and streamers hanging from the ceiling. When I rounded the corner, I noticed my locker was covered in *Happy Birthday* wrapping paper with a huge bow in the upper corner.

Spinning around, Jenna, Hilary, and Caitlyn were standing there, cheering like three baboons.

My face turned a bright red as my team members sang a chorus of the birthday song. I quickly rolled the numbers on my lock, hoping to crawl inside my locker, but instead, I discovered a little, dark-blue, velvet box with a pale-blue ribbon and a card tucked underneath the bow. I slowly lifted the box under the watchful eyes of my teammates.

My name was printed on the outside of the card envelope in the now-familiar handwriting. The front of the ivory card had two gold hearts intertwined together. The inside was beautifully handwritten, *"I hope you have a wonderful day, and may all your wishes and dreams come true. Happy birthday! All my love, Jackson"*.

I handed the card over to Jenna, knowing she'd end up seeing it anyway. She beamed and passed it on to Hilary and Caitlyn.

With all eyes watching me, I became very nervous about opening the box. I had no inclination what Jackson would have possibly gotten me that would have fit into a jewelry box. I was terrified to open it.

Like pulling off a Band-Aid, I did it quickly only to find a sterling silver ladies' pocket watch lying on the velvet. It was truly gorgeous. The numbers were inlaid on the cover, but it also opened. I had never seen anything like it before in my life. It was such a unique gift, and that made it more special.

I held it, momentarily speechless, and then I opened it and examined it closer. When I turned it over, I noticed there was something elegantly inscribed on the back. *"Time will reveal my love"*.

My body went completely numb with fear and shock. I slowly turned to Jenna with my trembling hand extended, giving her the watch. She gave me a confused look at the expression on my face before taking the watch out of my hand. She read it quickly while I watched the look on her face change as she comprehended what she was reading.

"Oh, my God!" Jenna handed the watch to Caitlyn, who looked at it then back at us both, stunned, and handed it to Hilary.

The four of us stood silent while the rest of the team gazed upon us with intense curiosity. Without any of us offering any explanation for our reaction to the gift, the rest of them dispersed to get ready for the match. The other three gathered around me, just as confused, and mesmerized by the gift as I was.

"Wow. That's quite a gift. I'm not sure what to say." Hilary looked from one face to another.

"Well, that makes two of us," Caitlyn added.

"How did he even get into the girls' locker room to do all this?" I waved my hands toward my overly decorated locker.

"Oh, that was easy. I asked Coach before lunch if Ethan and Jackson could get in before the game to decorate your locker for your birthday," Hilary explained.

"And I gave Ethan your locker combination last night when he asked me if they could do this. But I swear I had no idea about the watch." Jenna still looked as flabbergasted as I felt.

"What do you make of the inscription? I mean, isn't it a bit too soon for something like this? I've only known this guy for what, ten days and not even that, we've only *just* started dating. And this is, well…" I looked around at the three confused faces staring back at me, "a little much, don't you think?" I held the watch in my palm, gazing intently at it.

"Just a smidge." Caitlyn gestured, using her thumb and index finger to show just how small.

"I think it's gorgeous." Hilary squeezed my shoulder with a smile. "A perfect birthday gift."

"It shows he put a lot of thought into it," Jenna added.

"It's beautiful, so delicate." I whispered more to myself than to them, looking at the inscription and marveling at the details of the artwork. It was a truly amazing piece. "It almost looks like an antique."

"Ladies, I'm sorry to break up the party, but if we don't get changed and onto that court in the next ten minutes, Coach will have us running laps next practice," Caitlyn pointed out.

I carefully placed the watch back into the box and made sure it was securely tucked away between my clothes and locked up tightly before I left the locker room.

As soon as the team hit the court, I noticed not only my parents in the stands but Jackson's and Jenna's parents as well.

Jackson and Ethan were sitting a short distance away with Zak, Cody, Kyle, and several other guys from the football team.

Even Taylor's obnoxious behavior during the matches couldn't dampen my spirits. I realized for the first time how secure I felt in Jackson's feelings for me and that she was not even close to being a threat to my blossoming relationship with him. However, the rest of my teammates also noticed her hanging around Jackson and their sentiments were not so kind.

I rode home with Jackson, Mariah, and my brother. After we dropped Mariah off at her house and pulled into Jackson's drive, Ethan said his good nights and headed off across the street to our house. I could see through the lighted front window of Jackson's house that my parents were over there visiting with his parents again.

"Do you want to come over to my house since apparently our parents are congregating at yours?" I asked.

"Sure."

We quietly closed his car doors, hoping our parents wouldn't notice our return to buy us more time alone. We snuck across the street like two thieves in the night, trying our best not to giggle too loudly at our own immature behavior.

We made it to the basement alone. I could hear the shower running upstairs, and I knew Ethan was going to be down shortly.

"So, birthday girl, you never told me how you liked my surprise."

We flopped down on the couch, close to each other, but not too close.

"I'm speechless." I straightened up and turned toward him. "It's so gorgeous and unique. Where did you ever come up with the idea?"

"My father, actually. He bought one for my mother when they were dating in high school, and she said she knew then that she was going to marry him."

Wow. No pressure there.

"Did you see the inscription?"

"Yes, and..." *How can I explain this?* "It was so sweet."

"And terrifying? Is that what you are trying to say?" A sly grin slowly crept across his gorgeous face.

"Well ..., yeah," I stuttered.

"Jocelyn, I was not trying to scare you by the inscription or the gift. I only wanted to express how I feel."

He looked so sincere, but the sentiment still terrified me. After all, I was only in high school. I still had four years of college ahead of me and then graduate school. A serious relationship at this time in my life wasn't something that I saw as lasting the duration of my own personal goals.

"I love the gift. Honestly, I do. It's just, well, so soon." It was all I could say.

"I know it might seem that way, and I cannot explain it, but I feel as if I have known you for a very long time." He shifted and draped his arm over the back of the couch.

"It's funny you should say that. I feel that way about you." It was true. And I couldn't explain it either.

We sat in silence for several minutes, just looking at each other.

"Do you have any idea how badly I want to hold you?" Jackson's intense gaze made goose bumps run through my body.

"Yes," I barely squeaked out.

"Really?" He raised his eyebrows inquisitively at me.

"Yes, I do." I fumbled for words, feeling my face burn red.

A slow grin spread across his face, showing off his irresistible dimples. "Want to try?"

"Are you trying to kill me or just hospitalize me?" I laughed. "You know that if I pass out again that's exactly where I'll end up." I tried to laugh it off, but the truth was it also terrified me – the visions, the voices, all of it. But I couldn't share that with him or anyone else.

"No, but we have to get past this. Do you not agree?"

The pleading in his voice was wearing me down. I wanted to hold him so badly it was killing me. I could only dream about how wonderful it would feel to be in his arms.

"Yes, but I don't believe that this is the right time or place to test it."

"Why not? The house is empty except for Ethan, and he is still in the shower."

I looked deeply into his eyes, pleading what I couldn't bring myself to say.

"True, but my parents could be home any time. You realize it wouldn't be a good thing for them to walk in on us kissing or you trying to revive me." The image in my head made me laugh.

"Kissing? I said I wanted to hold you." The corner of his lips lifted in the lopsided grin I love. "Does that mean you want to kiss me, Miss Jocelyn?" I could feel my face burning red with embarrassment. He was truly enjoying himself.

"Thanks. Now that I've made a complete idiot out of myself, I think I'll head off to bed now." I smirked at him playfully.

I started to get up when Jackson reached out in an instant and grabbed my arm to stop me. The flood hit full force, and I felt a sharp pain on the side of my face before the world went blank.

I was suddenly sitting in my room, but it was different — very different. The bed was a huge canopy with sheer drapes tied back around the posts. There were flowers — lilies — on a large table and lilacs with violets on the mantel. A large vanity with strange-looking jars and bottles rested against the wall, and upon it was an old silver mirror and hairbrush. A large, black woman dressed in an old-fashioned full-length dress with an apron was carrying a tray to me.

"Good mornin', Miss Jocelyn. Did ya sleep well?"

"Yes, Mimi, I did." I heard myself reply. "Is Mother up?"

"Yes'm. She's downstairs wif Dr. Timmons n' da' study." This woman placed a tray on my lap and adjusted a napkin around my neck. It was then I realized the strange-looking nightgown I was wearing and the ruffles along the sleeves. I ran my hand over the thick quilt covering my bed. It was lovely and so soft and warm. Strangely, I felt oddly at ease.

I felt a numbing warmness covering my face. In a distant fog, I could hear Jackson's voice calling my name, bringing me back from the confines of the warm bed and pleasantries of the large, black woman. I reluctantly opened my eyes to see Jackson and Ethan hovering over me.

"Jocelyn, my God, are you alright? Lie still. You are bleeding!" Jackson's face was full of concern and hovering over me, but I couldn't feel anything. I was numb.

"Don't move! I've got to get Mom." Ethan's voice was full of panic. His hair and skin were dripping wet from the shower. It was obvious he hadn't toweled himself off. Jackson must have hollered for him, causing him to grab a pair of sweatpants and T-shirt. The smell of his Axe body wash was still strong and burned my nose.

"No," I squeaked.

"Jocelyn, I have to. I can't get the bleeding to stop, and it looks deep," Ethan pleaded.

"What? I'm fine." I tried to lift myself as a sharp pain shot through my head as if it were being split in two. Immediately Ethan's hands were on my shoulders, forcing me back down.

"I said stay." His voice was loud, and firm and I obeyed. The pain wouldn't allow me to fight him.

I looked over at Jackson's grief-stricken face.

"Don't let her move. I've got to get our mom." Then Ethan was gone.

Jackson's face looked like he was in as much pain as I.

"I am so sorry, Jocelyn. I did not mean to grab your arm. It was instinct. I would never..." His voice trailed off. "I am so sorry."

"I know. It was an accident. It wasn't your fault." I hated myself for putting that look on his face. I was so sick of this crap that was happening to me and pissed because I couldn't understand it.

Why can't I have a normal relationship like everyone else?

Within minutes, two sets of hysterical parents were hovering over me. I could no longer see Jackson or Ethan anywhere, even though I knew they were both still there.

My mom, who was extremely calm when it came to dealing with her patients and emergencies, was not quite so docile when it came to her own children. She stood there, hovering over me, and arguing with our dad about the necessity of making the trip to the ER. Emily held my hand and Robert behind her, looking concerned.

"Can't you just stitch her up here?" my dad questioned.

"Well, yes, but I believe we need to get an X-ray. She might have fractured her skull," she argued.

"She has a hard head, and it was just the coffee table. I'm sure she didn't fracture her skull." I could tell he was getting more irritated with her by the minute.

"And when did you get X-ray vision?"

Wow. It was rare that my mom ever spoke to him that way and in front of guests. She was pissed. And I also knew that this meant I was on my way to the ER.

"And how did this happen? Ethan? Jackson?" My mom demanded eyeing the two young men lingering in the background.

"We were just watching a movie and talking, and Jocelyn said she was going upstairs to make some popcorn for us when she tripped over the side of the couch and hit the corner of the coffee table," Ethan replied instead of Jackson.

I was impressed. He'd covered for me. Although Jackson was allowed over, I knew my parents would give me grief about us being in the rec room alone when they weren't home. I would have to remember later that I owed him a lot for this.

"Are you sure you two weren't wrestling around again, being stupid?" I could tell our dad didn't exactly believe his story.

I slowly opened my eyes again to see Robert and Emily exchange puzzled looks.

"No, we weren't. I promise."

Ethan and I were always being stupid and shoving each other into things. I knew that if they thought he was responsible for this he'd be grounded whether it was his fault or not. Our parents were constantly yelling at him about roughhousing with me ever since he'd hit a growth spurt three years ago. Ethan now towered over me and was easily twice as strong.

"Help me get her in the car," Mom said to our dad.

I felt my dad's arms under me, lifting me to him. I could smell his cologne and immediately felt safe and secure.

"Wrap your arms around me, pumpkin," he instructed.

I did my best to comply, but my arms felt like dead weights.

"Jocelyn!" His voice got louder but felt more distant than it should have.

Then everything went dark again.

Chapter 16

Friday, October 25, 1878

OLIVIA NEVER RETURNED TO SCHOOL. She missed an entire week of classes and every day I brought her assignments home and had Eddie deliver them since Olivia apparently didn't want to see me. I would have thought that by now she and I were beyond this and able to talk things out, but I suppose I was wrong in thinking so. Her behavior proved my naivety.

I did my best to be as excited about my upcoming party the next day as clearly my friends were. However, I could not seem to get myself in the mood. I was still upset about being shunned by Olivia and was half tempted to go over and confront her. But I knew that William and Jackson would be returning that evening and may already be there by the time I returned from school.

I knew William would be furious with me if I got into another altercation with Olivia, especially now. And I truly felt selfish for even considering it with all that she was going through. After all, she was the one who was going to be the bride next weekend. Not to mention the baby on the way.

The other girls were just as confused as I was by Olivia's absence from school and her irrational behavior. There was great speculation as to whether she would attend my party tomorrow or not. Elizabeth was the most understanding and sympathetic, but the others were not. In fact, they were angrier about her secret relationship and deception with William than I and felt that she had truly betrayed my trust.

It would probably be a good thing if Olivia did not show up tomorrow. I was not sure what type of reception she would receive. It was obvious that she did not want to see me or anyone else. I did wonder if she was experiencing horrible morning sickness, as Mimi had suggested might be the problem. Or if she was, in fact, too ashamed to face anyone, which is what I believed to be going on.

Both Jackson and William were at the house by the time the school day ended. They were sitting on the porch enjoying the mildly warm autumn afternoon and drinking tea when I approached.

"Hello, my love." Jackson walked over and kissed me on the cheek. He took the books from my arms and placed them on the table.

I returned with him to the swing and sat down beside him.

"How were classes this week?" he inquired.

"Wonderful. How did the examinations go?"

"Over, finally." He laughed. "I think I did well."

"I'm sure you did." I snuggled in closer to him suddenly aware of William watching us. "And how did yours go, William?"

"Fine," his voice was somber.

"Are you alright?" He did not look very well. He was pale and had dark circles under his eyes.

"I am fine. Please excuse me," he muttered and without another word, got up and retreated into the house.

"Is he okay?" I asked Jackson.

"Not really." Jackson shook his head as he dropped his eyes.

"Has he spoken to Olivia yet?"

"No." Jackson shook his head again. "I suggested he go over there, but he said he was not ready yet."

"He needs to speak to her. She needs him to be strong now." I was truly disappointed in William's behavior.

"I told him the same thing, but he is not listening. He is drowning himself in pity and not even thinking about what she is going through."

"There is nothing he can do to change it now but accept responsibility for his mistakes."

"Trust me. He knows that. It is what upsets him so much."

I snuggled into Jackson's arms, hoping they would protect me. I wanted desperately to believe we were immune from all their troubles, yet somehow, they kept showing up on our back porch. We sat there in silence, each lost in our own thoughts. We held onto each other, letting the time pass, enjoying the peace and serenity that felt so rare these days.

"Has my mother already started to decorate for the party?" I attempted to change the subject.

"What do you think?" Jackson laughed. He was all too familiar with my mother's love for entertaining and playing hostess.

"She does enjoy any reason to throw a party." I shook my head.

My mother always went out of her way to ensure everything was perfect and drove the entire household crazy in the process.

"My mother is even in there helping and the two of them together, well, let me just say that it is frightening to watch them work." He laughed. "Our Fathers are hiding across the street at my house. They were banned earlier by the women after they offered some suggestions."

"Sounds about right." I smirked.

Even I know better than to do that.

"We might want to join them. I am not sure it is safe for us in there." Jackson raised an eyebrow.

"William is probably hiding out in his room." I remarked.

That's certainly where I'd be if I were him.

"I would imagine so. Coward," Jackson laughed. "But I am also not brave enough to go in there. Our mothers are on a quest, and I do not want to get caught in the crossfire."

Jackson and I found our fathers playing poker in the atrium when we arrived. My father looked stunned at my arrival, knowing that Mother would have several harsh words to say if she learned of his playing such a game.

"Jocelyn! I was, um, well…" He tucked his cards under the table and turned crimson.

"It is all right, Father. I am not going to tell on you." I giggled. It was so far out of his character.

Robert on the other hand, did not seem bothered at all by our appearance and greeted us with his typical enthusiasm. "How was your day, Jocelyn?"

"Wonderful, thank you. And yours?" I grinned.

"Delightful."

"Are you two hiding from your mothers?" My father replaced his cards into view and settled back into his card game, relieved.

I stood beside Jackson, amused at their charade. "Yes. Jackson warned me before I made it into the house."

"Smart man," Robert laughed. "You could not pay me enough to go back over there."

"Well, we're going back inside. You two enjoy." Jackson took my arm and the two of us retreated to the living room.

We sat down in the parlor at the piano bench. I began to play softly while Jackson sat contently beside me. Susan, a younger woman who worked in the Chandler household, brought in a tea tray, and set it down on the table beside us. Jackson nodded thanks toward her, and she smiled and exited the room.

I played a while longer as the clock edged its way towards dinnertime. It was such a peaceful evening. This was exactly how I imagined our life would be after the wedding. Of course, I knew that it would not always be moonlight and roses for us, but I certainly intended to enjoy to the fullest those moments that were.

Our fathers joined us for dinner in the dining room where Susan served us almond chicken on rice with bread fresh from the oven. It tasted wonderful. The wine was flowing freely and that seemed to loosen the tongues among the men.

They were all in high spirits and had found their element to the extent that even my father seemed to have forgotten I was sitting across from him.

The conversation shifted to industrial development that was apparently booming all around us. New products were being thought up almost daily to make life easier and the railroads were going across the land at a tremendous rate. It was simply amazing how fast things had changed in the last ten years alone. It was exciting to watch it, even though most of it I only got to witness secondhand.

Three bottles of wine later, the four of us returned to my home well after dark. Robert, my father, and even Jackson, who had consumed his fair share, were feeling jovial. And I was enjoying the opportunity to poke fun at them every chance I got. However, I knew my mother was going to be annoyed when she realized the state her husband was in. That too was going to be amusing.

However, when we returned, Mother and Emily were too fixated on the party arrangements and ensuring that the decorations were perfect that they did not even seem to notice the erratic behavior of the gentlemen.

The downstairs of the house was covered with lilies and violets, and ivory bows hung on everything that stood still. There was ivy draped along the walls and wrapped around the spindles winding up the staircase.

My birthday cake was already sitting on the dining room table. It was three-tiered, red velvet with cream cheese frosting decorated with little violets and sage petals. Sarah had done a gorgeous job. She was so talented in her culinary skills. It really was a breathtaking sight. I was impressed with all the ladies had accomplished in a short amount of time.

Robert and my father quickly retreated into my father's office to stay out of our mothers' way, and according to them, to avoid a lashing over their obvious condition. Jackson and I took refuge in the parlor away from all the chaos our mothers were inflicting on the staff. It was the only somewhat quiet room in the house where we could speak without having to shout at one another.

It was almost nine o'clock when Jackson left. I slowly walked up the stairs to my room. I was truly jealous of Olivia. She only had a week left before she was a bride and I had two months left to wait. It felt like an eternity from now.

I snuggled under the covers feeling wide-awake and restless. I was anxious about the party and whether Olivia would make an appearance; and if she did, what kind of reception would she receive from our friends?

I hated to think about how Maryanne would surely treat her and not for what she believed Olivia had done to me — that was just the excuse she would use — but because Maryanne had a mean streak that she loved to unleash whenever the opportunity arose.

The glow from my fireplace illuminated my room, giving off a warm, soft glow. I climbed out of bed and wandered over to the mantle. I picked up the soft, velvet, blue box, quietly opening it. There lay my precious pocket watch. I ran my fingers softly over it, thinking about Jackson.

I picked up the watch and wrapped my fingers around it, enclosing it in my hand. Suddenly, I felt a wave crash over me, making me dizzy and sick to my stomach. The room began to spin around me. My legs felt so weak and could no longer hold my weight. I fell to the floor in front of the hearth.

I could see myself surrounded by strange girls in the weirdest clothing I could possibly imagine. Some were wearing pants like men. The others had pants that were cut up to their thighs. Their shirts were so odd, like nothing I had ever seen before. Some even showed their stomachs, and the material was the most unique fabric I'd ever seen.

I found myself in the strangest room surrounded by tall, yellow, and blue cages and wooden benches. The air was musty and smelled horrible. It was so loud, and everyone was talking all at once. The floor was cold and hard and the cage in front of me, which, strangely enough I knew somehow belonged to me, was covered in some type of paper with *Happy Birthday* written all over it.

I held in my hand the watch that Jackson had given me. I could not understand why it was *here* in this weird place. The girls around me were all excited about my watch, but I did not understand why.

One of them was speaking to me. Her voice and words were off. Her grammar was appalling. I handed my watch to one of them, who proceeded to pass it on to a couple of others. I had no idea where I was, but I felt so strangely comfortable. Finally, my watch was handed back to me, and I tucked it into the cage.

The images and voices began to fade around me. I opened my eyes, dazed, and completely confused. The sounds from downstairs were muffled and tunneled in my ears.

What in the world happened?

I scanned over my room, and it appeared the same as it always had. I could feel heat from the hearth burning the side of my face and realized I was lying on the floor.

Jackson's gift was next to me on the rug, where I must have dropped it. I looked at it for a long time shaking uncontrollably, too terrified to pick it up. I slowly inched away from it, feeling like it was going to strike out and bite me.

I climbed to my feet and made my way back over to my bed. Nothing made sense. There were no cages like that in any place I had ever seen before in my life. It was not a prison. I was somehow positive about that. And those girls, I knew them. But how?

They did not go to my school; I was sure of it. And the clothes? I searched my brain but could not figure out what was going on with the clothes. They were bizarre. The girls had on pants and even short pants and those shirts showed their midsections. It was unbelievable. I had never seen anything like that before.

I closed my eyes and pulled the covers up over my head. My head was now throbbing, and I felt sick to my stomach. I rubbed my eyes, attempting to make some sense out of what I had seen. It was so strange.

I was *there*. I swear it. And my watch, my gift from Jackson, I was holding it in my hand, showing it to these girls. *How is that possible?*

CHAPTER 17

Friday, October 23, 2015

I WOKE UP TO A DULL LIGHT glaring down at me. My head was throbbing, and I couldn't get my right eye to open. It felt stuck. I slowly turned my head, trying to figure out where I was but the movement instantly made me nauseous.

Noticing my movement, my mom was immediately within my field of vision. "Honey, you're awake. How do you feel?"

I tried to reach up to touch my head, but she gently took my hand in hers, stopping me. "No. Don't," she whispered in a soft voice.

"My head is killing me." I groaned. "What's wrong with my right eye? It feels like it's stuck. Can you wipe it? There's something in it."

"Sweetie, you fractured your right eye socket, and you have twelve stitches. Don't try to touch it." She sat down beside me, still holding my hand in hers.

"What? How?" I could barely remember what happened, but I knew I'd blacked out again.

"When you tripped, you hit the corner of your eye on the corner of the coffee table." She explained in her soft tone.

I could feel the tears pouring over and running down my cheeks. A strong hand took hold of my other hand while my mother tried to wipe away my tears.

"It's okay, honey. The stitches are right by your hairline and your mother called in a plastic surgeon friend of hers to make sure there would be no scar." My dad squeezed my hand tenderly.

"Let me get you something for the pain. I'll be right back." My mom leaned and kissed me on the forehead. I suddenly felt four years old again and didn't care.

"You know, honey, your friends and Jackson and even his parents have been here every day." I turned my head gritting my teeth from the pain and trying not to vomit, just to look at my dad.

"What do you mean every day? I just hit my head a few hours ago." Now I was really confused. "Didn't I?"

"Two days ago, actually. It's Friday evening, sweetie."

This fact only made the tears come harder and my head hurt even more if that were possible.

"Hey," he rubbed my arm to comfort me. "It's okay. Everyone's at the game right now, but you will see them soon. You've had numerous visitors. Your room is filled with flowers and balloons." He chuckled. "It's kind of ridiculous."

He paused, waiting for me to say something, but I didn't have anything to say, so he continued to ramble like he always does when he is nervous. "Can I ask you something without being too personal?"

"Sure, Daddy," I squeaked, feeling sick to my stomach. I just wanted someone to turn off that freakin' overhead light. It was killing my head.

He suddenly looked uncomfortable as he always did when he butted into our personal lives. "Is Jackson your boyfriend?"

"Yes. Why?"

"I thought so. I saw the pocket watch he gave you for your birthday. It was on the floor by you where you fell." He paused, waiting for me to say something. When I didn't, he continued. "I didn't show it to your mother, but I read the inscription."

Oh no, here it comes.

My dad paused again like he was considering his words carefully. "Jocelyn, you just met this boy." He fidgeted with my remote absentmindedly. "Now, I realize he's a nice kid and all, but I don't want you getting too serious with a boy at this age. Besides, you've only known him a short time and for him to engrave something like that... well, it concerns me."

"I know." I felt the same, but I couldn't explain to him how Jackson and I felt such a strong connection to one another. He would never understand that. But then again, neither did I.

"You realize your mother would have a nervous breakdown if she saw that inscription." His eyebrows raised in amusement.

"Yes." That I was positive of.

"Well, I tucked it into your nightstand under some folders and I won't say anything to her. I promise. But you must promise me something too, okay?"

"Okay."

"Don't give up on your dreams for some boy you just met. I know how it feels when you're young and in love, but you still have college ahead of you. I don't want anything stupid to happen to derail your dreams. So, be safe and smart, okay?" I had to smile despite the pain it inflicted. It was so difficult for him to talk to me about anything personal.

"I promise, Daddy." He leaned down and kissed me on the uninjured side of my forehead.

"And you know you still look beautiful, pumpkin." Now I knew he was lying, but I appreciated the effort.

My mother returned shortly thereafter, giving me an injection in my IV that took me out for the rest of the night. At least the pain went away for a while.

CHAPTER 18

Saturday, October 26, 1878

I ROSE BEFORE DAWN. I did not sleep well because of the strange episode from the night before. I felt tired and drained, and my head was throbbing. My body felt worn out and my mind was exhausted.

The party held no excitement for me. I was too confused and overwhelmed by emotions that I could not explain. I just wanted to spend my day in bed.

I reluctantly crawled slowly out of bed and put on my robe before splashing some cold water from the basin on my face. I quietly brushed my teeth and hair before I went downstairs.

The house was still quiet. I crept around silently, not wanting to wake anyone and lost in my own thoughts. I continually ran the episode over and over in my head trying to make some sense of it, but nothing helped. I could not explain it away. I entered the living room, where it was still dark, and wandered over to the front window. I pulled the curtain back and stared at Jackson's dark, motionless house across the street. It was obvious that everyone over there was still sleeping as well.

"What are you doing up so early?"

The voice came out of the dark corner of the room, frightening me to my very core. I jumped, spinning around, only to find that William was sitting in the corner, still dressed in the clothes he'd worn the day before. His face looked haunted and torn.

"William!"

"Sorry, Jocelyn. I did not mean to frighten you," he responded in a weak voice.

"I did not realize anyone else was awake." My heart was pounding so loudly in my chest that I was sure he could hear it.

"I could not sleep."

I walked over to where he was seated and sat down beside him. I hesitated for a moment, unsure of his reaction, but then placed my hands over his.

"I am sorry, William. I know you are going through a difficult time."

"I am only feeling sorry for myself, and I am so ashamed that I am. I thought I was a stronger man than that." He refused to make eye contact and instead stared down at our hands.

"You are a strong man, William. I know that. This would be hard for anyone."

"I am so ashamed of myself for having disgraced our family, for what I have done to Olivia, her family, and what this has done to our lives. This is not what either of us wanted."

I gently squeezed his hands in mine. It was all I could think of doing. I had no words of comfort for him. My heart broke for him. William had always been so special to me, and it was killing me having this distance now between us. We had always been there for each other, and I was helpless to give him any words that might bring some solace.

"I have made such a mess of things, and now I cannot make it right. I wish there was a way out for both Olivia and me."

"I understand."

"No, you do not, Jocelyn. I appreciate you trying, but you simply cannot understand what I am talking about." He took a deep breath and exhaled slowly.

I sat there numbly staring at him.

"Did you speak with Olivia last evening?"

"No." He shook his head slowly, with his voice barely above a whisper in shame.

"Why not?" For once, I wanted the truth and not speculations from others.

He still refused to look at me. "Because I am a coward."

"You are not, William. You have never been afraid of anything in your life." I assured him.

"I am now. I am terrified of getting married. And every time I look at Olivia's face, she gives me this look like she truly loathes me for ruining her life. And she has every right to look at me that way." Tears rolled down William's cheeks.

"Everything is going to work out in the end. She is just having a difficult time as well right now. It is a huge adjustment for both of you." I put my arm around his shoulder pulling him to me.

"Have you spoken to her this week?" He glanced up at my face with pleading eyes.

"No. She did not come to classes all week. I went to her house, but her mother told me she was not well and not receiving visitors."

He ran his fingers through his hair in exasperation. "I do not know if she would even see me if I went over there."

"I am sure she would." I tried to reassure him, but I honestly was not sure.

"I do not believe so. Did you invite her to the party?"

"Mother handled the entire guest list. I honestly have no clue as to whom she invited. I do not believe my opinion matters in such things." I laughed softly, "I do not even know whom Mother invited to my wedding."

"Sounds like Mother." William gave me a weak grin.

It was at least good that he tried.

"Yes. Perhaps you should go over there this morning and speak with her. Invite her to the party. I believe it will do you both some good to socialize a little."

"I am not so sure. I do not believe Olivia wants to be around anyone. Besides, I am not really in the mood for a party as well."

"William, it is my birthday party. It will not be the same without you," I complained.

"I am sorry, Jocelyn. I truly am. But in my current state, I am not up for it." He slumped over, resting his head on his knees.

"Perhaps by the time the guests arrive, and the party gets underway you will change your mind," I said hopefully, even though I knew he would not.

"Perhaps."

We sat there for a few moments in silence. The sun was coming up, promising a beautiful autumn day. I was glad to see that it was no longer raining and gray. Maybe the sunshine would improve everyone's mood and my party would be a success.

I heard someone, probably Sarah, rummaging around in the kitchen. "Sounds like breakfast is being started. You hungry?"

"Not really," he answered in a weak voice.

"William, I believe I am going to smack you!" I shook my head with irritation. "You are truly aggravating me this morning. Now, some food would do you some good. I am going to go get dressed. You go clean yourself up. You look horrible." I bumped up against him, making him smile. "And I will meet you back down here at the dining room table. All right?"

"I guess there is no fighting you, is there?"

I shook my head at his weak smile.

"Fine."

I searched relentlessly through my wardrobe for the perfect dress for my party. There were several that I loved, but I wanted something exceptional. Mimi opened my door and chuckled aloud when she saw the scattered array of gowns I had flung across my bed in my indecision.

"My dear chil, wha' ave ya dun?"

"You are looking much better this morning, Mimi." She appeared revived from her previous state.

"Ah's feels betta. Now let's fin somein' special fo ya ta ware." She stepped back out of my room and returned with a large, white box and set in down on the table. "Mrs. Chandler gives dis ta me las nite ta give ta ya dis mornin'."

I eagerly lifted the lid and opened the tissue paper to reveal the most beautiful maroon, velvet gown with ivory-colored lace at the collar and sleeves. I pulled it out of the box and held it against me in front of the full-length mirror. There was a dark, maroon, satin ribbon around the waist that tied in the back and darted pleats down the chest. It was perfect. The colors fit the seasonal spirit of fall — warm and welcoming.

"Oh, Mimi! It is gorgeous! I cannot believe Mrs. Chandler! This is perfect!"

"She wanted it ta be a surprise fo ya birthda'." She smiled; "Now, let's git ya reade. We ave lots ta do."

I quickly undressed and placed by nightclothes on the bed. I could not wait to get into this dress.

I descended the staircase carefully, not wanting to wrinkle my dress. It had taken Mimi and me almost two hours to get my hair done perfectly. I was elated with the results we had achieved. She was invaluable in her talents.

William and my father were in the dining room when I arrived.

"Glad I decided not to wait to have my breakfast." My brother chastised my tardiness.

William looked refreshed. He had taken a bath, shaved, and put on clean clothes and finally disposed of the ones he had been wearing for God only knows how long.

"But it was truly worth the time. You look stunning, Jocelyn." My father got up and pulled out a chair for me.

I sat down, and he patted my shoulder gently before returning to his seat. Sarah came in with a plate of ham and eggs with biscuits, orange juice, and coffee, setting them down in front of me.

"Thank you, Sarah. This looks wonderful. And thank you, Father."

"You are most welcome, darling." He took a sip of his coffee.

"Where is Mother this morning?" I asked, placing my napkin in my lap.

"Driving the staff insane" William laughed making our father smile.

"I see."

"Easy on your mother, William. She is not only making the staff insane. She is working on me as well. I am going to be hiding in my study until the party begins." My father picked up his morning newspaper and began reading again.

"What are your plans for this morning, William?" I took a long sip of my hot coffee.

"I am going to head over next door and speak with Olivia."

Mother entered the dining room looking frazzled and upset.

"What? William, please. Not this morning. I honestly do not want any drama during the party." She gave him a stern look and our father hastily put his paper aside.

"Mother, I am only going over there to speak with her. I have not spoken with her since last weekend." William had a confused look on his face.

"Could you please not invite her to the party this afternoon? I do not want any whispering or speculating amongst the guests." Mother gave him an apprehensive look.

"Are you telling me that Olivia and her family are not invited to my sister's birthday party?" William balked as his face was red with anger.

I looked at the three of them. This was not going to be good.

"Of course, I invited Olivia's family. Her parents and her brothers will be here, but her mother and I decided that Olivia would not be attending. We were just going to tell the guests that she is not feeling well."

"Is she banned from all social events until the wedding, or is this in effect until our child is born?" William looked as if he was ready to explode.

"I believe it would be appreciated by both families if she did not attend any social gatherings until after the baby arrives," Father interjected.

"Fine. If she is not welcome at my sister's birthday or apparently even her wedding, then neither am I." William got up so fast that he knocked his chair over and stormed out of the dining room.

"William, please. Try to understand," Mother called after him, but to no avail.

Father got up and picked up William's overturned chair. "Let him go, Annabelle. He needs to calm down."

"So, I suppose Olivia is not going to be my maid of honor?" I tried to act casually, but I was just as disappointed as my brother.

"Your father and I feel that you should probably have one of your other friends stand up with you at your wedding." Mother rang her hands on the apron she was wearing over her new gown.

"Olivia has been my closest friend since forever. I mean, I realize that recently we have drifted apart, but that never deterred me from wanting her to stand up with me at my wedding."

"Jocelyn, honey, Olivia will probably be noticeably pregnant by then and it would be inappropriate," he explained.

I placed my napkin down on the table and stood up.

"Please excuse me. I believe Jackson will be here soon."

Neither of them said a word to stop me.

I paced the living room for a short time while listening to the phonograph. The tune had drastically changed and no longer seemed enjoyable. My headache had almost disappeared during my time with Mimi but now it returned worse than before. I had no idea where William had disappeared to. I wondered if he had escaped to Olivia's or if he was hiding upstairs in his room. I was tempted to look for him, but I was not sure as to whose side I was on in this argument.

Traditionally, my parents were correct to try and save as much grace and dignity as possible out of the current situation, but William was also being ostracized from his own sister's birthday and wedding. I felt disheartened. I hated the entire situation and both William and Olivia for shifting the course of events for everyone, it seemed. This was not the way things were supposed to be.

Jackson finally arrived shortly before eleven. I answered the door quickly and caught a stern look of disapproval from Eddie. However, I did not care. I grabbed by shawl and bonnet and hurried out the front door before Jackson even had the chance to enter the house.

"Let's go for a walk," I said quickly.

"What is wrong?" Jackson looked clearly confused as I rapidly descended the front steps. He quickly caught up with me at the garden gate. "Is everything all right?"

"No."

Jackson halted in front of the fence along the walkway. I hesitated only for a second before I continued. He kept his step with mine, but I knew he was waiting for some answers.

"Jocelyn, please stop."

"I am sorry. I am just upset. My parents informed me that not only is Olivia banned from every social event until she gives birth, but I also must find another maid of honor." The words rushed from my lips with all the anger I felt towards everyone and everything.

"I figured this was going to happen." His words stopped me in my tracks.

"Honestly?"

"Well, yes. Under the current circumstances, I figured that we would have to change things around a bit. It would be most inappropriate for her to show herself in public in her stated condition."

Sometimes he truly surprised me.

"Seriously? Why is everyone being so backward? Accidents happen. I see no reason to be so obtuse. Are they not suffering enough?" I questioned him.

"Jocelyn, you are so sweet, but you must realize that what you are suggesting is impossible. There is simply no way we can expect our families to ignore the obvious embarrassment and allow Olivia to participate in social events."

I could not believe he felt that way, but I knew he was also right.

"I know, but now that she is ostracized, who am I supposed to have as my maid of honor?"

"What about Elizabeth? You and she have always been good friends," he suggested.

"True. Elizabeth would certainly be my second choice. What about you? Who is going to stand beside you?"

"William, of course"

"William stated that if Olivia could not attend, then he would not either."

Jackson looked stunned. "He really said that?"

I nodded.

"I will speak with him. Where is he?"

"I have no idea. He might be in his room or at Olivia's. He stormed out of the dining room earlier and I did not see where he went." Then I suddenly remembered. "Oh. Please tell your mother thank you for the gown. I love it." I twirled around showing off the dress to Jackson.

"You look lovely, my dear. My mother certainly knows how to design a dress."

"She designed this?"

"Yes."

"She made this from no pattern at all?"

"Well, she drew up the design, made a pattern for it then created the dress. It is something she enjoys doing. Sewing is her favorite past time." He smiled.

We continued to walk aimlessly down the pathway, following it to the park. The sun was shining brightly in the blue sky. There was just a hint of scattered clouds hanging around to remind us that autumn was now thick in the air.

The weather was exactly how I would have wished it to be for my party, had I thought of wishing for such things these days.

Jackson and I crossed the cobblestone pathway to the gazebo. The green grass was totally saturated with the amount of rain we had received lately. We climbed the steps and sat down on the benches.

"Jocelyn, are you going to be in a bad mood all day?"

"I am not in a bad mood. Honestly." I knew he could see straight through the lie, and I did not want to complain about my headache or attempt to tell him about what had happened last night.

"Then what kind of mood are you in?" He gave me a confused look.

"To be honest, I am not sure. Surprised, I guess, and I do not even know why. I mean, I should have expected this. But Olivia has always been such an important part of my life for as long as I can remember. It is just difficult to imagine getting married without her there."

"I understand."

"It baffles me that people can be so small minded about things. I know they made a mistake, but they are doing what they can to correct it. They will be married next weekend. Our wedding is still weeks away and I honestly hoped that things would have returned to normal by then." I shrugged my shoulders.

"I am not sure whether things will ever return to normal again or be the same between you and Olivia, I'm sorry to say." He wrapped his arm about my shoulders, giving me a gentle but firm squeeze.

"I am afraid of that," I admitted. "I got up earlier than usual this morning and found William sitting alone in the dark. I do not believe he went to bed last night."

"I assume he is not doing any better."

Recalling how he looked, I was assuming that Jackson knew he was not sleeping at school either.

"No. In fact, he is utterly miserable."

"I wish there was something we could do for them."

"So, do I. It breaks my heart to see William hurting so."

Jackson and I arrived back at the house shortly before one o'clock. My mother was in panic mode, while my father was still hiding safely in his study and William was nowhere to be seen.

The dining room table was covered with an ivory, satin tablecloth with my birthday cake perched in the center. Sarah and Mimi had obviously been cooking and baking since dawn, covering the table now with an array of dishes and desserts. I could not imagine how many people my mother must have invited to warrant such a spread.

We stood there in awe when she came through the dining room door.

"What do you think? Is it enough?"

"Mother, there is enough food here to feed an army. How many people did you invite?" I stared at her in disbelief.

"I lost count. Around sixty or so?" She took a deep breath and exhaled slowly.

"What? Why?"

"Jocelyn, this is your coming-out party. You are now officially an adult, and every young lady must have a grand coming-out party." She smiled widely and patted me on the shoulder. "By the way, you look elegant in that dress. Mrs. Chandler did a beautiful job creating it for you."

"Yes, she did. I love it." I twirled around again, enjoying the way the dress flowed and billowed around me.

"Now you two just relax and enjoy today. Everyone should be arriving shortly, and I have a few last-minute things to attend to, like finding your father for one. I believe he is hiding in his study again." She laughed, exiting the room.

Jackson's parents were the first to arrive. I thanked his mother repeatedly for the beautiful gown, expressing my love for her talent and the thoughtfulness of her gift. Emily was as gracious as always and thrilled that I loved the dress.

My eldest brother, Patrick II and his wife, Katherine were the next to arrive, followed by Jackson's siblings and spouses and children and then my other brothers, Jonathon and James with their wives and children. The house was filing up rapidly, and so far, only immediate family had arrived. This was certainly going to be the grand affair my mother had intended it to be.

Benjamin and Harriett arrived next, bringing with them their young sons, Kincade and Oscar, and minus Olivia. My father's younger brother, Monte, showed up with his wife and their sons alongside my father's youngest brother, Nicholas, and his family.

The house quickly became crowded, forcing the guests outside and onto the veranda. Elizabeth and her parents arrived next, with Maryanne and hers followed by Laurie, Christina, Thomas, and Theodore, with their parents and siblings. Even Reverend Jacobs and his wife and children made an appearance, along with several other families around town.

Our guests were having a wonderful time eating, drinking, and socializing with one another. There were so many conversations taking place I was unsure as to whether anyone was doing the listening instead of the talking.

Jackson remained close by my side as I received my guests into our home. I was indeed thankful that the rain had stopped, allowing people to mingle about the grounds.

Mother's estimate of approximately sixty guests was understated by a grand amount. However, she was enjoying all the praises from her guests on the food and decorations as she excelled in her duties as hostess.

Elizabeth and her date, someone whom I did not recognize, wandered over to us.

"Jocelyn, you look lovely. Where did you ever get such a gorgeous dress?"

Elizabeth was wearing a royal-blue dress that enriched the color of her eyes. For once, her hair was down in curls and flowed evenly over her shoulders and down her back. She looked so beautiful.

"Mrs. Chandler created it for me as a birthday gift."

"How exquisite." She gave me a gentle hug. "Happy birthday." She was radiant with excitement. "Miss Jocelyn Timmons, Mr. Jackson Chandler, I would like to introduce you both to Mr. Lee Miller."

The two men bowed towards one another as I curtsied. Lee took my hand and kissed it gently. "It is a pleasure to make your acquaintance, Miss Timmons. Elizabeth has told me so many wonderful things about you I feel as if I already know you." He was quite charming.

"Thank you. It is a pleasure to meet you also, Mr. Miller." I glanced over at Elizabeth a questionable smile as she beamed with pride.

"Mr. Miller just moved here from Indianapolis for his new position at Wilson and Riley. He is an architect," Elizabeth explained.

Clearly, Mr. Miller was a few years older than the rest of us. He was very handsome, with bright- blue eyes and sandy-blonde hair. His features were soft and boyish, making him appear younger than his true age.

"Wonderful. Welcome to Chicago." Jackson extended his hand and Mr. Miller took it. "Did you move here with your family?"

"No. My parents and siblings remained in Indianapolis. I recently bought a house over on Maple Lane," he answered politely.

"How do you like Chicago so far?" I inquired.

"Well, it is much larger than Indianapolis." He laughed. "But everyone has been very welcoming. I have only been here since mid-September and so far, I am finding it very enjoyable." His gaze fell upon Elizabeth, making her blush and look down.

"Would you gentlemen please excuse us for a moment? Elizabeth, may I speak with you briefly?" I asked.

"Certainly. Please, excuse us."

Elizabeth and I curtsied as the two men nodded.

We made our way through the growing crowd out into the far yard by the carriage house so that we could speak alone.

"So how did you meet Mr. Miller and why did not you tell me you were seeing someone?" I was intrigued.

Elizabeth blushed again.

"He is quite wonderful, isn't he?"

I nodded.

"And very handsome." Her eyes glimmered.

"Yes, he is."

"I was surprised when he showed interest in me."

"Elizabeth, how can you say that? You are very beautiful and the sweetest person I have ever met. Why would he not be interested in you?" Her lack of self-confidence always surprised me.

She shrugged as her eyes scanned over the guests lingering about on the veranda before she continued. "When I met him, he just seemed so nice. I thought he would only be interested in being friends with me. Boys have never really paid much attention to me before."

"That is only because you are always so serious with your studies. Every time the rest of us wanted to play, you were always buried in a book."

"I enjoy reading." She smiled softly.

"He seems like a delightful gentleman. But I am curious. How old is he?"

"Twenty-four."

"He looks so young."

"Yes, and he is so very sweet. We both share a love of literature and spend hours discussing various works we have read." Elizabeth's voice was giddy with blossoming love.

"I am so happy for you. It is wonderful to see you so happy with someone."

"My parents even approve of him. I never thought my father would ever approve of anyone for me."

"Are you two getting serious?" I grinned at her.

"I believe so. He invited his family for Thanksgiving to meet me. Of course, when he mentioned it to my mother, she insisted they all join us at our house for a proper Thanksgiving dinner." She looked shyly over at me out of the corner of her eye. "His family is quite large. I do not believe my mother anticipated having such a group. He has seven brothers and sisters. Most are married, some with children and they are all coming along with his parents. It should prove to be very interesting, to say the least." She halfheartedly laughed, clearly nervous about the upcoming event.

"I am sure it will be splendid."

"I hope so." Elizabeth glanced over the vast array of guests milling around everywhere once again. "I have not seen your brother, William, or Olivia. Are they here?"

"Olivia is still not feeling well. I believe William is over there with her." I lied. I hated lying to her. This façade was getting old quickly. Her believing the lie only made me feel that much worse about it.

"Of course. How thoughtful of him. I hope it is nothing serious. She has missed a great deal of school lately."

"Yes, but I am sure she is on the mend."

"Good."

"Elizabeth, can I ask you something?"

"Yes, of course." We wandered along the back fence.

"Well, as you know I am getting married to Jackson this Christmas." She nodded. "And I would be honored if you would agree to stand up with me as my maid of honor." I stopped and faced her.

"Are you serious?" I nodded. "I would be truly honored, Jocelyn." She embraced me tightly. "I thought for sure that Olivia would be standing up for you?"

"I am afraid that circumstances have changed."

Elizabeth nodded but did not push for any further clarification. "I am sorry to hear that, but yes, I would love to be a part of your wedding."

"Wonderful. Then it is settled."

"Jocelyn," Mother hollered from the back porch, "please, come in, dear. It is time to cut the cake."

"All right, Mother." I looked over at Elizabeth. "Guess we had better return to the party."

By eight o'clock most of the guests had departed, but there were still several family members lingering about. My brothers and uncles, along with their families, loitered in the living room, enjoying a lively conversation. There was still no appearance of William or mention of him, even from the family. It was quite disappointing. Jackson and I joined everyone in the room, taking a seat next to the warm hearth.

The night air had rolled in, bringing in a chill that belonged with the season. I felt drained from the chaos of the day. I leaned my head against Jackson's shoulder. The exhaustion swept over me quickly as I drifted off to sleep. I do not know how or when, but someone had gotten me upstairs into my nightgown and tucked away in my bed.

Chapter 19

Saturday, October 24, 2015

JACKSON WAS PERCHED ON THE CORNER of my bed, reading a book, when I awoke on Saturday morning. He looked sad, almost heartbroken. I could hear the rain pouring down outside my window. The sky was dark and gloomy, offering little light into my cold, sterile hospital room. The fragrance from the flowers was a bit overwhelming and as much as I truly appreciated the sentiment from my family and friends, I wanted to clear them out just to kill the aroma.

"Good morning. How are you feeling?"

"Better." I lied.

"I stopped by last night for a few hours, but you never woke up."

"I'm sorry."

"Why are you apologizing? You obviously needed the rest." His smile was so sincere. Then his expression changed, and his face clouded. "Look, Jocelyn. I am so sorry. I would never do anything to hurt you. I did not reach out to you to cause you harm. I was only playing around and reacted out of instinct when you stood."

"Jackson, I wish I could explain to you what happens when you touch me, why I faint." I was not about to confide in him the entire truth.

"I know," he said.

"So please, don't worry about it."

I mustered up the best smile I could for him, and a sharp pain shot through my head. I did my best not to wince so as not to make Jackson feel even worse than he already did.

"Are you sure you don't want to ask someone else to the Halloween party? Or perhaps we should change our costumes. Maybe I could go with

something more like Frankenstein's monster and you could be my bride."
That at least brought a smile to his face.

"You are going to look gorgeous in the costume my mother is making
you. Besides you cannot back out now. She has already started working on it.
Do you really want to explain it to her?" His beautiful, emerald eyes were
pleading with me.

"No."

"Then I guess you are stuck with me. And I honestly do not want to invite
anyone else because I already am going with the best-looking girl in school."

"Wow. I know I hit my head, but how hard did you hit yours?" I loved
teasing him.

"Stop it. I know I am right, and I really do not appreciate you speaking
about my girlfriend that way." His smile was so heartwarming.

"So how did the game go last night?"

"You are trying to change the subject," he accused.

I gave him a small smile. "Guilty."

"We won, but it was ridiculously close. Zak made a mistake in the fourth
quarter and threw the worse interception possible. They would have scored
too if not for your brother. He knocked the guy flat on the three-yard line so
hard his helmet flew off. The kid dropped the ball, and we got it back."

"Seriously? Wow. What was Zak thinking? He never makes such careless
errors."

"I believe he was not thinking. That was the problem. Besides everyone
makes mistakes but I believe the team taught him a lesson afterward. They
were really upset with him by the time we got to the locker room. I came here
straight after the game, so I missed the fallout." His laugh told me there was
something more to that story and I wasn't sure I wanted to know.

"What did those idiots do to him?" I could only imagine.

"I do not know, but I am sure that we will hear about it soon enough.
Ethan was there, so he probably knows all the gritty details."

As if on cue, my parents and Ethan arrived with a large pizza, breadsticks,
and a two-liter of Coke. I was so glad to see them, not only because I was
starving, but I also wanted the opportunity to ask Ethan about what they did

to Zak last night. However, I knew I couldn't question him in front of my parents, especially since he'd covered my rear the other night.

My family and Jackson settled in around my bed and had a little picnic.

"So, when do I get out of here?" I looked over at my mother. I knew she could get me released if she really wanted.

"Tomorrow, probably," she said a little too casually, which made me nervous.

"Tomorrow? Why not today?" I had this horrible feeling that she was up to something.

"Honey." She placed her hand over mine which made me more uneasy. "I know you're ready to go home, but I also know that this isn't the first time that you've had one of these fainting spells. I just want to make sure that your tripping wasn't contributed by another fainting spell. So, I've asked Dr. Clark to do a PET Scan in the morning."

It was too bad she couldn't order those tests conducted with Jackson holding my hand. At least that might give us all some answers. My eyes landed on Jackson, and I knew he was thinking the same thing.

My parents decided to head home for a while around three. Jackson promised them that he would give Ethan a ride home later so that he could stay with us. I believe my father was thrilled to leave Ethan with us so that Jackson and I wouldn't be left unsupervised, even in the hospital.

"So, tell me, what did you guys do to Zak after the game? Please tell you didn't do anything stupid." I gave Ethan my big sister look, as much as I could with half my face wincing.

"Oh, don't blow a gasket." Ethan plopped himself down in the recliner in the corner. "We didn't beat him up or anything. Just played a practical joke on him that will ensure that next Friday and thereafter, he will pay closer attention to where he throws the ball."

"What did you do?" I was ready to strangle him, but he was truly enjoying his torment.

"A couple of guys kept him busy in the locker room by, well, taking off with his clothes while he was in the shower. But only for about thirty minutes, give or take, while some of us put his car on blocks and stole his tires. By the time he made it out to the parking lot, his tires had left without him."

Both guys were rolling with laughter, and I cracked a smile despite myself.

"Please, tell me that he has his tires back now."

"Not exactly, but he will in time. We decided we wanted to be sure he looks next time before he throws." Ethan couldn't seem to get his laughter under control, and neither could Jackson.

"You little shit! How could you do that to one of my friends?" I tried to hide my own amusement at their stupidity and act like I was upset, but the pain shot through the side of my face.

"This has nothing to do with him being one of your friends, Jocelyn. This is about the team!" Ethan could barely get his laughter under control. "Got it?"

"Ethan is right. It's a team thing and not about you at all." Jackson sided with my brother.

"But you both have to understand. Caitlyn is one of my best friends and she's going to give me hell for this." I tried hopelessly to explain.

"No, I'm not." A familiar voice entered the room.

I turned my head towards the door at the sound of her voice to see Caitlyn, Hilary, Jenna, Kyle, Zak, and Cody all walking into my room.

"Why would you even think that?" Caitlyn came over and gave me a hug.

"Because my idiot brother was involved." It seemed like forever since I'd seen them and not just a couple of days. "God, it's good to see you all."

"You too. Although I will admit that you've looked better." Jenna laughed at the sight of my bruised-up face and stitches. "Geez Jackson, did you have to beat the crap out of her for her birthday? Most boyfriends would have given something a little sweeter."

"If she would learn how to control that mouth of hers, it would not be necessary." Jackson quickly responded making the entire room laugh.

"Great. So how long will it take for that rumor to spread across school?" I laughed.

"It should be all over town before school on Monday, which should make classes more interesting this week. Not that you have to worry much about that." Hilary came over, taking a seat on the other side of me.

"Thanks, but I'd rather be in class. This sucks. And I look so beautiful."

"Ah, honey, you still look beautiful." Caitlyn attempted to cheer me up.

"I don't know what you're all making such a big deal about. She looks the same to me." Cody shrugged, and Hillary punched him in the shoulder.

"Thanks. I appreciate that." I felt much better having them all here.

"Hey, asshole. Where the hell are my tires?" Zak approached Ethan, looking like he was ready to pounce on him. But instead grabbed him in a head lock and pulled him from his spot off the recliner. Zak quickly had Ethan pinned on the floor. The other guys stood back, and everyone started laughing and hollering. We were making so much commotion that two nurses came charging into my room with very unhappy looks on their faces.

"What in the world is going on here? You do realize that this is a hospital and not a playground."

The tall, older, nurse gave us all a stern look like we were little children making noise during a church service. Ethan and Zak immediately stopped and stared.

"Jocelyn, I realize that your mother is a physician here, but we do have rules. And you cannot have this many visitors at one time. Some of your friends are going to have to leave or wait out in the hall."

"Sorry." I tried to keep a straight face. "My friends were just leaving. Give us just a few minutes and they'll clear out. We'll keep it down, promise."

"Fine," the older nurse stated coldly and the younger one smiled at us as they left, closing the door a little louder than normal.

"Thanks for coming by guys. I appreciate it." I really didn't want them to leave. It felt so wonderful, so normal to have them all here.

"We'll be back tomorrow." Jenna leaned over kissing my forehead. "Get some rest."

Their laughter still lingered in the air, but their absence filled me with sorrow. Ethan had decided to catch a ride home with Jenna and Kyle because Jackson couldn't give him a timeframe of when he'd be heading home. I was thankful for some alone time with Jackson.

We sat alone in the semi-dark room, staring at one another. I knew the words I wanted to say to him, but I couldn't get them out. Jackson's hair was messed up from him constantly running his fingers through it. His eyes contained a strange combination of stress, worry, and lack of sleep. His face was tense and unshaven.

"It was nice of everyone to stop by." I tried to break the silence.

"They care and are worried. You know you have been the talk of the school for the last two days?" His smile returned.

"I didn't realize that fracturing your eye socket could be so interesting."

"Well, by the time the story had made it rounds, it had been embellished just enough to make it really interesting. You know how it works. I believe the last thing I heard in psychology class was that you were getting dialysis for kidney failure. But I also heard that you had ovarian cancer in third period, so I am not sure which to believe at this point." Jackson laughed aloud.

"Please, tell me you are kidding. Are people really that stupid?" Unfortunately, I already knew the answer before I even asked.

"High school." He shrugged halfheartedly.

"True."

"Please, do not worry about it. I am sure by next week there will be some other hot rumor everyone will be gossiping about."

"Also, true." I glanced over at the clock on the wall. It was almost seven o'clock.

"Are you getting hungry?"

"No. I'm more thirsty than hungry."

"Me, too. Would you like a Coke or iced tea?

"Iced tea, please."

"All right. I will check the cafeteria." Jackson got up and paused at the door. "Now, do not go anywhere while I am gone."

I tossed the box of tissues at him, but he ducked. "Very funny."

Jackson disappeared down the long corridor, leaving me alone for the first time today. The empty room felt cold and lonely, and I wanted Jenna here with me. I wanted so badly to confide everything in her. I wanted to tell her what I was experiencing and hear her wild speculations about it.

I wanted her outlandish mind to explain this mess of symptoms, fainting and visions to me and tell me why I felt so drawn, so close, and already so in love with Jackson. It made no sense to me. I felt desperate to be with him all the time.

But here I was, alone in this sterile, dim hospital room because his touch sent my body into a frenzy and not in the normal way love should. I was so confused by how I felt — like I'd known him for a lifetime — and the strange way

I was so comfortable and at ease with him and his parents, and how I knew that he somehow completed me.

I was so totally frustrated that I wanted to scream until someone came running in to give me the answers I so desperately desired.

I settled back in my bed and pulled the covers up around my chin, feeling lost and terrified. Closing my eyes, I drifted off into an uneasy sleep.

CHAPTER 20

Sunday, October 27, 1878

I CLIMBED OUT OF BED EARLY while the house was still silent. I could hear Sarah, Mimi, and Eddie moving around downstairs in the kitchen, but it seemed my family was all still lost in their slumber.

I put on my robe and took a seat in my bay window, pulling the curtain aside. It seemed as if all remnants of yesterday's sunshine and mild warmth had long since disappeared and had been replaced by the familiar, dark clouds and gray skies from earlier in the week. The rain had yet to make its reappearance, but that only seemed like a matter of time.

I rested my head against the cold glass, staring off into nothingness, wishing I could speak with Olivia. I wanted to at least check on her, clarify that she was at least surviving all this turmoil. William's words from yesterday lingered in my ears, making me feel horrible for both him and Olivia. I prayed that someday our lives would return to normal again. But I feared that that normal was forever lost and there was no going back.

William was sitting at the table alone, eating oatmeal and sipping on his orange juice when I arrived in the dining room. He gave me a weak smile as I sat down across from him. His face still looked hollow and the prominent, dark circles under his eyes remained. I could tell he had not slept well in weeks.

"Good morning, William. How are you feeling today?" I tried using a cheery tone in hopes of making him give me a real smile.

"Still breathing," he answered in a low voice.

"That is good news at least." I smiled as Sarah brought in some oatmeal with maple syrup and orange juice for me. I thanked her, and she retreated into the kitchen. "I wish you would have made it to my party yesterday. I missed you. Somehow it was not the same without you and Olivia."

"I am sorry, Jocelyn, but I had to take a stand." His eyes were cloudy and distant.

"I understand, and I completely agree with you."

"I am sorry I missed your birthday celebration and will miss your wedding."

His smile was weak and sincere, and I appreciated the effort, although it broke my heart. I could not imagine getting married without him and Olivia there, no matter what they had done.

"Have you spoken with Jackson about standing up with him? He seemed surprised when we spoke yesterday."

"Yes. Last evening after you had fallen asleep on the lounge. He was upset with me but said he understood," William explained.

"Did he mention who would be replacing you in the ceremony?"

"No. He seemed upset with me about being so stubborn."

I nodded. Being stubborn was unfortunately a family trait that we had all inherited from our father.

"Have you thought about who is going to stand up with you?"

"Elizabeth Maddox."

William nodded.

"Did you know she has a beau now?"

"Really?" He looked up at me as if I had said something absurd.

"Yes. He is very nice and handsome too. His name is Lee Miller. She brought him to the party yesterday. He seems to be quite taken by her."

"Good. I am happy for her. I always thought she was too shy to even speak to a man."

"Normally she is, but she seems truly taken by him." I paused as he continued eating. "Did you get the chance to speak with Olivia yesterday?"

"Yes. I spent the day and most of the evening next door."

"How did it go?"

"All right." He half shrugged.

"Is she doing well?"

"No."

"Is she going to return to classes tomorrow?"

"No. I do not believe she could stop sobbing long enough to do anything." He half rolled his eyes and looked back down at his almost-empty bowl.

"Please, tell me you were at least polite to her."

"Of course, I was. I am not an ogre."

"But I know you can be at times." I smirked at him.

"Only to you, dear sister"

"Aren't I the lucky one?" It was good to see a little life return to his face.

"Olivia does not want to see anyone. She is so ashamed. And let me tell you," William dropped his spoon down on the table with a loud clank, "none of this would be half as bad as it is if her parents would stop treating her with such disdain. I hate the way they speak down to her and treat her like she is unworthy of the common courtesy you would give a dog." His voice had turned hateful and angry. "And our parents are not much better." He rose quickly, causing his chair to screech across the floor loudly. "Please, excuse me." He tossed his napkin on the table and stormed out of the room.

A second later, I heard our mother call his name as they passed on the stairs, but I heard no reply from William.

My parents entered the dining room dressed in their Sunday attire and full of smiles.

"Good morning, Jocelyn. Did you sleep well?" my mother inquired as father pulled out her chair before taking his seat at the head of the table.

"Yes. Thank you."

"Why are you not dressed? We have to leave shortly for services," Father asked.

"I am not feeling well this morning." It was not exactly a lie. "I believe I am going to lie back down for a while. I thought that perhaps eating something would help, but I am afraid my head is hurting."

"Would you like me to have Sarah fix you something else?" Mother offered, but I shook my head.

"Please make my apologies to Jackson. He will be here shortly. Please ask him to come over this afternoon. I am sure I will be feeling better by then." I rose from the table. "Excuse me." I placed my napkin down on the table and left the room as Sarah brought in their breakfast.

"Of course, darling. I hope you feel better soon," my father called after me.

I hurried up the stairs quietly and sneaked into my room. I returned to my bay window to watch for Jackson to make his way over. I hated deceiving my parents, but I saw no other way to get an opportunity to speak with Olivia. I knew her parents would be leaving shortly for services as well.

Several minutes later, I saw Jackson cross the street and make his way up the pathway. I heard his knock on our door and then spoke with my father. Shortly thereafter, Jackson and my parents left together with his parents for church.

I jumped up and got dressed as quickly as I could. Then I rushed down the hall to William's room and knocked softly on his door.

"William, it is me. May I please come in?"

"Sure," his voice was soft and cold.

I found him sitting in the gloomy room with only the light from the fire to show any life left in the place. His head was bowed, and he had his pipe gritted between his teeth. William rarely smoked, only when he was really upset about something.

"William." I walked over to him and placed my hand on his shoulder. "Would you please do something for me?"

"Why are you not on your way to church? I thought I heard everyone leave a few minutes ago?"

"They did. I told them I was not feeling well. I wanted to take advantage of the fact that everyone will be gone for the next several hours."

"Why? What are you up to now?" He looked intrigued.

"I want to speak with Olivia. Her mother has not let anyone talk with her, and I want her to know that I am here for her and am still her friend." William's eyes widened. "I just want her to know that she is not alone, and I figured since everyone was at church, this was my chance."

"I believe she would appreciate that a great deal." He smiled up at me. "Come on."

William took my hand, and the two of us snuck down the stairs like we had when we were children. I grinned at the memories of us doing this so many times throughout our youth. It felt like a lifetime ago or someone else's memories instead of our own.

William silently opened the front door. We could hear Mimi and Sarah in the kitchen and Missy and Cora were somewhere, cleaning something. Eddie was gone, having driven the carriage to services. We crept off the porch over to the side yard. The grounds were covered in a heavy fog, which made our adventure seem more exciting and childish.

William knocked on the Adams' front door without hesitation. We waited impatiently as Grady, their version of our Eddie, finally opened the door. He greeted us with a strange look but allowed us to enter the house.

"Good mornin', Mr. Timmons 'n Miss Timmons. Ah's sorry, but Miss 'Livia's feelin poorly dis mornin' 'n not receivin' 'ny guests."

"Grady," William looked agitated. "Please go and get Olivia immediately."

"Ah's sorra," Grady started, but William stopped him short.

"I will not tell you again, Grady. Please, go tell Olivia that we must see her at once." His voice raised an octave.

"Yes, sir." Grady disappeared up the stairs and I looked at William with disbelief.

"William, I am surprised at you." I smiled, and he smiled back at me.

"I am tired of all this." He shook his head. "Here I am, supposed to marry this woman in six days, but I am not allowed to even speak with her. It is ridiculous."

I was so proud of him. This was the first time I had seen him behave like a grown-up.

Olivia came down the stairs in her robe, looking extremely pale and thin. Her eyes were red and swollen. Obviously, she was not faking being ill. I could see why she refused to attend classes. She was not in any shape to go anywhere. Her hair was down over her shoulders, brushed back away from her gaunt face.

William met her halfway down the stairs, taking her hand and kissing it gently.

"How are you feeling this morning?"

She gave him a weak smile. "Better." Her voice sounded hollow and foreign to my ears.

"Let us sit down in the parlor." William guided her over to the loveseat by the hearth and propped her feet up on the stool before covering her with a blanket. "Jocelyn wanted to speak with you." He sat down beside her, and I took a seat in the chair across from them.

"It is wonderful to see you, Jocelyn. How have you been?" She sounded like an empty shell of who she had once been.

"I have been very worried about you. Your mother would not allow me to see you, so I am afraid I had to fake being ill this morning to speak with you." I smiled.

"You honestly should not have done that, but I am glad you did." Even her smile looked as if it took real effort on her part. There did not seem to be any strength in her.

"I am sorry that you have been so sick."

"I am afraid that my mother suffered from intense morning sickness with each of her pregnancies." She let out a small sound that should have been a laugh. "I hear your birthday celebration was quite an event. I am sorry that I could not attend. I wanted to."

She looked down at her hands and I noticed that tears were now covering her cheeks. William reached over and took her hands in his.

"I really wanted you there, Olivia. It was not my decision." I did not know how to finish the sentence.

"I know. My parents will not allow me out of the house, not even to sit on the porches and get some fresh air." She kept her head down, staring at her hands that were entwined with Williams.

"Olivia, I want you to know that I am here for you. You are still my dearest friend, and I love you so much. Please, do not feel that you are alone."

Olivia nodded her head. "I am sorry that I seem so distant lately. Things around here have been a little tense. My mother will not even allow my brothers to come in and see me. I am alone in my room all the time." She sobbed.

My heart was breaking for her. I guess this wedding was going to be a blessing after all. At least with Olivia living under our roof she would no longer be a prisoner.

"I hate that your family is behaving this way. I want you to know that not everyone feels the way they do."

Her eyes widened at my words, and she finally looked at me. "Who all knows?"

Her words caught me by surprise. "Just us, Jackson and I and our families. No one at school or anything."

She lowered her head again and nodded. "Jocelyn, can I ask you something?"

"Of course."

"I realize that I can no longer be a part of your wedding but next weekend, it would mean the world to me if you would stand beside me when I marry your brother."

"Yes. Of course, I would be honored too. I am seriously disappointed, though, that you cannot stand up with me."

"I know. Are you going to ask Elizabeth?"

I nodded slowly. I did not have the heart to tell her that I already had, and that Elizabeth had agreed. I knew it would only make her feel worse.

"Good. She is very sweet and will be wonderful, I am sure." Olivia gave me a weak smile.

Her words were sincere, but I knew how much it was breaking her heart to be replaced. "Did you know she has a beau now?"

That news brought an even bigger smile to her face.

"His name is Lee Miller. She brought him to the party yesterday. He is nice. I like him, and she is very happy."

"How wonderful for her. She deserves someone who is going to be good to her." A little life glimmered briefly behind her clouded eyes.

"Yes." I got up and walked over to her. I knelt in front of her, placing my hands over hers and William's. "Olivia, I meant what I said. I am here for you. Nothing between us has changed, and I cannot wait until next weekend when you are truly my sister. Things will be so much better once you are living in our home and get away from this house." I squeezed her hands, and she finally gave me a smile that looked somewhat like her old self. "Now, we must be getting back before anyone notice's our absence." I glanced over at William.

"I know." He turned to Olivia as I straightened back up. "I will be back this afternoon."

William kissed her cheek and they both stood. Tears began to fall down her cheeks again. She wiped them away and sniffled. I embraced her lightly, afraid that she was as breakable as she appeared. I was horrified when I realized I was hugging nothing but bones. She had lost a great deal more weight than I had initially estimated. It was frightening.

"I love you," I whispered in her ear.

"I love you, too. Please do not be a stranger. I could really use some company," she pleaded.

"I will try. I promise. I will be here if I can get past your mother." I gave Olivia a teasing smile, but the truth behind my words no longer made it funny.

She only nodded then embraced my brother.

I laid down on my bed, waiting for Jackson and my parents to return from church. William had retreated into his room in his own search for solace. I could not get the image of Olivia out of my mind. It scared me how poorly she looked. I had never seen anyone who was still able to walk look so pale, weak, and grossly thin. I tried to push it out of my mind and focus on something else entirely.

I pulled a blanket up around me and stared over at the flames dancing around in the hearth. It brought me back to what I had seen the other night: the girls, the cages, Jackson's birthday gift. I climbed off my bed and walked over to the mantle. There in the box lay the silver pocket watch Jackson had given me. Eddie or Mimi must have picked it up and placed it back in its box. My fingers reached out to touch it. But I stopped.

Almost as if it too were flames and burn me if I touched it. I halted only inches from it, terrified that it had some enchanted power and was responsible for causing that episode. I lowered my hand back to my side and laughed softly. The sound echoed across the silent room. I knew I was being silly. There was no way for this piece of metal to be responsible for causing anything.

Voices echoed up the stairway, informing me that everyone had returned. I backed away from the heat and set off to find Jackson. As I descended the stairs, I noticed my brothers, Jonathon, and James, along with their families, had returned with our parents for Sunday dinner. Even Jackson, his siblings, and his parents had decided to stay for the afternoon.

I lingered momentarily on the stairs and scanned over the room and once again, William was nowhere to be found.

"Hello, my love. Are you feeling better?"

I nodded and approached Jackson, who took my hand and kissed it tenderly.

"Much. Thank you. Where is William?"

Jackson shook his head. "I have not seen him today. He probably went over to Olivia's to see how she is feeling."

I took Jackson aside and told him the truth about the morning's events. When I finished, he stared at me in disbelief.

"What do you think we should do? They cannot continue to treat her this way. They are literally holding her prisoner. It is not right." I narrowed my eyes in disgust. I had always had a good relationship with Olivia's family, but now I despised them.

"No, it is not. But what do you expect us to do? She is their daughter. They are not starving her or beating her, and she is not in harm's way. There is nothing we can do at this moment." Jackson faced me, holding my hands in his. His eyes were full of sympathy for Olivia's situation, but his face held as firm as his words.

"Can we not bring her here now? She's terribly distressed, and it cannot be good for the baby or her," I begged.

"We cannot interfere in this, Jocelyn. She will be married to William next weekend. Then she will move in here and everything will be fine." He tried to reassure me, but somehow, his words only felt patronizing.

"Are you serious? We are supposed to let them treat her this way. It is not right, and you know it." I raised my voice causing everyone to turn in our direction and stare.

"Please, lower your voice. This is not the time or place for this discussion." Jackson's face turned serious.

"Why not? This is my home. If I cannot discuss something like this here, then, where can I?" I huffed, placing my hands on my hips solely for emphasis.

"Jocelyn, you know good and well what I am talking about. Now will you please calm down?"

But his effects were fruitless. His parents were already walking over to see what was going on.

"Is everything all right?" Robert asked.

"Yes," Jackson responded lightly.

"No." I gave him a mean-spirited look before facing Robert and Emily. "I saw Olivia this morning, and she looked ghastly. Her parents will not allow her to leave her room. I have been trying to see her all week, but her mother never allowed me into the house. So, this morning when everyone went to church services, I decided to go see her. I was worried and tired of playing their silly games." I paused, looking at the two of them. "I apologize for deceiving everyone about being ill, but I had to know if she was all right. And she is not!" I glared at Jackson.

Emily put her arm around my shoulders to comfort and calm me. "Jocelyn, I understand why you found it necessary to see her. I would have done the same. However, in this kind of situation, there honestly is nothing that we can do. She is not married to your brother yet."

"But she is carrying his child, and the health and well-being of that child is in danger. They cannot treat her like this." I pleaded with Emily. I knew she was my best chance for understanding. "Olivia looked like a dark, hollow shell of who she was just two weeks ago. I know that morning sickness can have an effect, but this is much deeper than that. Her eyes are swollen and red. Her skin is so pale it is almost transparent. When I hugged her, she felt like a bag of bones. We need to get her out of that house."

"All right." Emily studied my face carefully for a moment and slowly nodded. Finally, someone got it. She looked at Robert and nodded again.

Robert walked over to our stairs and began climbing. Emily kept her arm around my shoulders as Jackson looked from his mother to me. The expression he held had a mixture of disbelief and confusion. Everyone in the room had become silent and all eyes were turned in our direction.

Robert descended the stairs with William in tow, looking utterly baffled and tired. As the two of them approached the three of us, my parents closed in the circle around us, demanding to know what was going on. My mother looked deeply concerned, but my father looked angry.

"What is going on here?" My father demanded in a not-so-subtle tone.

"Patrick, we seem to have a situation with Olivia," Robert began.

If there was any hope of getting anything done immediately for Olivia, I knew Robert was the only one to make my father get involved with the right frame of mind.

"What now?"

"William and Jocelyn just explained to me what condition Olivia is in," Robert began but my father immediately looked angry.

"We are all aware of what condition Olivia is in." My father glared at his son.

"That is not what I am referring to, not entirely. From what I understand, Olivia is gravely ill, and I am not referring to morning sickness. Both William and Jocelyn have expressed deep concern for her well-being as well as the health of your grandchild."

I knew his words were chosen carefully to have an effect of my father's sentimental nature as well as his innate desire to care for people as a physician.

"Benjamin never said anything to me this morning," My father stated flatly but my mother looked concerned.

Emily tightened her grip around my shoulder, and I held my eyes locked with Jackson's.

"Wait here a moment, dear." Robert placed his hand briefly on his wife's arm. "Please, Patrick. Let us talk in your study for a moment."

Several minutes later, we heard the office door open, and my father hollered for William to join them. William gave Jackson a terrified look then left the room.

"I wonder what they are talking about," my mother said to no one in particular.

Jonathon and James had gathered close to us, while their wives held back just a little, trying to keep their children occupied and calm. Jackson's siblings and their spouses looked extremely uncomfortable.

"I am not sure," Jackson responded.

"What do you think they will do?" I asked him, but he shook his head.

"Is Olivia in danger?" My mother's voice quivered a bit.

"I am not sure," Jackson answered. "I hope not. I hope we are making too big of a deal out of this and there is nothing to worry about."

"You did not see what I saw," I quietly added.

We all stood in silence, waiting for anything to happen and unsure as to what to expect. Sarah came in and announced that dinner was served. Mother nodded towards her, but no one moved into the dining room.

After several more long and grueling minutes, she asked the others to please take the children into the dining room and feed them since they were getting fussy and hungry. Soon, the only sounds were that of the staff in the kitchen and the muffled sounds from the children in the dining room. None of the adults in the room spoke, and the silence was deafening.

Robert, Father, and William had gathered their coats and hats before they joined us again. My father stepped in the doorway with troubled eyes over at my mother.

"Jackson, would you mind joining us? Alex, Jonathon, James, please."

The four men nodded and got their overcoats and hats.

Father walked up to my mother and gathered his hands in hers. "We are going over next door to speak with Benjamin."

My mother let out a small sound but said nothing.

"Not to worry. I only want to see Olivia with my own eyes and make sure she is all right. We will be back shortly. Please go and eat something, my dear."

I looked at Jackson, who gave me a smile to comfort me. I only hoped he knew what he was doing. Benjamin had a horrible temper. I knew he would feel like this was an intrusion and a personal attack on his family.

The door closed behind them and Emily smiled lightheartedly to the rest of us, trying to ease the tension. "Shall we have something to eat?" She tried to make her voice as light and cheery as possible, but she too, could not hide her nervousness.

"I am not hungry." Mother rang her hands together and walked over to the fire. I followed her.

"What do you think they are going to do?" I whispered to her.

"Nothing irrational I hope."

"I do not believe they will." Emily joined us, taking a seat in the rocking chair. "Robert, Alex, and Jackson are very levelheaded."

"Yes, they are," my mother agreed. "I am glad they went with them. Patrick is very passionate, and I sincerely hope that Olivia's only suffering from morning sickness."

My mother sat down in the other rocker, picking up her knitting to keep her hands busy. I paced back and forth, stopping occasionally to glance out the front window.

A short while later James's wife, Rachael and Jonathan's wife, Lizette, wandered back into the room with their children followed by Jackson's sister, Phoebe, with her son, Wallace. Rachael and Lizette took their children upstairs and tucked them away for their afternoon naps. Phoebe sat down with Wallace and gently rocked him to sleep. However, in the absence of their noise, the house was dreadfully silent.

Finally, Mother could not stand it anymore. "I am going over there," she announced, standing.

Emily rose to object, but Rachael was the one who interjected. "Mother, please let the men handle this. I am sure they will be back shortly." As she spoke, the front door opened, and the men walked in, looking upset, but satisfied.

William came in behind them all, carrying Olivia in his arms. Jackson closed the door behind him as they all entered the front room. Olivia was still dressed in her nightgown but had her robe on. There was a blanket wrapped around her and her bare feet were sticking out from underneath it. She had a corpse appearance around her that caused the women in the room to gasp upon laying eyes on her. Embarrassed and humiliated, Olivia turned and buried her face in William's shoulder.

Our mothers rushed over to Olivia, in horror at what they were seeing for the first time.

"William, take her upstairs to your sister's room." Mother turned to Rachael. "Please go and have Sarah fix a plate and take it to her, along with some hot tea."

"Yes, Mother."

Rachel rushed off, and Jackson and I followed William up the stairs. "What happened?" I demanded as William placed Olivia gently down on my bed. Olivia looked even frailer than she had this morning if that was even possible.

"They were starving her!" Jackson said in a hateful voice. "In their bizarre, sick, twisted minds Benjamin and Harriet thought that by starving her it would cause her to lose the baby and save their dear little family from shame."

I could not believe what I was hearing.

Who could do such a thing, and to their own child?

William sat down beside Olivia and held her hand. I walked around and sat down on the other side of her. My heart was breaking just looking at her. I gently brushed her hair away from her face.

"I am so sorry. I wish I could have done something sooner." I could not believe how heartless her parents were. I always thought of Harriet as a cold woman, but this was even beyond my comprehension.

"You did not know?" Olivia gave me a weak smile that looked foreign on her face. "I know you tried to see me, and William said that you sent them all over there. So, see, Jocelyn, you did! You saved me! Thank you."

Tears poured down my face. I could not find any words to say to her.

"Why did you not say anything to me?" William asked in a small voice. "I should have seen this?" He lowered his head in shame.

"No one would have ever thought this." Jackson stood behind him. "They told you it was morning sickness. You are not a doctor, William. You believed them. It is not your fault." Although he meant well, I could tell his words did little to comfort William.

All the women and the men had made their way upstairs and crowded into my room. Rachael carried in the tray and handed it to me. I placed it on my nightstand and William helped prop Olivia up on some pillows as I attempted to give her some hot tea. Our parents were whispering behind us as I tried to feed Olivia some small bites of mashed potatoes with a little gravy.

"I believe we have decided how to best handle this," my father announced. "I realize that it is improper to have Olivia stay here even under strenuous circumstances and since we have neighbors who all enjoy gossiping, here is what we propose."

Jackson, William, Olivia, and I all stared at him with curious expressions.

"Since Robert has agreed to assist us, we feel that instead of holding the ceremony next weekend, we should just have it now. What do you think?"

"All right." William smiled over at Olivia who nodded in agreement, but then turned solemn.

"I have no clothes," Olivia whispered looking down at her nightgown.

"Not to worry, I have the perfect dress." I leaned over and hugged her gently. "Now, if you gentlemen will please excuse us, the bride will need a few minutes to prepare."

I would not have thought it possible, but I knew that I was going to do everything I could to make this impromptu wedding as happy for the two of them as I could.

Lizette walked over to the door behind the exiting men and paused turning towards the women in the room. "I just thought of something perfect. I will be right back." She smiled and closed the door behind her.

"Can you stand?" Emily asked Olivia, who nodded and began climbing out of bed. "Be careful now. We do not want your supper coming back up."

But Olivia only smiled. "I do not have morning sickness. It was just what my mother told everyone. I guess she had it, but I've had a little nausea is all."

We all stared at her with disbelief, even more disgusted with her parents.

Phoebe helped Olivia over to my vanity table and began brushing out her hair. I retreated to my wardrobe, which was already opened by my mother and Emily, who were searching through all my dresses for something appropriate.

"Excuse me." I squeezed in between them and reached into the very back and pulled out a gown that was still covered for protection.

I had put it there several weeks ago to keep it safe until my special day arrived.

"Oh, Jocelyn!" My mother gasped, but I only smiled and took off the outer covering.

I carried it over to the vanity table and held it up for Olivia to see. Olivia turned and shook her head. "Jocelyn, no. I cannot. That is your wedding gown." She stood in front of me with big tears in her eyes.

"Now stop. You are going to make me cry." I hugged her again. "And you are going to wear my dress. Today, you officially become my sister and I could not be any happier."

"But Jackson cannot see the dress, Jocelyn. It is bad luck. I cannot wear it," she protested.

"Rubbish. Jackson and I already have luck and more importantly, we have love."

"Are you sure?" she asked.

"Positive. Now let's get you ready."

I helped her get undressed and all of us women fussed over her for the better part of an hour. We took turns making her sip chicken broth and tea. Lizette returned with some baby's breath for Olivia's hair along with some small violets which Emily expertly placed along the cascade of curls. Phoebe carefully applied a tad bit of rouge to add some color to her pale skin.

Olivia stood back in front of the full-length mirror as we all gathered around her. Despite her appearance upon her arrival, we did an amazing job. She still did not quite look like herself, but at least she was headed now in the right direction.

My dress fit her almost perfectly. It was a gorgeous white-satin gown with a lace overlay and white-pearl buttons down the back. The sleeves were full, but short and the white-satin gloves were full length, climbing up her arms. The gown cascaded down into a long, full train in the back.

"Are you ready?" Emily asked the nervous bride.

Rachael handed Olivia some flowers from my party that she had tied a light purple ribbon around.

I quickly changed back into the dress that Emily had given me for my birthday and placed my grandmother's broach on my chest for the special occasion. Phoebe added some baby breath to my hair for a final touch.

"I am a little scared." Olivia took a deep breath.

"All brides are. You should have seen me on my wedding day. I was a mess." Phoebe laughed.

"I would say so. I was ready to string you up that morning." Emily could not hide her amusement of the memory and started giggling.

"We all were." My mother placed her hands upon Olivia's shoulders. "Or will be." She turned back and smiled at me.

They headed back downstairs to forewarn the gentlemen that we were ready, leaving me briefly alone with Olivia at the top of the stairs. She turned to me with tears still running down her cheeks. I quickly wiped them away in hopes that her makeup would not smudge. She could not afford it.

Phoebe surprised us by playing the wedding march as we began our descent down the stairs. I walked slowly in front of Olivia but kept looking over my shoulder, fearing she would stumble in her weakened condition.

At the foot of the stairs, waiting patiently was Jackson and my father beaming up at us. I took Jackson's arm with a smile as Olivia reached my father. He looked at her and gave her a big smile.

"I know I am not your father, Miss Olivia, but I would be honored if you would allow me to give the bride away."

Of course, these words only brought about more tears, but she did manage to squeak out a low "Thank you," and took his arm. The two of them followed us into the front room. Robert was standing in front of the hearth with William nervously beside him. Everyone else was seated in arranged chairs, facing the two men. All the decorations for my party gave the room a festive, warm atmosphere.

Our families stood as we entered, walking towards my shaking brother. Jackson took his spot beside William, placing his hands on either side of him trying to steady him.

Father and Olivia approached, and he handed her over to William.

Robert made the service brief since it looked like we might lose the bride and groom at any moment. Both were green with nervousness and William was so shaken that he was rocking back and forth on the balls of his feet.

Sarah had reheated dinner for most of us and brought out what was left of my birthday cake. She apologized profusely to the newlyweds for not having the time to bake their own wedding cake. Neither seemed bothered by such trivial matters.

For a day that had started out dreary with fog, it had finally given way to a clear evening of celebration. I stepped back away from all the commotion and watched how happy my family seemed. I felt a rush of peace overwhelm me as Emily joined me in the corner of the room.

"It was so very sweet of you to allow her to wear your dress," she whispered softly.

"I believe after all she has endured recently, wearing that dress means more to her than anything else I could have done."

Emily wrapped her arm around my shoulders pulling me to her. "You realize that your interference may have possibly saved her life as well as the life of their child."

Her words choked me up, and I could only nod in response. I had not really looked at it from that point of view. I only knew that my dearest friend was suffering, and I had to help.

"And since you no longer have a wedding gown, I would be honored if you would consider wearing mine," she whispered.

I could not believe my ears. Emily turned me to face her with a loving motherly look.

"I realize that I am not your mother, Jocelyn, but I have always thought of you as a daughter. Phoebe could not get married in my gown since she is taller than me, but I believe that it will fit you perfectly. It truly is a lovely dress." She smiled and took my hands in hers. "I have been blessed with such a wonderful marriage and I believe that marrying my son in that dress will give you and Jackson the same magic to your marriage."

Again, I nodded my head and tried to ignore the tears running down my cheeks. Emily hugged me tightly.

"Please come over tomorrow after your classes and have a look at it. It will be our secret."

"I would be honored, Mrs. Chandler. Thank you." I whispered softly through my tears hugging her tightly.

She let me go and stood back, smiling. "Please, call me Mother. After all, you are marrying my baby soon and I could not be happier. You make him very happy, Jocelyn, and that is all a mother wants for her child. You will see."

"Thank you, Mother."

Jackson had to return to school before the end of the evening and I would not get the opportunity to see him again for several days. William was staying home tonight with his new bride and leaving for school early in the morning. Robert and my father returned to Olivia's home shortly after the evening wound to an end to retrieve her belongings and inform her family that she and William had been married. From what I understood of what father told mother upon his return, her parents were unemotional and glad to hand over her things to the men. I only hoped that Olivia did not hear their response. However, in my heart, I believe she already knew.

Chapter 21

Sunday, October 25, 2015

I FELT A WARM KISS on my forehead, bringing me out of the darkness. My mom's voice was soft and warm just like the blanket keeping me snug.

"Good morning, honey. How are you feeling?"

"I'm okay." My head still hurts, but not nearly as bad as before.

"Did you sleep well?"

Then it dawned on me. Jackson must have returned and found me sleeping.

I sat up, frantically searching the room even. "Where's Jackson? Have you seen him today? I must have fallen asleep when he went to get us drinks last night."

She placed her hand on my shoulder. "Don't worry. I saw him this morning with your brother."

Tears started rolling down my cheeks.

"Honey, he's not upset. He knows you need your rest."

"Maybe, but I wanted to see him."

"I'm sure he will be by later. I told him earlier that we were going to be running the tests this morning." Somehow that didn't make me feel any better.

The nurse arrived, pushing a wheelchair, looking too cheerful for my current mood status.

"Good morning, Jocelyn, Dr. Timmons. How are you ladies doing this morning?" Her voice was so sweet it gave me a cavity.

"We're doing well, Mindy. How are Michael and the boys?" my mom asked in her physician's voice. She knew about everyone in the hospital and always tried to make a point of keeping up with the personals. I wasn't in the mood for pleasantries this morning. I just wanted this over with.

I remained quiet and climbed into the chair. My mom helped me adjust the feet rests and offered to push me to the radiology department. The two women chatted down the long, bright corridors about their children and busy schedules. I did my best to shut them out.

It was one o'clock before I got back into my room. The tests were long and boring. My mom stayed with me the entire time, trying her best to lift my spirits, but the deafening noise from the tests had made my headache return worse than before. All I wanted to do was lie down and cry.

Several hours passed while I lay there alone, crying softly. I stared out the window to the gray world surrounding my existence. The Midwest winter was close; and I could hear the winds blowing across Lake Michigan, chilling the entire city of Chicago. I hated being confined to this room.

Jenna, Kyle, and Jackson woke me up at five with dinner. I was truly happy to open my eyes and look upon their smiles. It was a comfort to have them here.

Jenna flopped down on the foot of my bed while Jackson smiled and began passing out the food. "Let's eat. I'm starving."

"I agree," I said, instantly feeling better.

"Boy, I'll tell you I think you'd do anything to get out of practice." She laughed. "I think Coach is having a coronary with one of her starters in the hospital. She's terrified that you're done for the season, and she even asked me about basketball. Can you believe that?"

"What did you tell her?"

"I told her you were having tests done and we wouldn't know anything until then." Jenna shrugged her shoulders and dunked her chip into the artichoke dip.

"Mom said we should have the results back today but whether I go home today or tomorrow, I'm not going back to school until at least Wednesday. Not with this face!"

"You look beautiful." Jackson smiled from the foot of the bed next to Jenna while Kyle made himself comfortable in the chair pushed up beside the bed.

"You're not a very good lair." I grinned at him, tasting my loaded baked potato soup. It was fabulous, as were the rolls.

Jackson helped himself to some of the dip also. "That is because I am not lying."

"I'm hoping I'll look somewhat better by Wednesday, but I seriously doubt my mom is going to let me practice this week, let alone play in the match."

"You're probably right about that." Kyle knew all too well how over cautious my mom could be when it came to medical crap.

"Hopefully, I'll be back next week, and you can tell Coach she has nothing to worry about as far as her precious basketball season is concerned." I smirked at Jenna.

"Can I word it that way? Coach Smith would be so pleased." We all laughed, knowing exactly how pleased Coach would be with that response.

"If you like, but it's your funeral," I teased.

"Thanks."

Jenna tossed another roll at me, which I caught. Then my door opened again and my parents along with Ethan joined our little party.

"Looks like you're feeling better?" I knew my mom was referring to my spirits and not my physical well-being.

"I am." I grinned at my family. "Much better." I glanced over at Jackson.

"Well, I have some good news." My mom crossed over to my bed and leaned against Kyle's chair. "All your scans came back normal. So, you have been discharged and are free to come home."

"Oh, goody." Ethan rolled his eyes at me.

"Thanks for the support, little brother." I tossed at him the same roll that Jenna had just thrown at me.

"Hey, thanks," he said and took a big bite.

At the insistence of my parents, I had to ride home with them while Ethan rode with our friends. Thankfully, all of us were headed to my house so I wouldn't be left alone with my mom, who I knew was going to be fussing over me all evening. My dad agreed to allow me to rest on the couch in the basement and watch a movie with my friends if I agreed to stay put and not get too excited.

Once my mom felt satisfied that I wasn't going to die or fall off the couch or something equally as stupid, she retreated upstairs with her cell phone in hand, reminding me to text her if I needed anything at all. Jenna assured her several times that she would make sure I stayed put before she ran over to the wall unit and stuck the *X-MEN: Days of Future Past* movie in the DVD player, proud of herself for beating the guys to it. She bowed at me with a giggle and waltzed over to join Kyle in the recliner. Jackson sat down in the other recliner across the room from me making Jenna give me a confused look.

"Jackson, you can sit on the end of the couch with Jocelyn. She can put her feet on your lap," she offered.

"I am all right. I do not want to crowd her."

"You won't. Don't worry about it." I shot Jenna a disapproving look, telling her to drop it. Thankfully, Kyle noticed and changed the subject.

"What movie did you put in, babe?" Kyle put his arm tighter around her waist.

"*X-MEN: Days of Future Past.*"

"Again," he groaned.

"Oh, come on. I love this movie," I added in her defense. "It's easy on the eyes." I winked at Jenna who giggled.

Ethan came over and plopped down on the end of the couch, shoving my feet out of the way. I playfully kicked him, and he shoved me back.

"Part one of *Hunger Games, Mockingjay* comes out in a couple weeks. Would you like to go see it with me Jocelyn?" Jackson gave me that smile that turned my insides to Jell-O.

"Of course." I would follow him anywhere.

Jenna cleared her throat loudly, making us all look at her. "Me too, and you're going also." She playfully pointed her finger at Kyle's nose.

"I figured as much." He rolled his eyes at her.

The five of us settled back and enjoyed the movie. I had a difficult time keeping my eyes off Jackson throughout the film. What I couldn't believe was that every time I would steal a peek over at Jackson, I would always discover him looking back at me with a slight, knowing grin on his face. I firmly believed he knew more about what was happening to me than what he was telling me.

Chapter 22

Monday, October 28, 1878

ELIZABETH AND I WALKED TOGETHER in the fading sunshine. I was heading over to Jackson's, while she was going straight home to complete her schoolwork before Mr. Lee Miller got off work. The skies had somewhat cleared from the day before, but it was evident that winter was on its way. There was no warmth left in the sun as we both pulled our caplets tighter around ourselves.

Elizabeth was being rather elusive about her relationship with Mr. Miller, yet there was a new lightness to her step. She was so unlike Christina or Laurie, who simply could not stop themselves from talking about their beaus. Elizabeth was much more refined than the other two could possibly ever hope to be.

Although I was dying to tell her about William and Olivia's nuptials, I knew I could not; so, I was doing my best to keep the subject focused on anything else.

"Did Mr. Miller have a good time at the party Saturday?"

"Yes. He enjoyed getting to know everyone. He thought you and Mr. Chandler were very pleasant."

"He seems like a very kind man." A cold breeze blew through my hair, chilling me to the bone.

"He is, and I really like him." Her cheeks blushed, but not from the wind.

"Wonderful. Is his family still coming for the holidays?"

"Yes, and I believe Mother is quite nervous about it." She giggled. "I admit I am rather curious about them."

"Why is that?"

"Perhaps, because he seems so much older than he is." She shook her head.

"Yes, he does." I agreed.

"But sometimes there is still a hint of a child in him."

I remembered how that felt when a relationship was just beginning, the excitement and the thrill of discovery.

"You seem very taken by him."

Elizabeth's face got even redder, and she looked away shyly.

"I suppose I am." I saw her grin even though she was looking down.

"You know there is nothing wrong with that."

"I know, but I normally do not behave like this." She almost looked as if she were ashamed of herself.

"I believe he is good for you." I could not help but laugh at her.

"I believe he is too."

We parted ways in front of my house. I told her I had to speak with Mrs. Chandler and bid her farewell as I crossed the street. I could see the lights pouring out the windows, welcoming me. Their house was so beautiful and homey. I knocked on the front door and waited impatiently in the cold air. Emily greeted me warmly and offered me some hot tea in the living room to warm me.

We sat down in front of the hearth, letting the embers return my body temperature back to normal.

"How were your classes today?" she inquired in a warm tone.

"Good. Long." I sipped the tea. The heat was intoxicating. "I admit I could not wait for them to be over today. I am so excited about seeing your wedding gown. I am honored that you would want me to wear it."

"I am pleased to hear that. I was worried that I had offended you. I know how excited you were about your gown."

"Well, I was but I believe that Miss Olivia needed something special since she felt as if the entire world were judging her." I explained my reasoning even though I knew it was not necessary.

"She loved the dress because she knew how special it is to you."

"I know she made a mistake, but I do believe that we all make mistakes and need our families and friends support to help us get through them. I just cannot believe how her family and mine for a while, and even I reacted too. I feel badly for judging her when I heard." I looked over at the fire to avoid her gentle eyes. I was truly ashamed of my earlier behavior.

"We were all surprised. It is natural for us to be shocked by events such as these, but the important thing is we give the two of them all the support we can. They have a long and difficult road ahead, and they are going to need all of us." Her voice was smooth and caring.

"I still cannot get over her parents and what they did to her," I stated softly, recalling how Olivia looked when William carried her in.

"I know. Robert told me what happened when they returned to gather her belongings. It is heartbreaking." Her eyes dropped briefly.

"How can a mother do such a thing to their child?"

"I honestly do not know. Robert also told me that they are moving as soon as possible." She shook her head slightly.

"Really?"

Emily nodded again.

"Somehow that does not surprise me. Is Mr. Adams going to sell the bank?"

"I have no idea. I cannot imagine what this is going to do to Olivia. Perhaps it will in some strange way help." She wiped the corner of her eyes.

"For her sake, I hope so."

Emily stood and straightened the front of her dress as if she were shaking off the negative thoughts. "Well, future Mrs. Chandler, I have something special to show you."

She retrieved a large, white box from the dining room and placed it on the coffee table in front of me. She lifted the lid, setting it aside, and pulled open a mountain of tissue paper. There, underneath it, was a gorgeous ivory, silk gown. Emily pulled the dress out and held it up in front of her.

It had a boned, high-neck bodice with large gigot sleeves and a front chiffon insert at the yoke, waist, and cuffs. It had front hook-and-eye closures; and the skirt was gathered at the back that led down to a four-foot train with ivory, silk, lace-trimmed lobster tail bustle. The gown also had a flounced and ruffled petticoat under the hemline and a plain, taffeta slip. It was magnificent. Tucked away in the bottom of the box, Emily pulled out her satin pump shoes that had abalone ornaments on them and two bowed satin stockings.

"I cannot believe this. It is so elegant and gorgeous."

"Want to try it on? I know it will look beautiful on you."

With some tugging on the corset and nearly turning blue from holding my breath to get it fastened, the gown was finally on. Despite not being able to breathe, it looked amazing. I twirled around in front of the full-length mirror, looking adoringly at myself. As much as I loved my previous wedding gown, it held nothing to the exquisiteness of this one.

"I love it!" I gushed repeatedly. I could not get enough of the sight of myself. *I cannot wait for Jackson to see me grace this gown on our wedding day.*

"You look so beautiful, Jocelyn. I knew you would." She beamed.

"Oh, Mother." I rushed over and embraced her. "Thank you so much for this. Jackson is going to love it. I know he is."

I had to change back into my other attire before Robert came home for the evening and ruined our surprise. I hated retiring the gown back to the box to await my beautiful day. I asked Emily to keep the box here so as not to raise suspicion. She agreed and walked me to the door. I thanked and hugged her again for the gown and hurried across the street.

Olivia was waiting for me in the front room when I arrived. She was all bright and smiley, looking entirely different than she had only yesterday morning.

"Good afternoon. How were classes today?" She was knitting a pale, yellow blanket for the baby next to the fire. She was the picture of an expecting mother.

"Good. How was your day Mrs. Timmons?"

Olivia blushed at the sound of her new name.

"Lovely. Your mother helped me re-organize William's room to make space for my things. It feels strange, but wonderful."

"I imagine." I couldn't wait to be able to live with Jackson and wake up beside him every day.

"It feels strange being here without William." She said quietly and continued knitting.

"Why is that? You have been here your entire life and stayed with me countless times."

"I know, but it is different now that we are married."

Yes, I believed that. "You have been married less than a day." I sat down in the rocking chair opposite her and picked up a novel my mother must have been reading earlier and flipped aimlessly through the pages.

"Are the gentlemen coming home this evening?"

"No. Wednesday, perhaps." She held up the blanket to admire her work before she started again.

"Oh."

She leaned in closer to me and whispered, "Do you know what is really odd?"

"What?"

"Sleeping next to him last night and waking up beside him this morning." She giggled. "Your brother is certainly a bed hog."

"That I would not know." I laughed.

"Have you and Jackson begun house-hunting yet?" She sat back in her seat and continued knitting.

"No. We're planning on looking later this week during fall recess."

"You are going to stay in the area, right?" Anxiety rested on her gaunt face.

"Yes. Of course."

"Wonderful. I was hoping you were going to say that. I honestly want you to be close by. I do not know what I would do without you." She relaxed again over her knitting.

"Granted, I will no longer be down the hall, but I do not plan on going too far."

"I overheard Sarah tell Missy that my parents will be moving soon." Her head dropped down again.

"Yes. I heard that as well." I wished briefly that I could go over there and say my piece to her parents for doing this to her.

"I believe it will be good for them. They need a fresh start where no one knows what happened and they will no longer feel ashamed of what I have done." She continued to look down.

I noticed huge tears fall on the blanket she was creating for her baby, and it broke my heart.

"Olivia, I cannot comprehend what you must be feeling, but I do believe in my heart that you are better off here, surrounded by those who love you, then living in your parent's estate." My words did little to give her comfort.

"I know."

I could see the tears falling readily now.

"I feel horrible for all the pain I have caused them."

"I feel they have repaid you for that with everything they have done to you recently. You have nothing to feel guilty about." The thought disgusted me.

She barely looked up and whispered softly, "Jocelyn, I have not only shamed my own family but yours as well. I got pregnant out of wedlock. How can you say that?"

"I understand what happened better than you think I do."

"You and Jackson would never, have never." she interjected.

"No. Not yet, but I am very aware of and have felt that passion. I know how difficult it is to stop."

"You did stop. I did not."

Her objection had merit, but not as much as she claimed.

"True, but only out of fear, not a lack of desire."

We sat next to the fire together while she knitted, and I completed my schoolwork. We chatted about our friends and people from school. It felt almost as if things between us were on the mend. Yet I realized that our lives would never be the same again.

Too much had occurred for us to return to our former selves, but hopefully, the events of the last several weeks would make us stronger, closer.

I snuggled down into my bed as Mimi closed the door behind her. The fire was dancing lively, filling my room with warmth and a soft hue. I stared at the little, blue box that was still resting on my mantle.

In my head I could not easily dismiss those female voices and the imagines I had seen. For some unexplainable reason, they felt as real to me as the quilt covering my body. I loved his gift, but there was no way I was going to touch that thing again. I rolled over on my side and hugged a pillow tightly feeling alone and confused.

CHAPTER 23

Monday, October 26, 2015

AFTER AN HOUR-LONG ARGUMENT with my mother, she finally relented and went to work. She wanted to take the day off work and stay home with me in case I needed anything, which meant she would be hovering over me all day and driving me crazy. I finally agreed to call Emily and asked her if it was okay if I could call her if I needed anything. Of course, she politely agreed and told me to tell my mother she would be more than happy to look in on me.

I made myself comfortable in the family room with a fuzzy blanket, pillow, hot chocolate and the remote. I searched through the channels until I finally came across some re-run episodes of *Supernatural*.

Around nine, there was a knock on the sun porch door, and before I could even get up, someone walked into the kitchen.

"Jocelyn? It is me." Emily's voice rang out. "Do not get up, darling." She walked into the family room all bright and cheery. It was easy to see where Jackson had gotten his disposition. "How are you feeling today?"

I rolled over to look at her. "Good. And you?"

"Wonderful."

"You look nice today?" Emily was wearing khaki slacks with a mauve-colored shirt and a long, pink cardigan that hung just below her knees. Even her boots were stylish. I only hoped that I could look so amazing when I had three grown children of my own.

"Oh, thank you." She sat down in the chair nearest to the sofa. "How is your head feeling?"

I gave her a small laugh, which broadened her smile.

"Only hurts a little when I smile or move or talk."

"It will get better. Are you going back to school tomorrow?"

"Wednesday. Jackson is bringing me my homework."

"Good. I know you do not want to fall behind."

"No, but I also don't want to go looking or feeling like this either."

She nodded. "Understandable."

"So how do you like living in Chicago?" I thought that perhaps this was the perfect opportunity to get to know her and her family a little better, and I was dying to learn more about Jackson.

"I am adjusting," she stated in a soft voice.

"It must be hard."

I honestly hadn't considered before how difficult this move must be on her. She didn't work outside the home, so she really didn't have the opportunity to meet anyone or make new friends. Of course, that's why she's become so close with our moms, I thought. She's probably so lonely from leaving her home and her other children and family in Boston.

"It is. I really miss Boston a lot. I am hoping that Alex and Phoebe will be home for Thanksgiving with their spouses and my grandkids."

"I didn't know you had grandkids."

"Yes, three of them. Alex and his wife Leslie have two, Lucinda and Charlie; and Phoebe and Carson just had a little boy, Wallace." She smiled, "Wally. He is almost a year old, and I hate that I am missing it." Her eyes suddenly looked so sad.

"I'm sorry."

"It is all right. It was important to our family to move here, and I cannot let my own selfishness in wanting to be an overbearing grandparent take away from what is best for the family."

"You're a very strong woman, Emily. I'm not sure I could be so graceful."

"Of course, you could, Jocelyn. When it comes to your husband, there is nothing in the world you would deny him of, especially his dreams of providing a better world for your family."

"True." I knew I would do the same too.

"Is there anything I can get for you? Are you hungry? Thirsty?"

"No, thank you. I'm fine."

"Well, if you do not mind, can I keep you company at least until lunch? I hate to admit it, but I do get rather bored and lonely in that big house all day."

I wasn't sure if she was bored or just being a mother and making sure I was okay. Either way, I was more than happy to have some company myself. Besides, Emily wasn't like everyone else's mom.

"Of course, I'd love some company. Would you like some hot chocolate? I just made some, whip cream and everything." I grinned at her.

"Sounds wonderful. You fix the hot chocolate, and I will build a fire. It is a little chilly in here."

"Great." I got up and headed into the kitchen while Emily started a fire in the family room.

In no time at all, the room had warmed up to a very comfortable temperature, and she and I were truly enjoying the company of one another. I questioned her extensively about Jackson's childhood in Boston, his likes and dislikes, his siblings, anything else I could think of.

Emily proved to be a knowledgeable informant. I couldn't imagine my parents knowing so much information about me.

We spent the afternoon looking through old photo albums from my childhood, which she seemed to enjoy. She even ran home for a moment and brought back a photo album stuffed full of memories of Jackson's younger days. I loved looking at pictures of his life in Boston. There were photos of his early days in football, his first steps — a whole lifetime of firsts that Emily had carefully documented in loving detail.

I finally drifted off around three or so and woke after six to the most delicious aroma coming from our kitchen. Confused, I got up to investigate, since I knew it couldn't be my mother in there. Her idea of cooking dinner was something frozen she could bake in the oven for fifty minutes and serve with rolls from a bag and a pre-made salad.

Sure enough, when I walked into the kitchen, Emily was in there with Jackson and Ethan, cooking a homemade meal.

"Wow, it smells incredible in here." I leaned against the doorway.

"Thank you. I hope your mother does not mind. I sent the boys to the store a little while ago to get some fresh vegetables and a few other things since your mother called earlier and said she would be stuck at the office for a while longer." Emily was dicing carrots and cucumbers on a chopping block that I didn't even know we owned.

"Are you kidding? She'll be thrilled. She never cooks," I told her.

"Yeah. That's what I told her." Ethan laughed. "If it doesn't come frozen or in a bag, Mom can't fix it."

"True." I agreed.

"Do you know how to cook, Jocelyn?" Emily glanced up at me.

"A little bit. More than Mom, but not much," I confessed, embarrassed by my lack of knowledge.

"Every woman should know how to cook." She continued chopping. "Would you like to learn?" She glanced up at me.

"Yes. I'd love too."

I was impressed with how well Jackson functioned in the kitchen. He looked so knowledgeable and perfectly at ease with everything he was doing. Jackson's family had such an admirable dynamic that I was truly jealous of them. Their behavior was something that I had only read about in old novels.

Ethan gave me a sneer from the stove where he was still absentmindedly stirring something. I childishly stuck my tongue out at him in return.

"So, did you enjoy your day off, faker?" Ethan mock fainted with his hand on his forehead and falling to the floor.

"Get up, you idiot."

Ethan laughed and jumped back up on his feet but promptly threw an oven mitt, hitting me on the shoulder.

"Jerk." I smirked and took off after Ethan.

He ran around the corner, into the dining room, and through the living room across the foyer to the family room. I doubled back to catch him but in doing so, I collided full force with Jackson in the family room.

Darkness hit me first before nausea or light-headedness ever had a chance to appear. I hit the floor immediately with voices ringing loudly in my ears. I was no longer on the living room floor but could see my bedroom around me. The only distinguishing features about the place that made me positive it was my room was my fireplace and bay window. There were lilies and violets in vases on the mantel. It appeared the same as before when I had seen the large, black lady dressed in old-fashioned clothes. I was positive about it. I scanned around, trying to take in every detail.

But then she appeared again, the same large, black woman in an old, simple dress with an apron on. She smiled warmly at me as she approached. "Miss Jocelyn, ya'r ma's requestin' ya'r presence 'n da parlor."

I heard my voice respond, "Thank you, Mimi." I handed her a large sun hat. "Please tell Sarah thank you and that the picnic lunch she packed was delightful."

I could hear my own voice. I knew it was my voice. But the language was much too proper, foreign really to my own ears. *And this woman, where did she come from?* I still could not figure out who she was. A nanny, maybe. She held a kind and gentle face and spoke to me with love. I could feel my admiration and love for this woman, but I didn't know why.

I quickly looked around my bedroom again as I saw myself walking out the door; then the images began to become more difficult to see. I felt the urge to stay there, that this was a place where I belonged. I felt like here, in this place, I was truly happy and content with life. But it drifted away from my grasp as the dim light from the family room tried to bring me back to another place and time.

I could now feel the heat from the roaring fire and smell the fragrance from the kitchen.

Emily and Ethan were hovering over me, rubbing my face as Jackson handed a washcloth to his mother.

"Jocelyn, honey. Are you alright?" Emily's face looked frightened.

I tried to sit up, but they both held me back. "I just got the wind knocked out of me."

"You fainted again." Ethan gave me a nasty look. "You shouldn't have even been up. And now I'm going to be in trouble."

"This was not your fault because I didn't faint." I gave him a weak smile. "And don't any of you go and tell mom I did. Understand?"

I looked between the three faces, pleading for their understanding. My head still felt in a fog from what I had just witnessed, but in a strange way, it was also starting to become familiar. The only good thing was that at least this time it happened so fast I didn't have to experience the leading symptoms before blacking out. That part always drained the life out of me. This time it wasn't nearly as traumatic.

"Jocelyn, I understand what you are saying, but perhaps it would not be wise to keep this from your parents," Emily implored.

"My test results came back normal. There is nothing wrong with me. Please, don't say anything. It will only cause me more problems," I begged.

"If that is what you want, I will say nothing. But just for the sake of argument I will come over tomorrow and stay with you just to be on the safe side. All right?" Emily eyes were soft and full of concern.

"Deal." I gave her a thankful look. "Now help me up."

I held my hand out to Ethan, and he pulled me back up. I was still a little queasy, so I went over and crawled back under my blanket on the couch.

Emily and Jackson finished dinner while Ethan watched ESPN. I hated being confined to one place but wasn't sure I was up to running around either. I propped myself up and started in on the piles of homework that Jackson had brought me. I had mostly reading to do, but there were some assignments to complete for my calculus and biology classes.

It wasn't long before my father came home and was completely amazed that someone had used the kitchen for actual cooking. I don't think I'd ever seen him so happy coming home before. Normally, he was in a moderate-to-grumpy mood, and all of us knew to give him a good hour to unwind before approaching him with anything.

He happily snooped around the kitchen to see what she was making. "This is wonderful. Emily, you didn't have to do all this."

"I wanted to help. Amy called earlier and stated that she would be working late, so I thought it would be nice if she did not have to fix dinner when she returned home."

"Well, I really appreciate this. Where did you get all the ingredients? Your house?" My father laughed. "Because I know we don't have these things here." He walked over to the oven and peeked inside.

"I sent the boys to the store when they got home."

"Ethan in a grocery store? That must have been an experience. I can't let you pay for our groceries, Emily. What do I owe you?" Dad pulled out his wallet.

"Do not be silly, Shane. Friends help one another. Please, do not worry about it."

I wasn't sure, but it was almost like Emily was offended by my father's offer to repay her.

"Then won't you and your family join us for dinner? You made so much we couldn't possibly eat all this by ourselves."

"That would be nice. We would love too." She smiled gently.

"Wonderful. Is there anything I can do to help?"

My ears perked up at his words. *What's this? My father offering to help in the kitchen? The man can't boil water!*

"Nothing Shane, everything is under control. Just make yourself comfortable. Dinner should be done in about thirty minutes."

"Okay, then I'll just go change." My dad scanned the kitchen over once more, totally impressed.

The house was quiet for a short time. The only sounds were of Jackson setting the table in the dining room and Emily making the final preparations. It was strange to think how differently their household must function in comparison to ours.

Robert rang the doorbell around seven. He was wearing navy slacks and a collared shirt, but evidentially had taken his tie and jacket off before coming over.

"I got your note. How was your day?" He leaned over and kissed his wife.

She looked lovingly at her husband. "Wonderful, and yours?"

"Not bad. Busy. Still trying to get everything sorted out in the new office, but it will be fine." He gave her another kiss and squeezed her shoulders. "What would you like me to do?"

"Everything is done, darling. I only need to fill the drinks."

"I will take care of that."

My mom walked in the door a few minutes after Robert had finished getting the drinks on the table. She looked exhausted. She must have had a long day at the office. She spoke briefly with Emily in the kitchen before retreating upstairs to find my dad.

Emily had made lasagna, a spinach salad, and homemade garlic cheese bread. It was better than any restaurant food I had ever tasted. I was amazed that this had been created in our kitchen. Apparently, Emily had her own herb garden where she grew all her own spices and herbs.

This impressed my dad as they chatted about different recipes that Emily enjoyed making. My mom was pleasant enough, but mostly silent throughout the meal. However, with all the chatter from the rest of us, it didn't seem anyone noticed.

The Chandler's left after nine. My mom repeatedly thanked Emily for her help and offered to return the favor, which Ethan and I found extremely humorous.

I had a hard time relaxing as I settled under my covers. I couldn't seem to get Jackson out of my thoughts. Even though we'd spend the entire evening together, I'd never gotten the chance to talk with him alone. I crawled out of bed and wandered over to the bay window, staring at the house across the street from mine. I wanted to believe he was across the street, looking back at me.

CHAPTER 24

Wednesday, October 30, 1878

"HELLO, DARLING. HOW WAS YOUR day?" Jackson welcomed me home with a smile.

"Wonderful now that you are here."

I wrapped my arms around him as he kissed me gently on my forehead. "I was hoping you would come home with William today."

"How could I resist the chance to see my girl?" His arms felt so warm and strong around me.

I handed my schoolbooks, caplet, and bonnet to Missy and walked into the parlor with Jackson. We took a seat on the lounge next to the roaring fire in the hearth. The heat felt incredible after being in the bitter, cold rain. My body shuttered a bit, causing Jackson to pull me closer to him.

"How were your classes today?"

"Dull. It seems strange not having Olivia there with me."

"But now you get to spend time with her every evening."

"True, but what I find amazing is that no one ever speaks of her. Our friends are still under the impression that she is ill, yet no one has inquired about her."

"I believe they probably already know the truth and are too polite to say anything in front of you." He winked.

"How would they know? I have not spoken to anyone about her, not even Elizabeth."

"Northern Chicago is not that big, Jocelyn. I am sure there has been a lot of speculation, but no one is positive of the truth."

"People love to gossip." I shook my head. "It is sad that their lives are so boring that they find it necessary to speak of other people behind their backs."

Jackson shrugged his shoulders casually. "True. I would just continue going about your everyday routine like nothing has changed. Let them gossip. Does it really matter?"

"It is cruel," I stated sadly.

"Did you hear that the Adams' are moving?"

"My father said that Mr. Adams refused to say where his family is relocating and that they will be leaving before this weekend. I guess the house is already sold."

"To whom?"

"I have no idea."

"Did he sell the bank?"

"Yes."

"That was quick." This was purely not accidental. It was well planned since the news came out.

"I know. It makes me think that he must have been looking for a buyer for both the house and the bank since they discovered Olivia and William's secret. I do not believe they had any intentions of staying here."

I wondered if Olivia had known all along.

"I feel bad for Olivia. It would be so hard to have such cold and cruel parents." I looked off into the fire. "I always thought that Mrs. Adams was not the nicest or warmest of mothers, but Mr. Adams always seemed to love his daughter."

"I am sure he does. But this is none of our business, and I would not mention any of this to Olivia. She has been through enough already."

"Yes, I agree."

Jackson joined my family for dinner. The three men discussed business and politics, as usual, while Mother and Olivia talked over various baby names. I listened absentmindedly to both conversations but found myself utterly bored. I stirred the food around my plate as my mind drifted back to the pocket watch sitting alone upstairs. Curiosity was beginning to get the best of me.

A part of me wanted to go upstairs and hold it in my hand just to see what would happen. *Will the images return? Will I see the same girls, the iron cages?*

"What do you think, Jocelyn?" Olivia interrupted my thoughts.

"Sorry. What did you say?" I stumbled, trying to refocus my attention.

"What do you think about the name Ava for a girl?"

"Ava is a lovely name." I agreed.

"I think so too." She smiled proudly.

"What about a boy?"

"William Arthur, after his father."

"Perfect." I smiled over at her, trying to get excited also.

"Yes. I believe so," Mother replied.

The two of them continued with their conversation while I returned to my own thoughts for the rest of the meal.

The six of us retired for about an hour into the parlor and chatted about the upcoming house hunt for Jackson and me, along with the fall festival on Saturday. It seemed that Olivia living in our home for the last several days had softened my parents a great deal. Neither of them no longer had any objections to Olivia and William attending the festival together.

I was thrilled that the two of them would be joining in on the festivities with us. It would not have seemed the same if they were not there. It was strange to think that only last year Jackson and I had attended the festival with Olivia and Sean. The two of them were so happy that day as the four of us rode on the hayride together in the early evening before we got the life scared out of us in the haunted maze.

I glanced over at Olivia and wondered how often she thought about that day. I wondered if being there this year with William beside her would bring back painful memories of happier times she had with Sean. For her sake, I hoped not. *But how could it not?*

Alone in my room after Jackson returned to his house for the night, I walked over and stood in front of the hearth. There it sat, the little, dark-blue box with the silver metal gleaming up at me from the gentle glow of the embers. I slowly reached my hand forward and picked it up.

It felt cool in my fingers despite the heat from the fire. I closed my fingers around it tightly as the room began spinning again like before. I dropped on my knees on the rug in front of the fire and everything went dark.

I was running up the steps of my house with another girl who seemed to be about the same age. She had light brown hair that was pulled up in a blue ribbon hanging loosely down her back. She was wearing a light-yellow dress covered with little, blue flowers. The dress was tied around her shoulders with thin straps, leaving her shoulders completely bare.

I looked down and noticed that I was wearing something somewhat similar except mine was pink and I had a white, short sleeved shirt on made of a strange soft fabric. Neither of us had on any shoes. From the look of us, I thought we must be around six, maybe seven years old.

We were both laughing and holding hands as we ran into the house and out the backyard without pausing. There were all these strange things about the yard that I had never seen before, and the carriage house was gone.

I followed her over to this large wooden structure and sat down on this weird-shaped swing made of a substance I had never felt before that hung to this long wooden beam by chains. I watched this girl laughing and imitated her behavior, swinging back and forth. It felt amazing, so freeing.

My feet rose off the ground higher and higher. I could feel the heat of the sun on my face. My body shook with laughter. Then I heard someone calling my name from a distance. I squinted my eyes towards the back of the house.

There was a woman standing by the back door whom I knew was my mother, yet it was not Annabelle. This woman was very strangely dressed in short pants that showed her legs and a top that was extremely inappropriate. Her blonde hair hung loosely over her shoulders as she smiled brightly in our direction.

"Jocelyn! Jenna! Lunch is ready," the woman hollered at us.

The little girl next to me smiled and sang out, "Come on. Let's eat." She rose into the air and let go of the chains that bound her and soared into the air.

I watched her in horror as she flew and landed safely on her feet. She turned, smiling brightly at me.

"Come on, Jocelyn! I'm starving! Jump!"

I could feel the terror building in my chest as I clung tighter to the chains.

"Jump!" She hollered again with laughter.

I closed my eyes and followed in the same fashion that I had just seen her do. I could feel the air beneath me as I let go. It was the most liberating feeling I had ever experienced. I suddenly felt the soft grass under my feet as I touched the ground. However, I stumbled backward and fell on my rear. The girl laughed loudly at me and held out her hand. Her face began to blur from my sight, leaving me in the dark.

I could feel the rug beneath me, but I dared not open my eyes. I did not want to lose the feeling I had just experienced. It felt so real. I was *there*. I could feel everything, smell everything — the soft grass beneath my feet, the wind in my hair, and the sun upon my face.

I desperately clung to the feeling of letting go of the chains and flying. Nothing in my life had ever made me feel that way. I wanted it back.

Reluctantly, I opened my eyes to the room around me. The open yard and sunshine were gone. The little girl who was smiling beside me left me feeling happy and warm.

Strangely, she somewhat resembled a younger version of one of the girls I had seen in my previous episode. Her name was Jenna. That was what the woman had called her.

I climbed to my feet, leaving the pocket watch on the hearth rug. I stared at it for a few minutes, wondering how long I had blacked out for. Slowly, I crawled into my bed, pulling the covers up to my chin.

My room looked the same as it always had. I closed my eyes again, recalling everything I had just witnessed. The house from my vision, I was positive, was my house but it was strangely different. I tried desperately to retrace the events from the first moment I was running up the steps into the house.

I wanted to see every detail of the inside of the house, but I could not make the objects out clearly. I knew they were strange and different. Nothing appeared familiar, but the girl I was *there* felt it was all so normal. I was so confused.

The colors of the rooms were all different, as were the furniture and pictures. I could not, however, remember any details of the kitchen, even though I had run through it to the back door.

Frustrated and exhausted, I rolled over and wrapped my arms around an extra pillow. My body felt numb while my emotions were all over the place. Part of me felt oddly content and comforted while another was exhilarated.

I could not understand it. I did not know if the elaborate gift was possessed or evil or held some type of magic power. It was not normal. That much, I was positive. The back of my brain was screaming at me to get rid of it, but the rest of me desired the power that it held to take me to a world that was so completely unlike mine.

I knew I could never speak of it to anyone and honestly, I did not want to. It was a powerful secret and an amazing escape into something unknown that I was so incredibly curious about.

Chapter 25

Wednesday, October 28, 2015

WALKING DOWN THE HALLS before class was more intimating than ever. Even with Jackson walking near me and Jenna beside me, all eyes were focused on me. Every head turned and stared, noticing the yellowing, green tinge that crept across my face and the hideous stitches that still lingered.

I felt more self-conscious this morning than I believed I ever had in my entire life. I hated the way everyone stared, despite Jenna and Jackson's constant reassurances that I looked great. I knew the two of them were just being kind.

Jenna was sweet enough to come over early and help me with my makeup to cover the bruising. I knew she did her best, and it looked much better than anything I had done but I hated the staring.

I sat across the aisle from Jackson in Biology class, and he carefully slipped me notes throughout the hour, inquiring about how I was feeling and how my day was going. He made sure his hands went nowhere near me, as we both tried to be inconspicuous. It was sweet how concerned he was with my feelings and how people were reacting to me. He had come very protective in a romantic sense.

We sat across from one another in lunch because the chairs were too close together for us to sit next to one another. Our friends were gathered around, acting silly and behaving more like elementary school children than young adults.

It was refreshing that things had gotten back to normal except for the constant stares I was still receiving across the lunchroom from Taylor. She would look at me then whisper to Dakota, and the two of them would start laughing. I had to fight the urge not to punch her in the face.

As we walked out of the cafeteria, Hilary leaned in close to me. "Who the hell does she think she is?"

"I think we need to have a talk with her." Jenna leaned in on the other side of me.

Jackson stayed behind, doing his best not to get too close at school, afraid of what the repercussions might be.

"I agree." Hilary was clearly angry. "There are a few things I'd like to get straight with her."

"Guys, let it go." I stopped in front of my locker and turned to face the girls. "She's the least of my concerns." I turned the combination on my lock. "Jackson is mine; and she's just going to have to accept that fact or I'll just have to make it clear to her in a way that her tiny, little brain can understand it." I started switching out my books, trying to calm down. I was so incredibly sick of that girl and her arrogant friends, thinking they owned this place.

"I like this new you," Jenna said.

"And if you need someone to help you make that little wench understand, you know I'd be more than happy to help," Caitlyn offered.

"Thanks. I might just take you up on that. Do any of you know if she's coming to the party on Saturday?" I shut my locker.

"Of course. I heard she's wearing a Playboy bunny outfit. She stated very loudly in first period that once Jackson sees her in it, there's no way he's going to give you a second look," Hilary informed me. "I could probably get Cody to tell her that she and Dakota aren't invited, but that runs into the whole team thing with Trey; and there's already enough tension between Trey and Zak."

"True." I agreed.

"Well, I wouldn't worry about it. I have a feeling that things are about to change in a big way." Jenna bumped up against me, laughing. "Now, we better get to class. I can't afford another detention. Coach Smith was pissed the last time I got one and missed practice."

I hated watching everyone get ready for the match when I wasn't allowed to participate. My parents had agreed to allow me to sit with the team and attend practices this week, but I couldn't play. I had never missed a match in all four years or the two I'd played in junior high.

I watched from the bench as my team hit the court. Sitting next to Coach Smith, I finally understood how frustrating her job truly was. I hated the fact that I had absolutely no control over what was going on out there on the court. It was such a helpless feeling.

I glanced up into the stands and saw Jackson sitting with my brother, Cody, and Zak. I wish I could be up there sitting beside him, but I had told him in our psychology class earlier that I didn't think it was such a good idea. I knew we couldn't sit close to each other like everyone else, and I didn't want it to look strange that we weren't. Knowing how quickly gossip spread around our school, people were bound to speculate that there was trouble in paradise.

For the first time this season, our team lost, and Coach Smith was clearly upset. As soon as the final whistle blew, she placed her hand on my knee and whispered in my ear, "You'd better get well soon. We need you back on the court."

She patted my knee before rising to gather the team and head into the locker room. I remained on the bench as the girls walked past me. I stayed silent, not knowing what to say to my teammates. Both Jenna and Caitlyn looked angry enough to hurt someone, and Hilary's face looked like she was about to cry.

Jackson and I settled down on my front porch swing under the cover of darkness. The air had gotten cold, and the temperature was now idling in the mid-fifties. The smell of autumn was thick in the air. I could smell the fireplace burning inside the house and thought how nice it would be to be sitting in front of it, but my father was lingering about in the family room, making that idea impossible.

There was a good two feet of space between Jackson and me that felt more like a brick wall. I was feeling a bit sick to my stomach but was now getting used to it.

"I am sorry about the match tonight." Jackson was looking down at his hands.

"Yeah. Me too." I turned slightly in the swing to face him.

He glanced up and gave me a weak smile.

"What happened at lunch today? Why did you get up and leave?"

"I was tired of the looks from Taylor. She kept glaring at me, and I didn't want to get up and confront her or, worse, for Caitlyn to, so I left instead."

Jackson chuckled.

"What?"

"Taylor is nonexistent to me. I promise. You have nothing to worry about with her or any other girl, for that matter." He started to place his hand on mine but quickly placed it back into his own lap. "You should know that by now."

"I do. I just hate the way she's always staring at you. Then she looks at me with that glare and whispers to Dakota, and they both start laughing. It pisses me off."

Jackson let out a louder laugh this time.

"You are so silly, Jocelyn. She is only trying to get a rise out of you because she knows it bothers you. Do not let her get to you. You are a much better person than she is."

"True." I smiled and playfully flipped my hair over my shoulder.

"And you are so beautiful, Jocelyn. I could stare at you for hours."

I could feel the blush rising to my cheeks. "Ditto."

"Are you getting excited about this weekend? You know my mother is almost done with the costumes, and they look great. She really out did herself."

"I imagine. She asked me yesterday if I could come over tomorrow evening for a fitting."

"She is very talented with sewing."

"Your mother is very talented in many ways."

"Thank you. I believe so." I could hear pride in his voice.

"Why do you think that you have this effect on me when no one else ever has?" I was curious if he would be brutally honest with me, although I doubted it.

"I am not sure." Jackson turned sideways to face me, leaning his arm on the back of the swing; "But I have a few theories."

"Such as?"

"I do not want to say. You will laugh." His eyes sparkled, making me feel weak.

"I promise I won't."

Just then, my father poked his head out the front door, flipping on the porch light.

"Jocelyn, it's nine-thirty. Time to come in. You have school tomorrow and it's too cold for you guys to be outside." He hung out the screen door.

"Okay, Dad." *Damn it, what timing!*

"Say good night to Jackson."

"Okay, Dad!" I looked at him, pleading for more time, but he paid no attention to my stare.

"Now." His voice got a little stronger.

"All right." I turned my attention back to Jackson. "Guess I'd better get inside."

Jackson and I both stood up and hesitated.

"Good night, Jocelyn. I'll see you in the morning," My Dad said in a teasing voice as Jackson made his way over to the porch steps.

I walked to the door, giving my dad a playful, scorned look.

"I will pick you up in the morning. Sweet dreams." Jackson waved as he descended the steps.

"Thanks, Dad. Could you have been a little more discrete?" I gave him a playful nudge as I passed through the door.

"No." He smiled back.

"Well, try!" I hollered over my shoulder as I climbed up the stairs.

Lying in bed staring up at the ceiling, unable to calm my thoughts, I couldn't help but be immensely curious about Jackson's theories. I wanted desperately to call him, but I didn't want to seem anxious. I closed my eyes, knowing that I would have to wait until tomorrow evening, when hopefully, we'd be able to sneak some time alone to talk before I could possibly get any answers from him. Frustrated, I rolled over and flipped on some music to clear my head.

CHAPTER 26

Friday, November 1, 1878

CLASSES TODAY AND YESTERDAY were canceled for what our school called fall recess. It allowed all the children to celebrate Halloween last night and recover from their antics and overdose of sugar today. For us who were now past that stage, it was a nice reprieve from having to get up so early for classes.

I lounged under the covers, watching the sun break through my curtains and paint my room with bright colors. I peeked over at the mantle, and the watch was leering at me from its box as if it was waiting for me. Eddie must have returned it when he stoked the fire sometime throughout the night.

I wondered if I had enough time to see if the magic was still there before Mimi came in to check on me. I seriously doubted it. I knew she would be here shortly and if she found me lying on the floor, blacked out, she would most certainly panic, causing an uproar in the house, thereby ruining my entire weekend. I could not risk exposure of what Jackson's gift was doing to me. I did not understand it myself.

Jackson and I traveled about the area of northern Chicago yesterday, looking at various homes. There were a few that we liked but none of them screamed "home" to me. In each of them, I tried to imagine what it would be like to live there with Jackson and build a home. I imagined the look of the furniture I wanted, how I would arrange it, everything. The biggest trouble we were having was in finding a home that was close to our families that would not feel so foreign.

Jackson wanted to go out again today in search. I was having difficulty imagining myself living somewhere other than this house that I had spent my entire life in. I felt safe and secure here.

I slowly climbed out of bed before Mimi came in to greet me. I wrapped my robe around me and approached the fireplace. Eddie had kept it blazing throughout the night, as he always did once the weather turned cold. I wanted so badly to reach my hand out and just pick up the silly ol' watch. Half my brain was screaming at me not to, with the other inquisitive side was intrigued by everything it had to show me. Curiosity of the power this trinket held captured my soul. I turned my head towards the door at the sound of footsteps and quickly hurried out of the room.

William and my parents were already finishing breakfast when I arrived downstairs. The room was bright and cheery in the early morning sun. I sat down in my usual chair as Sarah brought in my eggs, bacon, toast, and juice. She poured me a steaming cup of coffee from the corner kettle. There was nothing comparable to the smell of bacon and coffee in the morning to make you feel at home.

"Good morning," I announced, and I took a sip of my coffee. The heat immediately flowed through my body.

"Good morning, darling. Are you and Jackson going house-hunting again today?" My father inquired.

"Yes."

"You do not sound so excited. Are you feeling well?" my mother inquired between sips of her own coffee.

"I feel fine. Just disappointed in the prospects we have seen thus far," I assured her.

"I am sure you will find something to your liking. It takes some time. It is a good thing that you both decided to start looking early," my father said without looking up from his morning paper.

"Yes. I suppose it is," I replied, knowing full well that he was no longer listening to me. "Where is Olivia this morning?" I glanced over at William, who was still lingering on a piece of bacon while also reading the paper.

"Upstairs, still asleep." He also did not bother to look up from his paper.

"Is she feeling all right?"

"Sure, I guess so," he responded, still engrossed in the morning news.

"We need to talk about what alterations you would like to make on your dress now since Jackson has seen it. We will need to completely change the look of it." Mother paid no mind to the men, as usual.

"Whatever you feel is necessary, Mother." I did not have the heart to tell her about Emily's gown. I knew there was no possible way that I could ever wear my mother's dress but still, I was unsure how she would react.

I placed my napkin back up on the table. I had barely touched my breakfast but really was not hungry anyway. "Please excuse me. I need to get ready before Jackson arrives."

Jackson and I spent the better part of the day wandering around, looking at various properties. There was so much construction going on; and newer, more modern homes were going up everywhere. They were beautiful but not exactly what I wanted. Honestly, I was not entirely sure what I wanted but I knew it was not any of the homes I had seen thus far.

Jackson noticed that my attention was elsewhere when we climbed back into the carriage shortly before four o'clock. I felt drained and could not focus my attention on anything but that pocket watch in my room. I felt almost possessed by it.

"Sweetheart, are you alright? You do not seem very excited about any of the homes we have looked at today." He took my hand in his ever so gentle way. His emerald eyes were full of concern, but I knew there was no way possible for me to confide in him about this.

"I feel fine, darling. I am excited about house-hunting, but my mind is just elsewhere." I cuddled up closer to him on the carriage seat.

"Olivia said you have been acting preoccupied for the last several days."

I pulled my caplet closer around me, acting innocent. "Really? I guess I have been."

"Are you worried about the dress?"

I looked at him, confused. "The dress?"

"Your wedding gown. I know you let Olivia wear yours last Sunday, and now you do not have a dress for our ceremony."

Oh. That dress. Of course. I offered him the best smile I could. "Yes, I am worried about the dress." It was the perfect excuse for my behavior. I only wish I had thought of it first.

Jackson started the horses off down the pathway with a look of confusion on his face. "I do not believe that is it at all." He shifted a little more towards me. "What is bothering you, Jocelyn?"

"Nothing. Honest. A lot has happened in the last couple weeks, and I am just enjoying the calm now."

"Would you tell me if something was on your mind?" His inquisitive expression bothered me.

"Yes. Why would I not?"

"Not sure. Did you like your birthday gift? I noticed you never carry it with you."

That is something I could never do.

"I love it. I do not carry it because I do not want anything to happen to it. It is so lovely."

"I see." Jackson turned his eyes back to the front.

We rode in silence for several minutes. There was still a slight chill in the air, but the warm sun on our faces helped a great deal. Jackson's derby hat was pulled down enough that I could barely see his eyes.

"Do you ever wonder what the world will be like in another hundred years?" His question came out of nowhere and blindsided me.

"Not really. I mean, sure, it has crossed my mind before; but I have never put much thought into it." *What an odd question.*

"I have. I believe it will be totally different than the way we live now." He held his eyes forward, making it impossible for me to read his expression.

"How so?" *Where is he going with this?*

"Well, I believe that there will be a lot more machinery to make life easier; and I am sure there will be larger cities, but the world will somehow seem smaller," he said casually.

"What do you mean by that? The world is not going to change sizes in the future." His statement made no sense.

"I do not mean literally, of course." He laughed. "I mean that advances in communication and traveling between countries will be easier, and that will make the world seem smaller."

"I highly doubt that. It takes forever to travel to Europe. Even mailing a letter across the country can take weeks." I challenged his ridiculous theory.

"Well, who knows? It is fun to think about, though."

I could not help but question his intentions for such an off topic of conversation, especially after the scenes I had witnessed in the blackout.

"Why is that?"

"Because it is. Look how much things have changed since the war ended. We now have the transcontinental railroad that extends from coast to coast. We even have a phonograph that plays music when you want and a telephone to talk to people in a different location. That is amazing. Do you not agree?" His face held a cocky expression that made me uncomfortable.

"Of course, but those things were bound to happen if only to make it easier to communicate and, yes, to make life easier and more enjoyable. But I do not see any huge changes anytime soon."

My statement made him burst out laughing like I was being absurd.

"What?"

"Nothing. I am sorry. I did not mean to laugh. But do you not think that every day something new is being discovered? New advances are coming about every minute that will change the world forever as we know it."

"I suppose so. I guess I have never really given it much thought."

"Well, I am speculating, of course. However, I do believe that progress is leaping forward, and the world within the next hundred years will resemble nothing of life as we know it." Jackson kept smiling as if he was truly enjoying this topic.

"I suppose next you are going to speculate that these women suffragettes will get their way and someday women will be allowed to vote and even have control over their own lives." I laughed aloud. "And even blacks will be able to vote without all these clauses and restrictions, go to school with whites, and have equal rights and protection under the law."

Jackson gave me the oddest look. "Sure. Why is that so absurd to you?"

"Because most men believe that a woman's place is in the home. Most women who do not have the financial means do not even know how to read. Men are not going to let them vote when they cannot even read. And as far as the other, well, from what I have overheard the gentlemen in our families say, the tension in the South has gotten incredibly high; and the whites down there are treating the blacks worse than they did when they were slaves." I had heard both our fathers' remark numerous times over the years about how bad things had gotten in the South since the end of the war.

"I know. I have had that conversation with them several times myself. But if we are speculating on things a hundred years from now, it is promising to think that the quality of life can improve for both women and blacks."

I had never thought of Jackson as much of a dreamer before, but his words struck me as if he was wishing for something that was never going to happen, at least not in our lifetime.

The evening edged on slowly. It felt like the hours could not pass quickly enough before I could retreat upstairs to my room. I pushed house hunting and odd conversation with Jackson out of my mind. I could not even concentrate on the conversation going on around me as my family was gathered around the hearth. Robert and Emily had joined us for dinner to discuss the various homes that we had looked at today.

I excused myself before eight o'clock, stating that my headache was getting worse, and I wanted to get a good night's sleep before our long day tomorrow at the festival. Jackson rose and followed me to the foot of the stairs.

"Sorry you are not feeling well." He wrapped his arms around me, pulling our bodies close together.

"I am sure it will pass by morning," I assured him before he kissed my forehead and rested his cheek upon my head.

"I love you, Jocelyn, more than you realize." His words were so incredibly soft and warm.

I felt the strongest passion to be with him. I lifted my face to his and pressed my lips over his. The heat that shot through my body was so intense I did not want to stop. I wanted more. My arms pulled his body tighter to mine as I felt his grip tighten. Our thirst for one another was unquenchable.

Finally, Jackson pulled himself away, breathless. "We must stop." His breathing was labored.

"I know. I am sorry." I blushed.

"Not me." A smile crept across his full lips. "I love that you want me as much as I want you."

"I do. I cannot help it." My blush deepened.

"You had best get upstairs before I am too tempted and drag you across the street to my empty house." He kissed me deeply again, flaring up the intense passion between us before he withdrew again. He held my quivering body tightly against his.

"All right. I do not want to wait any longer," I whispered breathlessly in his ear.

"Jocelyn, we must. You know we cannot." His mouth formed words, but his body and eyes said differently.

"We will be married in a few weeks." I purposely tempted him.

"Seven weeks," he corrected with a more mature tone.

"I do not care," I whispered, pulling him closer to me.

"Yes, you do. We do not want to find ourselves in a compromised situation like others have recently." He nodded his head towards the parlor, where William and Olivia were talking with both our parents.

We held each other for several minutes. Neither of us wanted to let go.

"Good night, my love." I reluctantly pulled myself away from his grasp. I ascended the stairs holding his hand as long as I could.

"Sweet dreams. I will see you in the morning."

I waited impatiently for Mimi to finish bustling around my room. It was obvious she was tired and worn out from the long day. I was trying to be understanding and polite, but I wanted her to hurry and leave so I could go to the watch. She tucked me in and turned down the oil lamps, closing the door behind her.

I jumped out of bed as quietly as I could and hurried over to the mantle. I paused long enough to make sure there were no sounds anywhere near my door. I picked up the opened blue box. I slowly lifted the trinket, wrapping my fingers tightly around it. The room began to spin. I laid my head down on the hearth rug, waiting for the darkness to envelop me.

It was loud. I was in my room. The windows and the fireplace were the same, but there were different drapes over the windows and bizarre objects on the mantle. The room was bright, illuminated by this weird-shaped thing by the bed with several burning objects inside covered by colored shades. There was a loud noise blasting out of a blue-and-silver, box-shaped object by the bed.

The vanity was covered with an array of colored things, some of which were even attached to the wall by some big, black strings. There were different pictures and papers of strange looking people all along the walls that were also a different color. But the strangest by far was this box in the corner where the pictures were moving about and talking. I had never seen something so incredible in my life.

Then I realized I was not alone. The three girls whom I had seen before in the room with the cages were all there. I was laughing and moving about in a strange way, sort of like dancing.

Two of the girls were standing on my bed with colored, dark glasses on and strange-shaped bonnets. One was even wearing a bright, pink, long, feather thing wrapped around her neck and shoulders. They were singing to the noise, and I even knew the words they were saying even though I was positive I had never heard it before. I certainly would not call it music. It hurt my ears it was so loud.

I noticed the third girl was trying on various articles of clothing from the wardrobe and singing also. The four of us were barely wearing any clothing, just some very short, soft, brightly colored pants made of this unusual fabric and tight, short-sleeved, or no-sleeved shirts.

We were all laughing and having a great time. I loved it. I felt so close to these girls, like we had all been friends for a very long time. We were bouncing around and behaving so silly and childishly. Then the girls began to fade, and the room started to become hazy.

I slowly sat up on the hearth rug to utter silence. The sudden lack of noise was a shock to my senses. The only sound I could hear was the crackling of the wood in the fire. I felt so alone in this big, empty room. The girls and their laughter were gone, as were the strange objects and the pictures and bright colors. My room looked pale and void in comparison to the vision I had just seen.

My foggy head began to clear, and the images were lost. I noticed the tears rolling down my cheeks; and I felt so sad — sad that the girls, the colors, the unexplainable objects, and the noise were all gone, and I was left in this empty silence that encapsulated me.

The silver pocket watch lay next to me on the floor, inches from my fingers. Its power was intoxicating. Nothing in my life had ever given me such excitement. Nothing had ever allowed me such freedom, given me such exhilaration. I craved it.

I left the watch lying on the floor and climbed back into my bed. I was tempted to hold it again to see what would happen. Something inside me, deep in my soul warned me to stop before I saw something that I did not want to see.

I closed my eyes, pulling the quilt up around my chin, completely terrified but having no clue as to why. My mind was whirling over each of the episodes I had seen, yet I could not connect the dots between them. They all felt so real to me, like a memory of my own. I sighed, knowing it was not possible; but I could not explain it.

Frustrated, I rolled over and tried to block out everything I had ever seen because of that possessed trinket.

Chapter 27

Friday, October 30, 2015

THE HOURS DRAGGED BY as they always do when you're anxious for answers. I didn't get the opportunity to speak with Jackson last evening since Emily had kicked both him and Robert out of the house before I came over to do my fitting. She claimed she didn't want Jackson to see me before my unveiling on Saturday evening.

As upset as I was about not getting the chance to be alone with him, it was so much fun to try on my costume. Emily had done such a beautiful job. It was hard to believe that she had created the entire outfit by herself. However, she refused to allow me to even peek at Jackson's costume. I had to follow the same rules she had laid down for her own son. It was difficult to argue with her considering all the hard work she had put into them.

When I finally saw him, Jackson looked amazing; and I found it difficult, as always, to keep my eyes off him. His black, long-sleeved shirt clung to his muscular chest, while the stones on his necklace added just the right touch to complete the ensemble.

The only difference now was that we were sitting next to one another in our shared classes, and it was more obvious when I looked at him. I couldn't just glance casually to my side without anyone noticing. However, when I did get the opportunity to steal a glance at his beautiful face, I always found him smiling back at me. I could feel myself blush each time, knowing I could never get tired of him and the way he made me feel.

As the final bell rang and we all began to pile out of the classroom, the excitement over the final football game of the season and Cody's Halloween costume party, which most of the school had been invited to, had the entire school in a frenzy.

The halls were covered in signs of school spirit, cheering our boys on to a defeat against the Rockwall Royals. The two schools held a longstanding rivalry, and every season promised a close game. Yet it was sad to think that this was my last high school football game that I would have as a senior. I knew I'd do my best next year, especially if I end up going to Northwestern, to come home and see Ethan play a few games his senior year but for me, this was it.

Of course, the team had to ride on the buses to the game with the cheerleaders. That much I hated. I loathed the thought of Taylor doing her best to sit anywhere near Jackson.

I was riding with the rest of our group, and we were planning on meeting up at Jenna's around four-thirty since it was over an hour drive to Rockwall. Poor Kyle was going to be the only guy with us. Our parents had agreed to let us drive on the condition that we follow them. My parents and Jackson's were traveling together, which surely meant it would take us forever to get there.

The aroma of perfume and hairspray hung heavy over my room. Each of us playfully pushed and bumped into each other trying to force our way in front of my vanity mirror, wanting to get our make-up perfect. Hilary painted Jackson's number — 88 — on my cheek, Zak's number — 10 —on Caitlyn's and then Caitlyn painted Cody's — 15 — on Hilary. We all threw on long-sleeved thermal shirts under our school hooded sweatshirts and pulled our hair up into ponytails with ribbons in our school colors.

We arrived at the game just in time to see our boys do their game tradition where the entire team went out onto the field holding hands, for the coin toss. After that, our boys huddled together and began chanting with Zak as the team caption in the middle of the huddle.

Zak shouted, "What time is it?"

"Game time!" The team shouted in unison.

"What time is it?"

"Game time!"

"The dogs in the House! The dogs in the House!" The entire team shouted together. "Oh, oh, oh!"

They all bounced around together as the referee blew the whistle. The team clapped their hands and ran back over to their side of the field and huddled together.

In unison the boys all shouted, "Work hard! Improve every day! Be unselfish! Be the best! Dogs ready! Break!"

The special teams ran out onto the field to kick off the start of the game as the crowd went wild. The visitors' side was as full as the home team. It seemed the whole school had made the trip.

At halftime, the score was 7 — 24, and our boys hadn't scored since the first quarter. Our season looked like it was going to end on a sour note. However, our boys bounced back, refusing to admit defeat, and with 1:29 left in the fourth, the score was 28 — 31. An amazing touchdown pass in the last six seconds sent our side into hysterics at our unbelievable victory.

We followed the caravan back with people honking their horns and music blaring the entire way. Nothing was going to kill the elation of this amazing comeback.

I think the entire school headed out to Mark's parent's property out in the middle of nowhere on the edge of city limits afterward. It had a small pond that was surrounded by several acres of open field. We partied there frequently, when Cody's place was unavailable, but normally only in the summer since there was no shelter. Tonight, however, it didn't matter.

Cars were parked all over the place when we arrived. It looked more like attending some huge, outdoor event or concert with the number of vehicles scattered everywhere. Someone had built a huge bonfire about fifty feet from the pond, and there were several kegs and ice chests set up around the parameter; and music was blaring from someone's car stereo.

It took no time at all to find our guys as we strolled up to the fire. Most of the team was still huddled together. Everyone had a drink in their hands and was laughing.

Hilary and Caitlyn ran up to Zak and Cody and threw their arms around them. Jackson was standing next to Ethan and Mariah, close to the others. I strolled over, grinning widely as his searching eyes landed upon mine. I wanted desperately to be able to show my affection and admiration for him like Hilary and Caitlyn had just done for their guys.

Why did I have to finally find a man who I am crazy about and have to experience such strange episodes every time we have physical contact? Why do I have to have a boyfriend who makes me sick and pass out? It makes no sense at all.

Jackson's smile was welcoming, and he looked as though he wanted to wrap his arms around me also. We stood looking at one another with a strained distance between us. I glanced over at Ethan and mouthed, "Congrats" to him. He gave me a warm smile and hugged Mariah a little closer to him. It was great to see him so happy.

The heat was pouring off the bonfire, making it feel more like a midsummer night rather than almost November.

"You guys pulled off a hell of a victory. That was probably the best game I've ever watched." I stared into Jackson's powerful, green eyes.

"Thanks." Jackson held up his cup. "Would you like a drink?"

"Is that beer?"

"No. Water." He took another long drink. He was clearly dehydrated from the game.

"Is there anything else?"

"I think so. Stay here so I do not lose you in this crowd."

"Okay." I nodded as he wandered off towards the area where all the drinks were.

My eyes traveled over at the crowd of kids whom I had known all my life. I was really going to miss them next year. It was strange to think that after seeing them almost every day that it was all going to be over in a few short months. By next fall, we'd all go off to separate universities around the country. The thought depressed me greatly.

Jackson returned and handed me a root beer. "This is all I could find that does not have alcohol in it."

"Thanks. I just don't believe I should be drinking the way I've been feeling lately," I explained.

"I agree. That is why I have water. I have to drive you home and want to make sure you get there safely." I loved the way he always thought of me.

"I appreciate that." I laughed. "You guys were very impressive tonight, especially you."

"I believe you are biased." He flashed me that lopsided, cocky grin that I loved so much.

"Perhaps, but I don't believe so. You looked great out there."

"Thank you."

"I mean it. I love watching you play."

"Well, I hope you enjoyed it, because the season is over and now you will have to get used to seeing me on the basketball court if I make the team." He smiled.

"You will. I have no doubt." There was nothing he wasn't good at, it seemed. I was sure the same could be said for his skills on the court.

"Are you playing this season?" Jackson inquired.

"Always."

The crowd was getting more than a little rowdy. The beer was flowing through everyone as fast as water. It wasn't long before you could tell that over half of the people in attendance were highly intoxicated. I just hoped that they would get home safely. It would be tragic if someone had an accident after such a celebration for the win.

As if he could read my thoughts, Jackson leaned in a little closer. "Are you ready to get out of here? It is almost one o'clock, and your parents wanted you home no later than two."

I had gotten special permission after the game because of the victory and the long ride home. I believe my father was so proud of Ethan and on such a high, that I could have asked to stay out all night and he would have agreed.

"Yes."

But right as I answered him, Mason, the team's center, who was more than a little intoxicated, stumbled into me, shoving me directly into Jackson. Jackson reached out and caught me, but the blackness devoured me as I collapsed in his arms.

I was suddenly inside of a beautiful, old church with flowers scattered all about. The stained-glass windows let the sunlight dance in a variety of colors over the guests. The pews were a hard, cherry oak, and there were people standing along the back, as the place was completely full.

I looked at the people around me. I was standing up near the altar, holding flowers next to several other girls. I was wearing a long, old-fashioned, light-pink dress like the other two girls, with lace around my collar and wrists.

They were gorgeous gowns; and I knew this was a very special occasion, although I couldn't quite make out yet what it was. Jackson was sitting in the second row with Emily, Robert, and others that I recognized from the albums Emily had shown me. Jackson was smiling over at me. Jackson!

Jackson was *here*, as were his parents! *Why? What are they doing in this strange place and time?* My breathing quickened as I scanned the church, trying not to scream out.

The woman I had before called mother was seated in the front row with tears in her eyes next to a man, I had never seen but strangely knew was my father. Somehow, I knew this woman's tears were for joy rather than sadness.

On the opposite side of the altar stood several men that I felt close to but didn't recognize. One of them looked like a slightly older version of the boy I had seen before that I had wanted to go fishing with.

All of them were smiling and wearing very nice, double-breasted suits. I realized that this must indeed be a wedding, but whose? I was not sure how I knew it, but I was not happy about this wedding. I had the oddest feeling that I did not like the bride, but the groom was someone very special to me.

The doors at the back of the church opened as the imagines began to fade. I could barely see the bride walking down the aisle with her father and her delicate, long, white dress with the flowing train. I wanted to desperately hold on to where I was at. I wanted to talk with Jackson, ask him questions, and demand explanations. My mind was clear enough that I knew something was amiss, and I had to figure it out before I lost my mind completely.

But then I heard Jackson's voice hollering at Ethan, "Do not ask questions! Please just carry her to the car."

I felt Ethan's arm under me, taking me from Jackson. I could feel his body against mine and smell his cologne as he carefully walked over to Jackson's CRV.

"Is she drunk?"

I could hear Mariah's clouded voice somewhere near me. I knew she had to be walking next to Ethan.

"She'll be fine," Ethan replied from somewhere deep inside the tunnel.

Jackson apparently opened the back door while Ethan did his best to maneuver me in carefully.

"Watch her head." I could hear the worry in Jackson's voice.

"Are you headed home?" Ethan asked. The door must have still been open because I could hear them although it was still muffled. I kept my eyes closed, hoping that I could return to the images I had just seen.

"My house first. I want to make sure she is all right before I take her home. I know Jocelyn will be upset if your mother finds out about this." I heard Jackson explain to my brother.

"I'll go with you," Ethan responded.

"No," Mariah interrupted. "I'm not ready to leave. This is a great party, and we never get a chance like this just to hang out." Her voice was whiney.

"Mariah, there's another party tomorrow night, and I'm sure a thousand more in the future. I need to be sure my sister is all right?" Ethan's voice was short.

"She has Jackson for that. She doesn't need you. Stay with me. I don't want to leave." She whined.

"Then stay!" Ethan shouted at her. He must have walked around and got in the passenger side door, because I heard it slam shut then the other doors shut, and Jackson started up the engine.

I slowly sat up in the backseat and rubbed my head. I felt foggy but not sick for a change, which was a relief.

"I'm fine, Ethan. You should have stayed at the party with Mariah."

Jackson glanced at me in the rearview mirror as Ethan turned in his seat to face me.

"Are you okay?" Ethan's eyes were searching my face for answers.

His words were becoming clearer.

"I told you I'm fine. She's going to be ticked at you."

"She's always ticked at me." He laughed. "Besides, it's getting late; and you are more important than any party."

"Thanks."

I was still rubbing the sides of my face, trying to clear my thoughts. My stitches and bruises were still a little painful; but other than that, I felt fine. My mind was centered on the fact that I had just seen Jackson and his parents in the beautiful, old church. I couldn't figure out why they would all be there in this strange, familiar world.

Ethan settled his back against the window, looking at the two of us. "I've been thinking of ending things with her for a while now. She's been getting on my nerves."

I didn't mean to, but a laugh escaped before I could stop it. "Sorry."

Jackson looked back at me from the rearview. "Are you sure you are feeling all right?"

"I'm sure." I smiled at his beautiful reflection from the dashboard lights. "You can head straight to my house."

"We have time if you want to stop by my place first and relax a minute to gather yourself before seeing your parents."

"No. Seriously. I'm okay." As much as I wanted to demand answers from him, I knew Ethan would not leave us alone; and I couldn't think of how to get rid of him now that he'd made such a point of making sure I was fine.

"All right." Jackson didn't push any further.

"What's going on with you? Why are you fainting all the time? Mom said your tests all came back fine, but it hasn't stopped. You should probably tell her about this."

I knew Ethan was worried. I noticed Jackson's eyes staring at me in the rearview mirror again.

I knew there was something Jackson wasn't telling me. I wanted to scream and holler at him. He still had not even given me the chance to question him about his theories in all this. I leaned my head back against the seat and stayed silent the rest of the way home.

Jackson didn't come inside when we got home. Instead, he pulled into his driveway, claiming that he was tired and needed to get some sleep before tomorrow.

He asked Ethan to help me home, making Ethan walk with his arm around me across the street and up the walkway to our porch.

"E, this really isn't necessary," I complained.

"Shut up or I'll tell Mom on you." He grinned.

"Fine." I pouted. "You can really be a pain. You know that?"

He leaned over and kissed me on the cheek, which for him was unheard of. "But you love me for it," he teased.

"Yes, I do." I couldn't help but smile. It was nice to know how much he cared.

Both our parents were waiting for us as we walked in. My father was overwhelmed with excitement and immediately started gushing to Ethan about the game. It gave me a nice escape to sneak up into the shower unnoticed.

The hot water felt amazing and soothing as it ran over my body, allowing the fog to completely clear. I couldn't get the images out of my mind.

As I lay in bed, I thought about the rooms in my vision and how different they looked, how one was strangely the same as our living room. The walls, the fireplace, the carvings on the mantel were like the ones in my home now. It was impossible. Then there were the people, the sounds, the fragrance; they all screamed at me to realize what they meant, but I didn't understand it at all.

I was certainly losing my mind. I had to be. Nothing else made any sense. I suddenly felt very upset with Jackson and his avoidance of being alone with me since our conversation on Wednesday night. He had promised to share with me his so-called theories but had yet to do so. I knew he was aware of more than he was letting on.

I fought the urge to go over to his house and demand some answers.

Instead, I pulled the covers up around my face and clicked on the radio letting the music wash over me and clear my thoughts of all the visions.

Chapter 28

Saturday, November 2, 1878

THE CLOUDS DANCED AROUND THE SUN as I awoke early in the morning. The house was still quiet except for the rumbling around in the kitchen below. I rolled over onto my side, and I could see the silver pocket watch gleaming in the morning sun on the hearth rug. Immediately I was flooded with memories of the episode from last night.

I closed my eyes and tried to concentrate on what it felt like last night at the foot of the stairs with Jackson instead. I felt something stir deep inside me as I longed to feel that passion again. I wanted to creep over to his house and crawl into his bed, something I knew I would never do; but it was great to fantasize about it anyway.

I crawled out of bed and picked up my robe off the vanity chair before brushing my hair. The watch gleamed at me out of the corner of my eye as if it were calling out to me. I tried my best to ignore it while placing a silk ribbon in my hair to pull it away from my face.

I walked over to the door, ready to open it when I turned slowly. Its power or my curiosity was simply too strong for me to resist. I had to see what else the watch wanted to show me.

I sat down on the floor beside the watch, debating on how long it would be before Mimi would arrive to wake me. It would be impossible for me to explain my fainting on the hearth rug to her or my parents.

My father would never buy it and I would end up being forced to stay in bed for the duration of the day and miss the festival completely. I decided instead to take the watch with me and lay back on my bed. That way, if Mimi came in, she would believe I was still asleep.

I carefully picked up the watch by the chain and placed it back into the box. I carried the box back over to my bed, throwing my robe over the end of it, and crawled back under the covers.

With the box hidden safely under my covers and my head rested upon my pillow, I closed my eyes and wrapped my fingers tightly around the pocket watch. Instantly, the spinning began again, and I could see the front yard of my house from the porch.

It was late evening after twilight and there were stars streaked across the sky. However, I noticed they were not nearly as bright as usual, and the yard looked very different. Even the road and pathway looked strange, and now the road extended up to my house and all the other houses I could see.

I heard a very familiar voice and jerked my head around. There, sitting on the swing beside me, was Jackson! *What is he doing here?* He looked weird; his clothes, his shoes, his overcoat were all out of place. *What is he wearing?*

I looked down and realized that I was wearing the exact same blue material pants as he, except mine were ripped in one knee and looked shabbier than his. I was also wearing some sort of soft material with a metal clasp down the front. I looked around utterly confused.

Why is Jackson here? Why is he speaking to me as if he hardly knows me? I heard myself answering him but felt vaguely like I did not really know him. It was almost as if he was purposely keeping a distance between us. *Did I do something to upset him?* I wanted to scream out to him, but I could not get the words to come out.

Suddenly, the area became very bright, and I heard the door open. Some kind of light with no fire that was oddly attached to the house was lighting up the entire area brightly.

A man stuck his head out of the door, telling me it was time for me to come in. Jackson was getting up and walking down the porch steps, heading towards his home; but he gave me no hug or kiss. He did not even tell me he loved me.

He said he would pick me up for school in the morning. *Why? Jackson and I do not go to the same school, never have. Why is he not at the University?*

The morning light pushed through the darkness of my front porch, and I began to see my room emerge around me. I closed my eyes even tighter and gripped the trinket in my hand even harder trying to bring back the scene I had just left. Nothing.

None of this makes any sense at all. Why would Jackson be in one of my visions, dressed so strangely and behaving so differently? Who was the man on the porch? A part of me felt as if I knew him, but I am sure I had never seen him before.

I slipped the watch back into the box and placed it on my night table. Sitting up, I looked all around my bedroom. I was positive that this was the same room as the vision I had seen with the girls. I am also positive that it was my front porch I had just been sitting on with Jackson.

I slowly got out of bed and put my robe back on, pausing only a moment to look back at the trinket before heading downstairs for breakfast.

Jackson, William, Olivia, and I set out about two o'clock towards the autumn festival, followed by Jackson's parents and mine in the carriage behind us. Several blocks around the city had been transformed for today and there were people milling about, making the streets become increasingly crowded.

I was wearing a navy, blue dress with my hair curled over my shoulders. My caplet and bonnet matched perfectly with the charcoal suit that Jackson looked stunningly handsome in. Mimi had also done an outstanding job fixing Olivia's long, dark hair this morning.

She was wearing it up with a few scattered pieces down to flatter her face. Her auburn dress was the perfect choice for the occasion and complimented William's navy suit. A week of Sarah's cooking had truly done wonders in restoring color to Olivia's face, yet her overly thin figure still held no clue as to the secret she and William were hiding.

We soon found our friends mingling amongst the crowd. Christina, Thomas, Theodore, and Laurie were sitting at a picnic table, eating barbeque with Elizabeth and Lee. They were all laughing as the four of us approached. The six of them seemed stunned to see Olivia and William but had the decency not to mention it.

"Good afternoon," various voices greeted our appearance.

"Hello. How is everyone?" I greeted my friends.

"Wonderful. Would you all like to join us?" Theodore invited us gesturing to the open spaces at the table.

The four of us sat down and joined in the conversations. Elizabeth, whom I was seated beside leaned towards me. "It is good to see the four of you out together."

"Yes." I agreed, smiling.

"Miss Olivia is looking much better." I nodded, and Elizabeth smiled slightly then addressed the four of us. "Will you all be joining us on the hayride? I believe it starts in about an hour."

"That sounds like fun." William chimed in. "Are they still running out to Foster's Orchard?"

"Always," Thomas replied. "I think I have gone on this hayride every year for a long as I can remember." He laughed.

"All of us have," Jackson stated.

"Well, this is going to be a new experience for me." Lee smiled.

"It is not overly stimulating, but it is fun. It is more tradition than anything else." I replied just in time before Maryanne and her fiancé, Dimitri strolled up and stood behind Christina and Thomas. Maryanne had that smirk on her face which told me she was up to something.

"Well, Miss Olivia. It is certainly nice to see you up and about again and with Mr. Timmons no less." Maryanne's tone was sticky sweet, making Olivia immediately lower her eyes to the table.

"What do you want, Maryanne?" William's voice turned harsh.

"Not a thing. I only thought I would come by and say hello to my friends."

Dimitri began to look extremely uncomfortable.

"So, Miss Olivia, from the look of you, you are not still ill; so, I am guessing that you will be back in class on Monday."

Olivia continued to look down, remaining silent while Jackson reached for my hand under the table and squeezed it.

When Olivia did not reply, Maryanne continued. "No? Well, I must say I am not surprised. Guess you are too busy planning on where you are going to stick the next knife in Miss Jocelyn's back."

"Maryanne, enough!" I glared at her. "You really should not speak of things you know nothing about."

"Really? Well, it seems that Miss Olivia's family is busy moving, and yet here she is. That seems strange. Of course, my mother said the only reason for her leaving school and not moving with her family is perhaps she is pregnant. Know anything about that Mr. Timmons or are you planning on marrying the mother of your bastard child?"

The entire table immediately fell into a stunned silence.

William's face went burnt red as he leaped up from his seat. Jackson jumped up after him, grabbing his arm, pulling him away from Maryanne.

"You truly are a cruel, heartless young woman!" William spat at her, but Maryanne only laughed — a sickening, eerie sound.

"Nice. Thanks for the confirmation, William." She turned to walk away, but Dimitri remained in place. "Come on, Dimitri. I guess we are not welcome here."

He looked at Maryanne with pure disdain much like the rest of us.

"I cannot believe you can say something like that to someone whom you have known your entire life." Dimitri shook his head in utter disgust.

"Honestly? Look at what she did. She betrayed her best friend, and now is going to ruin her wedding. How is that a friend?"

But Dimitri only shook his head. He glared at her with hateful eyes. "I have put up with your gossip and sometimes even cruel statements about people behind their backs because I blamed it on your mother. I honestly wanted to believe that you would not turn out like her. She seems to enjoy finding faults in others and using it against them. But I cannot do this anymore."

"Dimitri, what are you saying?" She looked at him coldly.

"I am saying that these are my friends also, and I cannot allow you to treat them in such a manner. I am saying that the wedding is off, Maryanne. I do not want to spend my life with someone who enjoys making others miserable," he said flatly.

Maryanne's jaw dropped open, but she could not find any words to reply with. She stared at the group of us sitting there, witnessing the exchange, pleading with her eyes for one of us to say something in her defense. No one did.

"Fine." She took off her engagement ring and threw it at Dimitri and stomped off.

He slowly bent down and picked it up, watching her leave. "I am so sorry, Miss Olivia, Mr. Timmons. There is no excuse for her hurtful words."

Olivia nodded slowly with her eyes still turned down toward the table, but we could all see the tears running down her face. Her secret was exposed for all to see, and both she and William knew it.

William angrily shook free of Jackson's hold and sat back down beside his wife. He wrapped his arms protectively around her and pulled her closer to him.

He whispered something softly in her ear, and she nodded without looking up. The rest of us remained silent, having no idea of what to say. Dimitri slowly sat down next to Theodore, looking extremely uncomfortable. Jackson rejoined me taking my hands in his.

"Mr. Dimitri, I am so sorry." Elizabeth reached over, touching his hand slightly.

He returned her words with a slight smile. "It was something I should have done a long time ago. I honestly wanted to believe that I could change her, and she would stop behaving like her mother. Are you all right, Miss. Olivia? I am truly sorry."

Olivia wiped her tears away with a handkerchief and smiled at all of us. "You have nothing to apologize for, Mr. Dimitri. I knew people would be gossiping about me, us, but I thought that perhaps my friends would have enough class not to confront me about my shortcomings."

"We do, Miss Olivia. Miss Maryanne obviously was not your friend. None of us are judging either of you." Elizabeth quickly responded. "None of us are perfect, and we all have done things we are not exactly proud of as well."

"At least not everyone knows about them." Olivia gave a small laugh. "Everyone now knows about mine."

The table went silent again.

"Well, I suppose you all should know that William and I are now married."

Those simple words changed the atmosphere in the short time it took them to be spoken.

"Congratulations!" A chorus rang out amongst the others.

"When?" Christina's upbeat voice inquired.

"Last weekend." Olivia, thrilled at their acceptance, glowed.

"How wonderful. And you knew about this, and you did not tell us?" Christina teased, looking over at me.

"How could I? It was not my news to share." I laughed. "And yes, I am very happy to have *Ms.* Olivia join our family. We are now truly sisters." I beamed across the table at William and Olivia.

"Well, I see that the hayrides are now starting up. So, is everyone coming?" Thomas nodded over in the direction of wagons lining up.

The eleven of us piled into a wagon by ourselves. For the first time in the last two years, Dimitri, instead of Elizabeth, was the odd man out; but he did not seem to mind.

Elizabeth leaned over to me shortly after we took off. "I understand if you would still like to have Mrs. Timmons stand up for you now that the secret is out," she whispered in my ear.

"I want you both to stand up with me if you are still willing." I whispered back.

"I would love to." She smiled.

We arrived at Foster's Orchard as twilight set in. We all unloaded the wagon and strolled over to the barn. The smell of apples was thick in the air. Jackson walked with his arm around my waist as he guided me through the rows of apple stands and pumpkins. People were clustered in the aisles, gathering various types of apples to purchase for different desserts. I wandered around, looking at the numerous items from jugs of freshly made apple cider, candles to homemade noodles, jellies, and jams.

Jackson bought me a beautiful, blue candle before we sat down on a wooden bench to each enjoy a caramel apple sprinkled with nuts.

"Do you think it is going to be all right now that everyone knows the truth?" I asked him.

"I believe so. I do not think that any of them will say anything about this to their families. I believe they have too much respect for Olivia and William."

"I agree."

"I think Olivia feels much better now. She no longer feels she has to hide in your parent's home, at least from her circle of friends." He took another bite of his apple, dropping some bits along his vest.

I laughed as he shook them off.

"You cannot even eat without making a mess. What am I going to do with you?" I teased.

"Marry me."

"Yes."

Jackson leaned over and kissed me on the cheek with his sticky lips.

"Oh, Jackson!" I laughed, wiping my cheek. "How could you?"

"Easy. It made you smile." He continued laughing.

We spent the next hour touring Foster's before we loaded back into the wagon to head back to the main festival. The incident earlier was not forgotten but was momentarily pushed out of mind for most of us with of course, the exception of Dimitri. He tried to put on a good front, but it was easy to see he was still upset.

The dusty ride back was much darker than the one to the orchard. The sun had completely disappeared, and the stars were now covering the sky. The air had cooled off a few degrees, adding more of a chill to the night. I snuggled in closer to Jackson and closed my eyes, not really paying attention to the conversation taking place between the others.

Instead, my mind wandered back to the scene earlier in the day when he and I were sitting on the porch. I tried to make some sense out of what it all meant, but there was nothing to connect the dots.

If I told him what his gift was doing to me, he would certainly believe I was losing my mind. I was positive about that, because I would react the same if he approached me with something so absurd.

Upon our return, the crowd had gotten larger and even more festive. There were now several bonfires scattered about, shortly off the main areas and I could see the haunted maze built from hay stacks off to the side.

People were also now adorning various masks of different creatures in fiction and fairy tales. Their homemade creations gave off an eerie atmosphere in the dark world around them with just the glow from the fires to give light. It seemed very surreal the way everyone embraced these childish traditions one night a year, when this type of behavior was considered normal.

Gathered in the foreground was a small group of local musicians playing various melodies for a large group of dancing couples. Everyone was in high spirits celebrating the pagan traditions.

"Do you and Jackson want to try out the haunted maze?" Elizabeth and Lee walked up beside us.

"We would love too," Jackson eagerly responded.

"I have never tried it before." Elizabeth's voice was a bit apprehensive.

"Really? Why not?" Lee asked.

"I have never had someone to go through it with. I was always too afraid to try it alone." She blushed.

"Understandable." I nodded, looking over at the line of people waiting to get lost in the maze.

Community members dressed up in terrifying costumes waited eagerly inside to scare the life out of us. Of all the traditions, this seemed like the most ridiculous but certainly one of the most fun. Mr. and Mrs. Sutton, who ran the haunted maze every year, were only allowing people in by twos and spacing them a couple minutes apart to add to the effects.

Jackson and I followed Elizabeth and Lee while William and Olivia waited behind us. I wrapped my arm through his, holding tightly to his bicep. We slowly crept around one corner and the next, occasionally hitting a dead end or someone jumping out of the shadows, screaming at us, scaring us within an inch of our lives. We would burst out laughing at our own silliness and attempt another direction.

As we rounded a black corner, I tugged on Jackson's arm halting him.

"Do you believe in magic?"

"What?"

"Magic, do you believe in it?"

Jackson looked confused by my line of questioning. "In what sense?"

"In the sense that it exists."

"Yes. I believe there are some things that occur that seem to be unexplainable. Why do you ask?"

His eyes narrowed in the dark, confirming to me that he knew something more than he was letting on.

I tried to shrug it off casually. "Just curious."

"Jocelyn, what is going on?" Jackson cocked his head slightly to the side and eyed me closely.

"Nothing."

"Something has been bothering you all week, and I do not believe it has anything to do with the dress," he stated.

"Do not be ridiculous. Tonight, of all nights, when everyone is celebrating various pagan traditions, it is a perfectly normal question or pursue a conversation out of the ordinary."

"Perhaps, but you do not normally ask such questions."

I could hear William's voice behind us. They were getting closer.

"Come on." I pulled his arm a little, making him follow me around the corner.

"Have you ever experienced magic or something you cannot explain?" Jackson whispered in my ear. I only smiled and shook my head.

We emerged on the other side of the maze to find Lee and Elizabeth waiting patiently for us. She was huddled in closely to him. Both were laughing.

"You made it," Lee greeted the two of us.

"Finally." I was still trying to regain my footing.

"We made several wrong turns as well." Lee laughed. "I had never been in a haunted maze before. It was great."

Elizabeth smiled but the look in her eyes betrayed her, she looked on the verge of tears.

Lee looked down at the young lady in his arms. "You are shivering, sweetheart. We should get you some hot cider to warm you up." He kissed the top of her head then looked at us. "Would you like to join us?"

"Of course," Jackson responded while I nodded my head.

William and Olivia came into view from behind us, laughing and Lee invited them also to join us for some hot cider.

The eleven of us gathered around one of the bonfires, sipping hot apple cider and laughing at our own childishness as we regaled tales of our experiences in the haunted maze.

My room seemed especially cold, and I could hear the wind hollowing outside my window and around the house. The fire was burning brightly off to my side, taking the edge off the chill in the air.

I rolled over to my side, snuggling down into the covers. The little, blue box sat waiting for me on the night table. I squeezed my eyes together tightly and rolled over in the other direction, putting my back to it. A part of me was so tempted to see what it would show me this time, but the other part of me was too terrified to risk it. I tried to ignore it calling out to me.

Its power felt so strong. In my mind, I could see each of the earlier visions. I tried to force myself to concentrate on something else — anything else. Jackson. His words earlier ran through my head. *Why did he not believe me about the magic? Why did his face hold that smirk when he whispered those words into my ear? Did he know what his silver trinket was doing to me? No. It was not possible. Or was it? What is he hiding from me?*

Chapter 29

Saturday, October 31, 2015

I JUMPED OUT OF BED shortly before nine. I was beyond excited about the costume party at Cody's. It had been so long since I really got all decked out for Halloween, and Jackson and I were going to look so perfect together. Emily had done an outstanding job on our costumes. They appeared so authentic. She had even offered to fix my hair and makeup for the party.

My costume had a full, floor-length, amethyst, taffeta skirt, and a wide black belt with a gorgeous white lace blouse. Jackson had told me he was wearing a charcoal, double-breasted suit. I hadn't seen it on him yet as Emily wanted to make sure every detail was taken care of before I got to see him in it.

I headed over to Jacksons at five minutes to three with my wet hair still wrapped in a towel from my shower, wearing old sweats. Emily had asked me to come over with it still wet. However, I felt extremely silly running across both our large front lawns and the street with a bathroom towel wrapped around my head.

Luckily, Emily answered the door instead of Jackson. I didn't want him to see me with a towel on my head. She looked more excited than I was.

"Hello, darling. Come on in."

"Where's Jackson?" I held onto the towel, so it wouldn't fall off. I gave her a pathetic grin. "I don't want him to see me looking so glamorous." I laughed.

"Of course." She gave me a warm smile and closed the front door. "Follow me." We walked up the stairs to her bedroom; "I sent the men out for some more candy for the trick-or-treaters to get rid of them for a while."

I had never been on the second floor of their house before. I was very curious as to what Jackson's bedroom looked like, but I didn't dare sneak a peek. I would have hated it if he peeked into my room when he was upstairs with Ethan. I was also positive that Jackson had too much respect for me to even think of doing something like that.

"How are you feeling this evening?"

As soon as she asked, I realized that Jackson must have told her I had another episode last night. Thank goodness, I had never shared with him the full truth of what was really happening, or he would have had me committed. Anyone would, and who could blame them? I was now embracing deep denial that the voices and images were just a part of my over-active imagination.

"Fine." I tried to play ignorant. I wasn't sure exactly how much Jackson had told her.

"Jocelyn, darling. It is nothing to be embarrassed about. Jackson told us what has been happening. He merely wanted a woman's perspective." She motioned for me to have a seat on her bed, and she sat down beside me. "He is very concerned about you. I believe my son is developing very strong feelings for you."

Instantly, I felt my face blush a deep crimson. Guessing how uncomfortable I was with what she had just said, Emily patted my knee. "Come on. We should get your hair started."

She got up and walked over to her vanity table, and I followed. Emily placed dozens of rollers all over my head after she had thoroughly soaked my hair with several different styling agents. She commented numerous times how she loved my thick hair with the dark, auburn highlights.

When she finished making me look like a porcupine, she wrapped a purple scarf around my curlers and began working on my makeup. She had more beauty products than most stores.

By the time she had completed my full forty-five- minute make-up transformation, I couldn't believe my eyes. I didn't even look like me.

The person who stared back at me looked incredibly beautiful. I was stunned by the magic she worked on my eye, and the yellowing blue bruises were all but gone.

As we began descending, Jackson and Robert arrived back home. Robert paused at the foot of the stairs smiling up at us.

"My goodness, Jocelyn. You look stunning." He grinned at us.

"Yeah, Jocelyn. Nice hair." Jackson teased and stepped around his father and raced up the stairs, meeting Emily and I near the top.

But the fog had already set in, and his words were muffled. I reached for the railing but missed it completely as Jackson's shoulder rubbed against mine. I tumbled straight past Jackson and Emily down ten stairs, landing at Robert's feet. Thankfully, Robert had the instant to half-catch me before my head hit the slate tile.

The bright sunlight was all but blinding. It took me a moment to realize that I was standing in a gazebo on a beautiful, sunny, spring day. The sun was warm on my face, and the lilies and violets were in full bloom all around the white gazebo. There were no clouds in the sky, only a brilliant blue. The grass was an emerald green, and there was a cobblestone pathway leading around the park.

Suddenly, I felt arms wrapped around my waist, but it didn't startle me. Instead, it felt wonderful, secure, love. A man stepped around in front of me. He was wearing very old-fashioned clothing; a blue, double-breasted suit, a white shirt, a strange, thin tie that somehow fit with the rest of his attire.

His blue derby hat was tilted slightly in a cocky, confident way. He knelt on one knee in front of me, taking my hand. He was shaking with nervousness and had his head bowed to where I couldn't see his face from the brim of his hat.

"Miss Jocelyn, you are everything I have ever dreamed of. You are my heart, my soul, my life. If you would do me the honor of becoming my wife, I promise you that I will spend every day of my life making you happy." His words were carefully chosen and full of love and desire.

My heart leapt in my chest. I squeezed his hand in mine. I couldn't breathe. I loved this man more than anything in the world.

"Yes! Yes! Of course, I will marry you!"

Immediately the man stood and embraced me tightly. He pressed his full lips firmly against mine, kissing me passionately. His lips were warm and soft. They felt so natural as they molded into mine. Then he stopped and smiled at me. My breath caught in my throat when I finally saw his face.

Jackson!

The images slowly faded, and I could hear Robert, Emily, and Jackson's voices nearby. I kept my eyes closed, becoming very aware that not only was my head throbbing again, but my entire body was full of pain.

I could feel the cushions of the couch under me and a pillow beneath my head. The rollers were digging painfully into my scalp. Someone, most likely Emily, had placed a cold washcloth on my forehead, probably ruining the makeup that Emily had so carefully applied.

But none of that mattered now. My entire body was screaming in pain. I flexed my muscles in both my arms and legs. Nothing seemed broken, just battered, and bruised.

"How could you be so careless?" Emily's voice was soft, but I could hear the anger in it. "Do you realize that she could have been seriously hurt? What were you thinking?"

"I am so sorry. I was just going upstairs to jump in the shower. I did not think about her episodes. I did not intend to bump into her. It was an accident." Jackson's voice sounded remorseful.

"Has she given you any details? Do you know if she is even seeing images or hearing anything?" Robert's voice was low and hard to hear.

"No," Jackson answered.

"She must be. There has to be something there, some kind of trigger, that has started breaking down the barrier." Emily spoke softly.

"Maybe she is having them but is too scared to say anything." Robert's voice sounded hopeful.

"Maybe." Jackson paused. "Jocelyn is very private. She is so different *here*. I mean, it is strange. I know she has always been passionate about her studies; but *here* she truly flourishes. This whole thing is going to be very difficult for her to understand."

"Jackson, we talked about this before. We all knew it was going to be hard. It was when you went through it, but it all worked out." Emily reassured him.

I could hear light footsteps, as if someone was pacing around the kitchen.

"We all experienced this. Living with this is both a gift and a curse." Robert's voice broke the momentary silence.

"I am just unsure as to whether she is ready for the barrier to be taken down. I hate trying to force it. I see what it is doing to her." Jackson's voice was weak.

"Do you truly love this woman, son?" Emily asked.

"Yes. More than anything."

What? I didn't understand what in the world they were talking about.

"Then the barrier must come down now. There is no other way." Robert's voice rang in my ears.

"Can we please explain it to her? She probably believes she is losing her mind. I cannot stand to see her suffering like this," Jackson pleaded with his parents.

"She would never believe us, son. You know that. Remember how hard it was for you to understand before you learned how to control it?" Robert answered.

"Can we please try?" Jackson's voice was breaking my heart, although I didn't know why.

"I am sorry, sweetheart. You must trust us. It is better this way. She must see it for her own. Only then will she be ready to listen." Emily tried to reassure him.

I closed my eyes tightly, trying to block out their words. I was terrified to hear anymore. None of it made sense. *What in the hell were they talking about? How could they know about the visions?*

My throbbing head couldn't put anything into perspective. Part of me wanted to jump up and confront the three of them, demand to know what in the hell they were talking about, demand to know what they were doing to me.

The other part of me was too terrified to move, didn't want to know what they were referring to. I'm not sure how much time had passed before Emily knelt beside me.

"Jocelyn?" She carefully rubbed my cheek. "Jocelyn, darling. Are you awake?"

Before I knew what was happening, tears crept out of the corners of my eyes, betraying me.

"Honey, are you hurt?" Emily's voice was full of concern.

"No," I whispered. "Just sore. My head is killing me."

"Would you like some ibuprofen?" She offered in her gentle, soothing voice.

"Please." I tried to pull myself up into a seated position, but my body was screaming, causing me to let out a moan in protest.

"Lie still. I will be right back," she said before rushing off.

I rested my head back against the pillow, completely baffled. Emily returned with a glass of apple cider and a couple of ibuprofens and handed them to me.

"If you would like, we can help you home. Robert or Jackson can carry you," she offered.

"If it's all right with you, I would rather not move right now, at least until my head stops pounding." I gave her the best smile I could muster.

"Of course, darling. You just let me know if I can do anything for you."

Emily started to stand, but I reached up for her arm. "Emily?" The dam broke, and the tears came pouring out with full force. "Please." I gently pulled her arm to make her kneel beside me again. "Please explain what is happening to me. I have to know." I sobbed. "Am I losing my mind?"

She leaned down and hugged me tightly. I wanted to scream out in pain but remained silent. She finally released me and looked very upset. "You heard us?"

I nodded.

"What's happening to me? I know it sounds absurd, but every time Jackson comes near me, I get lightheaded and nauseous. It's even worse when he barely touches me." I hesitated, not sure if I could go on without sounding insane. But I knew I had to. I had to get some answers. "I see things, hear voices, my voice. It's like a movie but not in the third person. It's like I'm there and they are memories. My memories. But they can't be."

"Oh, sweetheart, you are not losing your mind. You are very special with an incredibly special ability." Emily paused a moment, looking towards the kitchen. "Robert? Jackson?"

They were both lingering in the doorway behind me. I hadn't noticed them standing there. Both men came in and knelt on the floor on either side of Emily next to me. Jackson handed me a box of tissues with a weary smile. I did my best to clean off my face. I glanced at the tissue then up at Emily with an apologetic look that only brought about more tears.

"I'm so sorry, Emily. I ruined my makeup."

My sobbing over something as trivial as my makeup caused the three of them to chuckle.

"It is all right, darling. Do not give it another thought." She gave me one of her motherly smiles.

"Are you sure you are up for all this? Perhaps we should have you checked first. You took a very nasty tumble down the stairs." Robert's face was full of concern and hesitation.

"Please. I need to know." I did my best to get the tears to stop.

"All right." Emily still appeared concerned, but also determined. "Jocelyn, can you explain to us exactly what images you have been seeing and what you have been hearing?"

"Well, like I said, they feel like memories. I can't explain it."

I paused, waiting for them to look at me like I was crazy but none of them did. Instead, they all looked as if they knew precisely what I was talking about, so I continued.

"That day in the dining room, when we were studying, I saw myself running after a boy who looked about twelve years old. He was dressed funny, like from the *Little House on the Prairie* or something. He had dark, blonde hair and blue eyes. I was upset and wanted to know why I couldn't go fishing with him. I called him William; and I knew he was running off with Jonathon and James, although I couldn't see them, and I don't know who they are or how I knew that. William told me to go home, that fishing wasn't for girls, and I should go play with Olivia."

I shook my head in disbelief, but the three of them smiled and nodded their heads.

"The weird thing is I felt like I was close to him, like this William was very important to me." I took a deep breath and felt much better now that I was talking about my strange visions.

"What else have you seen?" Jackson asked.

"The second time was even stranger than the first. I was in my house, but it looked very different. But I'm positive it was my house. It was full of antiques. It had oil lamps, and the fireplace was burning. I was talking to a woman who was very pretty with long, blonde hair and blue eyes. She was very elegant and petite. She also was dressed in the same, old-fashioned style as

William was. But the most bizarre thing is that I called her mother, and I truly believed it." I sighed heavily before continuing. "It felt comfortable and normal. I asked her if I could go over to Miss Olivia's house before supper. She had agreed but warned me that I had to return on time and that if I didn't and she had to send one of my brothers to fetch me than I would be in trouble."

I looked at the three faces watching me intently. Everything I was saying didn't register as odd to any of them.

"Brothers? I only have one brother. I have no idea who this Olivia is, but I do. She is my closest friend. I don't know how to explain it, but it's something I know. I feel it."

"Is that all?" Robert asked.

"No. There were many others, some where I saw my bedroom, one with a wedding; and for some reason, I knew I didn't like the bride. It was truly weird because you were all there, even your other two kids that I've never met; but I recognized them from the picture album. There was one where there was this strange woman bringing me breakfast. I was very close to her. She was like a second mother to me, and I loved her dearly."

The three of them smiled.

"But the last thing I saw, what I saw tonight." I closed my eyes knowing I was blushing and didn't want to continue.

"You saw Jackson tonight, didn't you?" Emily asked in a very soft voice.

I could only nod.

"What did you see?"

I looked over at her, trying not to look directly at Jackson, not knowing what effect it would have on me. But then Jackson spoke up, surprising us all.

"You saw us in the white gazebo at the park, didn't you?" He was smiling.

It was a good thing I was lying down because his knowledge would have surely sent me to the floor.

"She saw my proposal," Jackson proclaimed, and I stared numbly at him.

How could he know such a thing? It wasn't possible.

His parents looked at him and then back at me for confirmation. My entire body was numb. My head was spinning, no longer throbbing.

"How could you know that?" I squeaked out, barely able to control my voice. The trembling had set in, and I wasn't controlling it as well as I would have liked.

I pulled myself up into a seated position, and none of them tried to stop me this time. I was on the verge of hysterics. He couldn't be inside my head like this. There was no way. Maybe I was talking throughout my visions. Maybe I was acting them out while I was watching them. It could be the only explanation.

"Jocelyn." Robert placed his hand on my shoulder, trying to calm me down. "Listen to me. I need you to be calm, because this is going to be difficult enough to explain and even harder for you to comprehend, but you must try. I am not telling you about this as a joke. This is serious, and I need your full attention. Can you do that for me?" He smiled gently.

I nodded at him, and Emily placed my hands in hers and smiled motherly at me with reassurance and trust.

"Jocelyn, you have a very special gift. The visions and the people you are having them about are very real and not in your head at all." Emily nodded, noticing the confused look that I gave Robert.

"How is that possible? I don't understand." I stumbled with complete utter disbelief.

Is this some kind of sick joke?

"You are a part of what is called *Essence Voyager Era* or as we refer to it, *EVE*. It is where you live a complete life on two separate yet parallel planes of existence. You have a full life *here* in the year 2015 or rather the 21st Century, everything compiled to make up a rather normal existence, correct?"

I nodded, looking at him stupidly.

"However, you also have all of that in the year 1878 or rather the late 19th Century. You have a family *there* — four older brothers, school, friends, parents who love you dearly, servants, and yes, a fiancé, Jackson."

Robert paused for my reaction, but I didn't have one. I was so baffled that I simply stared at him, so he continued.

"When you go to sleep every night, Jocelyn," he squeezed my shoulder, "You actually awaken in 1878." He smiled assuredly. "Not your body, of course, but your soul. You look the same, but your personality is a little different because you were raised differently in a different era. But you are very much you. You get up, eat meals, go to school, spend time with your family and friends, everything that you do *here*. That period is just as real and normal to you as your life is *here*."

"The visions you saw really occurred, and the people are very real. The wedding you saw where you say you felt like you did not like the bride was, I believe, the wedding of your oldest brother, Patrick II, to Katherine. And the woman who served you breakfast whom you felt very close to was Mimi. She has worked for your family since before you were born, and you two are very close," Jackson explained.

My mind could not comprehend all that he was telling me. There was no way this could be real.

"You see, when we moved here, we came here looking for you." Jackson slightly smiled at me.

"You came here looking for me? Why?" Now I was even more confused.

"Yes." Emily smiled and squeezed my hand. "We came here to find you. We had to set off some trigger between your two worlds to break down that veil between your two-consciousness making you aware of both aspects of your lives."

"But why? If all of this is real, if what you're telling me is the truth, why not just leave me in ignorance? Why did you have to come here and put me through all of this? I don't understand. Or why didn't you just tell me the truth from the beginning?" I felt like my body, my life, who I am, was not me any longer.

"Because, Jocelyn, we are all able to do the same thing as you. We, as well as our children, are all part of *EVE*. It is a genetic gift passed on through family members. There is someone else in your family who has this gift also. Can you think of anyone in your life or your visions that you have seen in both worlds besides us?" Robert smiled.

I shook my head.

"You inherited this gift from your dad's brother, Montgomery. Do you know him?" Emily asked.

"Barely. He passed away when I was young. He used to live in Boston and visited us on holidays. My father doesn't talk about him much. I believe he was close to his brother when they were little, and he took it hard when Monte passed away." I explained with my head still foggy.

"Monte did not pass away, Jocelyn. He simply made the decision to live solely in the 19th century. He is very much alive and well. He is married with several children of his own and lives down the street from you. He is very much a part of your life in 1878, and he truly adores you," Emily confessed.

"Wait. Uncle Monte is alive? That can't be. I went to his funeral. I saw him in the casket. We buried him."

"You have to try and understand. Your Uncle Monte chose to live solely in the 19th century." Robert took a deep breath, trying to find the right words. "When you are a part of *EVE*, your soul is what travels, not your physical body. All of us, even you, once you pass the point when the barrier in your consciousness between the two worlds is down and you become fully aware of both of your existences — depending on your bloodline, can decide which place you want to live in without the other. You do not have to, but it is an option. So, when your uncle decided to stay in the 19th century, it was because his wife, Vivian, did not have the gift. Many who are born with this gift make that decision when their spouses cannot travel with them, or their children do not inherit the gift."

"Uncle Monte has sons?" I muttered softly to myself. I thought he never married or had any children.

"Four, actually. You see, you are the youngest of five children and the only girl in the family. Your other two uncles on your father's side all have only boys. You are the only female, and everyone was so thrilled when you were born. Now they all dote over you and are very protective of you, especially your brothers." Robert tried to make me see the impossible.

"Mainly William." Jackson laughed.

"Yes, William. You and he are extremely close. You see, Jocelyn, you and William are only a couple of years apart in age. Although you are close to your other brothers, William, I would say, is sort of your favorite," Emily explained.

"How do you know so much about me and my life *there*? You haven't explained why you came here looking for me?" The throbbing returned, and my head was killing me.

"Because darling, you live in the same house in 1878 as you do now; and so, do we. We have always lived across the street from you since you were born. Your father, I mean your father *there* — Patrick — built that house for your mother — Annabelle — in the summer of 1860. Ours was built during the same time. Patrick and I grew up together in Boston and moved here together before the beginning of the Civil War. Your mother was pregnant with you at the time. Patrick is a physician who served as a doctor in the Union Army during the war. Even though he was not on the battlefield, he was still away from home for several years shortly after you were born. I served in the Union Army also, and we kept track of each other," Robert explained.

None of it was sinking in completely. It was too much.

"You're telling me that I live in the same house now that I do or did or whatever in 1878? How is that possible? Does my father, I mean Shane know that it is his, what, ancestral home?"

"Yes. Of course. He went to great lengths to buy the house as soon as it became available. His great-grandfather sold it shortly after the fire that burned down the carriage house back at the turn of the 20th century; before your father was ever born. The house needed a lot of updates, and his great-grandfather did not have the money to invest in it. The house had no electricity, the plumbing was outdated and having a lot of problems. Many other things that were going to take a lot of time and expense needed fixing. He had the opportunity to sell it for a small fortune; so, he jumped at the chance, although it killed him to let it out of the family. Your father, Shane, grew up hearing stories about the house and how grand it was. So, when your parents moved to Chicago, he was determined to purchase it and vowed never to let it out of the family again. Monte explained all this to us. Shane has no idea that we know."

Robert tried to give me as much information as he knew so I could understand everything.

"But he's never mentioned any of this to us, I mean my sister or brother."

"Shane is a very private man. More so than most I would say." Emily offered. "When we met them for dinner and were discussing the vast history of this area, he barely mentioned that the house was your ancestral home. But your mother is aware of it because the news did not surprise her any." She laughed. "You know one thing your mother did tell me. She said that when they were researching Shane's family line years ago, she came across the fact that Patrick, your *other* father, had built the house when his wife Annabelle, your *other* mother, was pregnant with you. Amy discovered that Annabelle had named you Jocelyn Alyssa and she thought it was the most beautiful name. She decided then because they got the house back in the family when she was pregnant with you, that you should also be named Jocelyn Alyssa."

"What? Are you serious?" Robert and Emily nodded, smiling widely. "Are you telling me that I am named after myself?"

"It is a little strange, I admit." Robert laughed, and Jackson and Emily joined in. "A little unusual, perhaps."

"You think?" This was all too much information to even begin processing. My head was swimming, and I couldn't piece it together. "Are you telling me that I could perhaps look myself up on the internet for the 19th century and find out what happens in my life?"

"I would not recommend doing that. People have done that in the past, and it has led to some dire consequences." Robert gave me the stern father look and the voice to match so I immediately dropped it.

"This is all so unreal. I don't know what to say. And you have not explained why you came here looking for me. Why now?" The three of them looked at each other and hesitated.

"Remember the vision you said you had tonight," Emily began. "Jackson's proposal?"

Instantly, my face turned crimson. I hadn't as much as kissed this man, and yet I was having visions of it; and somehow, I was engaged to marry him.

"You and Jackson are due to be wed on Christmas."

"Christmas. *This* Christmas?"

"Yes." Jackson gave me the most loving smile that took my breath away.

"And?"

"Well, the problem with it is that when you both announced your engagement at Easter last spring, Monte came over and explained to us that you also had the gift of *EVE*. He, of course, was aware that we had the gift also. You see, he stayed in Boston when your family moved to Chicago when Shane got promoted, because Boston is traditionally historic. A lot of us who have inherited this gift feel more comfortable in the New England area. That is why we live there also. But what became clear when he told us about you having this gift also is the problem of your wedding night, to be more precise."

Robert looked suddenly uncomfortable, and the look on his face told me that he was hoping I could figure out what he was trying to say without him having to spell it out for me.

But I was lost. Sure. Our wedding night. So, what? That was clearly between Jackson and me, or at least I thought so. I would imagine that in 1878, I was still a virgin. I had no memories or flashes to contradict that impression. I was certainly still a virgin in 2015, so I didn't understand the problem.

"Isn't that between Jackson and me?"

I looked between the three of them. Robert and Jackson clearly looked uncomfortable with having to explain the obvious.

"That is true. However, the ramifications of it could strongly impact your life *here*, I am afraid," Emily began. "Jocelyn." She squeezed my hands gently. I could see she was trying to carefully choose her words to make the explanation as painless as possible.

"Birth control in the 19th century consists mainly of the rhythm method. I am sure you are aware how largely ineffective that is. With you and Jackson both having the gift of *EVE,* I can guarantee that your children will have the gift also. Therefore, if you conceive a child in the 19th century, the child will be with you in the 21st century. Trust me. I carried all three of my children in two separate time periods, and I was just as pregnant in each of them. It did not matter where I was. We came here looking for you because we were afraid that once you two are married you will become pregnant. That would add the obstacle of explaining it to your family *here*. The impact of a pregnancy in 2015 would forever alter your life *here*. Do you understand what I am saying?" Emily looked so motherly and sincere.

"Yes, I believe so. You're saying that if I become pregnant *there* after Jackson and I are married then I will also be pregnant *here*. Correct?"

Emily nodded.

"But how can that be? Robert just said it was my soul that travels not my body. If my body can't travel and only my soul does, how can a baby travel with me in both periods? That doesn't make sense." Now I was really confused.

Emily squeezed my hands in hers, attempting to comfort and reassure me, but I was way beyond comforting.

"I am honestly not sure why it is. I cannot explain it. I am sorry. I truly wish I could. But I know I carried my children in both periods and to be honest, it was different to say the least. Therefore, I know you will experience the same because you both have inherited the gene."

"We came to Chicago hoping to trigger the existence of your *other* life into your reality *here*. It would be very difficult to explain how a virgin teenager became pregnant. Wouldn't you agree?" Robert laughed, feeling better that he didn't have to explain the details to me.

"True. I can see where that would cause some problems." I couldn't imagine how I would have reacted if halfway through basketball season I discovered I was pregnant. The fact that I am still a virgin would clearly have gotten me admitted to the nuthouse. "So, what do we do now?"

"Well, you have two options." Emily took a deep breath lost in thought.

"Such as?"

Emily looked uncomfortable but continued. "Well, darling, I am sorry to have to ask this, especially in front of the men, but are you by any chance taking birth control pills? I am not saying that you are not a virgin, some women take them to relieve menstrual cramps or just to regulate their cycle."

"No." This conversation had taken an embarrassing turn for the worse. This was not information that I shared lightly with anyone.

"Once that barrier is completely diminished, you will become fully aware of both worlds like we are. At that time the adjustments won't um, what is the word I am looking for?" Robert looked extremely uncomfortable again.

"Are you saying that if we take precautions *here*, then I will be able to make love to Jackson *here*, just not in the 19th century where we are actually married? Am I correct?" I attempted to ease Robert's pain. "But I thought condoms already existed during the Civil War?" I couldn't exactly remember where I had read that, but I was certain I had.

"Well, yes." Robert looked ready to bolt. "But they were even less effective at that time than they are now. And they were mainly used as a prevention for sexually transmitted diseases, not to prevent pregnancies."

"Still, one slight problem though with that theory." I smiled over at Jackson. "I faint and apparently have flashbacks whenever he touches me."

"Once both sides of your consciousness are joined, eliminating the barrier between your two worlds, the fainting and all other symptoms will disappear. I promise." Emily reassured me.

"But how long will that take?"

"I am not sure, to be honest. Everyone is different." Emily shrugged. Much to my own dismay, it became clear she had no concrete answers to give me.

My body screamed in protest as I shifted myself around, draping my legs over the front of the couch in the proper position. I looked around for a moment at the three faces staring back at me as I tried to absorb all I had heard in the last thirty minutes.

"So, let me get this clear. I apparently live in my ancestral home, am named after myself, and have a genetic defect called *EVE* that makes it possible for me to live two perfectly normal and complete lives on parallel planes over a hundred and thirty years apart with two separate families. Oh, and I am engaged to Jackson and getting married this Christmas. And these flashes that I experience are really memories of my own from my *other* life in the 19th century. Plus, as a bonus, not only am I getting married at eighteen to an eighteen-year-old; I faint every time he touches me. And once we're married and want to consummate that marriage, we can only have sex *here* on a plane where we're virtually strangers who've only known each other for two weeks." I exhaled deeply at the absurdity of it all. "Is that right?"

"Pretty much," Jackson chuckled at my simplification of the subject, "with one exception. I am not eighteen. I will be twenty-two years old on December 6. I lied about my age to go to school with you. I am almost done with law school in 1878 and was, up until three weeks ago, in my first semester of law school in Boston. I finished my bachelor's last spring."

"Great. Anything else about you a lie?" I was quickly becoming frustrated. "I'm sorry I just didn't expect to find out any life altering events today. I was just expecting to get dressed up and go to a Halloween Party." Then it hit me. "My costume isn't really a costume at all is it? Neither is yours?" I looked directly at Jackson.

"Well, yes and no. I mean, they are costumes for the party tonight, and my mother did sew them from scratch for us; but they are replicas of outfits that we both already own in 1878. I thought that maybe they would trigger something in you if you put on the dress and saw me in the suit." Jackson looked like a sinner at confession. "See, we did not know if you were experiencing flashes or not or if my presence had any effect on you besides the symptoms, I had witnessed so I was attempting to push the envelope. I am sorry. Truly I am. The costumes were my idea. My parents did not want to try it. They thought the costumes might be too strong a trigger and could produce undesired results. But I pushed the issue since I was unaware of the magnitude of what you were experiencing." He moved next to me on the couch just inches from me and for the very first time it didn't have any effect on me physically.

Instead, I felt nothing but an overpowering love for him that was even more confusing to me than the lightheadedness, nausea, and cold chills.

"Jocelyn, you have to believe me. I love you more than I can possibly explain to you at this moment. You are my life, and I would never ever do anything that I truly believed would cause you physical or emotional pain." Jackson looked at me with his gorgeous, green eyes, pleading for my understanding.

"I know." And somehow that I couldn't even explain even to myself, I knew he did. I felt it. Stranger still, I felt the same way. "And you want to hear something even stranger?"

I smiled at him and then at both his parents, who sat in front of us. Robert still had arm wrapped around his wife.

"I'm not experiencing any symptoms; none. What happened?"

The three of them looked as puzzled as I felt.

"Can I try something?"

I smiled at Jackson who nodded in return. I leaned over as if I was going to touch him to test my own reaction, but as if on impulse, I gently pressed my lips upon his.

Jackson responded passionately, pulling me closer to him.

Reluctantly, I pulled myself away, trying to catch my breath. My face immediately turned crimson.

"Well, it is nice to see you have gotten over the nausea and fainting episodes." Emily smiled.

"Yes," I blushed further. "But why?"

"Because your mind knows what we have told you this evening is true," Robert stated proudly.

I looked over at Jackson, and he nodded in confirmation.

"So, this is real?"

The three of them nodded in unison.

"Can I ask a question then?"

"Of course," Jackson answered.

"How long have we been together? I mean, as a couple *there*?"

"Three years."

"And we're getting married over Christmas?"

"Yes."

"Are we very much in love?"

"Very much so."

"And I have a happy life *there*?"

"Yes. I mean it is like every life. It has difficulties, but yes, you are very happy *there*."

"I can't believe this." I shook my head. *How is any of this possible?* "I have so many questions I don't know where to begin." I laughed.

"That is only natural, Jocelyn dear." Emily reached over, placing her hand back on mine.

The phone rang out, startling the four of us. With a brief sigh, Emily got up and disappeared into the kitchen to answer it.

"How are you feeling? Does your head hurt?" Jackson touched my cheek lightly and tucked a few stray strands of hair that had fallen out of the curlers behind my ear. Then he wrapped his arm protectively around my waist. It felt so wonderful, so right. Natural. I loved the fact that the symptoms he normally evoked had disappeared.

"The ibuprofen helped a lot. But my body is sore."

Jackson's green eyes danced as he whispered in my ear, "It is so wonderful to finally be able to hold you."

I didn't have the chance to respond before Emily waltzed back into the front room. "That was Amy. Your parents will be here in about an hour." She sat down again next to Robert, watching Jackson and me. "So, what are you two going to do?"

"I would still like to go to the party if you feel up for it." Jackson flashed me that lop-sided grin I loved so much.

"I suppose so." My voice was still weak.

I really didn't want to go. *How could he think about going to a party tonight of all nights? Not after everything I had just learned.*

"Would you rather be here when your parents arrive?" he asked, recognizing the odd look I gave him.

"Dinner? Ah, right. I forgot." My parents were supposed to be here for dinner tonight. "I guess we're going to the party, then." I took a deep breath and signed. "Emily, would you mind fixing my makeup?" I turned back over to Emily, who nodded.

"I will get dinner started, honey." Robert got up kissing his wife and headed off to the kitchen.

"I am going to take a shower." Jackson followed his father's example and kissed me briefly before departing himself.

Emily and I returned to her vanity to repair the damage my tears had done to her masterpiece.

It took her almost thirty minutes to completely redo my makeup and take the curlers out of my hair. She had styled my hair in the appropriate fashion, which was beautiful and elegant.

I stood back in her full-length mirror, staring at a version of my *other* self, completely in awe. I barely recognized myself. The clothes felt so foreign to my skin. I tried to imagine myself wearing these every day of my life, but the thought even seemed absurd.

I spun around and faced Emily, who held this mischievous grin across her face.

"You look so lovely. If I did not know better, I would swear I was standing in front of, the *other* you." She laughed.

"This feels so strange." I took a full spin and stared at myself again in the mirror. She came up behind me, still smiling; "Do I really dress like this, in all these layers?" I ruffled the skirt a bit. The gown felt heavy. I couldn't fathom wearing all these layers in the humid summer heat.

"Yes, every day." She placed her hands on my shoulders. "Do not look so glum. I wear them also."

"But it's so heavy. What about the summers? And no air conditioning? It must be miserable!" I exclaimed.

"Yes, the summers can be. But when it is something that you are accustomed to, you honestly think nothing of it."

I turned back to face her. "I have so many questions I want to ask you." My eyes pleaded with her for answers.

"We have plenty of time. Do not worry about it right now."

How could she possibly be serious? Not worry? I could think of nothing else.

Jackson came up behind us, also dressed in his full Victorian attire. The sight of him literally took my breath away.

"Wow. Jocelyn, you know you look amazing. You look exactly like, well, you." He laughed. "It is uncanny."

"I know. That is what I said," Emily agreed, turning towards him. "I am going to help your father with dinner. You two better hurry and get out of here. Stop in the kitchen before you leave. I know your father wants to see you both and take some pictures." Jackson nodded, and she left us alone.

"You ready?" He held out his hand to me.

I took his hand in mine. It was so strange and wonderful to be able to touch him without bizarre reactions. I loved the feel of his skin —warm and smooth. His hand molded into mine with a firm grip.

I took a deep breath and looked lovingly at the man who, in another life somehow, I was going to be married to in a few short weeks.

"I'm nervous."

"Why?" He gave me a puzzled expression.

"This is just too much to process," I exclaimed turning back toward my reflection in the mirror. I stared for a long moment at the vision of this *other* me who lived in an era that I could not begin to understand. She resembled me, obviously. But she was somehow not me. "I feel like I don't know who I'm supposed to be."

Jackson wrapped his arms around my waist. "You are my Jocelyn. And regardless of where we happen to be, nothing can change that fact." He leaned down and rested his head on top of mine. His eyes held mine attentively in the reflection of the mirror. "I truly love you, Jocelyn. I realize that your consciousness *here* has only known me a couple of weeks and hearing me say that seems overwhelming, but I promise you that we are very much in love."

I placed my hands over his. "I know." I slowly turned to face him. "Jackson, I know. Somehow, I feel it in the very essence of my soul. I love you too." I smiled slightly, feeling embarrassed.

Jackson held my face in his hands and gazed at me intently. Our eyes locked, and I was struck again by the brilliance of the green in his eyes. He tenderly brought his lips to mine. The intensity between us heightened as our bodies pressed together passionately. Gently yet firmly, Jackson pulled himself away from me. He struggled to maintain his even breathing and smiled lovingly at me.

"We have to go." He gently pulled me towards the door, ending our brief encounter.

Robert and Emily smiled as we entered the kitchen. "My goodness, Jocelyn, you look so beautiful." Robert came around from the stove.

"This certainly feels very odd to say the least, to see you dressed in that attire, *here*."

"Yes, it does." Emily agreed. "Now would you two please stand over by the fireplace so I can take some pictures before you leave?"

We drove in silence for several minutes. I rested my head against the cool window, trying desperately to grasp some smidgen of reality. My mind was whirling in a thousand different directions. The cold window felt amazing against my forehead, but even though my headache was gone, I could not find any solace.

"Are you alright?" Jackson placed his hand over mine.

"No."

"Everything is going to be fine. I know you have been through a lot this evening, but you must trust me when I say that I do understand. I remember when I learned about all this how confusing and lost, I felt." His words did give me some comfort.

"How did you get through it?" I looked over at his striking profile, pleading for the right words to make this all click in my head.

"It took some time. My family helped me more than anything else." He gave my hand a gentle squeeze as we turned the corner onto Cody's street.

"There's so much to try to put into perspective that my mind cannot process it all."

Jackson guided the car into a spot along the already crowded curb and turned the engine off.

"It does get easier, I promise. However, I am not sure how much information I should give you or if it is better for you to discover some things on your own." He faced me with a soft expression.

"But I want to know everything."

"Such as?"

I didn't even know where to begin. "Are there a lot of people who have this, this *EVE* thing?"

"I honestly do not know. I only know of the few in my own family and your uncle Monte. My father told me once that there were many more, but it is impossible to know exactly how many. He has a lot of theories about all of it that you would probably find very interesting. You should ask him to explain it to you, since I cannot give you an accurate account." He glanced at the people walking past our window towards Cody's house.

"When did you go through this?"

I wanted to keep him talking and make him tell me everything he knew.

"I was nineteen and away at Boston U when the barrier began breaking down between both sides of my consciousness. I started having visions of a world I did not understand, and it lasted for months before I ever told my family. I was positive I was losing my mind. The visions and the people in them were so real to me, and I felt very close to them. It scared the life out of me."

I halfheartedly laughed, recalling my feelings over the last few weeks.

"I am so sorry that you had to experience all of this, but honestly there was no other way. I mean if you think about it, how would you have reacted if my family moved in across the street, I befriended you, and then tried to explain to you this bizarre story about this concept of *EVE* without any proof?" He chuckled.

"I would have thought you were insane and stayed as far away from you as possible." I laughed, knowing it was true.

"Exactly. You had to experience it for yourself. I am only sorry that you got hurt in the process. That was never my intention at all." Jackson gently ran his fingers lightly over my cheek that was heavily coated in makeup to hide the bruises.

"I understand what you are saying, but" my eyes held his intently. "I cannot help it if I am curious about my *other* life and knowing that soon I will be fully aware and living as one conscious mind on two parallel planes across some one hundred and thirty years. It somehow doesn't seem possible."

"I know."

More people drifted by his CRV, giving us strange looks as to why we were sitting in the car alone on the side of the road.

"Come on. We should at least make an appearance." The corners of his lips slightly turned up.

"We don't have to stay long, do we? I'm really not in the mood for a party."

"A half an hour at most. We need to keep up appearances, after all. Then we can go somewhere and talk, and I promise that I will answer all your questions as best I can." He leaned over and kissed me gently before opening his car door.

The house was overflowing by the time we arrived, most already intoxicated this early in the evening. We spotted Kyle and Jenna who were dressed up as Scarlet O'Hara and Rhett Butler from *Gone with the Wind*. We pushed through the crowd and made our way over to them.

"You guys look great!" I shouted over the music at them.

"Thanks, so do you two!" She shouted back.

Jackson left me momentarily to find us a couple of sodas. Jenna and Kyle were in high spirits and rambling on a mile a minute. I only caught a few words of what they were saying.

A moment later, Caitlyn slid in beside me, dressed in her sexy Jasmine attire and elbowed me in the ribs, nodding towards the ice tub across the room.

"Can you say relentless?" I glanced over in the direction she was looking and there stood Taylor in her tiny, black playboy bunny costume, flirting with Jackson. She was hanging on his arm and giggling like a hyena, flipping her hair over her shoulder. She looked ridiculous.

"How pitiful. Does she honestly believe she has a chance of taking him from me?" I asked.

Jackson looked over at me with apologetic eyes. He said something to Taylor and firmly shook his arm free from her and headed back towards us. Taylor shot me the evilest look before stalking off in the opposite direction, making Caitlyn, Jenna and I laugh all the harder.

"That girl does not understand the concept of no!" Jackson rolled his eyes. "I am afraid I might have insulted her this time."

"Oh, what a shame!" Caitlyn couldn't hide her enthusiasm. "I hope you didn't hold back any punches."

"I told her that I am very happy with Jocelyn and that she has no chance whatsoever of me ever being interested in her." He shrugged one shoulder and slightly raised his eyebrows as a slight smile spread across his lips.

The three of us roared with laughter. Jackson leaned over and kissed my cheek, enjoying the momentary lapse from the reality that we had left behind us in the car.

"Oh, I wish I could have been standing there just to throw in a few comments of my own," Jenna added.

"Me too," Caitlyn chimed in.

"Hopefully, now she will leave us in peace," he said in a hopeful tone.

I could not afford to be so naïve. I knew Taylor better than that.

"You cannot be serious. Your rejection will only make her more determined," Caitlyn assured him. "She will enjoy the challenge of breaking you two up."

"She can try all she likes. It will never happen," I said with upmost confidence. Both Jenna and Caitlyn looked at me with surprise.

The night was dreadfully dark, and the wind had picked up in intensity, bringing a chill that went straight through our clothes. The clouds hung heavy over the sky, blocking out any stars. The leaves were drifting freely from the trees and blowing softly across the ground. I snuggled against Jackson's warm body as we made our way back to his CRV.

We pulled into his driveway, and Jackson turned the engine off. The lights were blazing from his home, and we could see our parents through the front window still gathered around the dining room table playing cards. I turned toward Jackson and took his hands in mine.

"Okay, now answer this for me. I know we're engaged. I know how you proposed and that we've been together for three years." Jackson nodded. "So, tell me, what is my life like *there*?"

"What exactly do you want to know?"

"Everything."

"Well, like we told you earlier, you go to school, church, you have friends, and a very large, close family."

"You're being very general. Tell me details like what do I do? How do I spend my days? Who do I hang out with?"

"You read a lot, play the piano, you spend a lot of time with Elizabeth, but Olivia used to be your best friend."

"Used to be? She's not anymore?"

"You two are still working things out, but after the recent scandal, your relationship has been strained somewhat." He tilted his head slightly.

"Recent scandal?"

"Yes, your brother, William, and your closest friend, Olivia Adams, seemed to have gotten themselves into a bit of trouble before the wedding." He raised his eyebrows at me.

"Really? And how did that go over?"

"Not well. See, Olivia lives in Jenna's house, and she and your brother were sneaking around behind everyone's back, seeing each other. Your brother and I share a dorm at Northwestern, and he had confessed to me at the beginning of the fall term of their courtship. However, they were afraid to tell you because each of them has such a close relationship with you. They feared how their relationship would affect it. When you found out a couple of weeks ago, I am afraid you did not handle their betrayal very well."

I listened intently as Jackson explained the couple's fall from grace. It amazed me how intriguing my life was *there*. I couldn't believe how strangely similar my life was *there* with friends and family yet incredibly different. It was funny that despite the large span of time difference between the two worlds, some things truly didn't change.

"You want to know something funny?" I asked him, trying to absorb everything. "I'm afraid to go to sleep tonight." It felt silly to confess something that sounded so trivial, but after this evening, going to sleep no longer seemed trivial at all.

"You have nothing to fear, my darling. Tonight, is no different than any other night."

"But it is." I fought back the tears I could feel welling up behind my eyes. "I know now that things are different."

"Nothing is going to change, my love." He kissed my forehead.

"I'm sorry. I know it sounds ridiculous." The tears rolled down my cheeks, making me feel incredibly childish.

"I would not say that. Your reaction is perfectly normal."

He pulled me closer to him and whispered in my ear, "My cell phone is on. You call me if you need me no matter what the time. Understand?" He kissed my cheek lightly and gazed deep into my eyes. "You are not alone. I am right across the street."

Jackson came around and opened my door. I took his hand, stepped out, and wrapped my arms around his neck. "I'd better get home."

"All right. I will walk you."

"No. Thank you, I want to clear my head."

We gazed into one another's eyes for a moment before he leaned down and kissed me softly. "I'll see you tomorrow, okay?"

"Of course." He smiled. "I will call you in the morning. Call me tonight if you need me."

I nodded and slowly let him go.

I tossed and turned, clutching my cell phone in my hand. I wanted so badly to push the button that would connect me with Jackson, but I hated being weak and refused to do it.

The entire day played out in my mind like some twisted movie. *Could everything they said be true? Could I possibly be part of this EVE thing? How could any of this be possible? Were the Chandlers telling me the truth or simply screwing with my mind?* I didn't want to believe that, couldn't believe that. I felt it in my bones that they would never do that to me.

I felt so odd, cold, and out of place. I didn't know where I belonged. I wrapped my arms around my extra pillow and hugged it tightly, feeling lost.

CHAPTER 30

Sunday, November 03, 1878

I SNUGGLED AGAINST JACKSON'S CHEST after supper and rested my head down upon his shoulder. He folded his arms around me tightly, pulling me closer to him. We sipped our coffee and discussed various events with William and Olivia. I did my best to pay attention to the conversation around me, but my mind was focused on the pocket watch upstairs. I could almost hear it calling my name, beckoning me to come to it to witness everything it wanted to share. It was hard to remain still. I shifted constantly to the point that Jackson sighed heavily at my restlessness.

"Sorry," I whispered up at him. "I cannot get comfortable for some reason."

"Are you feeling all right?"

"I am fine, just restless."

"Is something on your mind, darling?"

"No. Not really." I lied.

The hours crawled by, and every single frustrating minute was pure agony. I felt so incredibly torn between wanting to run upstairs in hopes of another vision or remaining safely here in Jackson's arms.

I settled once again into Jackson's chest. I rechanneled my energy into hearing nothing but the words of those around me.

By eight o'clock our families started to say their good nights. Group by group, they dispatched to their respective homes, leaving only the current residents and Jackson behind.

"I hate to see you leave," I whispered into his chest.

"I know. I will try and come home one day this week."

I nodded as a silent tear drifted from the corner of my eye and landed on his vest.

"Baby." He gently listed my chin forcing me to meet his gaze. "I know something is bothering you and that you feel you cannot discuss it with me. But, sweetheart, no matter how bizarre or strange or complicated you believe something to be, you can confide in me." His peculiar choice of words baffled me.

"Really, it is nothing. Please try to come home this week." I kissed him quickly before he could say another word.

With everyone now gone and William and Olivia retiring to their quarters for the remainder of the evening, I climbed the stairs slowly, still confused by Jackson's odd choice of verbiage.

Mimi turned down the oil lamps and closed the door behind her. I remained silent for several minutes, listening to the familiar sounds of the staff and my parents moving about the house. When I was sure that I was going to be left alone for the rest of the evening, I reached over and lifted the pocket watch out of its resting place in the beautiful, blue velvet box. I was careful just barely to touch the chain as I sneaked it under the duvet.

I snuggled back into the pillows and closed my hand tightly around it.

My head felt clouded, and my body went numb. I could no longer hear any sounds from the rest of the house. The world around me suddenly disappeared, opening into a bright field surrounded by large buildings that looked nothing like anything I had ever seen in my entire life.

The air was hot and muggy; I knew it had to be summer. I was walking across a grassy meadow of some sort surrounded by people who were excessively loud. These people were dressed in bizarre fashions. I was stunned when I looked over and saw that the women were wearing that same style of short pants that showed their legs and in public no less.

Their blouses were an odd fabric and weird styles that I could never remember seeing before. But when I looked down, I realized I was wearing a similar fashion to theirs! I paused a moment, trying to figure out what was going on. Everyone walking around me was wearing something similar. Not one woman was wearing a skirt or dress!

And the noise. It was so loud. Sounds engulfed me from every imaginable direction. Things I had never heard before.

To my left there was the strangest thing I had ever seen — horseless carriages. They were all different sizes and shapes and colors. I couldn't take my eyes off them. *How is that possible?*

"Hey, Jocelyn. What's wrong?" A tall boy with dark, blond, messy hair asked me.

"Excuse me?" I shook my head, trying to place who he was and where I was. I felt like I knew this young man. For some strange reason, I felt like he was my brother. I tilted my head and squinted my eyes into the sun to get a better look at him.

"Why'd ya stop? Something wrong?"

"No. I am fine." I stepped up my pace to walk beside him, having no clue as to where we were headed.

"Man, I am so jealous. I can't believe that you might be going here next year." I looked up at him now, totally confused.

I closely studied my surroundings for some sort of inkling as to our location. On the corner, I noticed a large concrete sign that read Indiana University. *Could that be right? Why am I down here?*

"Are you speechless or what?" The boy elbowed me in the ribs.

"I am fine. Why do you keep asking me?"

"Because you're acting weird. What's up with you? You were so excited earlier about seeing the campus. You can't tell me you don't like it, it's perfect. Plus, you have the bonus of being far enough from Mom and Dad that you won't have to worry about them bothering you once the semester starts." He stated with obvious envy. "For that reason alone, I was thinking about going to school on the west coast."

"The West Coast?" *What in the world is he talking about? There are no schools on the west coast. There is nothing out on the west coast.*

"Yep. Sun, fun, parties, and girls. And maybe I'll attend a class or two."

"For that reason alone, you will be attending a school a little closer to home." A man's voice from behind us interrupted with a teasing tone.

"Sure, Dad," the younger one replied, still grinning.

We walked over to a large fountain encircled by a beautiful garden of flowers. The four of us stopped long enough to fully absorb our surroundings. I could not believe the things I was seeing, the majority of which made no sense whatsoever. I was afraid to ask questions since these people obviously didn't seem to believe anything was out of the norm.

The older gentleman placed his hands on his hips and looked all around him. "So, Jocelyn. What do you think? Is this where you'd like to go?"

"Are you serious?" I looked at him strangely. *He couldn't possibly be serious. Me? Attending a university? Patrick would never allow such a thing!*

"Well, I'm sure with your grades and athletics you wouldn't have any problem getting in." A serious-looking woman added, "They have an outstanding pre-med program."

"Pre-med?" *This was too much. Me? A female doctor? Who ever heard of such a thing?*

"Look, I know you haven't decided yet, and you still have another year of high school before you make your decision, but I want you to think about it. I love the program they have here, and it would be so wonderful for you to follow in my footsteps and become a physician too." She smiled lovingly at me.

"But you know that you can pick any major you want. No pressure." The man gave the woman a hard look. "As long as it's practical." He turned his focus back on me.

I nodded to them stupidly. "I am not sure exactly. But I know it will be something in science." It fell out of my mouth before I realized what I was saying. My mind was whirling in a thousand different directions, yet in my heart and soul I had been dreaming of this very thing for as long as I could possibly remember.

"Somehow that does not surprise me," the man stated with a chuckle. The woman smiled but remained silent. The younger man was busy watching every female that walked by.

"Let's get something to eat before we check out the other end of campus." The woman casually started strolling back towards the area in which we'd just come.

The heat began to fade, and I could feel the coolness of my bedroom return. The bright sunlight was growing fainter, and I reached out my hands to physically hold onto it. I could feel the air escape from my lungs as I fought desperately to grasp the world that was slowly fading before my eyes.

"Jocelyn? Jocelyn! Wake up! Open your eyes! Jocelyn, look at me!" William was gripping my shoulders tightly and screaming inches from my face.

"No. No. No!" I sobbed. "It's not fair!"

"What is not fair?"

I slowly opened my eyes, realizing that I was sitting upright in my bed, covered in perspiration, and screaming madly. My brother was seated beside me with a look of terror in his eyes. I closed my eyes tightly, wanting the world back that had just slipped through my fingers. It held all my dreams and everything I was denied. This strange new world held the key to my happiness, and I was determined to get back there.

Author Bio

A. L. Waddington has her master's in military psychology and is currently working on her doctorate. She is an avid reader and researcher, has a slight coffee addiction and when she is not lost in a world of her own creation, she enjoys spending time gardening, hiking, and traveling with her family. Waddington and her husband, Eric, live in East Texas with their daughters and three spoiled puppies.

PERCEPTION, BOOK 3

My hopes, my dreams, and most of all me . . .
we will finally be set free.

Questions, questions, and more questions ... they consume Jocelyn Timmons' life — both of them. Questions that never seem to have an answer. They haunt her, eat at her, and dreams of a normal senior year of high school have finally floated away into nothingness.

Inheriting the gift of *EVE* (Essence Voyager Era) has become both a gift and a curse. One that Jocelyn doesn't know if she wants or can accept. The world she once knew and thrived in has all but disappeared in the last two months. And now she wonders if she can ever find her way home again.

Her fiancé, Jackson Chandler, and his family seem to be the only ones who understand what she is going through besides her uncles, both of which she's grown very close to. But even they do not fully grasp how turbulent the situation has become. Will Jocelyn survive the torments of her mother and brother? Or will she find a hidden key to finally unlock her golden cage?

ILLUMINATION, BOOK 4

Can time predict the future?

In the gripping conclusion of the bestselling *EVE* series, Jocelyn and Jackson come face to face with the challenges of living combined lives on both planes. While Jackson struggles under the demands of his chosen profession, Jocelyn discovers hidden branches in the family tree. But the more she uncovers, the deeper she finds herself and her family in an uncharted realm that no one considered possible. Can EVE not only skip around with family members but also switch branches?

The happy couple soon learns that a branch, like time, has the tendency to bend in the most unexpected direction and occasionally break. When that happens, lives are forever changed, the forces of destinies altered, and fates derailed. The fluidity of time begins to take on an obscure meaning as the barrier between the two worlds fades into darkness.

AND DON'T MISS THE EXCITING SPIN-OFF SERIES

TRANSCENDENCE, BOOK 1

THE SPIRIT QUEST SERIES

A storm is brewing . . .

Several years ago, Sidney learned that she, like her sister Jocelyn, inherited the gift or curse of EVE — the ability to live parallel lives on two separate planes of existence two centuries apart as their soul travel nightly. A prospect she has yet to fully embrace.

Sidney's 21st century life consists of her boyfriend Landon, completing her residency, and following in her mothers' footsteps to becoming a doctor. She has worked hard and sacrificed much to get where she is, and she is proud of all she has accomplished.

But the actions of her 19th century self-threatens to jeopardize is all. As the treat of the looming American Civil War darkens her world, she is consumed with her limited abilities as a woman. Unrest and tension surround her Boston home as her neighbors speculate what the future holds. How can she remain silent in her knowledge when her husband Keifer, and all those dear to her will soon be in jeopardy?

Is losing the life of someone you love to save your future in another world selfish? Can she be so selfish? The storm is brewing, and she feels powerless to stop it.

DISHEARTENED, BOOK 2
THE SPIRIT QUEST SERIES

"I do not know which is worse — sitting on the edge of a Civil War you know is coming or watching your country implode from within on the verge of another that could happen at any time."
~ Sidney Timmons-Marshall

Gifted or cursed with the inherited ability of E.V.E., Sidney is forced into the inconceivable — her 1860 self-watches on the eve of the American Civil War as the Northerners and Southerners dismantle the fabric of the nation. Whereas her present-day self-witnesses the extreme Progressives and Liberals shred away the decency of the American Culture on a world-wide stage and make the USA the laughingstock of the globe.

Sidney is heartbroken watching everything her loved ones and countrymen from her other life fought to preserve be undone by a minuet mindless minority of entitled fanatics and a political party so hell-bent on spreading hate, they would rather burn the nation to the ground than relinquish power.

But what can she do? Can one small voice change the mind of millions with hate in their heart? Can she find her way back to the solace she once treasured in both her lives?

ScarlettInkPublishing.com.
Alwaddington.com